Three Ravens Publishing
Chickamauga, GA USA

Credits:
Cover art by: Dimitri Walker https://www.paintingsbydimitri.com/
Edited by: Jesse James Fain & William Joseph Roberts

It Came From the Trailer Park: Double Wide Volume 1 by William Joseph
Roberts /Three Ravens Publishing – 1st edition, 2025

Ebook ISBN: 978-1-966507-26-0
Trade Paperback ISBN: 978-1-966507-27-7

Table of Contents

Trailer Park Fun

By: William Joseph Roberts
"aka Hillbilly"

These Trailer Park stories came about while me and Chris Woods were shooting the shit and I was doing the dishes. I honestly can't think of what it was we were talking about, but he'd stopped in after swinging over to Toni's place (Baen Books) to sign contracts for the LibertyCon anthology when it hit me…

It Came From the Trailer Park.

It wouldn't be anything serious, but instead something fun. Something I could do with a few of my buddies and we'd gut chuckle out of it. Hell, I really didn't care if I made anything on the first one. I wanted to do it *because* it was going to be fun. I never in my life thought anyone would fall in love with these stories as much as I have, but it happened.

I can't say the Trailer Park anthologies are making us bank, but they do have a strong following for a small press. People generally enjoy them, or you get those select few that absolutely hate everything to do about it, but when you read the reviews, you wonder why they even picked up a copy other than to find something to be offended about so they could write and *Karen* review.

That's their problem. All I know is that folks enjoy reading the stories, folks enjoy writing the stories, and I'll continue the series all because it's fun.

Be Still, Deer

By: J. T. Arralle

The transmission screamed as he downshifted, slowing for the turn, and slamming the accelerator as he shot out of the curve onto the hard packed dirt road. The straightaway came into view and he cycled through the gears, gaining speed and ground between him and the pursuing sheriff.

Lights ablaze, the car behind him could fit into an old cop drama on tv. It was ancient compared to modern cruisers. All hard angles, long, low engine compartment complete with shiny hood ornament. The rack of lights on top a single bar instead of the gumdrops seen on more recent vehicles. A car that old meant one thing. Sheriff Benjamin was trying to relive his glory days.

True to form, the older cruiser lost its steam as the gap increased between the two. He lost sight of it as he took three turns and the cruiser seemed to vanish behind him. The road straightened out in front of him and he gunned it. The old cruiser didn't have the horsepower to keep up.

Sitting on a pure four hundred and fifty horsepower engine custom built for this kind of speed, there wasn't a car in the county that could catch him. Let alone an out of repair sheriff's department cast-off.

"Eat this, you used up has-been!" He stepped onto the accelerator hard. His engine's growl turned to a roar as he opened it up. Fire flooded his veins as the thrill of the chase wore off and his adrenaline rush crashed. His arms felt heavy.

The former logging road cut about two hours off his expected trip time. At this late hour, no one was using it. There wasn't any signage or street lights to guide you along. No one driving it on the regular ever needed any of that, though. His tires bounced across the random pothole as he drove deeper into the woods.

He glanced at his passenger seat, ensuring the packages were still in their bag where he set them. Anything not belted in got sent flying around the vehicle. The gym bag was still there, tucked against the seat back, the zipper still open from him inspecting, weighing, and counting the containers. The translucent sides did nothing to mask the crystal growths inside. Three bottles full of tannin colored whiskey sat nestled into their bubble wrap and tucked snug beside the containers.

He lacked the time at pickup to pack it into the secret cargo spot behind his back seats. If he could shake loose of the sheriff, he'd pull over and conceal them. His clients preferred their product not sitting in view.

The roadway danced in front of him as his vision began to spin. The crash was getting worse.

Dammit! I don't have time for this! I need to focus.

He picked up his self-lighting pipe he had loaded before setting out with a good sized crystal. A press of the button on the side and the little burner lit under the chunk, melting it as he inhaled.

The sweet smoke filled his lungs, the bitter edge spiking on his tongue as he stopped and held his breath. After a minute, he blew out a thick cloud of smoke and could feel the warmth tingle across his body. He took a sip of his soda, then returned it to the cup holder.

Everything came into sharp clarity; the road took on definite lines he could follow. The trees blurred into each other, but that didn't bother him. He wasn't planning on driving through them.

He punched the accelerator again. The siren faded in the distance. It was a good thing the local sheriff was a disgraced idiot. Otherwise, he'd have a dozen cars on him by now.

"Yes! Fail harder, pig! You can't catch me!" He tapped his palm on the steering wheel, counting the seconds until he was free and clear. The end of the logging road was only three or four miles away and once there, the sheriff was beyond his authority and couldn't follow him. The siren continued to fade.

On the right side of the road, a brown blur was shaping itself into something more recognizable. He wasn't sure what it was, but felt like he should know. At the edge of the road, the brown blur bobbled and staggered around.

He'd heard rumors of the demon of the forest over the past year or two. People went missing, some turned up dead, others were never found. Could this thing be the demon they talked about?

The haze inside the car did nothing to help with visibility. The thing on the side of the road turned to look at him. Its glowing red eyes peered into his soul from within a mane of black smoke. It opened its mouth, the fire in its eyes dimmed as it screamed. The sound made his teeth hurt. His ears went numb as the wail rose in pitch. Soon he couldn't hear it, but his hair tingled as he felt it.

"Not today, demon! You ain't getting me."

As he closed the distance, the demon shape twisted, blurred, and shifted. The red eyes always watching him. It shrank in on itself; the smoke roamed all around its body like a tornado. Spears grew out of the tempest as long as his arm. With loud cracks, they bent and split into antlers.

The swirling vortex resolved itself to a large stag, though it stood with its legs splayed at odd angles, as if trying to keep its balance. The red eyes were now black as coal. Its rear was lower than the front, tossing its head at something on the other side of the road, but when he looked, he couldn't make anything out.

"Where'd the demon go? Is it still after me?" He couldn't believe his good fortune. First, losing the sheriff, now gunning past the demon of the forest and living to tell about it. Today was his lucky day. He puffed another lungful from the pipe. Just in case he needed more focus.

The flat road stretched before him, clear of obstacles. Another demonic scream resonated with his few remaining teeth. His heart raced as he looked in the mirror looking for the demon. It was racing after him!

Another loud crack caused him to look in the mirror. The demon had grown its shroud of black smoke again. It jumped in the air and kicked, before turning and jumping into the woods.

Panic gripped him as his car seemed to gain a mind of its own and veered off the road onto a side track as if following the demon.

"Stop controlling my car, you evil spirit!"

He stomped on the brakes to slow down. The road seemed to drift to the side. His tires sounded like a broom being swept over rough concrete. Trees slid sideways in front of him as his car turned in a slow arc, still flying down the narrow road.

"Oh, no!" He fought the dirt, wash boarding, and potholes for control of his car. The road resisted his attempts to right his vehicle. He turned his wheels all the way to the right, hoping once traction came back he'd be facing the right direction.

His passenger side wheels hit a large divot on the road. For a moment, he felt weightless. He rose out of the seat as far as his seatbelt would allow him. His pipe floated up by his face. Delighted at the opportunity, he grabbed it and puffed. The view outside the windows smeared to an indecipherable mess.

His passenger side window shattered, spraying glass inside the car. He tossed his pipe away and tried to wipe glass fragments off his clothing, only to have his hand fly up and hit the roof.

"Ow!"

The roof followed his hand down, stopping shy of making him a shorter man, though it made a mess of his hair. The windshield was nothing but a white mess of glass kernels and wrinkles. Something threw him against his door as the sound of the tires popping reached his ears.

"That's not good."

He shot up and bounced off the roof of his car, his seat belt flying free. Still holding the steering wheel, his stomach decided, right then, to remind him it was present and wanted to empty itself. He fought the urge to vomit as a demonic force pushed his face into his window. Somehow, this glass held throughout the whole experience.

The steering wheel kicked him in the chest. His seat punched him in the back and threw him into the steering wheel again. Somewhere in the distance, he heard a loud crack. Something big kicked the car, followed by something pressing into his back, shoving him forward.

The entire world seemed to roll around him, like when he used to fish on his father's boat.

A soda can floated up into view, then slammed into his side.

Several minutes went by and the world seemed to slow down and right itself.

The engine of the car rumbled, shook, shimmied, shuddered, shivered, and died with a backfire.

Silence slammed into his ears.

"Time to go." His voice sounded strange.

His door refused to open. Something solid held him as he tried to move. He punched whatever it was and pulled a soda can out. He slipped over to the passenger seat, put his feet on the windshield, and shoved. The broken glass peeled away from his feet in a large section.

"Good enough."

He slipped through onto the hood, reached back inside and groped for his bag. His hand found the strap, and he pulled it through. A quick check of its contents showed nothing missing. Some containers busted open, but everything was still inside the bag.

The humid air was going to be a problem. He removed his jacket and tossed it inside the car, and another idea occurred to him.

"They can't track my scent if I ain't got any clothes on. Them dogs always smelling for clothes."

He slid off his hood, and his pants followed his jacket.

"I'll keep the shirt a while. These skeeters are nasty."

He leaned a moment on the massive tree stump his car faced while he took off his shoes.

"Can't let em find my shoe prints either."

Satisfied the sheriff could no longer track him, he headed away from the wreck towards his destination. At least, he thought he was on the right path. Small animals ran away from his approach, squirrels chittering at him in the trees.

The road looked like the kind loggers used to drag trees to their trucks. He'd get to higher ground and figure out which direction he needed to go to get his delivery done.

As he hiked, he could feel his shirt getting tighter. His breathing was difficult, but he expected that from the hike. He wasn't much of an outdoorsman; he preferred to drive everywhere. That got him thinking about his car and how he was going to get it fixed, and that thought led to the demon chasing his car.

He jumped and turned around to check if the demon was on his trail. Nothing obvious stood out and he relaxed.

His shirt constricted further, his breath coming short. He felt lightheaded. If he could sit for a minute, he'd be okay. He could feel a clicking in his chest as he breathed. That was new, chests aren't supposed to click.

He found a tree with a root large enough to sit on and lean back against the trunk. He set the bag down and leaned back. It felt good to sit. He could breathe easily for a few moments. Evening was settling in. He'd have to wait for the moon to come out or he'd be wandering blind.

His shirt was squeezing him, making it impossible to get another breath. He sat up and pulled it off. That felt better. He sniffed the wet spot on the side. A coppery sweet, sugary odor, blended with the scent of earth and greenery. The soda on it was drawing the critters to him. He tossed the shirt to the side.

Night time settled in and darkness closed around him. He would rest a bit. Maybe after a brief nap he'd get moving again. He settled himself against the tree. That was good, only a little nap.

Old man McHenry sat bent over the copper kettle he was cleaning. His deft application of the rag and cleaning spirits left no part of the inside untouched. The sun glinted off the polished copper surface as he inspected his handiwork.

"Yep, that'll do it, deer," he said.

He liked this spot in the woods. A small clearing he'd converted into his personal refuge. He'd built a small shelter he disguised with logs and branches, old leaves and grasses. Any further away than the middle of the clearing and you'd miss seeing what it hid.

The old man moved onto the cap and inspected it with his discerning gaze. He applied more spirits to the rag and ran it over the inside. He gave a knowing grunt and set it on top of the kettle.

A bump at his elbow startled him. He turned and saw his deer friend standing beside him, wearing what looked like a playful grin. He rubbed the deer on the head, between his antlers and gave him a playful shove. The deer danced back, tossed its head, and pranced a moment.

Next up was the column. He inspected it and poured some spirits in to rinse it instead of scrubbing. He didn't expect anything there to cause problems, but he wanted to get it nice and clean.

While he was staring down the column, he felt a wet nose poke behind his ear and a warm tongue lick his neck. He shivered as that creepy feeling crawled up his spine and caused him to squirm. He shoved the deer back, but this time, instead of dancing away, the deer held its ground and pushed back against his hand.

"Dang it, Deer. Let me get this started. You'll get your drink soon enough."

Once he finished the cleaning and inspecting, he stood up and stretched. The sun dipped behind the trees, though truth be told it hid like that a short while after noon. There was still plenty of light to work by.

His small lean-to housed a sleeping bag, lamp, two sealed buckets, a large pot with a spigot, an ice chest, and a small stool he used for a table when he wasn't sitting on it. A small pile of firewood he collected for the still lay next to the sleeping bag.

He stepped over to the lean-to and opened the small, squat stove next to it. A quick shoveling of ash out from the hollow in the stove prepped it for its next run. He set the kettle on the stove, reached over to his bedroll, and retrieved the bucket.

A clang at the stove made him look over his shoulder. The deer was trying to knock the kettle off the stovetop. Its hoof had kicked the door of the stove closed while it tried to climb up.

"Dang it, Deer! Knock that off, you alcoholic! I told you, you gotta wait."

He opened the bucket and inhaled the sweet aroma. The murky fluid inside the bucket gave off a bouquet of odors, from corn to barley, a bit of sweet wheat, and a lot of sugar. The sharp tang of alcohol poked at his sinuses. It was ready.

The deer stepped over behind him. He could feel it standing there, breathing on him, sniffing the air. He felt a gentle nip on his elbow, then the tongue on the back of his ear, the velvet muzzle tickling him.

"Fine! You asshole." The old man grabbed the deer in a half headlock, careful to avoid the antlers, and shoved its face into the bucket. He felt the deer's throat working as it drank. After a minute, the deer started tossing its head, making it hard for the old man to hold.

He released the deer and watched as it staggered away. The alcohol content of the wash couldn't be higher than twenty percent, but for an animal, that was plenty. He laughed as the deer stumbled a few times and swayed as it stood, trying to get its bearings.

First laying a screen over the kettle, he emptied the bucket into the copper pot. A few pieces of corn, wheat, and barley landed on the filter and once the bucket was empty, he flicked them away with a swing of the mesh.

He secured the cap to the top of the kettle and locked it in place. He checked the pressure relief valve he added after one mishap almost cost him his still. A couple of yanks on the stem verified the spring still worked. Satisfied, he gave it a curt nod.

He looked around for the deer, but it was gone. It must have wandered off while he was setting up the kettle.

He moved the assembly to the top of the stove and stuck the column on top of the cap. After latching that in place, he set another small pot next to the main kettle. This one he filled about halfway with some water.

He finished attaching the various pipes and tubes, ensuring the chiller was stocked with water and ice from his ice chest, then stood back to inspect his handiwork. He placed his capture jar, and the burner was ready to light up.

After loading the stove up with dry wood from his lean-to, he got to work with a small butane torch. This thing was a blessing. It used to take forever to get the fire in the stove going. Now it was nothing. The torch worked well to light the odd cigar he enjoyed as well.

He had two buckets of wash to run this evening. It was going to be a long night. Good thing his lamp had fresh batteries, and he had his stash of nudie magazines to read.

The page fell open, unfolding from the center of the magazine. By the light of the lantern, the brunette staring at him from the page had the most marvelous eyes, among other assets that were, by no means, hidden.

"Hello there, Miss July." Old man McHenry savored the display for quite a few moments before sighing and folding it away to turn the page. He snapped the magazine a bit to get a better grip and read the article.

It had something to do with moonshiners being a blight on the honorable profession of distilling quality whiskey. He couldn't stomach more than a paragraph or two of bloviating by the author.

"You should remember, little man, that we all used to be moonshiners. Some just put on a suit and kissed the government's ass. All it takes to ruin a fun hobby and side business is a bit of regulation."

He looked over and saw his latest capture container nearing full. He swapped the vessel with the next empty and sealed the mason jar. Placing it on the small table next to the others, he counted out eighteen quarts.

"Not bad. Almost done with this batch. About time to pour in the last bucket."

The still was flowing at a decent rate now. The next quart should be the last one before it slowed down. He set the next empty near the spout so he could swap it fast and not lose too much of the tail end of the run.

He sat down on his bedroll and grabbed the magazine for another glance at Miss July. Her glittering eyes were too alluring for him to not want to gaze into. He flipped back to the beginning of her layout and relished each picture.

"It says here you like long walks on the beach. Imagine that, me too! I wonder if we have anything else in common? Other than me being too old, that is."

He was almost at the centerfold again when the strangest scream ripped across the small clearing. The jolt it gave his heart, not to mention the rest of him, caused him to toss the magazine over his head into the depths of the lean-to.

He picked up his lantern and held it up high to see who or what made that awful noise. Nothing beyond the glow of the lantern was visible. He stepped into the center of the clearing.

"Y'all better stop screwing around. This here is serious business. Mess with me and you'll regret it."

It was all bravado, of course. He couldn't remember the last time he'd been in a fight. What he remembered of it didn't go well for him. He dimly recalled being woken up by someone he didn't recollect fighting.

Another scream. This time closer.

He dimmed his lantern. He wasn't sure if we wanted to know what made that noise any longer. In fact, if his still wasn't in the middle of his run, he'd not be there right now. In all his decades making shine, he'd never heard this kinda noise before. It was frightening.

A shadow took form at the edge of the clearing. White, glowing eyes peered back at him. Not wanting to be taken by surprise, he raised the light level of the lantern in slow increments. Inch by inch, the shadow resolved into the form of his deer friend. Though something looked wrong.

"What's wrong, Deer?"

The deer screamed at him, that terrible noise. His tongue curled upwards as he did. He tossed his head and stamped the ground. Ever closer, the stamping brought the buck towards him. The light seemed to make him worse.

"The light bothering you? I'll put it out. Come over here, let me see what's gotcha all worked up."

He dimmed his lantern as the deer was close enough the fire in the stove illuminated him. Everything looked fine. He couldn't see anything on his legs that might cause him pain. He was still staggering, but McHenry chalked that up to him still being drunk.

The whitetail screamed again, lowered its head and darted towards him, pulling up short of ramming him to stand still and stamp his hoofs. The deer pranced around like he was trying to keep away from some frolicking bunnies.

"Stop fooling around. Here, have a drink."

Not sure what else to do, McHenry grabbed his wash bucket, ripped the top off, grabbed the deer in a headlock, and put his snout into the liquid. The animal got two gulps down before bucking in a wild frenzy that forced the old man to let him go.

One jump swung its backside around and plowed the old man to the ground. His wash bucket flew away. A couple more bucking kicks and its hooves landed on the old man's back. The deer started stomping trying to regain his balance, but the old man's body was in the way.

The buck leaped away and pranced around, eyes rolling all over. Tossing its head every direction. As the old man stood, shaking his head to clear it and looking around for the wash bucket, the deer stopped, staring at him.

"Oh, don't you dare! I ain't putting up with that! Not after last time!"

The whitetail lowered its head and charged, turning its head at the last second. The old man went flying, landing on his table, flipping the contents into the shelter. Now broken, the table landed on top of him as he stumbled into the shelter. One jar of moonshine wasn't closed tight and spilt its contents across his favorite magazine.

That did it. Now he was angry. He stood up, saw the deer charging across the clearing again, grabbed the stool and threw it to the side, hoping the movement would distract him.

The stool hit the platform his collecting jar sat on, sending the jar flying away from the spout, and spraying its contents into the stove grill. The resulting fireball engulfed the small still, lit the area, spooked deer and old man alike, then whooshed out of existence.

By the time the old man's eyes readjusted to the darkness, the deer was gone, and he had a burning pain in his stomach. He felt where the pain was and his fingers came away red. Looking down, he had several large curved pieces of glass sticking out of his abdomen. Small lacerations covered his arms where the antlers caught him.

"Damn… Musta landed on one of them jars."

The old man was extra careful as he collected all the jars he could find intact and put them in a canvas duffel, then hiked out of the clearing. He'd have to do some repairs on the still when he got back, but it should be fine until then. The stove had pretty well extinguished itself with that big fireball.

"Aw hell, the cleanup is going to take forever…"

"Quiet down, ass-assassin. They'll hear us if you can't shut your gob," Jack hissed at his brother.

"Why you using so many words, douche-tit?" Chip stared at him, daring him to say another word.

"Don't stare at me like that, rump ranger." Jack picked his way through the bushes a couple dozen yards away from the family camped in the small clearing.

"I'm not staring, just trying to figure out how you're so ugly you can make a blind baby cry," said Chip.

"Yeah? Well, you're so fat your shadow casts a shadow," whispered Jack. They were too close now to continue their game.

The parents looked like most parents. Older, tired of each other, and looking like they'd rather be anywhere else than near the other. Their teenage daughter helped to haul stuff from the truck to the tent. They looked like the kind of riff-raff they often dealt with from Little Bethlehem.

The small town was the closest thing that could be called civilization to the trailer park, though the trailer park residents called it Little Methlehem. Jack knew that most of the townies, as they called them, were addicted to something called meth, but he didn't know what it was. All he'd been told was it messed with your teeth.

He liked his teeth and had no intentions of messing with them. Messing with the townies though, that was always fun. Him and Chip had plenty of plans for this evening. It was worth the hiding they'd get from mom. The full backpack on his back held so many possibilities.

"Slow down, pecker head," whispered Chip.

"Shut your face, knob slobber," hissed Jack.

They never used their real names. It was a game they always played, and with them being teenage boys, their made up names needed to be creative.

"Why don't you, dick fart?" Said Chip.

That was a new one. "You been cheating and reading insult books again? Oh wait. Reading. You. Ain't happening," said Jack.

"No, butt munch, just proving I'm smarter than you."

"As if! If you were any smarter, you could be an idiot. Let's go. They're not looking."

The boys crept, each step careful and quiet, into the bushes surrounding the campsite. On one side of the big campfire sat three stumps. They looked fresh cut. Their tops still damp from the saw releasing the sap. Looked like the dad forgot to shave the bark off.

The campfire had enough wood piled on it to start a small bonfire. The mom busied herself removing some of it. She was muttering to herself the whole time she worked. Dark circles under her eyes showed how tired she was.

Next to the truck sat an ice chest, Jack assumed stocked with the family's food, drinks, and ice.

The bed of the truck held quite a few bags and boxes of supplies. Too many for a short camping trip. Maybe they planned on being here a while?

The dad brought a roofer's torch from the bed of the truck along with a propane tank, turned the gas on, and lit it with a welder's sparker. The orange flame belching from the nozzle sharpened and turned a rich blue as the dad adjusted the gas.

He held the lighter to the biggest log. The damp wood crackled, sparked, and popped as the sudden and drastic change in temperature caused the sap inside to explode. Even with his torch, the fire struggled to light. Several minutes later, the largest log maintained its flame and helped catch the rest of the logs.

The fire provided a warm illumination to the campsite, and the crackling seemed to settle the family. The mother seemed happier, but still appeared not pleased to be there. She called her daughter over and the two of them set about pitching the tent.

Jack and Chip settled into a large bush that gave them sufficient cover, but allowed them to spy on the campsite. The mother and daughter, busy with the tent, weren't of much interest. The father, off to the side, held some kind of device aimed at the woods, it seemed strange and caught Jack's interest.

Jack pointed at the dad and said, "Looks like he's using a fish finder."

Chip scowled and whispered, "Why would he be using a fish finder in the woods, you idiot?"

Jack clamped his mouth shut on his reply. The dad seemed to look in their direction, but he wasn't sure. Anyway, he didn't have a clever retort figured out yet. He needed something epic to not only embarrass Chip, but prevent his immediate reply with something even better.

He settled for studying the campsite again. The dad stood on the other side of the fire, preoccupied with whatever device he held. The mom and daughter were inside the tent, arranging things, the flaps closed.

"I got an idea. Wait here," said Jack as he slipped out of the backpack and nestled it at the base of the bush.

Jack crept through the shadows cast by the campfire, moving in a slow circle, careful not to step on any branches or piles of leaves. He made good time, his only worry being seen by the dad. At last, he hovered over the ice chest.

With deft fingers, he opened the cooler and almost giggled at his luck. He grabbed two bottles of beer and retraced his path back to the bush. He handed one bottle to Chip and made a big show of twisting the cap to let the pressure out with a whisper rather than a pop.

Chip followed his example, and they settled into drinking their pilfered pilsners while watching for more opportunities to mess with the family. He had a few ideas, but he was watching for the right time.

The dad, either bored or finished with his device, turned and let out a yelp. He marched over to the ice chest, checked its contents and bellowed, "Who took my beer?"

The mom poked her head out of the tent and asked, "What? Peggy and I have been in here trying to get this damn bed setup. No one took your beer. Did you remember to pack it?"

"Of course I remembered to pack it. The ice chest was open. Did you rummage through it?"

"No. I've been in here, jackass."

Jack and Chip struggled to keep their laughter in check. This was too good.

"Whatever, woman." The dad slammed the ice chest closed and moved it closer to where he was using the device.

Jack watched Chip rummage around in the backpack and pull out a small orb with a green fuse. He smiled. That was a good idea. The wind was just right. Chip flung the orb in a tall arc. It sailed through the air and bounced off one of the blazing logs in the campfire before dropping out of view.

In seconds, a thick smoke poured from the campfire and drifted across the area. The mom and Peggy coughed and gagged as the smoke invaded the tent. They emerged from the shelter, the mom furious.

"What did you put on the fire? You know you can't use green needles; they stink and everyone will know we're here."

"I didn't put anything other than wood on that fire. You watched me build it!" shouted the dad.

"Then what's stinking? It smells like rotten eggs!"

The brothers looked at each other, smiling. That was good for now. They had plans for later after they went to sleep, but that was a while off.

The eerie half-light of dusk faded to the deep darkness you can only experience away from civilization. Even the lights of Little Methlehem couldn't penetrate the nighttime gloom shrouding the campsite. Unseen critters made their presence known through chirps, croaks, and minor rustling in the bushes. Silence swallowed the night noises whenever a camper walked near the bushes, but the calls resumed after a few moments of peace.

That tranquility wasn't sitting well with Chip Jessup. He and his brother hunkered in the big bush near the campsite. Their ill-begotten beer bottles lay in a small pile at their feet. Each brother took a turn fetching a new set when they ran out. They were feeling pretty good after a few drinks each.

He had several ideas on how to disrupt their evening. He'd shared a couple with Jack using hand-signals they learned in scouts. Those signs came in handy when they could see each other, but were too far to hear.

The family they were watching sat around the campfire. Their moods calmed now the campsite was set up and the fire roaring away. The amount of food the twins discovered made them think the family was planning on being there for at least a week. They'd ensure that never happened.

"Oh! I know what we need. Honey, you stock up the fire while I go get the ingredients." The mother stood and sauntered over to the tent. After closing the bug screen flap, she illuminated the small lantern and busied herself looking for something. After a few moments, she called out, "Peggy, come help. I can't remember which bag it's packed in."

"Momma, I told you, it's in yours. I seen you put it in there." The young girl scrambled over to the tent and let herself in.

The dad, by himself at the fire, drained his beer bottle and tossed it into their trash bag. He rose, stretched, and yawned, his teeth glinting in the campfire's light. To Jack and Chip, he looked like a giant of a man. He wore the same type of clothes you'd expect the townies to wear, but he wasn't gaunt like most of them. Maybe he was new into town?

Chip and Jack froze as the dad wandered over to their bush, unzipped his fly, and withdrew the largest member they've ever seen before; letting loose a torrent of warm, foul smelling urine… all over Jack. They dared not move lest he notice them.

While the splashing sprinkled him, he watched his brother Jack's clothing turn black with the soaking he suffered. Both boys held their hands over their mouths, for different reasons. Chip's shoulders shook as he resisted the urge to laugh his ass off, while Jack struggled against screaming and running.

At last, the stream relented, and the man walked away in search of more firewood. Jack stared at Chip, his eyes flashing a dare to even mention what happened. Chip allowed himself a giant grin, but held his tongue. Jack did a quick check of the backpack and breathed a quiet sigh of relief that none of the fireworks were wet.

Chip extracted a small orb from the backpack. A just revenge for the dousing the man delivered. With the man out of sight, he tossed the firework into the ring of rocks surrounding the campfire. Fortune smiled on him again as the orb landed near a log, but not on the coals, a moment before the man dropped another bundle of sticks on the fire covering where the firework lay. The dad disappeared into the trees again, this time with a hatchet he fetched from the back of the truck.

A few moments later, a loud bang threw sparks skyward as the father dove to the ground. The mother and daughter poked their heads out of the tent. A smile crossed Jack's face as he wrung his shirt out. Chip smirked at his brother as he wiped his arms.

"Stanley! What did you put on the fire? I knew I shouldn't have left it to you to get the wood for the fire. I swear you're useless outdoors."

"What are you talking about, Nel? I tossed some sticks on and added a couple logs just now." Stanley tossed the two split logs in his arms onto the fire and watched as the sparks flew up and around until they extinguished themselves, stepping on the few that made it to the ground.

"Some of that wood had to be good. Are you able to find anything without pine needles on it or sap pockets?"

"Why would pine needles smell like your cooking? You sure you didn't throw any rubber on it?"

"What, I've been in the tent the whole time? How dare you! You can sleep in the truck tonight!"

"Whatever. I have no idea why the hell the agency would hook us up. We can barely stand each other." Stan grumbled as he wandered over to the truck, grabbed another beer, and sat on the front bumper, drinking.

Jack got another idea, prompted by the stink bomb earlier. He signaled to Chip what he wanted him to do. Chip nodded, and pulled the small lidded cup from the backpack, and slipped out of the bush.

Chip returned half an hour later with a cup full of stink bugs and handed it to Jack. Creeping low to avoid detection, Jack slipped over to the tent and unzipped the bug screen over the door, folding it out of the way before emptying the cup of stink bugs into the tent. Nel and Peggy were in the back of the tent, fussing over two bags. Jack crawled away from the tent and returned to the bush, and gave his brother the thumbs up.

"Aha! I found it. Let's go cook 'em at the fire."

Their shadows crossed in front of the lantern in the tent. "Peggy, why didn't you close the bug screen? We're going to get ate up by mosquitoes."

"I did close it. I zipped it right up."

"Then why is it open and folded out of the way? Stan, did you do that?"

"Momma, what's that smell? Gross!" Peggy ran out of the tent and past the truck before her stomach got the better of her and she puked.

"Who put all these stink bugs in here? Stan, help!"

Stan laughed as he stood. "Serves you right. You help yourself. I need to make my bed."

"You asshole. Did you do this? How did you even find that many stink bugs? I can't sleep in here."

The can of bug spray hissed as Nel sprayed it all over inside the tent. "Dammit. I'm going to be cleaning for hours now."

A shrill scream tore across the campsite. High-pitched and full of terror.

"Peggy? Why you screaming like that?" Asked Stan.

"I didn't, daddy."

Chip looked around the campsite. He couldn't make out the direction the scream came from. It sounded like it was everywhere at once. His brother's eyes were wide, searching around as well.

Another scream, louder than the first, ripped across the clearing.

"Stan? What was that? I don't remember any animal that sounds like that."

"Shush. I'm trying to figure out where it is," said Stan, crouched on one knee.

"Don't you shush me."

"Shut it, woman." Stan moved to the rear of the truck, moving boxes around. Opening a few, looking inside before casting it aside. He was searching for something.

A demonic, inhuman scream filled the campsite, seeming to originate near the tent.

Another scream joined the cacophony in near harmonic chorus.

Stan raced from the truck and barreled into the tent.

Peggy screamed and ran past the campfire and circled behind a large tree.

Chip grabbed a brick of firecrackers and tossed the whole bundle into the campfire.

Something plowed into the tent from the backside. The fabric billowed and twisted as the attacker thrashed around. Both parents, caught by surprise, fell as the tent twisted around them. Fabric tore as the tent fasteners ripped from the ground.

The firecrackers went off, a slow cascade of pops at first, then faster as the rest of the brick ignited. Small cracks followed by louder bangs, chased by one deafening boom. Stan flew from the fabric of the tent and, somehow, pulled Nel with him. Both landed on the ground, hard. Air exploded from Stan as Nel landed on top of him. He must have still had his wits about him as he rolled Nel over and put himself overtop of her, shielding her from whatever was thrashing in the tent.

Firecrackers zipped all over the campsite, cracking away at anything nearby. Several flew towards the tent and popped, spooking whatever was tangled up inside it.

The tent flowed over both parents, muffled screaming streamed from the tent. Several thuds sounded from where Stan and Nel lay before the tent seemed to stumble away. The billowing fabric jumped, spun, and danced away from the campers and out of the clearing. Another muffled scream chased the tent.

All that remained was the portion held fast by the bags the campers brought.

Stan groaned and rolled off Nel. He held his hand up and examined the dark smear of blood. He looked at Nel and felt her abdomen.

"Nel? Hold here, Nel. I have to put you in the truck." He stood and carried her to the truck. He fastened the seat belt around her and called, "Peggy! We have to go! Mom's hurt. Peggy?"

No response from the girl. Chip looked around and didn't see her emerge from the tree.

"Dammit, Peggy! I got no time for this. There's food in the ice chest. I'll be back as soon as I can."

With that, Stan jumped in the driver's seat, gunned the truck, and took off. Several boxes and containers spilled out the tailgate of the truck as he sped through the trees, heading for the main road.

Chip looked at Jack, and without a word, both brothers decided they accomplished their mission and snuck out of the bush before rushing back home.

"Rusty, hurry. Commercial's almost over," called Harry.

Rusty returned from the kitchen with two tumblers and a half-full mason jar. The clear liquid in the jar danced as he set everything on the table between their armchairs. The ice clinked in the tumblers when Harry grabbed his cup and settled it onto the coaster.

Rusty opened the jar and poured Harry a shot before filling his cup halfway. He emptied the rest of the jar into Harry's cup and set the empty jar down with a sigh.

"We're gonna have to get some more. Hopefully Old Man McHenry has more to sell. We still need to return his jars."

The screen on the tv faded from whatever toothpaste they were selling now to the show he and his brother have been waiting all month to see.

"Here it is!" Exclaimed Harry. He took a sip of the moonshine Rusty poured him and started coughing. "This stuff is stronger than last time."

Rusty nodded as he took a sip from his own tumbler. The smell caused his eyes to water.

A large ring faded into view. The announcer's deep voice sent chills up his spine. "And now, the event you've all been waiting for. The tenth annual Federated Ultimate Championship. This is the event of the year! FUC X!"

The camera panned around the audience, going wild. Many held up signs showing their support for their favorite wrestler. One rather muscular guy, wearing shades and a ball cap, held up a sign that said, "I don't know why I'm here."

Harry saw the sign and said, "To watch Mr. Indestructible. That's why!"

Rusty laughed, "Mr. Indestructible won't survive the night. Artemus Asp will annihilate him."

"No way. Artemus uses illegal moves. The ref will ban him if he pulls another table into the ring."

"We'll see. We gotta get through the junior cards first. Broken Badger is facing Howie Horton. I'm taking Badger in that one. Howie doesn't know how to break out of holds. In fact, I bet Badger is going to win with a KO."

"He sucks. His worst enemy is the ref. Always tries to clothesline his opponent using the ropes. Almost never works."

"Almost ain't always." Rusty took a sip of moonshine. The fire burned down his throat. Whatever recipe Old McHenry used always made it taste like liquid lava. He wouldn't have it any other way.

The match with Broken Badger and Howie Horton started. The two exchanged a few slaps and punches, then rushed at each other, embracing in a fierce collar and elbow tie-up. Each man, stepping and stomping, pulling and pushing, jostling the other for position. After a couple minutes, the ref stepped forward to break up the tangle of limbs and men, but before he got close enough, Howie twisted to the side and threw Badger into the ropes. Broken Badger flew off the ropes and jumped as Howie tried to execute a backhanded clothesline on him.

Instead of a toppled Badger, Howie caught a flying ass on his shoulders and landed face first with Badger mounted on top. The match ended with Howie being helped out of the ring by one of the medical staff. Badger picked something off the mat and held it aloft. It was a tooth.

Badger made a big show of putting the tooth in his pocket. Howie stood up, checked his mouth, and raced back to the ring. He rolled under the rope and executed the best flying kick he'd ever performed. He landed on the mat as Badger went stumbling into the ropes before being tossed back toward Howie.

Howie Horton rolled towards the tottering Badger as he crossed the ring. Broken Badger tripped over the prone Howie and hit the mat chest first. Howie rolled onto Badger's back and grasped his head before banging it into the mat several times, leaving a smear of blood behind.

Howie shoved Badger to the side and picked up something small from the mat before brandishing it to roars from the audience. It was Badger's tooth. He waved the small object in Badger's face before pocketing it and leaving the ring. Badger sat up, shook his head, grabbed his mouth, and fell over, still dazed. Another of the ringside doctors rushed to the mat to help him stand.

The referee grabbed Broken Badger's hand. The announcer's voice booming over the audience. "Victorious by fall…Brooookeeeeeen…Baaaaaaadgeeeerrrrrr!"

The audience went wild! Jumping and screaming approval. Boos rolling across the stands from a group of disappointed Howie fans.

The ref raised Badger's hand, throwing him off-balance, and the EMT had to catch Broken Badger as he fell. A ringside doctor pushed a stretcher onto the mat and the medical technician loaded Badger into it before two men hauled him away.

Four ring techs rushed the stage and stripped the mat canvas, tossing another over the surface and securing it before hauling the old one away and blending in with the rest of the staff.

"See! I told you Badger would win," said Rusty, sipping from his tumbler.

"He might've won, but it wasn't by KO. He also needs to see about getting his tooth back." Harry emptied the last of his shine and set his glass on the coaster.

"Maybe they could arrange an exchange of hostages?" Asked Rusty.

The next two matches went by with nothing notable. The unknown wrestlers were trying to make a name for themselves in the already crowded field. None of the junior crowd impressed Rusty. Most of them looked like copies of existing wrestlers, minus the talent.

"And now. Ladies and Gentlemen. This is it. The event you've all been waiting for."

"Oh, here it is Rusty! Hit record."

"I'm doing it, I'm doing it." Rusty looked at the remote. He pressed the red button and the whirring of the VCR on top of the TV set disappeared into the background as the lights went out around the arena.

Harry sat up, "aw, man! That was awesome! Mr. Indestructible could have done better. Why'd he team-up with that loser Silver Slasher?"

"Just goes to show, even two decent wrestler's can't beat Artemus Asp."

Rusty stood and stretched. The room swayed for a moment. His back reminded him he wasn't supposed to sit for so long.

"We best get over to Old Man McHenry before he forgets to give us our supply and drinks it all," said Rusty.

"You think that's safe? Old Man McHenry makes potent stuff."

"I'm not drunk, Harry. Just buzzed. I'm fine."

Rusty pocketed his keys and wallet from the small table next to his recliner.

He walked over to the door and said over his shoulder, "Hurry up. It'll be dark before we get there."

"Alright, Rusty," said Harry as he ran to his room to dress.

Rusty opened the door and saw someone had thrown an old mattress on his steps.

"Now why would someone do that?" He asked.

The mattress was old. It had stains in places he didn't want to think about. The fabric worn where the springs were trying to break through.

"Damn Jessup boys. Its gotta be them. They're always causing trouble. I'll have to tell their momma about this."

Rusty stepped through his door to fetch the mattress. Not having looked down, he never saw the small cord stretched taught across his doorway right at ankle height.

His foot caught on the tripwire, and stalled. His momentum, already leaned forward, forced him to catch himself with his other foot. That one also caught the tripwire and snapped it. Panic set in as he fell forward. Nothing he tried to save himself worked.

Resigned to his fate, he sucked it up, knowing he was helpless.

He hit the mattress hard enough to feel the steps beneath. The springs in the mattress were still good enough to bounce him head over heels and he landed on his back at the base of the steps.

Looking up at the afternoon sun, he pictured himself chasing, catching, and torturing the Jessup twins. They deserved it for every prank they pulled on him. They were lucky more pressing matters occupied his time right now, or he'd be employing some of his more creative imaginings.

Harry poked his head out the door, a gym bag slung over his shoulder, and looked at him. "Why are you laying down? Don't we need to get going? Did you fall down? Good thing someone put that mattress there or you coulda been hurt."

"Get in the truck, Harry." Rusty climbed to his feet and put the mattress over by his trash cans.

Rusty held the ignition on while the engine turned over, complaining about being woken up cold and revved without mercy. After twenty or thirty revs, the truck belched black smoke and started up. The rough idle shook the truck enough that it reminded him of that time he treated himself to a massage. He tapped the gas whenever he heard the engine struggling until the idle smoothed out.

"I thought you were going to fix the truck?" Asked Rusty.

"You need a starter. I told you that last month," said Harry.

That's right. He did. He should order that soon.

"It'll be okay for today." Rusty backed the truck out of their carport and turned onto the main road of the trailer park. It was at least a forty-five minute drive into the woods to where the trail that led to McHenry's camp started.

Rusty turned the radio on and the familiar voice of his favorite female jockey blared from the speakers.

"Aw, man, not this garbage again. All the music you like sounds the same. How many times can a guy lose his wife, his truck, or his dog, before you want to hear a new song?" Complained Harry.

"You just don't have no appreciation for good music. All that stuff you listen too is what's diluting good ol' fashioned country music."

"At least it's more than just some worn out old man putting his bad choices and depression on display for everyone else."

"Fine, Harry. One song and you can change it to your station. I get the radio on the way home, though."

Rusty turned out of the trailer park, waving at Sheriff Benjamin sitting in his aged, dusty patrol car opposite the entrance. The sheriff glared at him as he turned onto the highway.

"I'm glad they put him to work, but did it have to be here?" Asked Rusty.

"No one else wanted him. He hates everyone, us especially."

"I know, but I don't get why. We haven't done anything to him or even broken any serious laws."

"The way I heard it, it was part of his agreement to retire. The union wouldn't let the county fire him, so they made a deal. He gets us and the park, they get to get rid of him."

"At least the only thing they take seriously from him are the few speeding tickets he writes."

The song ended, and Harry punched the button for his station. "Finally."

The twang of electric guitars filled the cab with the singer crooning modern country rock. It wasn't terrible music, as far as country went. Rusty preferred the older classical sounding country over the modern variants.

The forest road came into sight. He slowed and turned into it. The compacted dirt road bore fresh gouges from someone tearing it up driving too fast.

"Looks like someone was in an awful hurry," said Rusty.

"At least two cars, one was a cop," said Harry.

He never knew how Harry could do that. He saw the tracks, and it looked like a jumbled mess to him. Harry could look at them and tell you, not only how many, but which brand of tires each car had.

"Driving that crazy, it had to be one of the Little Methlehemites, or one of their dealers," said Rusty.

The gloom closed in as the sun dipped and the trees grew denser. Shadows played tricks on his eyes with the tracks in the road. As they rounded the bends, the tracks seemed to fishtail wide. That car must have been moving.

"Look there! You think the demon of the forest got them?" Harry pointed at a break in the tree line. The bushes broken and trampled by something big.

"That's just a myth. There's no demon of the forest. Must have gone off the road. I don't see anyone needing help. You sure one of these tracks belongs to the cops?"

"Positive. They're the only ones that use Goodyear Eagles out here."

"I'm sure they stopped to help, then."

"Maybe. But they'd have to turn around. Their tracks are still headed that way," said Harry pointing down the road ahead of them.

"Aw, hell, that means we should stop and see. It's possible they didn't see the driver go off the road. If he's from Little Methlehem, it's possible he didn't even see the road go away."

"I'll never understand why anyone wants to use that stuff. I mean, it don't take long before you need four buddies with you to get a full set of teeth."

Rusty pulled over and put the truck in neutral. "Run back there and see if you can see a car or a person in need of help. Wave at me if you do."

Harry jumped out of the truck and ran to the break in the bushes. He disappeared from sight for a minute before emerging again and running back to the truck and hopped into his seat.

"There's no car. Looks like another logging road down below. Maybe he gave the cops the slip?"

Rusty pulled onto the road again and gunned the engine.

A small semi-circle cut into the side of the road, used for turnout and turning around, marked the head of the trail for Old Man McHenry. Rusty pulled into it and turned the truck off.

"Here we are."

Harry already had his door open. He slung the gym bag containing their empty mason jars over his shoulder and wandered over to the trail.

Rusty joined his brother as they picked their way along the old animal trail. The critters in the woods scrambled away from them as they stepped on twigs and branches. The soft, green leaves made no noise. His pa always taught him and Harry to make some noise while walking in the woods to scare away wildlife that could ruin your day.

He enjoyed hunting, but he knew he wasn't any good at it. Harry had a hard time eating anything that didn't come from the store in a box, bag, or can. Hamburger Helper was the main dish around their place. Good thing there were so many varieties to choose from.

The deepening shade made it difficult to keep to the animal trail.

With the sun almost set, they burst from the trail into the clearing with the old man's camp.

The camp was a mess. Both brothers stood still taking in the chaotic scene. It looked like someone came along and trashed the place.

"No way this was the cops. They would have taken everything," said Harry.

"No way this was kids, the most likely ones would be Chip and Jack, but not even they were this stupid. Something else happened. Let's look around."

Harry stood in front of the lean-to examining it.

Rusty put his hand up to the still.

Cold.

"Fire's been out a while."

"Look, here, Rusty. Old Man McHenry left his magazines out."

"He wouldn't do that unless it was an emergency." Rusty poked his head under the edge of the shelter. Titus liked those magazines too much to leave them exposed to the weather.

He moved the sleeping bag and saw two jars full of shine, sealed and calling to him.

"We'll take these for, uh…evidence."

"Evidence? You sure you don't just want to drink them?"

"Of course, we're going to drink them. If they're good, they probably came from before whatever happened."

"Sure, Rusty." Harry set the gym bag on the bedroll and stared at something on the ground.

Rusty shook the jars and watched the bubbles settle on top of the fluid.

"This is good stuff, Harry."

His brother ignored him, absorbed in what he was seeing on the ground.

"What are you looking at?"

"I think this is blood. It's so dark I'm not sure."

"See if you can find more of it. Track it like you're hunting an injured animal."

"That's gross," said Harry as he walked in circles and stopped a few feet from the original spot.

"More over here. Just a little. Maybe the wound isn't bad? Oh, no. It's bad." Harry bent over and picked up a large shard of curved glass covered with blood.

"The camp looking like this with blood on the ground means we should follow it and check on him. Make sure he's alright."

"Good idea, Rusty."

Rusty followed Harry as he found more blood spots. The trail led them to the head of a smaller game trail through denser bushes. The blood trail stained the green leaves.

"Knowing the old man, he knows all the trails around here. This one is probably the fastest way back to the trailer park."

Rusty and Harry emerged from the game trail back on the main logging road, though quite a ways down from where their truck waited for them. Rusty wasn't sure how long the hike down the new trail was, but he thought it couldn't have been over thirty minutes.

Harry crouched at the edge of the road and studied something he found. After a moment, his brother waved him over. "Look here, Rusty. This blood drop looks different from the rest."

"What do you mean? It looks like a smear, just like all the other smears."

"This one is pressed into the dirt."

"What? Pressed?"

"Yeah. I think the old man got into a car. One with Goodyear Eagle tires."

"Great. So a cop picked him up? What cop would pick up anyone out here?"

"The only one we know is Sheriff Benjamin. He'd only come out here, for the same reason we did. Unless he was chasing the car that got away."

"Well, we can't follow the tracks on foot. We need to go get the truck. We can check with Ms. Grace at the trailer park in the morning. Nothing to be done about it tonight."

"Alright, Rusty," said Harry as they walked up the road.

Darkness descended on the roadway. The tree canopy blocked the stars from lending any light. Rusty wasn't concerned. He'd grown up in this darkness. It was like an old friend. The night time critters chirping away, singing their songs. The cicadas clicked away in a desperate cry for a mate.

Fingers of ice ran down his spine as a loud crack of a branch broke behind them. A scream filled with horrors beyond his imagination peeled across the road.

"I told you the demon was real!" Harry ran ahead in the darkness, not caring if he could see.

Rusty chased after his brother, not wanting to meet whatever was so tortured as to scream like that.

The cab light illuminated as Harry ripped his door open and shut it behind him. A moment later, he locked the door.

Rusty opened his door and jammed the key in the ignition. The engine started revving.

"Oh not now," said Rusty.

A dozen more revs, and the engine started, only to die a second later.

"What the hell, Rusty? It's gonna eat us. I don't want to get ate."

"Not now, Harry."

Rusty turned the key again, the engine revving like it had all the time in the world.

The engine started, the idle rough as ever.

"What are you waiting for, Rusty? We need to get out of here. It's getting closer!"

"If I drive now, it'll die and the engine won't start. It needs to idle a bit."

Rusty gave the engine some gas as it struggled to smooth out the idle. This helped, and the engine settled into a gentler purr.

Rusty slammed the truck into drive, whipped around, and headed down the road, back towards home and safety.

Muffled pops in the distance seemed to escalate as they drove. After a few moments, it sounded like an all-out war raging in the forest.

"What's that?" Cried Harry as Rusty stomped on the brakes.

A figure raced into the road from the trees, twisting around, flowing every direction at once. Bright colors flashed around it as it danced in the beams of their headlights.

A bang in the middle of the battle, louder than the rest, crackled in front of the truck. The figure in the road crossed to the other side and disappeared into the woods.

Rusty gunned the truck and flew past where the ghost disappeared, his headlights shining on an empty road.

"You think someone was hunting the demon? Sounds like a lot of them."

Morning arrived with a chill unheard of in the middle of May. Rusty sat up and shivered. He looked around his room, but didn't see his robe anywhere. His breath misted as he exhaled. They needed to get an early start, his worry for the old man eating at him.

He grabbed his quilt and wrapped it around himself before donning his slippers and heading to wake up Harry. His brother slept like a log. He'd need a bit to wake up. He opened the door, but found an empty bed.

Now where did he get himself to this early? Rusty thought.

He needed coffee. In the living room, he found a pile of pillows and cushions, with sheets draped over the childish structure.

Now that's something he hasn't done since we were little.

He saw Harry's giant feet sticking out of the opening of the pillow fort. Not wanting to drop his quilt while waking his brother, he pulled it up over his head. He reached down and grabbed Harry's ankle.

"Come on now. Get up."

He couldn't see the foot that hit him in the head, but he sure heard the scream Harry let loose.

"Don't you come near me, demon! We ain't in your woods! You can't eat me here!"

Rusty fell backwards and landed in his armchair, the foot rising to its full height as his weight settled back. Staring at the ceiling, stars filling his vision, he contemplated leaving Harry in his fort while he checked on Old Man McHenry by himself.

No, I can't do that. Harry needs me.

"Calm your tits, Harry. It's just me. Why's it so cold in here?" Asked Rusty.

"The demonic chill you brought in with you, demon? You ate my brother! Don't eat me!"

"Ate—No one ate me, you moron. Help me up so we can get some coffee on and go check on the old man."

Rusty pulled the quilt off his head and saw his brother looking at him like he'd grown another face.

"Rusty?"

"Yeah, Harry?"

"You ain't the demon of the forest? Here to eat me?"

"Do I look like one?"

"What does the demon look like during the day? You kinda did wrapped up in your favorite quilt. Like what almost got us last night."

"I dunno, Harry. I think I'm quite a bit smaller than what we saw last night, don't ya think?"

"Not sure. When I saw you grabbing me, I couldn't think. I had to act. Sorry, Rusty. Are you hurt?"

"Nothing I can't handle. Let's get some coffee made." Rusty sat up and threw off his quilt. The chill reminded him why he had it on. He stepped over to the thermostat and saw it set to 50 degrees.

"Fifty! Why on earth did you turn it so low, Harry?"

"It got hot and stuffy in my fort."

Rusty shivered and turned the unit to a more reasonable seventy before heading into the attached kitchen. He loaded the coffeemaker and filled the top with water. One button press later and the machine set about its task of brewing up liquid gold.

Rusty grabbed a set of somewhat clean pans and set about making a couple egg sandwiches for breakfast. He grabbed bacon and eggs from the fridge then slapped several strips on one pan. Next up, he coated the surface of the other in butter and cracked two eggs in it. Bacon on a couple slices of bread and an egg on top. He handed one sandwich to Harry on a plate and wolfed the other one down.

He fetched two coffee cups from the little stand next to the coffeemaker and filled both. He set one next to Harry's plate and fixed his coffee with creamer and sugar. Harry drank his black. He'd never understand how his brother could.

Breakfast done and over with, it was time to see Ms. Grace. They'd be lucky to get out with nothing more than a lecture.

After a short walk to the office, Rusty and Harry stared at the sign still showing "Closed" in the window.

"Isn't Ms. Grace supposed to open up by now?" Asked Harry.

"Most days. She practically lives in the office," said Rusty.

Rusty stepped to the edge of the office porch and looked over at the trailer behind the office. It was unusual for Gracelyn Whittacre to have the curtains drawn closed at this hour. She was an early bird, always at the office before Rusty and Harry were even awake.

"Guess there's nothing we can do but check on her. It could be serious."

"She's not gonna like that, Rusty. She always yells at us when we bother her at home."

Rusty tried the office door.

Locked.

"Well, what else are we going to do? She don't trust us with the keys even though we've worked here for ten years."

Harry shifted from foot to foot. It was one of his nervous ticks. "What if she yells at us real bad this time?"

"I've been yelled at before."

"Not like she does it! She terrifies me."

Rusty heaved a sigh. "What would you rather I do?"

"Why not go talk to the Sheriff? At least he isn't as scary as Ms. Grace."

Rusty shook his head. "We should talk to Ms. Grace first. Why don't you wait for me by the swings."

The swings were part of the pathetic attempt at creating a scenic play area for the kids. The biggest problem was there weren't many kids in the trailer park to enjoy it. Most of the park residents ignored the park. Rusty could count on one hand how many times he'd seen someone using it other than the Jessup twins.

He knew he was in for it as soon as he knocked on that door, but he'd feel worse if something happened that he could have done something about.

He walked over to her trailer. His knocks sounded muffled, like the trailer was smothering his hand as he tried to let Ms. Grace know he was there.

Right. This time with confidence.

He rapped on the door three solid knocks, confident that he was doing the right thing.

"I'm coming! This better be good!"

The door flew open, and the hissing opossum in her arms greeted Rusty, its teeth bared, looking like it wanted to bite his head off. Rusty took a step back, in case it tried its luck.

Gracelyn Whittacre stood all of five foot four inches and was meaner than an angry Rottweiler. She could tear a man apart with a glare, which seemed to be a permanent fixture on her face. Her hair rested in a no nonsense pony tail and was as gray as the cloud of menthol laced smoke haloing her head. Her old cardigan might have held some color in the past, but had faded to a dark gray, either from age or ash.

The one accessory no one expected was the small opossum she always carried. It hissed as she faced him, clutching it to her chest. The small diaper it wore bore little blue flowers. It hissed again as he took a breath to speak. She cut him off before he got the chance.

"Oh. I should have figured it'd be you. Where's that idiot of a brother of yours?"

Kindness was not one of Gracelyn Whittacre's virtues. She ran the trailer park with ruthless efficiency. Even when it involved talking to people. She seemed to save the acid for Harry and him.

"Good morning, Ms. Grace." Rusty smiled and tapped his hat in greeting.

"Morning already? Dammit. Why are you bothering me? Isn't it enough I was already woken up in the middle of the night and kept awake by the Sheriff and Lily calling me?"

"Lily called? What about?" Lily Jessup was the prettiest girl in the trailer park, but her boys were the worst trouble makers Rusty had ever dealt with. Those boys had changed his mind a few times about the obvious attraction he and Lily shared.

"What else, you idiot? Those boys of hers. Always causing trouble around here. If they ain't blowing something up, they're breaking something else. What they need is a good father. Though I can't expect a moron like you to understand that. They didn't come home last night until well after midnight. By then, Lily had called twice."

She eyed him as she said that. Rusty knew what she was referring to, but it ain't none of her business. If only he could tell her that without his voice cracking.

"What did the sheriff call about, if I may ask?"

"Do I look like I speak drunken fool? The old sot was blabbering on about something, but he was too deep in his bottles to make any sense. Why don't you go ask him? You know where to find him. Maybe you can remind him I'm not the type of lady that takes callers after 6pm."

That he did. In fact, everyone knew where to find the Sheriff. All day, every day, right in front of the trailer park. When he wasn't there, you had only to wait a few minutes. He spent his days making the residents' lives as miserable as his own.

"Ms. Grace, have you seen Old Man McHenry? We visited him at his campsite and found a heck of a mess. I think he might have been injured, but we haven't seen him."

"No, I haven't seen him. I'm not his babysitter, you dolt. He pays his rent on time, unlike some of you folk."

"Not sure what you mean, Ms. Grace. We're paid up three months in advance." Rusty was proud of that. Harry sat down one night and showed him the numbers and they seemed to make sense. So far, no bill collectors came to bother him, so it must be working.

"You are, but some others are behind quite a few months. It's not like I can evict them though, who in the world would choose to live here?"

Rusty couldn't disagree with that, but for himself, he liked it there. Their small community felt like a family. All dysfunctional, like the rest of them. Even those families had their trouble makers, like they had the Jessup twins.

"Are you done questioning me, Detective Dimwit? I'm taking today off." The opossum hissed at him again.

Rusty jumped. "Thank you, Ms. Grace. I'll go check on the Sheriff now."

"I don't care what you do," said Ms. Grace as she slammed the door.

Rusty walked over to the park and found Harry sitting by himself on one of the two swings. The rusty chains clinked as he sat down on the empty saddle.

"The Sheriff is our best bet to finding out what happened to Old Man McHenry. He called Ms. Grace last night. So did Lily. Said her boys were missing."

They had no choice now. The Sheriff was their only lead. The Jessup boys had returned the night before. Who knows what they were up to? They wouldn't get a straight story out of them. It was useless to try.

"Missing?" Asked Harry. "They're right over there, coming this way."

Rusty looked where Harry pointed and saw Chip and Jack running towards them.

"Rusty! Harry! We knew it! The forest demon was real. We saw it!"

Saw it? What are they talking about?

"What'd it look like?" Asked Harry.

"It was huge! It kicked the ass of some campers in the woods before running away. I guess it didn't want them in its woods," said Chip.

"Who's camping in the woods? You two sure are acting strange. Why haven't you insulted us yet? You always start off our conversations with an insult. I feel cheated." It'd been a long time since anyone other than Old Titus dared camp out in the forest.

"Some family of townies. They must be new. We haven't seen them before and they have all their teeth."

They must be recent transplants. Not everyone uses meth in town, but most do. It was the easiest way to tell where they lived. The number of teeth left was a good indicator of how long they lived there. The longer they stayed the fewer they had.

"You sure they're townies?" Asked Rusty.

"Had to be. Who else would try something so stupid?" Said Chip… or was it Jack? He never knew.

"Just about anyone can do something dumb. Like you two. Why were you out so late? Your poor mother was worried sick," said Rusty.

"We were doing stuff, old man. In fact, I think our actions last night chased the forest demon away from the trailer park," said Jack… or was it Chip?

"If it's a forest demon, why would it come to the trailer park?" Asked Harry.

"It just would. Why're you so stupid?" asked Chip… Jack?

"I dunno, boys. Things don't seem to add up," said Rusty.

"Fine. All we know is it tore up their tent, kicked the shit outta the parents, and chased off their daughter before we scared it away." Jack… Chip? Beamed in pride at this.

"Tell us where this campsite is. I want to get a look," said Rusty.

The boys did their best to describe how they got to the campsite. Rusty had a hard time translating their path on foot to roadways he knew in the area. After a while, he got a good idea of the area they were talking about.

He thanked the boys, and said, "You best head home and be extra nice to your mother. She does a lot for you two. You don't know what she goes through."

"Thanks, dad!" Chip sneered at him. At least, he was sure it was Chip this time.

The boys ran off into the park. Rusty hoped they would head home, but doubted it. He wished they'd treat their mother better. She deserved it. Those two were more than a handful for a single mom. He knew if he stepped in the picture, he'd end up in jail after he issued appropriate discipline. Lily was beautiful, but those boys…

"We best get the truck. If the Sheriff picked Old Man McHenry up, he probably took him to the hospital," said Rusty.

The old police cruiser gleamed in the morning sun. The sheriff sitting behind the wheel glared at the two of them, almost daring them to approach. Sheriff Benjamin may not care much about taking care of himself, but his car was something else.

He used to make Harry and Rusty wash it when they did something wrong. He called it his diversion program. Rusty thought he did it to get a free car wash.

Rusty parked away from the car to avoid being given an opportunity to experience his youth again. He didn't want to spend three hours washing that car.

Rusty stepped up to the driver's window and said, "Morning, Sheriff. We'd like to report a missing person."

Sheriff Benjamin lifted the mason jar he held to his lips and took a long pull. "Why would you want to do that? Today was looking to be a fine day, until you two showed up."

The sharp scent of shine rolled off the Sheriff in waves. Rusty's eyes stung and threatened to water on the spot. A car rolled past. The sheriff looked at his speed gun, grimaced, then turned back to Rusty.

"You been drinking? I smell it on you. Strong."

"No, Sheriff, I haven't been drinking today."

"You sure? I haven't used my breathalyzer today."

"No, sir. Drinking and driving ain't right."

"Damn right, it's not! I'm here to make sure none of you losers do it! Not even one sip! That's all it takes." The sheriff's words slurred around and lurched to a stop.

"Just one?"

"Just one. That's all I had. Just a single sip. I wasn't even impaired. That car came outta nowhere. Now I get to sit here and babysit a bunch of idiots and retirees. How is that fair?"

"I—I dunno, Sheriff."

"It's not! That's what I'm trying to tell you! It's not fair. Why should I be forced to patrol such a small area? I used to run the county! I was good at it!"

"You sure were, except all those break-ins and robberies and the drugs. Everything was wonderful then."

Rusty meant it. Sheriff Benjamin was terrible at his job, but when he ran the county, he'd never bothered them in the trailer park. He had no reason to come out here. Even if they called for help, he'd never show up.

Then again, he was never around to harass them like he does most days now.

Rusty looked in the back window. A jacket he recognized lay on the seat. Smears of blood stained the cloth. Some had transferred to the leather. The torn fabric lay in a rumpled ball, as if discarded by someone in a hurry.

"Sheriff, is that Old Man McHenry's jacket in your back seat?" Asked Rusty.

A long silence filled the space between them as the Sheriff took a slow sip from the mason jar.

"What do you know about Old Titus McHenry?" The Sheriff's eyes seemed to clear, intense gaze focusing on his face. Rusty felt confused and embarrassed. He knew little, but he knew saying that would only prolong the questioning.

"Not much, sir. Just asking because I recognize the jacket in your back seat."

"Is that so? What's wrong with the jacket?" Asked the Sheriff.

"It looks torn and bloody," said Rusty.

"How did it get that way, junior?"

"I dunno, Sheriff. Maybe the old man had a bloody nose?"

"Or maybe you and your brother attacked him and you're here to see if my investigation is onto you."

"That'd be silly, sir. My brother and me were out driving last night in the woods."

"Isn't that interesting. That's were I found him. Why were you driving in the woods?"

Another sip from jar wet the Sheriff's lips. Sheriff Benjamin let out a small burp.

Rusty winced. That's wasn't helping them get out of there anytime soon.

"We were looking for Old Man McHenry, but we got attacked by a ghost!" Said Harry.

"A ghost, huh? You on the meth now, son? Maybe the marijuana? Addled your brains more than usual?"

"No…The ghost was huge! It attacked us and then ran off. Maybe it attacked Old McHenry, too?" Harry nodded at his own statement, as if to lend it credibility.

"Why'd you call Ms. Grace last night, Sheriff?" Asked Rusty trying to deflect Sheriff Benjamin from questioning them further.

"You spying on me now? What's it to you? How'd you know I called her?" Benjamin took another sip from the mason jar. It was almost empty.

"She told me this morning. Said to tell you she don't take callers after 6 o'clock."

"Oh. It was related to my investigation of the attack on Old McHenry. You wouldn't understand it."

The Sheriff was right about one thing. He'd never understand what he saw in Gracelyn Whittacre. As mean as she was, Rusty couldn't imagine Sheriff Benjamin lasting a week. These late night calls waking her up seemed to come on the regular about twice a year. She must have given him an earful last night.

"The old man was plenty out of it when I found him. He couldn't tell me anything about his assailant. That or he wouldn't. I have yet to figure out which. I dropped him off at Mercy Memorial. Now go away, even if you did it, none of the boys at the station will drop by to take you in. About the only thing I'm good for these days is writing tickets."

Sheriff Benjamin looked at Rusty and said, "Stupidity's not against the law. Exercise your liberty to leave."

The sheriff leaned back in his seat, cranked his air conditioner fan, and rolled the window up sealing Rusty and Harry outside of his world. In a couple moments, he was snoring loud enough to be heard through the glass.

"Mercy Memorial," said the bored woman on the phone, smacking gum loud enough for Rusty to hear.

"Hi, I'm looking for a friend of mine. He was dropped off last night by the Sheriff," said Rusty.

"Honey, we get all kinds dropped off by many deputies. I'm going to need a little more to go on." The smacking of bubble gum punctuated her statement.

"Older man, named Titus McHenry."

"I can't give out personal details. I have a few older men dropped off by deputies last night. Two drunks, checked out this morning. One overdose still here. One cut up real bad."

"That's probably him. That last one. When are visiting hours?"

"Unless you're family, or power of attorney, I can't give you the room number or allow you to visit. All I can say is he was brought in by the old Sheriff that's always drunk. To be honest, I'm surprised they got here alive considering how sauced the Sheriff was. Everyone could smell it when he walked in."

"Thank you for your help." Rusty hung the phone up.

"I don't get why we can't go visit, Rusty? We're the closest thing old Titus has to family," said Harry.

"It's the hospital trying to protect itself. At least he's getting looked at. I don't know how he'll afford the bill, though."

"Maybe—"

A loud knock at the door interrupted their discussion.

Rusty opened the door to the sight of the loveliest woman in the trailer park.

Lily Jessup, her wavy red tresses hanging loose over her shoulders. A smattering of angel kisses across the bridge of her nose lay atop rounded cheeks. Her shirt was losing the struggle to contain her ample assets, the flower print on her brassiere visible through the stretched fabric. A pack of cigarettes stuck inside the strap above one cup. Bright red lipstick emphasizing the big smile she wore. She leaned against the doorframe granting him a better view.

"Hello, Rusty. I don't know what I'm going to do. My boys have run off again. They came home close to three in the morning last night, and even after I grounded them, they up and leave when I'm not looking."

Her mascara rimming her eyes had small rivulets where she'd been weeping. That caused a stirring in Rusty. Down below. His discomfort rose like a wave of fire from there to light his cheeks up. Her own cheeks glowed with a light rouge that enhanced her beauty.

"Hi, Lily. How can I h-". Rusty cleared his throat and still squeaked out, "help?"

Her bright green eyes were like magnetic emeralds. He could stare into them forever.

"Would you be a dear and send them home if you find them? I'm worried about them."

Rusty couldn't take his eyes off her face. She was the prettiest girl he'd ever seen, and he didn't want to stop seeing her.

"Get a room, you two," called Harry from his armchair.

Rusty's cheeks burned even hotter. Lily dropped her eyes, a small smile playing at her lips. She heaved a big sigh that sent Rusty's head spinning.

"I have a big meal planned for tomorrow night. If you can get my boys home, you're welcome to join us. You can bring Harry, as well."

"That's awful nice of you, Lily. I'd love to join you for dinner. We'll get right on looking for your boys."

"Oh thank you, Rusty. I don't know what I'd do without you." She batted her eyes at him and his heart soared.

"It's no trouble, Lily. I'm glad to help."

"You're so precious, Rusty." She smiled as she left.

Rusty closed the door, and leaned his back against it, waiting for his heart rate to slow down.

"Rusty…"

"Hush up a moment, I'm picturing life with Lily while the boys are in military school."

"What am I doing in that dream?"

Damn. He hadn't thought of that. Harry was his responsibility. Had been for a long time and even if he got with Lily, Harry'd be right there. He couldn't be anywhere else.

"Don't worry about it Harry. It's not gonna happen. Just nice to think about, sometimes. Let's go see if we can find Chip and Jack."

At the bottom of their steps, a loud hiss startled Rusty.

The opossum in the arms of his employer favored him with another greeting, this time adding a swipe in for good measure.

"Ms. Grace, is there something I can help you with?" Asked Rusty.

"I doubt it. You can't even help yourself in noticing that young woman's flirting. It's as obvious as you are stupid." Gracelyn shifted her pet from one arm to the other.

Rusty knew better than to speak up in defense of his intellect. It would only worsen the punishment dished out by the frail old woman. He'd made that mistake a few times. Instead, he stood there smiling…like an idiot.

"We're all free to act stupid sometimes, but you seem to enjoy abusing the privilege. What's wrong with you? She's into you and you keep blowing her off. Her boys need a good father figure too, and since one of those isn't around, you'll have to do." Ms. Grace sniffed her disdain for him.

"As a matter of fact, Ms. Grace, she came over asking for some help finding her boys. Have you seen them?"

"Of course I have. Saw them about an hour ago. They had another youngster tied up marching around like soldiers. I don't know where they went, but I heard something about camping and a demon. They headed off towards the forest a bit ago." The opossum gripped her collar tighter and sneered at him.

"Before you head off, have you finished your jobs for today? Mr. Miller's plumbing issue? What about Hannah's phone line? Or how about Charle's mower?" She arched a thin eyebrow at him.

Harry spoke up from behind him, and said, "we're waiting on parts from the hardware store for the plumbing. We can't fix the phone line, that's phone company property. The mower works fine, Charlie don't know how to start it is all."

"Figures, you have an excuse every time, don't you?" She glared at Harry.

"The invoice is on your desk in the office. I dropped it off myself, Ms. Grace," said Rusty.

She harrumphed at him, gave another wicked glare, then wandered off.

"We should get out of here while she's busy. We need to find the boys."

"Stop pulling so much!" Peggy slowed her pace and allowed the small twine cord tied around her waist to loosen.

"You idiots are the ones that have me tied up. I can't help it if I walk faster than you bungling bumble-footed buffoons."

"We can't let you escape. How do we know you didn't sick the demon on your parents?" asked the one not holding the rope.

"You two really are feebleminded, aren't you?" She looked over her shoulder.

The twins stared at her, then looked at each other, then back at her.

"Hey, no one calls us stupid but each other," said the one holding the cord.

"Does it matter? Does it make it less true?"

She saw an opportunity and skipped a couple steps, pulling the cord hard. The twin holding it stumbled.

"Knock that off. All we want to know is what you saw."

"I don't know. All I saw was the tent moving. If you saw it, how do I know you didn't turn whatever it was loose on us?"

"We saw something, alright," said the empty-handed one. Looking away, his cheeks flushing. "We were hiding in a bush near the campsite."

"Really? Which one? Were you spying on me?" Peggy widened her eyes in mock terror.

"No. We were spying on all of you. We don't want you in the woods. Look what happened and you didn't even get to spend one night."

She picked her way through the shrubs blocking the path. Not far now, if she remembered the way right.

"Oh I spent the night in the woods, alright. My pa taught me all kinds of survival skills while we were overseas. I slept in a tree."

"Over— where?" Asked the one holding her lead.

"Overseas. Not sure, but that's what pa always called it."

She fingered the knot in the twine. It was loose. So loose, in fact, if she pulled on the cord, it'd come untied.

Those two really are morons. Can't even tie a basic knot.

She held the knot in her fist. She didn't want to give away one of her advantages too soon.

"Why were you over there?" Asked Chip, curiosity flashed in his eyes.

"My pa is an assassin. I saw him kill two agents from another spy group. They even stabbed my pa, but he killed them anyway, then he sewed himself up and is peachy keen."

"You're lying. If they stabbed him, he'd be dead."

"Am not. And you saw my pa last night, so you know he's alive."

"We saw him, alright," said the one with the cord elbowing his brother. His impish grin was cute. She'd like him if he weren't so stupid.

The other one turned beet red, glaring at his sibling. One fist balled up ready to be thrown. He must have thought better, because he unclenched his fist and walked past her. "This way. We need to hurry to get there before dark. I don't want to run into what attacked your camp."

They marched on in relative silence. The crunch of the leaves and twigs under the feet were the only sounds. Even the forest life seemed to abandon this place.

She tried to get another conversation going, "What about your pa? You know about mine and how badass he is. I don't know nothing about yours."

The one holding her leash said, "We don't either. He's been gone a long time."

"It's over here," said the other twin.

They stepped into the clearing, the campsite before them.

The tent remnants lay cast off to the side of the site, torn apart and shredded. Two suitcases lay near the fire, their contents strewn about the camp. White campfire ashes lay cold inside the circle of stones. The truck was nowhere to be seen, but the scattered contents of the boxes dropped from the bed mixed in with the rest of the belongings all over the camp.

It looked like a cyclone had come through after everyone ran away. The disaster left nothing untouched.

The sun dipped behind the tree line. Peggy looked at the sky and saw clouds rolling across. She watched the two boys as they fussed at each other by the large bush at the edge of the camp. The lead lay on the ground, unattended.

She wrapped the twine cord around her waist in a loose coil. She stepped on rocks, thick branches, and large patches of moss or dirt, and circled the tree while the two argued over who left the bag behind. Neither was looking in her direction.

Quiet as a mouse, she snuck away, putting distance between the camp and the two morons. Once she couldn't hear them arguing any longer, she sprinted down the game trail she found the night before. She knew the perfect hiding spot.

A scream from the campsite, joined by the sound of the boys yelling, gave energy to her legs as she ran. She wanted nothing to do with that haunted place.

The wreck came into view; the light was getting dimmer by the minute. She hoped the jacket was still in the back. She'd slept there the night before and looked forward to her secret sleeping spot. The walk through the forest listening to the doofus brothers had exhausted her. She needed time to think about how to find her parents.

She crawled into the wreck through the window, avoiding the small kernels of broken glass as best she could, and climbed over the tree branch stuck crosswise through the body of the vehicle. The backseat was cold to her skin, like the night before. The jacket was where she left it. She was thankful for it. The night's chill was already setting in.

At the top of one of the back seats, she found a lever and pulled it. One side of the back seat popped loose. She pulled it to see what she'd opened and found a space big enough for her to stretch out. She wriggled into place and explored the surfaces with her fingers. Her inquisitive probing found a small knob and twisted it.

Light shone from the hole. Peering through she could see the path leading up to the car. It also let in some fresh air. That was a bonus. She set the knob off to the side. She'd put it back later.

She felt around some more. Some kind of netting met her fingertips. She pulled the back seat closed, but not latched. She wanted to be sure she could get out. Wrapped in the jacket, she felt warm and snug. She'd almost say she was comfortable.

The snapping of twigs outside the car woke her. She strained to listen for more. Silence met her attention. She might have imagined it. Her own mother told her she'd get in trouble with her imagination one of these days.

Another snap. The light coming in through the hole was dimmer than before. She couldn't have napped for long. She peeked through the hole and saw a figure standing on the path. Tremors shook her body as ice clamped over her heart.

Its fur was green and curly, not all straight like her dog's coat. Antlers grew at odd angles all over the creature. It stood taller than her dad, with long arms. She couldn't see its feet, but she suspected they bore claws as long as her fingers.

The most terrifying part of the creature was its face. Wide near the top, where two horns curled out from the temples, it descended to a narrow jaw, sharp fangs jutted down from bottom. Set deep in hollow sockets, she could see its eyes shining.

"Unidad uno, regístrese."

The creature's voice was deep. She couldn't hear anyone speaking to it.

"¿Ya revisaste el auto?"

Motion near the car startled her. She stifled a whimper.

"Sí. Lo comprobamos ayer."

She couldn't understand a thing they were saying. Its alien language mystified her. Fear crept in at the edges of her thoughts. She had laughed when the boys spoke of forest demons—just stories to pass the time. But now… now she wasn't sure. It didn't sound like demons—but then, what did a demon sound like? A nervous chill crept along her spine.

Another one stepped into view from beside the first.

"No hay señales del ciervo aquí. Todavía nos queda un sector por limpiar."

The first one nodded its head and said, "Veamos si podemos enviarlo hacia la unidad dos."

It reached under its face and a shrill scream full of terror filled the air.

She covered her ears, praying they didn't hear her in the car.

A loud crack cut the scream off with a deep grunt. A large animal ran into the clearing and slammed into the screaming creature, throwing it to the ground. It delivered a couple good stomps, then bucked and jumped towards the other demon.

Peggy couldn't understand what she was seeing. The beast twisted and jumped, flipping around what looked like a second head. She knew it was angry and was thankful she was in the car. It moved too fast for her to see what kind of animal it was.

"¡No dejes que se escape!"

The monster still standing on the path dodged the charge of the animal. Standing between the two still on their feet, the wild terror stomped, snorted, and tossed its heads. It charged the one by the car and slammed into the side door.

Peggy jumped. She clamped her hand over her mouth to keep herself quiet.

The four legged, two headed monstrosity spun and bucked. Kicked every direction and refused to stand still.

One back leg kick caught the shin of one fiend. The other raised some kind of black object and followed the beast with it. The two demoniacs kept it between them as best they could, but it was racing around, making it difficult.

Hooves stomped on the back of the downed creature as it stirred to life. Startled by the movement, the terrible animal reared up on its hind legs, ready to head-butt the prone creature. It took two steps, then jumped to the side.

She didn't understand what happened next. The devil on the ground sat up and pointed something small at the monster. A loud snapping boom made her ears hurt as the animal jumped to the side. Broken glass flew from the window as the demon standing between the monster and her hideout flew backwards and slammed into the door before sliding down and laying still. The two-headed beast was nowhere to be seen.

"¡Mierda! ¿Qué diablos pasó? ¡Le disparaste a Hura!" shouted the standing creature.

After the fallen creature climbed to its feet, it pointed at the car and said, "¡Maldita sea! Compruébalo. ¡Todavía tenemos que atrapar a ese maldito ciervo!"

"Él está muerto." The creature joined its companion, and the two of them left in pursuit of the fleeing beast.

She waited until she couldn't hear their footsteps anymore, then to be sure, she waited until she counted to five hundred.

Around one hundred and fifty, she got bored and decided it was safe enough. She was thankful the seat was silent as she pushed it open. Getting out was a noisier endeavor, but no one heard. She saw it as a win.

Antlers stuck up above the edge of the window she crawled into the car through, convincing her to use another. Outside the vehicle, she hunkered down and listened. Nothing rustled the bush or broke any twigs.

She exhaled and made her way around the wreckage. Next to the body of the creature she studied it in the faltering light. Tremors shook her thin frame as she wrestled with her fear. She worked up the nerve and reached out, poking the body.

No reaction.

The fur felt weird. It almost felt like string. She grabbed a fistful of fur and pulled.

It was an outfit.

It wasn't fur at all.

Her hand felt cold and sticky.

She looked at her palm. Something thick and dark red that smelled rank covered her hand.

Whatever it was, it covered the being's entire chest.

"Only one thing left to do, Peggy."

She pulled the creature's face up.

The skull face came off in her hands.

It was a mask.

The staring eyes of the dead man looked past her shoulder. At first, she glanced over her shoulder, thinking he was watching someone approaching, but then realized he couldn't see anything.

His eyes had dark makeup around them. His skin was darker than most people she knew. He had a thin black mustache and goatee. The small bit of hair sticking out of the hood he wore was black and straight. He had something in his ear, but she didn't know what it was.

She could see he attached the antlers to his outfit with cords. He wore black gloves, and she could see his feet now. Seeing the black boots instead of the razor-sharp claws she imagined disappointed her.

She wiped her hand off on a clean spot among the threads of the man's outfit.

Not sure what to do now, she contemplated crawling back in the car, but decided that wasn't a good idea. Not with the possibility of them returning for their companion. She didn't want to be anywhere near here when they returned.

One thought crossed her mind. She toyed with the cord around her waist. She could tell them. Lead them here and see how brave they were or if they'd run away like cowards.

The faint sound of snapping twigs and crunch of leaves helped her decide. She scampered from the wrecked car and away from the noise. She had a couple boys to impress.

Rusty halted the truck next to the ragged hole in the brush. A large vehicle had passed through, tearing up the vegetation along the embankment. He mapped out the path back into the woods and got confused. He couldn't understand how Harry did this. Just thinking about it made his head hurt.

"Harry, what do you think happened here?"

Harry was already looking at the tread marks on the road. His brother dropped a clump of grass he'd been staring at and pointed at something in front of him.

"See these tracks?" Asked his brother.

"No, you're in the way."

"Oh." Harry shifted, putting his body further in the way.

"These tracks are made by off-road tires. They cross the others, kinda tear em up, so they're newer. Musta been a big truck. It drove out of the woods. Made a hard turn towards town. See how the outer edge of the track is deeper?"

"No, Harry. I can't."

"Are you even looking?" Asked Harry.

"Big truck?" Rusty looked at the road and couldn't see anything that was obvious about a truck.

"Yeah. Wheel base is too wide for a car with those tires."

"We should probably follow the tracks backwards, see where they came from." Rusty followed the path plowed by the truck.

The walk wasn't long, maybe three hundred yards, before they found what they were looking for. A trail of tools, supplies, and empty boxes led to the remnants of a campsite. Refuse lay scattered all over. The ice chest lay on its side. Animals had gotten to the food.

"What's that smell?" Said Harry.

Rusty had been trying not to smell the malignant odor. "Maybe the campers were sophisticated folks that like complicated food? I heard some of that stuff smells real bad. Like that cheese you don't like."

"If complicated food smells like this, I don't want none." Harry pulled his shirt collar over his nose.

Whispered snickering reached Rusty's ears. He couldn't tell which direction it came from.

Rusty picked his way through the mess, looking for clues as to the whereabouts of the owners and their identities. It looked like more than animals tore through the site. Boot prints mixed with the animal tracks. Smears of dark blood were everywhere.

Harry knelt down to study the tracks in a semi-dry area.

The sound of nails on tree bark unnerved Rusty. He looked around, but couldn't see anything watching him.

Rusty checked the remnants of the tent. The damage done looked worse than anything an animal could have. He'd seen places that looked like this on the news. It was always another country where the people were fighting over the same scrap of nothing.

"You know, Harry, I'm really hoping we don't find the boys or their friend here. I don't think I'd be able to tell Lily. I'd hate to be the one that broke her heart with the news."

Harry stood and said, "I don't think you have to worry. There's a jumble of prints here. Some are like dad's old boots. Newer, but same tread. The rest look like sandals and sneakers."

Rusty wandered over to the ice chest. Scattered around it were empty beer bottles and spoiling food. The ice was gone, saturating the ground, turning the dirt into soggy mud. The rotten egg odor was stronger by the fire as he walked around it.

Laying against the inner edge of the rocks was a small, burnt orb he recognized. It was cool to the touch. The twins were here, alright. They must have seen what happened. Rusty had been the victim of one of their stink-outs. It took a week for his truck to air out when their prank landed on the floorboard.

"Looks like the boys were telling the truth, for once." Rusty held up the used stink bomb.

Harry stretched and wandered over to a tall tree. Rusty could hear him watering it as he walked to a small path hidden by the bushes. Something shiny flared in the weeds near the trail. He picked it up. It was a spent rifle casing.

"Poachers…Got to be."

Harry's scream startled him. "What happened? A snake bite you on the dick, again?"

"No! Something tried to jump on me from behind! I heard a sneeze. I thought it was you, and was about to bless you, then something hit the ground behind me."

Rusty circled the tree and looked around. He couldn't see anything moving. Black stains crusted the trunk. He pushed the weeds around and a red wrapper caught his eye.

"Look here. This must be what got ya." He held up a brick of firecrackers.

It was the brand the twins carried around. He recognized the smiling face of the animal on the side with the little bubble promising the loudest explosions ever heard. The pack was dry. Morning dew hadn't marred the thin paper wrapper at all.

"This hasn't been here long. If the twins threw it, they woulda lit it first." Rusty looked up.

Sitting on their own branches, hidden from view, were the twin brothers Chip and Jack. One wore a backpack with the flap open, fighting with the zipper and fireworks about to fall out of it.

"Hi, boys. Come on down."

Rusty imagined the trip down from the tree took less effort than their initial climb. He remembered being their age. Things like climbing and running came a lot easier, then. Once they were down, they sat on the stumps around the cold fire pit.

"Go ahead and tell us what happened. I want to know where the girl is," said Rusty, doing his best to look like an authoritative father.

"We left our backpack here, so we came to get it. We brought her with us since we weren't sure if her family was here, or if she was controlling the demon," said Chip.

"Controlling the demon? What kinda nonsense is that? No one controls demons, but the devil." Rusty scratched his head and looked around.

"How'd y'all get up in that tree? There isn't a branch low enough to grab onto," asked Harry.

"Your guess is as good as mine. When we heard the scream, we thought the demon came to claim us. Next thing I knew, I was sitting on that branch and Chip was on the other one."

"Do you understand how dangerous what you did was? What woulda happened if her dad saw you with his little daughter tied up? It's called kidnapping. He coulda gone apeshit on you and no one would know." Rusty's concern for the kids was showing in his voice. He needed a moment.

The boys, for their part, looked at the ground and seemed to shrivel.

Harry asked, "Did you see what direction she ran? Was it before the demon got here or after?"

"We noticed she was gone after we got our backpack out of the big bush. Then we heard the scream," said Chip, his voice small.

"Then the demon rushed into camp and tore the place up. It was running all over, too fast to see what it looked like. We stayed quiet until it left."

"What did it look like?" Asked Harry.

"It was big. It had two heads, a long body, ran like a horse," said Jack, Chip nodding his agreement.

Jack looked at Chip, like he was asking a question. After a moment, he shrugged. "We think there's more than one. The scream we heard at first was different than the ones that came after. Once the first demon left the camp, others came through. Horns everywhere, they were yelling, but we couldn't understand what they said. Sounded evil. One of them screamed a couple times. Its voice loud enough to scare everything away. We think they're hunting the first demon."

Rusty shook his head. Their story was not only confusing, but made no sense. Why would demons hunt each other? Weren't they all working together? What was going on? These boys needed a good lecture.

"Now, boys. Having an imagination is a good thing. Yours runs a bit wild, though. You sure you ain't making some of this up? Be honest, now."

Both boys looked at him, fire burning in their eyes as they denied making anything up.

Rusty ignored Harry wandering away while he focused his attention on the trouble-makers. He knew he'd given his brother plenty of these lectures and didn't blame him for not wanting to hang around for someone else's turn.

"What would your mother think about you kidnapping a girl? How do you think she's going to react? If that girl goes to the sheriff and tells him you tied her up, what then? What if her father comes looking for you two?"

Each point he made caused the boys to shrink further, looking like they'd rather be anywhere else. He felt sorry for them. Kids are kids, but these boys wronged folks. They'd have to come up with something to make it right.

"I'll tell you what. If you two promise to head home, right now, straight there, I'll consider finding a way of breaking the news to your mother in a way that she won't be angry. Not promising she won't be furious. Just promising I'll try."

Rusty dismissed them. The boys took off like the devil himself was chasing them.

"Rusty. I think I got something." Harry stood at the head of the small trail where Rusty found the shell casing.

"What's there?" Asked Rusty, remembering he'd need to report the poachers to the sheriff.

"Small foot prints. Larger ones, too, but small ones ran off this way."

The prospects of finding the girl rose with Rusty's hope.

The trail wasn't hard to follow. The girl made no attempt at hiding her flight from the campsite. Broken weeds, bent limbs, footprints, all signs of someone leaving in a hurry. The only thing Rusty hoped for was they found her before the poachers. At risk of vanishing in the fading light, they followed the trail as fast as they could.

"Wait. There's another trail. This one joins it, but I can't tell which direction it goes." Harry stood at the intersection, puzzling over the path.

"Which one is smaller?"

"The one this way is smaller and less messy," said Harry.

"Let's follow it, then. Time's running short."

The sunlight was almost gone as they rounded a bend, and Harry stopped again. "There's more blood."

"More…blood? I didn't know there was any to begin with!"

"Oh. I thought I told you."

"No, Harry, this is another of your you-only conversations."

"Sorry, Rusty. There's more blood smeared on the leaves here. We should hurry."

Harry stopped after a while, standing still, looking into the woods.

"More blood? Or maybe a piece of clothing? What about a body part? Did you see one of those back there you want to tell me about now?"

"No, Rusty. There's something standing over by that big tree. I can't see what it is, but it looks like it's eating something." Harry pointed.

In the gloom, Rusty could make out a faint shape, but nothing concrete.

He stepped as light as he could to sneak closer without startling whatever it was.

Harry joined him, crunching leaves and twigs as he stepped.

Rusty whispered, "Do you want to walk over there and step on some leaves and twigs you might have missed?"

The creature didn't seem to hear them, as it hunched over whatever lay at the base of the tree.

They crept closer to another thick tree. This time, they could see the body of a man leaning against the base of the tree. Blood smeared across his side. Bloat twisted his facial features to be unrecognizable.

"He's not wearing any clothes, Rusty. Who'd do that?"

The creature stood over something beside the body. Crunching and smacking drifted from the creature. Several empty bottles of liquor lay beside the bag.

"I think it's eating something. I can't see what it is. Something's wrong. I think it has two heads." A tremor caused Harry's words to waver.

"Nothing's got two heads, except maybe that deformed snake that almost killed itself. Let's catch it and I'll prove it," said Rusty. "I'm going to sneak around, see how close I can get. Gonna try and grab it. When I give the signal, step on the path and talk soft at it. That should scare it into my trap."

"Okay, Rusty. What signal?" Apprehension thick in Harry's voice.

Rusty moved slow and careful through the underbrush with a lot less noise than Harry could ever manage. Cloud cover shrouded the moon, plunging the area in darkness. Rusty moved by feel, listening with every step to ensure his target hadn't noticed him.

The clouds moved on, taking their own sweet time. Silver light lit the trees up as Rusty slipped into position. He waved his hat to signal Harry, but he doubted whether Harry could spot him. He waved bigger and harder.

The slim figure of his brother stepped into view, the two-headed monster between them.

Harry raised his arms and waved back.

Rusty waved at him and motioned for him to speak.

Harry mimicked Rusty's motions and then started chicken dancing.

Rusty acted out smacking Harry with his cap.

Harry pretended to pitch a ball at him.

That's it!

"You supposed to call him to you!" Shouted Rusty.

Almost as if his voice banished the clouds, the moonlight flooded the area with bright light.

The creature raised its heads and looked at Rusty. Froth surrounded its mouth as it snorted and reared, hooves striking the air in front of it.

It screamed a terrible wail, turned, and charged up the path towards his brother.

"Rusty, watch out! It's growing another of itself!" Shouted Harry.

The creature screamed as it ran straight at Harry.

The creature plowed into Harry, cutting short his scream and tossing his body to the side.

Harry hit a tree with an audible thunk of flesh, smacking something solid.

"Harry!"

The creature screamed again as it fled the area.

Rusty rushed over to his brother's side and knelt.

Blood covered Harry's chest.

The shirt looked black in the moonlight before another cloud hid the lunar body.

The sharp, metallic tang carried an air of putrescence with it.

"Harry!" Rusty cried as he pulled him onto his lap.

"Rusty? Where are you, Rusty? I can't see you."

"I'm right here, Harry. Can you feel me holding you?"

"My chest hurts, Rusty. It hurts real bad."

"Don't you worry about that. It'll be alright, Harry."

"It's so dark, and cold, Rusty."

"That's cause it is dark, Harry."

"Rusty! It's hurting worse. Feels like it burns."

"Where does it hurt, Harry?"

"Right under my heart."

Harry gasped again.

"I think it's moving."

"Moving? What do you mean, Harry?"

Pfffffffffffft.

The loudest, wettest fart he'd ever heard come from his brother erupted into the silence.

"It don't hurt no more, Rusty."

The cloud rolled away from the moon and by the moonlight, Rusty saw that the blood on the shirt was old, filled with grass and leaves…and not Harry's.

Rusty shoved his brother off his lap.

"Get up you idiot. We still have a little girl to find."

Rusty strode over the body to get a better look.

He'd say the man looked like he was middle-aged, but the bloating in the injuries to his face made it hard to tell. There was also a large gash across the forehead, though this one didn't look like it was fatal.

He saw the source of the blood on his torso. The broken end of a large branch stuck out of a hole in his side. That wasn't the only injury Rusty found as he looked at the man's neck. The edges of the gash were smooth, as if sliced by something sharp. Someone cut his throat.

No blood leaked from the wound.

That was good; that meant he died beforehand.

Harry joined him at the body, took one look and threw up.

Rusty felt sorry for Harry. The smell wasn't pleasant, but hadn't reached full ripe, yet.

Rusty turned his attention to the bag. Inside the haversack, he found a couple of large plastic containers. The lids were missing from the containers, and something had torn open the paper wrapped bricks inside. Translucent crystal fingers lay in a jumbled pile. Rusty pulled a couple of plastic tubes out, cracked one, and shook it.

Orange light filled the area, giving a better view of the body.

Two teeth stuck out of its mouth at odd angles. One upper, one lower.

"Meth user." Rusty looked at the bag. "Correction…meth runner." That means those crystals were meth.

Damn.

"We need to go the other way up the trail. The little girl didn't come this way."

Harry nodded and followed Rusty. The orange glow stick helped them find the trail and follow it back to the intersection. Harry jumped at every noise. Some real, others imagined.

A much shorter hike, the other direction, ended at a car wreck. Leaning against the front door of the car was the body of a man. Rusty shone the glow stick over his body and found the blood-soaked chest. A small hole near the top of the staining looked to have entered just below the heart.

He'd fastened several types of antlers all over the ghillie suit he wore. A bone mask lay next to his body. The eye makeup did nothing to hide him being Hispanic.

Rusty turned his head and saw the earpiece and attached boom mic. He followed the cable to his waist and found the radio missing. Whoever it was, they were careful to not leave anything to identify them by.

Not too careful.

Rusty examined the rest of the body and found a rifle under its right side. The sleek, black rifle was too weak to be hunting elk, or bear. They intended this for something else.

Rusty shone the glow stick around. The only thing he found was more footprints.

"Harry, can you tell which way they went? What about the girl?"

Harry took the glow stick and looked around for a long while. He circled the car, then around the body, the back to where Rusty stood. A loud boom ripped across the forest. Both brothers stood still for several moments before resuming their tasks. It was too far away to concern them now, but it emphasized the danger.

"Yeah. She was here, but she headed that way. I think back towards the trailer park." He pointed past the car. "Whoever did this, went that way, but doubled back and headed up over here."

"How far is it to the park?"

Harry ticked off his fingers one at a time then said, "About an hour, if she knows the way."

"Then we need to find out who these guys are. There's no way this was an accident. We can't have them out here poaching, they'll hurt someone."

"What about that rifle? We could use it for protection," said Harry as he examined the black metal gun.

"No. We can't take it. It's evidence. If that gun has been used to hurt anyone and the police catch you with it, you go to jail. No, thanks. I'm fine skipping that trouble. Plus, it's empty and all the magazines are missing."

"But Rusty. We might need it," whined Harry.

"What are you going to do? Use it like a club? No, and that's final."

"Fine…" Harry sulked as he followed Rusty.

Under the warm glow of the orange light, the trail was easier to follow. The black stains on the shrubs and undergrowth made it clear which way the creature and poachers went. The flatted grass left an obvious trail.

After walking a while, Rusty found another spent casing. The brass was cool to the touch. Parts of it were still polished. Up ahead, another dozen steps, he found a large section of antler. The antler's end had splintered and appeared to have a small hole at the base.

The trail widened into a small clearing of flattened grass and torn up earth. Boot prints trampled the animal tracks in a line across the clearing. Animal tracks ranged all over the small circle.

"Rusty? What's that?" whispered Harry, pointing to a shadowed blob at the side of the trail.

"No idea. Let's check it out," said Rusty.

A large body of a deer, its front legs caught among the narrow spacing of the tree trunks lining the side of the path, lay unmoving. Rusty grabbed a stick and poked the backside of the animal.

No reaction.

"I think it's dead," said Rusty.

Harry shoved his way through the trees to the backside and said, "Rusty! I think the demon tried to eat it! Its head is missing."

Missing head? A picture of what they were dealing with was forming in Rusty's head. He wasn't sure, since he'd only heard about it and never seen the phenomenon. He wanted more information to be sure before he said anything or Harry's imagination would run wild with theories.

"Let's get a move on. We need to find the poachers." Rusty continued along the trail on the other side of the clearing.

Not far ahead, the blood trail ended at the missing head of the dead deer. One of its antlers was a nub of splintered horn. Whatever ripped the head off was strong. His theory was falling apart. Every instance of this he'd ever heard of the deer was dead for days or weeks before the surviving one could rip the dead head free.

The trail was harder to follow now that the severed head no longer marked it. The bent grass and broken branches were still leading them onward.

"Mierda. Malditos árboles. ¿Qué hice para conseguir esta tarea? Persiguiendo a un maldito ciervo."

Harry and Rusty froze. Rusty shoved the light into his back pocket and pulled Harry off the path behind a tree. The whispered cursing and voice, though he couldn't understand the language, he knew when someone was upset, came from further up the trail.

Rusty clamped his hand over Harry's mouth as another man in a ghillie suit, antlers strapped on all over, walked into view. He held his rifle across his body with an air of experience and willingness to use it.

The man paused in front of their hiding spot. Held his hand up to his ear and said, "El rastro está claro. No hay señales del animal. Asustándolo a tu manera."

The ghillie clad man, moved his hand to his throat and let loose a demonic scream that drove ice down Rusty's spine and made his teeth hurt. Harry struggled in his grasp a moment, before giving up and settling down.

The man held his hand to his ear, again, before running back up the trail. Up ahead, he screamed again, the fading sound letting Rusty know he was moving away fast. Rusty counted to ten to be sure he was gone before he let go of Harry's mouth.

"What'd you do that for, Rusty? You know I can't breathe out of my nose right." demanded Harry.

"I know how you get when you're scared. I was scared too, but he didn't see us, and we're safe." Rusty looked down the path the man used. Something caught his attention. It looked like a light, but he wasn't positive.

As Rusty and Harry snuck along the path, he noticed the trees were thinning out. Up ahead, Rusty saw a lance of light cut across the sky. It was a spotlight on a tower.

Who puts a tower out here?

Why would anyone put a tower out here?

There's nothing around.

It's a forest.

Rusty and Harry made their way closer, staying behind trees and bushes whenever the light roamed their direction. It was like a dangerous game of hide and seek.

At the edge of the forest, the grasses and most trees were gone. In their place lay an enormous field. In the center, what looked like an old fire watch tower stood shining a spotlight around. A man wearing fatigues turned the light, paused, and took a long pull from a bottle. He was looking for something, focusing on an area to their left.

Five pointed leaves, every teenager was familiar with, grew on the crops in the field. The smells of the forest were being overtaken by a familiar odor. At last, it dawned on him what they were dealing with.

It wasn't poachers.

"Harry, it's pot. This is a growing operation. Looks like they've been here a while." Rusty pulls out the bundle of firecrackers. "I got an idea. Wait here."

When the spotlight moved away from them, Rusty darted across the clearing into the tall stalks of the crops. He opened the package of firecrackers and unwound the common fuse and put it in his pocket. The brick disintegrated into the individual crackers.

He roamed all over the crops, pausing when the spotlight roamed near him, stuffing the bangers into the plants. It took far longer than he'd hoped, but in the end, he used up all the firecrackers in the brick.

As he snuck through the crops, he found himself near the central tower. At the base of the tower, a small crate lay next to the ladder. Above him, the man in the tower finished another gulp from his bottle, and set it on the ledge.

Rusty lay prone among crops as the man shined the spotlight on the edge of the woods. The man put a radio to his face and said something Rusty couldn't hear. A burst of excited chatter sounded from the radio and the man slammed the light to another section of woods.

The violent wrenching of the light caused the tower to sway and the half-full bottle of liquor to fall to the ground. Glass shattered as the bottle hit the leg of the tower on the way down and rained golden alcohol all over the ladder and dirt at the base.

The light operator cursed and slid down the ladder. At the bottom, he opened the crate and grabbed another bottle. He popped the lid off and took another drink before returning to his post.

Rusty crept over to the crate and took two bottles, then opened the rest and laid the common fuse from the firecrackers into the top of one, dangling it out over the edge. He secured the fuse with a bottle lid and the top of the crate.

Rusty took extra care, moving back to where Harry waited for him. Both bottles held good quality tequila. He wanted to enjoy one later.

"Okay, I got a plan. It ain't great, but it might work. Here's what we're gonna do—I'll be a…"

Rusty watched a deer sneak out of the woods, head over to the plants, and start snacking away. The bright lance of the spotlight was meandering its way towards where the deer stood. Rusty pointed at the spotlight and the deer.

Harry picked up a large branch and broke it over his knee. The sound cracked across the clearing and startled the deer. It snapped its head up and looked their direction. It stomped its foot and tossed its head.

A crack of a rifle exploded near them.

Several leaves flew off the plant near the deer's head.

The bullet crashed into the trunk of a tree near them.

The deer screamed and jumped, its hoofs flailing the air as a man in a ghillie suit emerged from the crops.

The deer landed, reared up, and lashed out with its front hoofs. It struck the rifle to the side as it slammed its head down into the man's face. An antler cracked his mask, with several others finding ways past it. Blood leaked from his face as he fell. The deer stomped on him until he lay still.

The spotlight landed on the deer. Shouts in that unknown language rose over the crops as two men emerged, one on either side of the deer. The man at the deer's backside dove to grab onto the animal and received a stiff kick to the chest.

He landed, unmoving, on his face.

His partner lunged forward and grabbed the deer by its antlers. Big mistake on his part. The deer spun around and pulled him off his feet, then slammed him to the ground before driving forward with its entire weight.

Antlers ripped through his shirt with ease. The man screamed as the deer tossed its head and tore him open. The deer looked skyward and screamed before charging into the crops.

Rusty heard more voices joining the fray. Only one thing to do.

He opened one of the two stolen bottles, took off his shirt and stuffed part of it in the opening.

"Harry, give me your lighter."

"What are you gonna do with it?" Asked Harry as he fished it out of his pocket.

"I'm going to give them something else to worry about other than that deer and us."

Rusty collected the lighter and lit the end of his shirt. He wasn't sure how these things worked, but he had the thought that he didn't want it anywhere near him when it did its thing. The fabric struggled to catch.

He closed the lighter, removed the shirt, flipped ends, then stuffed the dry end inside the neck of the bottle. This time, the small amount of alcohol helped the fabric catch the fire. In one smooth motion, he threw the bottle as far into the crops as he could.

A whoosh of flames erupted in the crops as the bottle landed and broke open. The alcohol driven fire engulfed the dry crops, the intense heat driving the guards out of the crops, sending them running. The man in the tower slid down the ladder and ran towards a shack Rusty hadn't noticed before.

For its part, the deer ran around the raging inferno, ramming errant men as they tried to control the fire. One swung a shovel at the deer and received a spiking from its antlers as a reward. The rest ran away from the rampaging animal.

A cloud of white fog covered the flaming crops, the fire diminishing as the fog intensified. The man cursed and threw the empty extinguisher aside. The raging inferno spread over more of the crops.

As the fire spread across the crops, the guard from the tower pointed at Rusty and Harry, drew his sidearm, and pointed it at them. The flames crept towards the tower as Rusty and Harry raised their arms.

He waved them over with his free hand, shouting instructions neither understood. The crops here had already burnt to a char and were smoldering. Smoke and fog were thick, making it hard to see beyond the man. The gun shook as the man struggled to contain his rage. Veins on his arms and neck bulged.

The man wanted nothing to do with their surrender. He fired his gun. The bullet went wide and fell far short of where they stood. He fired two more shots, but the forest swallowed both. Unsure of what to do, Rusty ducked and pulled Harry to the ground.

Rusty saw sparks behind him, near the tower. "Cover your ears, Harry."

Harry, who was already covering his ears, gave him a look that asked if he was blind.

The sparks disappeared into the crate at the bottom of the ladder. A fireball belched forth from the crate, wrapping around everything in the area, the fringes grabbing the angry man with the pistol.

Flames and hellfire engulfed the tower as it climbed skyward. The shockwave of the explosion threw the man to the ground, his pistol flying away. He hit the turf hard and rolled over, struggling to get back to his feet.

Rusty, ears still ringing, stood up. The earth swayed under him as he saw a shadow dancing in the smoke. The figure moved like a person, but it's staggering rush made no sense to him.

Wind whipped across him as the fire blazed. A gust cleared the haze long enough for him to see Hugh Howie standing there running at him.

"Hugh Howie? What the hell are you doing here? Ain't you supposed to be recovering at the hospital after tonight's match? Why are you guarding a weed crop?" Asked Rusty.

Hugh threw his arms wide and tackled Rusty to the ground. Sitting atop him, the guard punched Rusty in the face.

Rusty put his arms in the way and tried to buck the man off him.

No luck.

Rusty's stomach heaved a moment, but he forced the bile back down.

His ears were ringing like a church bell.

Every sound echoed like he was standing in a giant cave.

Another figure charged through the smoke and tackled the guard to the ground.

Broken Badger returned the favor and punched Hugh Howie with a couple good shots to the ear.

Badger stood and stomped on the prone man's stomach before extending a hand to Rusty.

"Get up Rusty. Get back in the fight."

For some reason, Broken Badger sounded like his brother.

"What are you doing here Broken Badger?" asked Rusty.

"Broken Badger? Rusty, it's me, Harry. What are you talking about?"

"I don't what's going on. Why's your voice sound like that?"

A blur of movement crossed in front of Rusty as Hugh Howie tackled his brother, looked his way, and called out, "Help me take out Broken Badger, Rusty! We can win the match!"

Excitement drove Rusty to Hugh's side. He threw a punch at Broken Badger and connected with his nose.

Badger screamed, "What are you doing, Rusty? It's me, your brother."

Broken Badger's thrashing forced Rusty to step back as Hugh Howie asserted his position on the fallen wrestler's torso.

That gave Rusty pause. Why was Broken Badger claiming to be Harry? Come to think of it, where was Harry? Rusty looked around and couldn't see his brother anywhere.

A gurgle brought his attention back to the fight. Hugh Howie sat straddling Broken Badger, choking him.

"That's not right, Hugh. You don't choke them, that's dangerous. You supposed to pin 'em. Where's the ref?"

Rusty looked around but couldn't see the official anywhere.

"Don't worry. When I'm done with him, I'll finish you," growled Hugh Howie

Rusty looked at Broken Badger, his face red but turning blue.

"The hell you will. That's not a fair match at all."

Rusty stepped up and slammed his fist into Hugh Howie's head, following it with a solid kick to the ribs.

The wrestler fell off the gasping Badger, hitting the ground hard. Hugh smiled, rolled to his feet, and stepped forward to charge them. Something shoved the wrestler off balance, and Rusty saw the shadow of the deer as its back feet landed from the kick it delivered. Howie turned to face it, but the deer was gone.

He offered a hand to Broken Badger, whose face resembled his brother's more than he remembered.

Rusty helped Badger stand up. They looked at each other, the glimmer in both their eyes said the same thing…

"Backyard Wrestling Federation!" both shouted in excitement.

Hugh Howie turned and said, "What the hell are you talking about?" Before charging them.

Rusty and Badger clasped hands and charged past the man, arms held at shoulder level.

"Tag-team clothesline!" Shouted Broken Badger.

Rusty thought it was weird that the echoey voice Badger spoke with sounded like Harry's.

Their linked arms smacked into Hugh below the neck and took him off his feet.

Howie hit the ground, and the air exploded out of his lungs.

Hugh curled on his side, reaching behind his head, rocking back and forth.

They stood over the dazed man as he turned over onto his hands and knees.

Badger positioned himself near the man's head and grabbed it between his thighs. He squeezed hard as the man struggled against the powerful grip.

Broken Badger held both hands up, posing for the non-existent crowd. Rusty cheered him on, then helped flip the man up and held his legs upright as Badger jumped up in the air yelling, "Pile Driver!"

The crack of the man's neck worried Rusty that they might have killed him, but the groan Hugh gave when Broken Badger let him go assured Rusty the wrestler was alive.

Rusty grabbed Hugh and rolled him onto his face. He picked him up by the belt and kicked the guy's feet under him. His victim made a feeble attempt at grabbing him, but Rusty knocked his hands away.

Badger stood to the man's side and helped lift him up for Rusty.

Once the wrestler was vertical, held up by Rusty, he cried out, "Suplex!" As he fell over backwards.

The impact with the ground was enough to rattle Rusty's teeth.

Hugh, on the other hand, looked to have left a few teeth behind.

Rusty rolled onto his hands and knees and gave a nod to Badger. Broken Badger wasted no time.

He stepped up on Rusty's back and leapt towards the man screaming, "Atomic Elbow Drop!"

The man curled inward, rolling onto his side before retching.

Badger and Rusty pulled him to his feet and spun him in circles.

The guy struggled to walk and kept tripping over his own feet.

"Last one, it's a combo. Let's set it up," said Rusty, the biggest grin he'd ever felt plastered on his face.

Every sound roared over his heart pounding in his ears.

Badger nodded, stood behind Hugh, and planted a solid kick between his legs.

The man squealed like a stuck pig and dropped to his knees.

The poor soul's mouth moved, but no sound came out, other than the faintest squeaking.

Rusty stood in front of the kneeling man and planted his hands on the ground before throwing his legs over Hugh Howie's shoulders, and locking his ankles behind the wrestler's neck.

In wheelbarrow position, Rusty cried out, "Trip to Skid Row!" and started bending his knees and pulling with his legs as fast as he could, jamming Hugh's face into his ass over and over.

The man started sobbing.

He lacked the strength to resist the beat down any more.

Rusty, lost in the moment, cried out, "And for the finisher! The Fumigator!"

Rusty pulled the man's face tight to his ass-crack.

He ripped a fart that would impress his brother.

The rumbling, airy, odorous finisher did just that.

Hugh Howie, cheeks wet with tears, passed out.

Rusty let go of his prey and allowed him to fall to the side.

He stood and looked around for Harry.

"Badger, help me find Harry. We need to leave."

Smoke filled the impromptu arena and cast everyone as shadows to Rusty's impaired vision.

Badger called from the thick haze, "I must leave now, Rusty. It was a good match."

Panic seized Rusty as the smoke thinned.

"Harry! Badger! Where are you?"

"What are you talking about, Rusty? I've been here the whole time," said Harry.

Sirens alerted Rusty to the imminent arrival of law enforcement. This was the last place they wanted to be caught. He grabbed Harry and ran back to the trail he and his brother arrived from. He picked up the remaining bottle of tequila.

"Man, I got a story to tell you. Let's get outta here."

The deer walked by the trail, nostrils flared, tips of its antlers glistening red.

"I think I recognize that deer," said Rusty. He stepped toward the deer and held up the bottle.

The deer looked at him and tipped its quivering nose towards him, testing the air. Rusty unscrewed the lid from the bottle and poured a bit into his palm. The deer, cautious but thirsty, approached while stretching its neck out to lap the liquor from his palm.

Rusty and Harry led the deer away from the blazing wreckage of the pot plantation. From the woods, they heard the chopper approach, then the large splashing of water as the chopper doused a majority of the fire with the first bucket.

"Rusty, can we get Griddle House?" asked Harry. "I'm hungry for some waffles."

"You and me both, Harry. You and me both."

Old man McHenry cleaned and assembled his still with his usual careful observation of the details. This task was harder with his arm in a cast and sling. The wrapping around his middle didn't help either. Doctor said he shouldn't lift anything more than a few pounds while he healed.

That never stopped him. He grabbed his old gas syphon hose, fresh out of the disinfecting tub at home, and stuck it into the wash bucket. He gave the hose a few sharp pulls, and the murky fluid surged from the bucket, snaking into the still kettle.

Once that was full, he set the hose aside and sealed the still. After he reassembled the tower, he checked the thumper's water level. Satisfied everything was ready, he grabbed the kindling and stocked the burner.

McHenry looked up at the sky. A beautiful day to be alone in the woods, enjoying his hobby of making good drink. He looked around the clearing, but saw no sign of his friend.

That's a shame.

He missed Deer.

He lit the kindling and got the fire going. As it cooked, the thumper made small thuds. Everything was working as expected.

A loud crack of a branch startled him. He spun around, his ladle in his hand to fend off whatever threat approached. To his surprise, he saw the idiot brothers, Rusty and Harry, leading a—

"Deer!"

The buck danced a moment and ran over to him, licking his face. Its velvet soft nose felt good. A reminder of before it went crazy and attacked him. The affection lasted only a moment before it was nuzzling the old man's bucket.

"It's been a right strange week, Titus," said Rusty

"Oh? Were you two trying another hair-brained scheme to make yourselves smarter?"

"Not this time," said Rusty. He then explained the events that led up to his deer solving the big mystery of the demon of the forest, along with the disappearances.

McHenry pointed at the bag on his table and said, "That's yours. Thank you for bringing Deer back safe. No charge, today."

"Thank you, Titus. That's mighty kind of you. We'll be on our way. We have some work that needs doing," said Rusty.

"Have a good one, boys."

McHenry grabbed the next wash bucket, sat down on his stool and listened to the still and thumper working. Everything was right again. His friend's steps mixing with the occasional crunch of vegetation as the deer grazed were soothing.

As he sat there listening to the sounds of nature, he felt the velvet nose on the back of his neck and felt the tongue brushing his skin.

Dammit, just like before.

He ripped the top off the wash bucket, and holding it with his feet, he grabbed the deer in a headlock, being careful to avoid the antlers, and shoved its face into the wash.

A bit of drinking and the deer shook his head free and stumbled away drunk.

Amongst the Drek

By: J.F. Posthumus

For as long as Tara could remember, she had been able to sense the presence of ghosts, demons, and angels. Among other things. She had an additional gift, or curse depending on one's viewpoint, of being able to sense the history of an object. The stronger the emotional attachment to the object, the clearer the history.

Most people able to do such things called themselves 'mediums' or 'psychics'.

Tara called herself a weirdo.

Now she stood at the front of what appeared to be an abandoned trailer park that the wealthy had once-upon-a-time used as a getaway. The battery in her car had finally died just as she'd pulled up to this place, and she kept wondering if it was an omen. Two weeks ago, she'd received a call from a lawyer stating she'd inherited a property located at Rosewynd Estates. From what she'd gathered from the lawyer, it sounded like a glorified trailer park. A place where people "retired" or something they used as a summer cabin of some sort.

If it had been houses instead of modular homes, Tara would have thought it was just another rural community. There were single wide modular homes to her left and right with a very run-down double-wide directly in front of her at the end of the overgrown drive. Other than a slightly worn path to her right, there was nothing to indicate a vehicle or anything had traveled along the path in the recent past. Probably not even in the past month, judging by the knee-high weeds.

Nothing appeared to have been touched by anyone in years. Every sign of just another dead end in her life.

She silently chided herself a fool for even considering coming here. More so, since it looked worse than she'd imagined it would be. She'd packed everything she could fit into the car, had sold anything that wouldn't squeeze in with room for her to drive. So foolishly optimistic of her. As if she would sleep here, like it was just another hotel or other unfamiliar place to stay for a bit. That had become far too routine for her in the past years, maybe. But she'd even brought the only gun she'd ever been comfortable with. Which currently sat on the floorboard of the car, of course. Maybe, Tara pondered, she should go back and get it.

"Can I help you?" A male voice came from behind her and to the left.

Tara jumped and spun to face whoever had spoken. She found herself staring at a tall man, maybe a few years older than her. He wore a rock band t-shirt tucked into a pair of snug blue jeans. A pair of work boots and ball cap completed the typical 'country boy' look. His broad shoulders stretched the material of his shirt, and while there weren't rippling muscles coming out of the sleeves, there wasn't flab, either. At least he wasn't wearing a huge silver belt buckle with the black belt. Then her visions of a southern "hick" type would have been completed. Strands of honey blonde hair fell from around the ball cap. His face was boyish with blazing blue eyes staring at her with suspicion.

At least they had that last thing in common, since she was sizing him up as a possible threat at the same time. Tara rarely thought she looked like a threat, but she'd put enough time in at ranges and defense classes to at least go down fighting. Unlike in her "old life."

"Oh, I'm Tara McClure," Tara replied, toying with her car keys. "I, um… got a call a couple weeks ago about inheriting my great-aunt's house." She paused for a moment. "Who are you? I thought this place was abandoned."

The man laughed. The grin illuminated his face like a lighthouse's beacon.

"Nah. Not completely. You must be here about Juliette."

Tara nodded. He held out his hand after she had done so. "Thought so. Juliette was the only other person living here. I'm sorry about your loss. I'm Roscoe Delaney, but everyone calls me 'Ross'. Guess you can say I'm the owner and operator of Rosewynd Estates. Or, rather, what's left of it."

"Pleasure to meet you," Tara said, shaking his hand briefly. "And thank you. Do you know what happened? The lawyer I spoke to made this place sound as though it were…" She trailed off, unsure of how to politely describe the place.

A shadow passed over Ross' face. But the smile remained. "People decided they preferred campgrounds and resorts, I guess. It's been like this for almost a decade. Maybe longer."

Tara's eyes shifted away from his and to the dilapidated modular homes surrounding them. Weeds and grass overtook much of the area, including around the former homes. She wondered if a good strong wind would topple them all like a delicately stacked house of playing cards.

Something was not quite right here at Rosewynd Estates. Ignoring the overall lack of human activity and maintenance of the properties didn't erase the sensation. All of the *other* senses that Tara had dealt with, since she'd spotted her deceased pet cat curled up on her bed, blinking slowly at her when Tara was only four years old, were tingling. But beyond that, even the air here seemed wrong.

You didn't need to be a medium to figure it out.

"So, um, where is my great-aunt's place?" Tara asked.

The longer she stood here talking to Ross, the more uneasy she felt. Something about the man was setting off alarm bells as well. So far, it was more of a Yellow Alert ringing in the back of her mind than the 'prepare for battle, Red Alert' claxons. Small comfort, in her estimation.

Or maybe it was all due to the fact she was in the middle of nowhere, alone with this stranger with only her car keys as an easy-access weapon.

Doubtful, but it was a better thought than the long shadows that appeared to hide dark shifting figures despite the mid-summer noon sun that shone down in all its hundred-degree sweltering heat.

"I'll take you there," Ross said, his eyes flitting over her briefly. "You can come back for your car after I show you the way."

He began walking down the dirt path that might have once been a road.

"It's not far?" she asked as she followed him.

He shrugged. "Her place is in the very back. Had the two plots that adjoined her house. It's the closest to the forest at the back." He chuckled. "Said she preferred her privacy. Even if her only neighbors were ghosts."

"Then… where do you live?" Tara asked as they passed house after dilapidated house. "Or is there someone else here you haven't mentioned?"

"Oh, I live on the far left of this place. Back in the woods. I inherited Rosewynd from my folks years ago. They lived in that big house at the entrance."

The sole building that had solidified Tara's unease when she had first arrived at the gates of Rosewynd Estates. It had been a large two story Tudor, sat to the left of the opened gates. The dozen windows of the home had felt like all eyes glaring down at her. Even though there hadn't been ghosts wandering around or in it.

Unlike almost every place they had passed here.

The apparitions wandering, sitting or standing all around had barely glanced in their direction. Like neighbors who were still, after death, more absorbed in what each other was doing than anything new or from outside the estates.

"Why not hire a lawn service for the place?" Tara asked, maybe a bit too cheerfully. "Or are you planning on selling now that my great-aunt no longer lives here?"

Ross stopped and turned to face her. He shook his head slowly. "Who would want to buy this place? I guess someone could try developing it, but it's not like Deerfield is a wealthy area. Not a whole lot of jobs to be had around here either." He gave a snort. "Besides, these roads are hell in the winter. You'd need a four-wheel or all-wheel drive to get here when it snows. And you don't even want to think about when it's icy."

It was on the tip of her tongue to ask just what he did for a living. Then she thought better of it. Some questions should not be asked. And not simply because they're considered 'nosy' and rude. He was also pleasant enough to look at for her. But, she didn't want to come across as needy for conversation.

Oh, how the mistakes of the past kept trying to insist on repeating themselves.

Instead, she replied with, "That's fair." After a short pause, she changed the topic. "So, how well did you know Juliette?"

Ross gave her a slight smile, turned, and began walking again. "I think she lived here since the place opened. Or shortly after. Knew my folks really well. They knew her, too, and so did I. Never did find out why she moved here, though. She never said why, and we didn't asked. She only ever said this place was a way to start all over for her."

Not exactly an answer to the question, Tara grumbled silently.

"How well did you know her?" Ross asked in return. "As far as I know, no one ever visited her, and she never went anywhere aside from the store and the rare trip to the post office."

"I didn't even know I had a great-aunt," Tara replied, honesty in her voice. "Grandma never mentioned a sister. Though, to be honest, most of my relatives didn't get along. Stupid internal jealousies and mistrust between most of them. So I never met a lot of my extended family."

Ross made a noncommittal sound.

They continued walking towards the back of the estate, passing one rundown trailer after another. Some appeared to have held up to the elements better than others. But not by much.

The weeds brushed against her bare skin and poked at her feet.

"Is her power still turned on? What about the water?" Tara asked, ignoring her increasingly itchy skin.

"Julie kept everything paid up in advance. As far as I know, everything is still on and working." He gave a short laugh and pulled at his single layer of clothing, flapping the rock band logo as he did. "At least you don't have to worry about the pipes freezing right now."

Tara replied with a laugh of her own. "Very true!"

Considering it was the middle of the summer, there was no threat of anything below sixty on any normal day. Maybe mid fifties at night during a summer storm. Or if a tropical wave made it up to the Virginia border. Rare, but not unheard of.

"Did you have any problems finding the place?" Ross asked, almost as though he didn't want to deal with a long silence. Not that she could blame him.

"I grew up in Crawford Manor," she said, trying to ignore the houses they passed. They damn near called to her, though. Echoes of violent moments, great sorrows, or both flowed from several of the dwellings. Some had an even darker history that wanted to devour anyone who got close. Like an emotional black hole parked up on cinder blocks. There was anger here. But also sadness and happiness. The mix of feelings from the whole place threatened to overwhelm Tara.

"Graduated from Buffalo Gap high school, then went out west to college." she forced herself to say, trying to push off the crushing, engulfing sensations.

As the houses grew further apart the brush and weeds became taller and thicker. Wild rose bushes, mountain laurel, and berry bushes turned the lawns into nearly impassable thickets. Trees towered far above them, giving shade to everything near them. Their shadows shifted in the sunlight.

Every so often something would rustle in the weeds along the path.

No birds sang in the trees. No squirrels scampered around or scolded the birds. That was never a good sign. It was then Tara realized something that made her question the intelligence of her original plans.

"Here we are," Ross said as he stopped in front of a yard that wasn't quite as badly overgrown as every other one. He turned to look at Tara. "You have a key, right?"

Tara moved to stand beside him. She nodded as her eyes swept around the yard. Fishing the key out of her pocket, she held it up.

The modular had brown siding almost mimicked a log cabin-type house. Bay windows on the left, while double-paned windows revealed at least two rooms on the right. A porch, two rocking chairs with a table between them were on the right side. A porch swing was on the left.

The yard had an ancient chain link fence that was covered in vines. No gate, though. Tall flowers that looked an awful lot like sunflowers grew along the sides of the house, giving them the look of a naturally grown fence. Around the porch, marigolds grew in a pair of rows.

The walkway up to the front door was dirty and had weeds growing here and there, but it did show signs of being used. Maybe not in the last two weeks or so, but it wasn't as empty and desolate as the rest of the trailer park from first glance. In fact, it looked somewhat inviting.

And yet, she felt as though someone should have been standing in the doorway yelling 'go away'. Perhaps it was the particular shade of purple that the door had been painted with.

"You okay?" Ross asked. Concern colored his words.

"Yeah," she lied. "It's a bit surreal, I guess. Walking into someone's home who I'd never met before."

Hiding her emotions was easy. She'd learned from an early age to keep her true feelings hidden. Otherwise, people got creeped out when she told the truth. Or, like when she told about being able to see the spirit of her dead cat around the house, laid out punishments for 'lying' to them. Actual lying was just a byproduct of her dealing with the ability, along with the living people around her.

"Uh huh," Ross said.

Tara glanced at him. He was staring at her intently. She could have sworn he was inhaling deeply. But maybe it was just her imagination. The unease of what she'd find inside didn't help either.

"Julie wasn't a stranger to me," Ross stated. His voice softened as he added, "Would you like me to show you where everything is?"

Despite every instinct screaming for her to run and never look back, Tara nodded. She found herself saying, "I'd like that."

Ross grinned and took the key gently from her fingers. The smile on his face and his twinkling blue eyes made her wonder what was going through his mind. Her mind was certainly starting to trail off into the proverbial gutter just from that look alone. There was a subtle scent that her nose was picking up that she hadn't noticed before. It was almost intoxicating... was he wearing a cologne and she hadn't noticed it before now?

As he headed towards the door, she found her eyes drifting down to his rear. A smirk curved her lips, and she followed after him. Pity her life sucked right now. The last thing she needed was any sort of romantic interest.

In fact, that's what got her into her current mess.

Oh, well. Maybe, eventually, she wouldn't be such a failure. The daily affirmation she'd be doing for months included telling herself every morning that she was worth happiness, and pretty enough in all the ways that mattered to be attractive to others that would treat her well. Or at least better than she was used to.

Then again, there was nothing wrong with a one-night stand, she considered as he held the door open for her. Just before stepping through, she reminded herself that the door was painted in a shade of purple. Tara held her breath before stepping in. She anticipated more than the usual unpleasant sensations of crossing someone's threshold without invitation. She wasn't a vampire, lycanthrope, or other being in that category. Nor was she, strictly speaking, any style of witch.

None of those facts had altered her past experiences, however. Crossing over an established threshold, whether made by intentional magic or otherwise, had been anything but pleasant. The worst left her feeling coated in plastic, webbing or worst, cold mud. A purple door, or even the smallest sigils was usually a sign of some manner of magic user. But here she discovered an entirely new sensation.

It was as though she had been welcomed into the home. Crazy, since the occupant who had lived here was dead. Her eyes shifted to Ross, and she wondered if he had been considered 'family' to her aunt. If so, maybe that would explain the threshold and why it hadn't affected her.

Like most modular homes, the doublewide had an open floor plan. A clawfoot dining table with chairs sat directly to the left of the door. A large antique hutch was to the right. Photos of Tara's family filled the wall on the far left. There was a bar with a marble counter in the middle of the room and a standard kitchen on the opposite side of the marble counter.

As she was taking in the pleasant visual aspects of the place, the emotional presence of the home engulfed her. Air caught in her throat and she choked out a barking cough. The sensation of being slowly smothered began to ebb, but it felt like an eternity before that happened.

Tara drew in a breath and let it out slowly. There was so much sadness filling every space of the interior it almost knocked her back outside.

Ross touched her arm and her mind went blank.

For the first time ever, Tara couldn't feel anything. Only the warm fingers that rested on her upper arm. She inhaled sharply. Ross slid his fingers away, rubbing them together almost as though he was rubbing her scent in.

That was fair. She suddenly wanted to rub him all over her. Except in a completely different way.

"Uh, the master bedroom is over here," Ross said suddenly, moving to the door to their left. He opened it to reveal a bedroom. "There's a bathroom with a walk-in shower in there."

"Um, thanks," Tara said. The sadness she'd felt earlier grew thicker. Looking away, she clenched her teeth. "What's on the other side?"

"There's a little office or foyer area through the doorway there on your right. Then three more bedrooms. There's a small back porch, too. Straight ahead in what Julie called the 'den'. It's where she kept the tv and her consoles." Ross moved back towards Tara, eyeing her thoughtfully. "You're like Julie, aren't you?"

"What do you mean?" Tara asked, refusing to give ground as he approached her.

Ross inhaled deeply, his eyes closing halfway as he did so.

He was kinda cute like that. But a bit creepy and definitely weird. And then Tara mentally smacked herself for acting like a love sick teen.

"She could feel things. Sense them. Called herself a medium," he replied. He opened his mouth to say something, but shut it instead. After a moment, he added, "She said it was a family thing."

"Oh," Tara said, looking away from him. "She told you about that? Wow, she must have really trusted you." Or Julie completely lost grip with how people react to that, she thought. Her abrupt lust for this guy was unsettling, which made her impulse to say anything to him that might hold his interest suspect as well. After another moment of internal struggle, she decided that instead of being a school girl, she'd tell him to try and pry more information. "Yeah. I'm like her in that way. Not sure if Grandma or Mom could do it. But I can sense feelings and stuff. Never really told anyone, though. Not since I was a kid and… a friend freaked out over it."

"My folks said Julie used to do fortunes and such at the county fairs," Ross said, a slight smile on his face. "She'd dress up, use a different name, and did it to make extra cash in the summer."

"My parents never took me to the county fairs," Tara said wistfully. "I've went a few times, but…" she trailed off with a shrug. "It's not a lot of fun to go alone. Last time I went, it was with friends back in high school."

"I'd imagine it can get overwhelming," Ross suggested, leaning against the bar. His hands were shoved in his pants pockets.

Tara forced her eyes to stay on his. What the hell was wrong with her? Had he drugged her somehow?

"Sometimes," she admitted. "But by then I'd learned to control it. A few years into college, I realized I could do more as someone who helped people deal with loss. So I changed courses, finished up my time in college, and became a grief therapist."

Ross' brows rose. "Impressive. So you use your talents to help people."

"As much as it's possible," she admitted. Glancing around, she sighed. "Think Great-Aunt Julie would mind if I stayed here while I figure things out?"

"Doubtful," Ross replied. "But wouldn't you rather stay in your place? Or with your folks?"

It was Tara's turn to snort. "I don't exactly live in the area. And I would rather get a hotel instead of staying with my parents."

Ross winced. "That bad, huh?" Tara nodded. "Well, if you need anything, Julie had my number near the phone in the den. I'm not that far."

With that, he turned and left. Leaving Tara to more deeply investigate the house alone.

Her steps were loud within the empty house. The sadness that lurked was thick and cloying. Shadows shifted and grew, despite the fact most of the windows faced the south.

Heading into the kitchen, she found the fridge held only unopened cans of soda. The freezer, though, was fully stocked.

Did Julie know she was going to die? Or had someone come in and cleaned out the fridge for her?

Through the kitchen was a small washroom and to the right was another room with a deep freezer.

Stepping further into the side room, she found a folding door concealing a half bathroom.

Turning, she headed back through the kitchen. Peeking into the den, she found a tv, entertainment center, lots of physical movies stacked together. Next to the multi-use remote, however, were a long pair of crystals. A basket next to the recliner had odd lengths of wood, a few with intricate carvings etched into them. Twine, copper wire and a pair of cutters had been laid next to the sticks. She meandered through the rest of the house, finding the other rooms and furniture. The place certainly looked as those someone was going to come home and make use of the place. Lots of filled bookshelves around, including a room with a roll top desk that Tara presumed was an office of sorts. Just the one tv was found, and no other modern electronics. Her cursory search didn't even reveal a cell phone charger. Each room, including the washrooms, had a small hanging object somewhere. To Tara they seemed like tiny potpourri containers, filled with dried leaves and herbs. Returning to the office, Tara opened the door leading to the back porch. A table sat in the far corner and there was a cabinet directly beside the door.

Her skin began to crawl. The hair on the back of her neck stood on end.

Something wasn't right.

Her pulse quickened at a noise to her right, and her heart leapt into her throat. Turning towards the noise, she glanced around, not finding anything odd.

Moving further onto the porch, she heard another rustle. Swallowing hard, she moved towards the step to the back yard.

A thud sounded behind her. She jerked around. Something jumped towards her.

Shrieking, she leapt back, ramming into the wood railing of the porch.

A cat hissed at her from a bar stool beside the cabinet and yowled before racing off into the back yard. The black and white tuxedo cat vanished into the thick vegetation, leaving Tara to stare at it in shocked disbelief.

She held a hand to her chest as she gulped in deep breaths of air. Laughter bubbled up and threatened to spill forth.

Walking back into the house, she closed the door behind her.

A cat. Either a stray or maybe a companion of her late great-aunt. Probably pissed at Tara for invading "their" space. Regardless, the feline definitely had gotten the better of her.

She'd been scared by a freaking cat. Wasn't she just having a grand ol' time?

Turning to the rolltop desk, she slid the top open. Little pigeon holes lined the left and right sides with long, narrow slots in the center. There was a long drawer just above the chair and deeper drawers to each side. She smiled as she slid out a wide piece of wood that would've been used to write on. Sliding it back in, she turned to the stacks of paper in the desk.

A photo slid free, and she picked it up. It was a photo of two girls with long pigtails. They wore short-sleeved shirts and knee-length skirts. One was a few inches taller than the other, but otherwise, they looked identical.

Tara's fingers tingled and she could hear the laughter from the two girls.

Jules. Missy.

The names rang out in her mind.

There was some sadness from an older woman mingled with the girls' laughter.

Swallowing hard, Tara gently placed the photo back into the desk.

Flipping through the notes, they appeared to be lists of things to do. Appointments. Nothing of importance.

Opening one of the drawers, she found pens, pencils, and other similar items. Closing that drawer, she opened another. Nothing interesting there, either. Nor was there anything in the other desk drawers.

Footsteps reverberated against Tara's ears. Light and gentle. With a slight scooting to them.

It took her a minute to realize they were echoes of her great-aunt.

Turning, Tara followed the echo to the master bedroom. The ghostly steps vanished in front of another set of accordion doors. She walked over and opened them.

Clothes hung on hangers directly in front of her and to the left. There were shelves at the top and bottom. Shoes lined up beneath the bottom shelf that held sheets, pillow cases, and blankets.

There were a few shoe boxes on the top shelf. Grabbing a bar stool, Tara climbed up on it and grabbed the boxes. Opening one, she found folded newspaper articles.

Sitting on the bar stool, she sat the box on her lap and began going through the news articles.

Each one had a headline about a massacre.

A massacre at Rosewynd. The dates were all in August and September of 1952.

Well. That certainly explained all the ghosts. And why no one might live here until the scenery changed. That kind of notoriety would last for ages.

Had my great-aunt lived there during that time? Or had she moved in after the massacre? And why had no one else mentioned it? Most people loved to tell stories about the macabre. Either as a warning or to scare little children.

Or maybe not.

It *had* occurred before the internet and a lot of the people involved would be dead. Or in nursing homes. Or just not care anymore. She randomly recalled reading about a nearby prison being refurbished into an expensive gated community. Plenty of locals avoided the very idea of that place. But it apparently drew in renters and investors, still. So, general apathy was alive and well in the area.

There was very little mentioned in the articles. Aside from how many people died and the location. The police didn't have a suspect. Or any ideas on why someone would kill so many people. Only a handful of people survived.

The owners. Betty Sue and Richard Delaney. Their son Roscoe Delaney, who had been severely injured in one attack. Her great-aunt, Julette McClure, who hadn't been at Rosewynd Estates at the time it happened. She'd been visiting family in Charlottesville at the time. At least, that's what the article claimed.

Wait… what? Tara thought, her brow furrowing. Rereading the articles, she looked up and stared at the hanging clothes. There was no way the Roscoe in the news article could be the same Roscoe who met her. The Ross she'd met didn't look more than a few years older than her. And she was twenty six. The Roscoe in the article would be in his seventies.

Tara shook her head. No, the Roscoe she knew must be the son or grandson to the one in the article. It was the only thing that made sense.

Closing her eyes, she opened herself up to whatever the clippings had to offer.

Anger. Sadness. Regret.

Sadness she understood. But anger and regret? Those two emotions she did not get. Did she regret not being there? Anger at whoever had done it?

So many questions. And yet, there were no answers. At least not in this pile of news articles.

Shoving the box on top of a stack of sheets, Tara turned to the task of going through her aunt's clothing and the rest of the closet's contents. She'd move the car closer before dusk fell. But for now, she had a task to do.

A few hours later, Tara had a large pile of her great-aunt's clothes stacked neatly on the dining room table.

Most people might have felt weird going through a complete stranger's things, but Tara was not most people. The longer she remained within the house, the more she felt the echoes of Julette's life. There was the lingering loneliness of having no friends nearby, added to the sadness of what family was around wanting to have no contact with her. Estrangement atop of seclusion, with none of it being by preferred choice.

Tara couldn't help but feel as though she had a lot in common with the great-aunt she'd never known. Or, maybe, screwing up was a family trait. Maybe one that came with being a medium.

As she crawled further under Julette's bed, a knock on the door interrupted her attempt to grab yet another box of who-knew-what. Hitting her head on the frame, a reminder of where exactly she was, Tara crawled backwards from beneath the bed.

Dusting her hands on her pants, she peeked from the bedroom.

Another knock.

Not being able to sense who was on the other side of the door was weird. There was only one person who knew she was here. Did Ross have something else to ask or tell her, perhaps?

Uneasily, she crossed to the door and looked through the decorative glass design. She could see a blurry figure the same height and build as Ross on the other side.

Opening the door, something dashed past her and into the house. She jumped back, biting back a shriek as she turned towards the direction the dark blur ran.

Ross, standing on the porch, laughed. "That's Lucybelle. Julie found her a couple years ago. She was a tiny, bedraggled kitten that looked half-dead when she showed up here. Julie took her in and saved the little psycho."

The "little psycho" turned and meowed demandingly at them. It was only then Tara noticed two small bowls tucked under a short stand just on the other side of the entryway into the den. Both were empty.

"I'm guessing you've been caring for her," Tara stated, eyes narrowed on the black and white cat.

Ross shrugged, but the smile on his face didn't fade. "Julie would haunt me in all the worst ways, until my dying day, if I didn't care for the furball." The smell of freshly baked pizza had her turning towards him. He held the box up, almost as an offering. "I thought you might like some pizza and drinks."

Tara's stomach rumbled, and she realized she was starving. When was the last time she'd eaten? She couldn't remember. Glancing at the table, she stepped back and gestured for him to enter.

"The table's a bit full, but we could always eat at the bar," she said. It was then she noticed the cooler at his feet.

Reaching down, she grabbed it the same time he did. He beat her to the handle by only a few seconds. When her hand touched his, she experienced another wave of blissful emptiness. It was followed by warmth and the sound of only what was around her.

A furry head appeared between her and Ross, followed by teeth to her hand. The cat was reminding Tara *she* was there, and *she* wanted to be fed. Standing, Ross grinned at her.

"I'll put this on the bar, then we can feed Madam Demanding here," he said. "Otherwise, I suspect she's going to think the pizza is for her."

Tara laughed, hiding her unease and confusion behind his joking. "Sounds like a plan. I'll need to know where Julette kept the food, anyway. Otherwise, I suspect Lucybelle will riot and decide to do more than nibble."

Heat flashed through Ross' eyes and Tara could have sworn they changed color. She blinked a few times, but his eyes were still their dazzling blue. Not the yellow-gold she thought they'd turned.

Maybe she needed to look up a good optometrist while she was in the area.

Ross moved past her and placed the pizza boxes on the bar counter. She hadn't realized he'd brought two. Yet, there they were on the counter beside the red and white igloo cooler.

After depositing the food and cooler, he continued to the pantry, returning with a can of cat food.

"Since you're here, I guess you can feed her instead of me. Or at least give her attention while she waits," Ross said as he handed the can with a convenient pull tab to Tara. "There's a bag of dry food along with the box of canned stuff for the little psycho at the bottom of the pantry. Should be enough for at least a couple of weeks, if you still plan to stick around."

Tara looked down at the cat twining between her legs. Her black and white fur was soft against her skin. For whatever reason, she'd never been able to sense much from animals. Maybe it was because they worked off more primitive feelings. She had no clue. It was probably for the best. The idea of touching things and not knowing if the echo was from a human or animal was very disconcerting.

Ross dumped the can of cat food in the food bowl, much to Lucybelle's delight. The tuxedo-colored cat hunkered down and began to chow down.

Grabbing a glass pitcher from beside the sink, Tara filled it halfway with water then poured it into the other bowl. Lucybelle took a moment to examine the freshly poured water before turning back to her dinner.

Opening the cabinet doors beneath the sink, Tara found a roll of paper towels, cleaning products for a household, and a wire rack loaded with still clean cloth towels. Another sign that her great-aunt lived like there would be another tomorrow for her in this place for the foreseeable future.

Grabbing the paper towels, she turned to find Ross had grabbed plates from a cabinet. He'd placed the plates on the counter and was opening the boxes. The logo on the front was from a local pizza place, not a chain restaurant.

Opening the lid to the cooler, Tara found several bottles of Bold Rock hard ciders, a couple bottles of water, and a few sodas. She lifted her gaze from the contents to Ross.

"Do I actually look my age?" she asked, cringing as she said it.

Ross laughed. "Figured you were at least twenty-one, from what you said. Besides, most kids around here are drinking cheap beer and boxed wines before they graduate high school." His gaze shifted towards the door and he nodded once. "Not like anyone is around to tattle on us if we get a little loose and loud. Unless you decide to go driving after having a couple, of course."

Shaking her head, she twisted the top off a Bold Rock. "Nope. I've got nowhere to go."

There was a deeper meaning to those words, and she suspected Ross knew it, if the tilt of his head and narrowed eyes were an indication. She took a long pull, hoping to drown the thoughts that threatened to bubble up.

"You've got family you could visit? Friends?" he said. He dropped his gaze to the pizza boxes. "Wasn't sure what you'd like, so I went with cheese and a meat lovers' pie."

Tara snorted. Her eyes drifted to the ceiling briefly before returning to him. "Until I found out I was mentioned in Aunt Julie's will, which I would have never expected, there was never a reason to come back to this state. My parents don't know I'm here and I'm not sure I want to tell them. I was an outcast in high school. So I don't have anyone I really want to see in the area."

He made a noncommittal sound as he gestured towards the pizzas. She grabbed a slice from the cheese pizza and placed it on her plate before grabbing a slice from the meat lovers' pizza. It was hot and dripping grease.

"Is that why you went out west?" he asked, taking a slice from the meat lovers' pie. She nodded. "That sucks. Sorry."

Tara shrugged. "My parents didn't understand my… gift. Curse. Whatever you want to call it. Mom ignored it. Dad told me to never speak of it. As far as I knew, I was the only one who could do what I did." Her eyes drifted around the room. "Guess I was wrong."

She bit into the pizza. It was as delicious as it looked. Full of melted cheese, tasty bread, and the perfect amount of grease. Because good pizzas were greasy and cheesy, in her opinion..

"Damn," Ross said quietly. He shook his head, the slice of pizza hovering in front of his face. "Julie would talk to my parents about her sister sometimes. Said her sister, Gloria, was able to do the same sort of thing. Said it had been a family trait that went back generations. She said she's got diaries around here from her mom and grandma."

That made no sense at all to Tara. She slowly finished chewing and swallowing her mouthful of yumminess. Taking a long pull of the hard cider, she studied Ross.

"My grandmother, Julette's sister, never mentioned being able to do anything. My mom hated that I could," Tara stated. "Why would Grandma lie about something like that?"

"Maybe she didn't like it," Ross suggested. "Maybe she didn't want to be 'weird'? Lots of people allow talents to atrophy for dumb reasons. Let alone because they'll be the target of bullies and hazing. For that, maybe it skipped your mom and she was secretly jealous. Folks have plenty of odd and frail excuses for their behaviors."

"I guess." She shrugged. "So, um, I found some news articles. They mentioned there had been a massacre here."

Ross' expression didn't change. "What'd they say?"

"Only that there had been a massacre. Bunch of people died. Only survivors were the owners and their son. Who had the same name as you…" she trailed off. For the first time in a long, long time Tara wished she could sense what he was feeling. Talk about a great time for her ability to not work.

"My father," he said easily. "He was seriously injured. Almost died. Stayed at the ICU over in the Charlottesville hospital for a week or so. The famous one, I mean. I don't think the others were around back then."

It sounded like the truth. He didn't shift or squirm or give any other tell to signal he was lying. Yet, there was something making Tara believe it was a flat out lie.

Scratch. Scratch. Scratch.

Tara turned slowly towards the door. Lucybelle was perched on the dining room table staring at the door.

Scratch. Scratch.

She turned back to find Ross staring at the door. He wasn't moving. At all. She wasn't entirely certain he was breathing.

More scratching.

The owner and operator of Rosewynd Estates slid soundlessly from his bar stool. His steps were silent as he moved swiftly towards the door. Tara followed soundlessly behind him.

Considering she was barefoot, it was pretty easy to do.

He flipped the porch light on. She couldn't see anything outside.

Pushing her behind him, Ross slowly opened the door.

A tiny black nose appeared. Quickly followed by a tiny, furry black head with tiny little ears. Blue eyes looked up at the pair as the kitten cautiously crept into the room.

Lucybelle meowed before hopping down from the table. She trotted over to the kitten and promptly began washing its head.

Ross stuck his head outside and looked around before stepping out onto the porch. He bent over and when he stood up he held a pair of kittens. His right hand held a gray kitten while his left held a black and white kitten.

"Looks like Lucybelle has been a bit busy," Ross joked. "Congratulations. You're a grandmom." He held the kittens out to her.

Laughing, Tara accepted the kittens and cuddled them close. "Wow. I didn't even have to deal with labor pains! This is great!"

"Just wait until you have to buy them food," Ross retorted as he looked around a final time. Giving his head a slight shake, he stepped back inside. "Not to mention when you give them baths."

"Ugh. Maybe I can just toss them into the walk-in shower and hose them off that way?" she asked. Kissing each one on the head, she put them on the floor. The pair rushed to their mom, who promptly curled up on the floor with her babies. "I guess I'll have to find a vet for them."

"Gonna keep the fluff balls?" Ross asked.

Tara shrugged.

He laughed. "Come on. Let's finish eating. If you want, I'll come by tomorrow to get the clothes and stuff you don't want to keep." A sadness swept across his face. "If there is anything I can do to help? Let me know."

"Does that include helping to rearrange furniture?" Tara teased, hoping to make him smile again.

"We'll see," he replied, laughter brightening his face again. "I might be persuaded to move anything except that rolltop desk in the office. That was a beast to move when she wanted to put it in her office space!"

The conversation turned to more mundane topics. From favorite foods and drinks to movies.

As the time wore on, Tara realized she hadn't been this relaxed and at ease for ages. Not since she was a little girl. It wasn't until the pizzas were half-gone and all the Bold Rocks had been finished that she realized it was dark outside.

So much for moving the car closer, she thought. Not that she really cared. She could always move it in the morning.

"It's getting late," Ross said needlessly. "Guess I should be going." She was about to say he didn't need to when he stood and headed towards the door. "I'll drop by tomorrow."

"I'm looking forward to it," she replied without thinking.

Ugh. Bad, Tara, bad! She thought, mentally kicking herself. *Just beg him to stay, why don't you? Too eager!*

"Have a good night," he said, opening the door. He paused, glanced down at Lucy and her kittens, then up at Tara. "Uh, make sure to lock the doors. And don't go out. There's a lot of wildlife around here. You wouldn't want to run into a bear or anything."

There was a decided pause between 'bear' and 'or anything'. But Tara didn't say a word. She'd lived near the mountains for almost her entire life. She knew there were plenty of things that lurked and hunted in the woods at night. Not to mention the people who liked prowling around in the dark.

"Sure. No problem," Tara replied. Ross gave her a nod and smile, then stepped onto the porch. "Good night."

"Night, Tara," he said.

She closed the door. It wasn't until she turned the lock that she heard him leave. She watched him walk away through the large windows until he was swallowed up by the darkness and the shadows of the houses.

Fireflies blinked in the dark, causing her to smile slightly. She'd need to get some little solar lights for the yard. Maybe some she could use to decorate the porch.

With her thoughts on how to decorate the yard, Tara turned to putting away the leftover pizza and drinks. Afterwards, she turned to finishing up emptying out everything from under her great-aunt's bed. She'd need to grab a shower and figure out where to sleep, since she wasn't about to sleep in her great-aunt's bed. Not without changing the covers, at the very least.

A few hours later, Tara was staring at the piled-up dining room table. Keeping her hands and mind at least mildly occupied kept her from dwelling on dark memories and feelings. Perhaps she should have been unpacking her own things, or at least bringing them to this house. But rummaging through unknown items in a new place didn't remind her of what she'd lost. Or still had, along with the memories of betrayal, healing in hospitals, spending time learning "unladylike" skills to prevent more of the former. Or being alone after standing up for herself.

Here, she hadn't found any old diaries, but she had found plenty of spiderwebs and dusty boxes of junk. Unmatched socks, rusty tools, and nicknacks were just some of the things in the boxes Julette had shoved under her bed.

There was no way Tara was going to sleep without grabbing a shower and some clean clothes. Along with a few other items.

Lucybelle was curled up on a pile of clothing. Her kittens were racing around the house, chasing each other. They seemed very content and happy. For a brief moment, Tara envied them.

Looking out the windows, the brilliant full moon was shining. There were enough trees to hide the path she and Ross had taken to her great-aunt's house. Everyone knew the vast variety of animals that lived in the mountains. Fox, deer, bear, coyotes, even bobcats and the occasional mountain lion. Though the latter two were harder to prove.

She wasn't afraid of the night. Or what the darkness hid. Over the years, she'd seen the terror that humans could inflict upon each other, and the grief that could be created and passed along. There wasn't an animal around that would terrify her the same way another human could frighten her, as far as Tara was concerned.

Grabbing a flashlight she'd found while looking through the cabinets, she flicked it on. The brilliant white light broke through the darkness and shadows. Grabbing her keys, she opened the door and stepped onto the porch. Making certain it wasn't locked, she closed the door behind her and headed for her car.

The gravel, weeds, and dried brush crunched loudly in the silence of the night. Dew had already begun to settle on everything, causing the night air to be cool and damp. The dark shadows from the houses were still. The vinyl siding appeared brighter and cleaner as the moonlight glinted off it and the broken windows. The breaks in the siding were evident. Everything looked nice and welcoming at a glance. But when you looked closer, you could see it was false, and the houses were dilapidated, dark and abandoned.

It would've been the perfect setting for any horror movie.

A snap of a branch had her jerking the flashlight to her left.

Sweeping the flashlight side-to-side, she didn't see anything. But there was an eeriness to the night. It was too silent. To still. Even the ghosts weren't moving.

Shivering, she picked up her pace. She continued to sweep the brilliant white light from side to side.

Something growled in the shadows of the trailers.

Tara stilled completely. Her pulse quickened even as she felt her heart jump into her throat. Swallowing hard, she forced herself to calm down. Fear would only cause whatever it was to come towards her. But damn if it wasn't hard to stop herself from racing away.

Another growl sounded out in the darkness, this time a little closer.

Not a raccoon. Not an opossum. Not a fox or dog.

Those facts flashed through her mind in seconds. As well as the fact she was equal distance from her car as the house.

A third growl sounded from her right.

That growl was decidedly deeper and longer. She flicked the flashlight to that side.

A dark form flashed from behind one house to the other.

Screw it. She had a lever action rifle with ten rounds of .44 Magnum loaded into the ammo tube. The trusty Henry rifle that she had bought years ago, wrapped in oilskin and laying on the floorboard of her car. "Mister Henry" could handle whatever was growling in the shadows.

Tara knew that if she took off at a dead run, whatever it was would attack. So she began to slowly walk towards her car. She did not turn the flashlight off. Whatever was out there might see just as easily in the dark as she could in the light. Instead, she continued slowly forward until she was hidden between two of the houses.

Then she made a run for it.

A roar echoed around her. Rattling the siding of the houses. Broken glass in window frames shifted. Followed by the sound of it shattering.

A howl broke through the cacophony of sounds.

Sticks broke. Metal rattled.

Tara ran as though her life depended on it. It probably did, but she wasn't going to dwell on that fact. The glint of her car in the flashlight's beam was a welcoming sight. She didn't stop pushing the button, even as she skidded to a stop beside the car.

Ignoring everything around her, she grabbed the door handle and jerked it open. She slid in and slammed the door behind her, flipped her headlights on, turning them to "high beam". But there was nothing to be seen. Locking her doors, she turned the key to the ignition.

The car started, and as she placed her hand on the gear shift, she paused.

Her great-aunt Julette, known as Julie, had lived here until her death. Ross lived here alone. Aside from the cat, Lucybelle, anyway.

Was she going to allow some unknown creature to send her running away?

Oh, hell no. She hadn't packed up and left the disaster her life had turned into out west just to be chased away by some critter who wanted to terrify her. She'd been drifting, and lost too much, already. Might not be much, but there was a slim chance at starting a new life here. She had to stop half-assing the work of not repeating the past.

Tara climbed into the backseat of her car, no small feat for any adult. Even one who was barely over five feet in height. But she managed without falling, breaking an arm or leg, or stepping on the rifle in her floor board.

Unwrapping her pride and joy, she checked it over. Grabbing extra ammo, because she'd been taught that any smart firearms owner kept extra, she shoved those shells into a pocket. Going back over the seat, she turned the ignition off, but she left the headlights on.

Unlocking the door, she stepped outside the safety of the vehicle.

Moving until she stood in the middle of her car's headlights, she held the rifle in a ready position. She could hear two large creatures moving around her.

Reaching out with her senses, she was able to connect with something. It was unhappy. Confused. And very large.

Twigs snapped from her left, and she turned to face the sound. But she couldn't see anything, despite the moonlight illuminating everything.

She waited for a few minutes. But nothing came towards her. Then the headlights dimmed and faded out to nothing. She really wished she'd listened to the mechanic and replaced the old battery when she had the chance.

"Oh, fuck this," she muttered.

She racked the rifle's lever and returned to the car. Grabbing her flashlight, she cradled the rifle in one arm. She'd spent enough time being taught defense by paid instructors to be confident she'd be able to drop the flashlight and fire quickly.

Maybe dealing with my ex hadn't been worthless, after all, she thought. *It got me to start looking after myself.*

Aside from her great-aunt's house and the one Ross' parents had lived in, there was only one other house that lacked ghosts. It had appeared less run-down. But at the same time, it had a distinctly creepy and unwelcoming feeling to it. More so than the houses with the ghosts. All of whom seemed to now be hiding.

So, she did the opposite of what any sensible person would do: she headed for that one. It took an effort, but she kept a steady pace all the way to that house's entrance.

Just as she reached for the door handle, she felt a hand on her shoulder. Shrieking, she turned to find Ross standing beside her.

"What are you doing out here?" he demanded. He seemed to have no concern for the rifle less than twelve inches from his face.

"I wanted to get my clothes from the car," she retorted. "What the hell is going on around here?"

Ross shook his head. He hunched forward, his hands in fists at his side.

"Get back to the house," he ordered her.

"No," she stated.

"I suggested you stay indoors, and that was for your protection," Ross said. His teeth were clenched, as if he was in pain. Such made his speech harsh and rougher. "Get to the house and stay there. If anything comes around, feel free to shoot at it. Unless you open a door, it can't come in."

Without answering him, Tara moved the rifle's barrel. She pivoted it away from his face and towards the front door.

"I don't smell the right ingredients for that to be of much use against what you'd find inside." Ross declared. "Presuming you're a decent shot, of course."

"Oh, I am," she answered defiantly.

"You don't appreciate the level of control I'm exerting to contain this situation, Tara. And that's alright. My concern is your safety. Now, please," he continued, "for your safety. Get back to Julie's place, your place, right now. As fast as your feet can carry you. Keep the doors closed."

Tara was torn between wanting to trust Ross, and letting her anger win at maybe being bossed around by yet another person, especially a man. Torn long enough for Ross to move himself, more than a bit forcefully, between her and the door. She prepared to object, and argue, just before realizing she'd be arguing to his back. Just below his shoulder blades, actually.

Had he been this tall all along?

Then the weirdness of everything around her intensified. Tara found it difficult to breathe, and smells that were heady and not unpleasant began to gag her throat. Before she could be overcome by it all, she hauled ass for her great-aunt's place. Just as she remembered that she'd brought Mister Henry but nothing else out of her car. She had to have her overnight bag, at least. The change of course was a minor one.

Fuck this as well, Tara decided, she'd go for it.

Course correcting a whole three steps to her right, Tara pushed her legs for a bit more speed. Even though she recognized both the risk and somewhat questionable motive of her actions, she'd committed to it. That did not mean she felt that doing so put her in less danger. Quite the contrary.

She also understood that if she didn't grab the bag with basic toiletries, at least one change of clothes and a few other necessities, she'd never stay indoors all night. No matter how much she might need to.

At least she knew where the bag was in the car. Passenger side, front seat. Right under the glove compartment. She was almost there. Keeping a firm grip on her gun with her left hand, she pushed the unlock button on her car remote. Still a precious couple of seconds away from the vehicle, Tara realized she'd forgot the battery was dead..

Keys put away, grab the door, get the bag, she chanted in her head before accomplishing each task in order.

"What the hell are you thinking?!?" A new voice shouted in her head.

Tara barked an incoherent shout of surprise even as she turned the rifle towards the flicker of a person in her peripheral vision. The overnight bag hung from the strap, which was mashed between her hand and the gun's forestock.

The .44 magnum barrel was pointed at the center of a ghost standing at a window of the nearest home. The ghost was of an elderly man who definitely fit every trope of a southern "hick" to her mind. Right down to a grizzled beard and faded "Newey's Garage" cap. He stared at her with an unmistakable look of disbelief and disdain.

She held her ground, silent and a bit confused.

"You gonna die over lipstick and makeup?" the "hick" challenged.

Tara rolled her eyes and lowered the gun.

A nightmare landed between her and the ghost. The being's back was toward her, unless this thing's wide, leathery wings had grown out of its chest. The head was smooth, with enormous, she guessed ears, on either side. The body, from what she could tell, was bipedal, covered in coarse fur, and otherwise naked. A thin, sinewy arm appeared ahead of one wing, then slashed back out of sight. Glass shattered and wood splintered, accompanied by two sounds she didn't understand. A light popping noise and a gurgle.

Then, she felt the absence of the elder ghost. He was just gone. Not into the light or whatever. Just no longer there. Tara sighted the rifle and fired before she had reason or sense about her.

The bullet struck where she had intended. At the base of the thing's presumed skull, where the stem would attach to the brain of a human. A single lurch from the creature. It slumped heavily, and began to turn towards her.

Where the ghost had been, the window was destroyed. The upper part of the frame looked broken as if struck by a sledgehammer, and only small shards of glass clung around it. The ghost was absent. In the damaged part of the frame, the bullet had bore a smoking hole through the wood. She shifted her focus to the creature now facing her. The middle of its bat-like face was torn apart. Flaps of ragged flesh above the tragus swayed with the almost drunken movement of the head. There were no eyes. Nor was there blood.

Lastly, it wasn't dead. Injured to some extent, perhaps disoriented, but very much living in some manner. The mouth opened and it shrieked. Other shrieks responded from multiple directions, along with what might have been a roar. Despite the ringing in her ears, those shrieks cut through.

Racking the lever to load a fresh round, Tara reconsidered her options and started running for her great-aunt's house.

With her eyes set on the purple front door, Tara kept making her legs pump as hard as they could. The distance felt like miles despite the reality of the house being less than one hundred yards from the front gate. During the seemingly endless trek, some creatures did come into her narrowed field of vision. Her hands came up and fired the rifle at them. Most shots looked like they might have hit, but she took no time to notice much more than if one of the human-sized bat creatures continued to come at her. Vaguely she acknowledged that more than once her hands had to deliver a follow up round. Once it took three to make the creature veer off.

As she slammed the door of her inherited place and began to take in deep gasps of air, Tara caught up with events that she did not remember. Her clothing had gotten torn at least once. The training she'd been diligent of had allowed her hands to remember to load the extra shells she'd grabbed. The pocket she had stuffed them into was empty.

Further evidence that she had fired more than the ten rounds originally sitting in the tube? The barrel of her beloved Henry rifle was so hot she could not stand to touch it. Repeated occurrences of reloading her gun in a slow and methodical manner while practicing at ranges gave her memories of the barrel's warmth after a tube's worth had been fired. That amount of heat was greater. She could hear almost nothing but the ringing in her ears. Any other sound was vague.

Something pressed against her leg as she stood against the closed front door.

Tara knew she screamed but could only hear the sound of her voice as an echo in her head. Her hands did their job again, pointed the gun dangerously close to her leg and pulled the trigger. Nothing happened, even as she felt the click of the trigger against her finger. A good thing, since she would have burned her leg, wrecked the floor right beside it, and likely splattered the gray kitten all over the rest of said floor. The little shit had rubbed up against her. Maybe to seek attention, or possibly to welcome her back. The kitten's mouth opened in what had to be a meow up at Tara. It sniffed the end of the barrel but then went right back to rubbing Tara's leg.

Goddamn psycho, she might have said aloud. She went to pick the kitten up, but remembered to rest the rifle against a nearby wall. It was apparently empty and had no use at the moment, after all. Once the kitten was in her hands and pressed against her, she could feel the critter vibrating with a content purr.

Grateful for the soothing and surprisingly comforting presence of the gray furball, Tara looked around to take in her surroundings. Almost immediately she spotted the mother and daughter team of tux cats. Each was perched by a different closed window. Both were looking very displeased. Fur raised and hissing, although she could not hear them, at something or some *things* outside. Their presence gave her a small comfort.

What else could be seen of the household's interior did not reflect the chaos, violence, or other lousy characteristics of what had been experienced outside.

Aside from the persistent ringing in her ears, Tara might have been able to convince a desperate part of her mind that all was well. Inside this place reflected a calm environment, even with stacked boxes and clothing around.

Of course, she knew better. With no clue of what those creatures were, there was no question of their existence. Tara would have believed in what had happened even if she had not spent a lifetime dealing with ghosts and other things that many considered to be fantasy or mere delusions.

Most of all at that moment, Tara wished the ringing in her ears would ease off or go away. Ross had told her that as long as she did not invite anything or anyone in, she and the felines would be safe. There was no desire to learn if even looking at whatever might be outside could be considered an invitation.

When something impacted against the house, the force was sufficient to shake the place. Taken by surprise, Tara took one hand off the kitten and reached for the rifle. Her reasoning was that it would serve as a club if nothing else. When it was long moments later before a second impact happened, Tara forced herself to relax a bit.

By the fourth impact over the course of the night, she could hear things rattle in the house. If anything crashed she wasn't hearing it, but the ability to hear dishes and such rattle set her to believe that such would be heard. She could approximate where the impacts were located by then as well.

Power had not been disrupted, so she put down the kitten and tried to do something that would help occupy her. After a slow and careful consideration, Tara remembered where the coffee had been in the pantry and set about making a full pot in the older machine her great-aunt had used.

While waiting for the pot to finish brewing, she gave the cats a late meal. They were keeping her company, after all. As a good host, she could at least feed them for their troubles. Wondering if she should be sure to get a litter box and litter in the daylight gave her a chuckle. Thinking like she was going to stick around. Wonders never ceased, she supposed. At least she was fine with cleaning up a mess or three if the mom and kids couldn't wait until it was safe to go back outside.

Which probably meant daylight. Tara realized she had no idea what time it was, or how long until the sun made a proper appearance again.

There had been an old windup clock on a wall in the kitchen. She hadn't even thought to look at it. She went there, while the fur babies chomped at their offered meal.

12:21am was the time. Tara stared at the old clock and its swinging pendulum, willing it to be later. She knew doing so was useless, but that felt more productive in the moment than mentally preparing herself for what would likely be a very long night.

With her hearing returning, Tara could discern more of what was happening outside. Less of the shrieking than she had anticipated. Only a single thump against her house since she had begun moving around. Another sound that could have been a type of roar, and another. She couldn't feel the ghosts roaming around, but they didn't feel gone. Not like the old fellow was. These were the observations she had made mostly to herself for the past hour since checking the kitchen clock.

Physically, that hour had been occupied by more cleanup and organizing of what she had piled in the dining area and table. Along with liberal periods of affection for the cats, who seemed pleased with her attempts to be a proper human for them. No great surprises had been revealed while shuffling through the boxes and piles.

Her intent had been just to occupy herself. A part of her mind did not want to become too engaged with discovery within the home. The very real possibility of something outside becoming an inside problem kept her from wanting to commit, even partially.

At some point she had located her phone where she'd left it, and learned that daylight was supposed to happen at 6:48. Internet signal was spotty at best, which didn't surprise her. The prospect of another five hours of trying to do as little as possible nagged at her.

Knock. Knock. Knock.

That came from the back door.

The mom and babies walked past her, heading towards the sound.

Taking a moment to grab a cleaver she'd unearthed in a kitchen drawer, Tara approached the rear entrance cautiously. Instead of speaking, she knocked once against the door before taking a long step away. The cleaver was in her free hand, ready for more primitive use.

"It's Ross." his voice sounded tired, strained, but not threatening.

"Prove it," she demanded.

Momma cat mewled at the door. The kittens sat and stared at the door, their eyes half closed.

"The three psychos know it's me. They hate those flying bastards."

"Uh huh," Tara replied, not convinced. "They're cats. For all I know, they might want me served up by those flying bastards as dessert."

"You haven't fed them?" he replied, and she could hear the restrained humor.

"I gave them a can of food to share," she rejoined.

"Oooooooo, big mistake. Momma wants her own can, every time. Or a separate bowl of dry food. But yeah, she might want you as after dinner scraps since you did that."

"Ungrateful wench," Tara reflexively replied.

"She *is* a cat. And queen of the roost, as far as she's concerned."

At that, Momma cat meowed more insistently. Her children joined in.

"I'm trusting you three," Tara said down to the furry trio, "and if you get me killed… well, I *was* starting to like y'all."

As the door came open just a bit, Tara peered defiantly out. Ross stood about a foot away, wearing a pair of gym shorts and the same boots he'd had on earlier. A different rock band adorned the extra baggy t-shirt he'd put on. He held up his right hand to where Tara could see what he had. A full box of .44 magnum ammo. One of hers, as she recognized it as one of four boxes she'd packed into her car.

"Thought you might want these," he said, "and it's not safe to leave your car unlocked."

"Get in."

He slipped in quickly, making sure the door was tightly shut behind him. Once that was done, he again held out the box of ammo to her.

"Those were buried under two suitcases, in a box that also held my fancy soaps and candles," she declared. "So you've been snooping through my car. How much of a mess did you make?"

"I replaced everything neatly, as I found it. But after you blazed off all those shots, figured you might be running low. So," he continued, "I went back and grabbed a box for you before I came here."

"Uh huh," she drolled, "and just how did you know you'd mind more ammunition in my car?"

Ross shifted his feet, looking uneasy for the first time.

"I, ummm, smelled it. Kinda odd being mixed in with lavender, almond, dandelion, coffee beans and such. But gunpowder and jacketed hollow points have a very distinct scent," he explained, his voice a touch quieter as though he was admitting to stealing warm cookies from the kitchen.

"Smelled them. Out of all the stuff I jammed in around them. And everything else that's crammed in that poor car of mine. Going to confess to being a werewolf, now?"

His blue eyes shot up, wide and possibly relieved. "Oh, no ma'am! Not a wolf at all."

"What, then?"

"A bear?"

"Are you asking me, or telling me, Ross?" she joked.

"Heh, telling you. Thanks for making it easier."

"This would fall under 'important information I could have used before nightfall,' Ross."

He shuffled and looked at his feet for a moment before answering, "Yeah, but I didn't want to be rejected before I had a chance to explain everything going on here."

"Fair. I have a long and illustrious history of rejection without even bringing my… abilities into a conversation."

"Abilities, eh?" Ross countered, talking through his smile. "That sounds a lot more accepting than 'curse' or 'gift' does. Maybe I should use that. Well, not that I have told anyone." He shrugged. "Learned from my father and grandparents how badly that usually goes. People aren't much more accepting no matter how many more labels are thrown out."

"Want coffee?" she interjected. "This conversation is getting too comfortable for standing at a doorway."

"Would love some. Julie keeps honey at the back of the cabinet above the coffee maker," Ross replied.

Unable to stop it, Tara barked a laugh.

"Honey for the big bear, huh? C'mon, Pooh. To the kitchen."

"Are those things done for the night?" Tara asked from her side of the kitchen. She leaned against the counter where the coffee maker sat, mug of coffee in one hand. Ross was opposite her, leaning at the counter closest to the fridge, also with coffee.

"The surviving ones are still out there," Ross admitted. "The lot of them will go to nest within an hour of daylight. No matter if I'm a bear or, at my biggest, a hybrid? No way I could take all of them out before they'd cut me down."

"I'm guessing the ones I shot aren't among the deceased, then?"

"Unfortunately," he observed, "you can't kill them with lead. No matter how big or fast the bullet is."

"Figures. What about what you said earlier? About not smelling the right ingredients?"

Ross paused from taking a sip of coffee, seemed to ponder the question before stating "Oh, yeah. Marigolds and, damned if I'm lying, mothballs."

Fortunately, Tara did not have a mouthful of coffee to choke on or spew all over the kitchen floor. It took her a moment to gather herself and reply.

"Why the hell haven't you, just surrounded that nest in marigolds, mothballs, or both?" she blurted. "For that matter, do you have to coat your claws in either to kill them? You don't smell like flowers or old clothes."

"Oh, it's got to be administered internally to poison them," he admitted, "and I'm a lousy shot with a bow or gun. Also? It's slow acting. They don't collapse into dust, like a vampire from a show or movie."

"That doesn't answer why that house isn't surrounded by marigolds or reeking of mothballs," Tara rejoined.

"Neither one is a deterrent. Whatever kills those bastards, there isn't enough of it to be effective at the airborne level." Ross explained with a disgruntled tone.

"Nothing else works?"

Ross took a long drink and put the mug on the counter.

"Not that I can say with confidence," he said. "My claws damage them, much like your bullets do, but don't always end them. Also, they have no organs to destroy, which may be part of the issue with killing them."

"But they can't enter a place without an invitation? What even are they?"

"I don't know what they are called. None of my family did," Ross admitted. "They're an ancient race. Likely the reason for an unreasonable fear of bats. Probably helped develop the mythos of vampires. Imagine early humanity trying to cope with encountering or even seeing those bastards!"

"Unlike dealing with werewolves or even werebears, you mean?"

"Not all that different in how people respond to us, no. And you know how thresholds work, right?" he gestured around the room. "Julie was a practitioner, and added wards to this abode. Put some on my family's place, and what she could to some of the other homes, here. Although, they can't enter a living being's place without invitation, as far as my family has seen. As long as ghosts aren't noticed, they are safe inside a former home."

"So that old fellow made himself a target by communicating with me."

"Daryl Emmet? I don't know why he did that. The bastards had a long grudge against him. One of the first residents in this place, and first to manage to end one of them. Bagged a few more before his mortal demise. Wasn't anything noble in his actions, though. He hated them for making it difficult to go outside and take a piss at night."

Tara put her mug on the counter close to her. "On that note, I'm going to go check and reload my rifle." She grabbed the box that Ross had brought, from its location further down the countertop.

"Mind if I keep you company?" he asked.

Walking towards the front of the house, she answered over her shoulder.

"Just keep your distance, okay?"

He stepped in behind her when she was three paces away, but asked "Still don't trust me?"

"Whenever you get close to me," she grumbled, "It's like I'm a horny teenager. I don't trust that."

"My apologies, that's not intentional!" Ross quickly replied. "Because of my particular condition, I exude a heavy musk. Especially when I'm in a good mood. You aren't the first person that's been bothered by it. Nothing I can do to tamp it down, unfortunately."

"Not the first person?" she teased. The rifle was where she'd left it, so Tara picked up Mister Henry and opened the chamber. She blew air down the barrel's interior. "A hit with all the ladies in town, are you?"

"Nothing that bad," he amended, "but sometimes it will affect a person in a real powerful way."

Satisfied that nothing visible had exited the barrel, Tara went about looking down the barrel's interior for debris and residue. There was nothing of significance. Once the chamber was closed, she began opening the end of the tube magazine.

"Alright, at least you're admitting to it," she said. "Back to the winged bastards. When did they first come around?"

While she had been checking the gun, Ross had opened the box of shells and taken a single one out. He examined the hollow tip as he replied to her.

"They were responsible for the massacre. Don't know what the couple in that place, where the nest is now, were doing. But pretty sure they managed to summon or at least attract the first ones."

While he spoke, Ross dug his free hand into a back pocket of his shorts. When the fingers came back into view, they held a small ball of lint. Ross began pushing the lint into the hole at the top of the bullet. His expression was one of concentration, but he continued his narrative.

"Four of them. That's all it was, at first. My family smelled them coming but had no idea what they were. The couple that got their attention were killed. Almost everyone was lounging out on their porches and in their yards. Most of those didn't have enough sense or survival instincts to run inside when the bastards showed up and slaughtered the first couple."

"Did your family try to stop them?"

"They sure did. Found out the hard way that the bastards didn't bleed, didn't have organs in any way they understood, and even tearing them in half didn't always do the job."

She gestured for the bullet he'd been toying with. "Great. Awesome. Start handing me ammo to load this baby."

Instead, Ross held up the bullet close to her eyes. The lint he'd gotten was jammed into the hollow area. "I'm wondering if we can put bits of mothball, or dandelion, in these, like the lint I've got here. Seal them over somehow."

"It wouldn't have to do anything but keep the 'bastard poison' in, right?" She said thoughtfully. "Maybe some kind of wax? Once the bullet is fired through the barrel, as long as there's some to enter their bodies, that should do what's needed?"

"Alright, alright, we may just have a plan. Or at least the start of one!" Ross exclaimed.

Coffee was consumed, stashes were revealed. Ross had certainly spent plenty of time in great-aunt Julie's place, because he showed Tara where her relative kept a large mortar and pestle, the hidden shelves in a closet where multiple herbs, flowers, and the like were stored.

Ross went back to his home to grab a handful of mothballs and some marigold from the plants outside the porch on the way back.

While he was gone, Tara searched all the way back into the cabinets and food pantry. She hadn't seen a need to see what every article in those had been. Figured that to be a task for another day, or when she was really desperate for food.

Should have known better, she reminded herself. Putting anything off had almost never worked out for her. She'd used the one percent of the times it had as a way to justify her doing it the other ninety-nine percent.

Amongst the many metal cans there were some surprises. Actual canned jars of potatoes, pickled eggs, tomatoes and whole strawberries were the first discoveries. A container, partially used, of paraffin wax. Sealed bags of roots and dried sage, hibiscus, vanilla and more had been tucked all along the back of the cabinets. Four faded Altoids tins held various crystals in many sizes had been tucked into a corner. When Ross had mentioned that Julie had been a magic practitioner, he hadn't indicated just how much of one she'd been.

The more she learned about great-aunt Julie, the more Tara wished they had been a bigger part of each other's lives. Maybe her "gifted" relative could have talked her out of some bad relationships. Or helped hide the ex's body.

Tara had done well enough of that on her own, but it would have been nice to have someone help. Prevented her from having to learn how to do it on the fly. Or maybe it was better that she came to know Julie this way, after making her own mistakes and really learning about herself.

Three knocks on the back door. Tempted to just yell for Ross to come in, the circumstances of Rosewynd Estates prevented it. Tara walked back to the door and knocked once from her side.

"Yes, it's me," Ross answered, "I come bearing mothballs and marigolds."

As she opened the door, she cheerfully declared "Come in!" to Ross's smiling face.

Over Ross's right shoulder, on the roof of the home across from the back door, sat one of the winged bastards. Tara's eyes locked right onto it.

The large ears curved towards her and the head tilted just enough for her to notice.

The bastard shrieked.

"Oh shit," Tara gasped, her eyes darting to Ross's.

He pushed the box of mothballs and plucked marigold flowers into her hands. His eyes had become that husky yellow that she thought she'd seen earlier.

"Close the door!" Ross demanded. He was turning away, pulling off his shirt and doing an odd dance. The sense of lust struck her so hard she felt unable to do anything for a moment. His bare back was riddled with scars and fresh cuts. The dance had been him dexterously stepping out of his boots without using his hands. Only now did she realize that his legs were as battle worn as his back. And then he did a little jiggle with his hips. The shorts promptly dropped to his ankles.

Musk or not, Tara was too busy taking in the sight of Ross's bare ass to acknowledge anything else. When his hand, easily twice the size it had been before, pushed her further into the house, she looked up as if woken from a trance.

"Stay here!" the now over-sized Ross commanded with a lower, savage voice. As he pulled the door shut in front of her, Tara's brain acknowledged two more things.

First, Ross was still growing, even though he was easily a foot taller and wider than he'd been around her.

The second was the winged bastard flying towards the back door at a hellish speed.

She stood, somewhat dazed, staring at the closed door. Until it jarred as something enormous slammed against it. The door held, but the home shook around and beneath her from the impact. A definite bear roar came from just outside, and then she was moving to find the closest window. The flowers and box fell to the floor, completely forgotten.

Once the quaint curtain was pushed aside, Tara could clearly see the entire area behind Julie's house. The winged bastard was attempting to crawl or climb over the shoulders of an enormous golden haired humanoid. Ross's head was obscured, but there was no mistaking that he stood at least eight feet tall and six feet wide. Fur the texture of a bear covered every visible inch of the caretaker, golden and honey blonde as the hair on his head when he was in human form. The bear hybrid's massive arms were wrapped around the lower torso of the winged thing, keeping it from further progress.

The wings flapped. The thin, inhuman arms ended in long taloned fingers that sunk into the pelt of Ross's back. The wings started to provide lift for the creature and the pair of enemies began to rise clumsily into the air. As Ross's back paws left the ground, the entwined bodies began to turn.

Ross's hybrid transformation gave him a face that looked like a cross between a klondike bear and a mastiff. Still there were recognizable features of the human that she had met. While her mind worked to make sense of those contradictions, Ross opened his muzzle wide. The impossibly large teeth crunched into the joint where the right wing joined into the bastard's back.

The snap of the joint giving way under Ross's bite was loud enough for Tara to hear in the house. Unable to fly or hover via a single wing, the creature smashed against the ground, Ross's full weight was on top of it. Tara felt her feet vibrate through the floorboard.

Ross tore the whole wing free with his jaws and tossed the amputated appendage away with a flick of his massive head. A gaping, ragged hole several inches deep gave proof that something had once been there, but no more. The bastard screamed, reminding her of what she had heard through the ringing of her own ears as she'd put bullet after bullet into that thing's fellow beings not so long ago.

Finally, Tara noticed the other winged bastards. Five of them, perched on different rooftops all along the road nearby. One in particular was atop the roof of the nest house. They were facing towards the fight. Each ear was extended out further than she'd seen them previously. Quick movements from one or another as if they were preparing to join in the fray, followed by each settling back. Perhaps reconsidering the idea since their fellow bastard had just lost a major part of itself and was now having the wounded area shredded by gigantic claws. The sounds being made by the wounded one were enough to make Tara think about leaving the window and seeing if there was anything to make tea with. Maybe taking up one of the many books that Julie had left behind.

Moments later she was grateful that she'd stayed put.

The winged bastard at the nest made a new sound. Part shriek, part cough was how Tara's ears interpreted it. The others responded immediately to whatever was being said. Each of the remaining four climbed across the roofs they had been perched at. One flew directly at Ross's unprotected back and strafed its talons through fur, which left deep red gashes. Despite being in the throes of tearing apart the remaining wing of his foe, Ross as the hybrid arched sharply in pain and gave a cry that was nearly human. The still unengaged trio were preparing to make their runs at him.

Her feet and legs weren't moving fast enough, yet again. Tara felt too slow as she skidded to a halt near the entrance to the dining area to grab Mister Henry and a half dozen shells that had been laid out earlier. The plan had been to grind the flowers and mothballs together, fill the hollow points with the stuff, cap the rounds with some kind of wax. The paraffin that she'd found would be perfect for it, at least as a first trial. No more time for any of that tonight. She'd have to settle for inconveniencing the bastards for now.

Hurrying to the back door, Tara loaded the six rounds through the rifle's loading port instead of trying to argue with the tube magazine. She finished stuffing in the last round as she got to the door. The situation outside sounded bad to her. More cries from Ross than shrieks or other noise from the bastards. She worked the lever to load the first round, and noticed the dropped flowers and spilled box of mothballs. An idea struck her.

When she threw open the back door, part of her took note of movement against her calves. Tara quickly hoped the cats weren't psycho enough to come out in this madness. Then she spotted two bastards tearing into Ross while the one he'd severely wounded was crawling towards the nest house. Ross was up on his back legs, taking sloppy swings at each of his foes. They, in turn, were waiting for Ross's swing at the other one to slash another wound in Ross's enormous form.

They definitely had the upper hand in the fight.

So, Tara shot the one giving the orders. The bastard perched on the nest house took the round right where she'd aimed for. Its so-called mouth, muzzle, whatever was pushed inward by the force of the magnum slug punching into it. The leader swayed and listed to its left. Tara moved on to her next target while jacking the lever to prepare the next round. The sights settled on the bastard to Ross's right.

Tara nearly shot the gray kitten for the second time that night. The furball appeared right in front of her sights, covering the chest of her intended target. Momma cat and her mini me were clawing their way up that same bastard's legs. Tara pivoted her aim and shot the one to Ross's left in mid torso. The bullet hit a little off from where she'd intended. Couldn't afford to miss much more than that. Only four bullets left, she scolded herself. No chance of getting back to the house to grab more. The exit wound must have breached near the wing joint of the right wing, because that one sagged uselessly.

Good enough for the moment.

A fresh round loaded and Tara was on the move. As she made her way, her rifle and eyes swept around, looking for the remaining pair. She found them circling high above, gliding like a nightmare version of vultures. As much as she wanted to try and snipe them out of the air, she didn't want to risk missing. Besides, she had reached the one that Ross had torn up.

The heavily wounded bastard was using its less wounded hand and mostly intact leg to drag itself to the nest and had made it more than halfway there. The handful of mothballs that Tara had stuffed into her pocket was in her secondary hand. The primary held the rifle against her shoulder.

With a scream that she could barely hear with her report-beaten eardrums, Tara mashed the mothballs into the gaping hole where the wing had been ripped out. She straightened up and stomped the mothballs deeper with one sneakered foot. As she gave a second stomp for good measure, she became aware of a shriek that was almost the same key as the ringing in her ears.

It came from the bastard under her shoe. Its whole body arched backward and convulsed. She took a few steps back from it, turned her attention to the rest of what was going on around her.

Not as much of a mess as she'd feared. Not great, but not as bad.

The leader was still tilting to one side and not making a sound. It moved, but the movements were sluggish and lacked confidence. Nor had it moved from the roof of the nest.

Victim number one of the tres' psychos was curled into a fetal ball, nowhere near Ross or the cats. The long talons looked to be trying to piece together the body's maimed torso and legs. The head twitched and was torn up enough to resemble a stuffed toy that a cat had tried to eat the stuffing out of.

Victim number two was still being mauled by the trio of furballs. It was crawling toward the nest on all fours. Momma cat was gnawing on the back of its head, all four paws sunk claw-deep into the neck of the bastard.

The kittens tore into the still active wing's membranes. Tara could see several long slits in each of the thin areas.

Above, the two untouched winged bastards circled slower, but not closer to the ground.

Lumbering towards her, Ross was a bloody mess. He had shifted into an actual bear. Still honey blonde, still bigger than life, but wounded all over his back, head and limbs. The four legs were wobbly but kept moving his body forward. He stared at her with his golden eyes, panting loudly.

Pointing directly at him with her now free hand, Tara gestured to the open back door of Julie's place. Ross shifted in an unsteady manner but made his way towards it.

Looking between the wounded and unwounded bastards, she took position at Ross's retreating back. She made a kissing sound with her lips. Remarkably, the cats immediately disengaged from their crawling scratching post and came to her. One by one they gathered around her until they formed a circle. Each faced a different direction.

They held their positions, Tara and the tres' psychos, until Ross had managed to fully enter through the back door. Tara walked slowly backwards, keeping her watch while the felines strode at her sides.

Once the back door was closed and all five of them were inside, Tara placed the rifle next to the door and looked around.

Momma cat, her mini me and the gray psycho sat around the now human and very naked Ross. His breathing was labored, wounds crossing each other all along his body. From what could be seen, his skin was already trying to knit back together, and blood was not flowing freely from most of the wounds.

"Hey," she called to Ross, "you're bleeding on my floor."

"Oh, it's your floor, now?" he wheezed. "Send me a cleaning invoice. And the cats still like me better."

Daylight eventually came. The cats went out with Tara, only to return less than five minutes later. They meowed loudly to be let in. Once inside, the kittens laid around Ross, who was still on the floor. He had put his shorts and shirt back on after Tara had found them. Momma cat sat next to Tara. All three felines purred loudly.

"So, werebear, huh?" Tara began the morning's conversation.

"Yep."

"Going to do some kind of healing hibernation on my floor? Be in the way for days on end?

"We heal a bit faster than that, even if that was the worst I've ever taken before," Ross admitted. "If you don't mind, I would do better by not moving around too much until noon or so. Should be able to finish healing while resuming normal activities at that point. If you don't want to feed me, no problem. Helps with healing, but I can manage."

"Looks like the little psychos have made those decisions for me," she observed, nodding to the pair curled up against him. "I suppose you're welcome to stay until you can leave on your own two, or four, feet."

"Ugh, the bear jokes are just going to keep coming, aren't they?"

"You're pretty tough, Pooh," she said with a smile. "You'll survive."

Ross flopped his head against the floor. The smaller tux took that as an invitation to start chewing on Ross's hair.

"Speaking of staying," he rejoined. "Are you going to bother to unpack your car? Maybe hang around and see if you can stand to live at Rosewynd Estates?"

He began to rub the kitten's head. It promptly began to playfully bite at his fingers. The gray one, sensing there was not enough attention being paid to it, jumped at Ross's free hand.

Tara looked around the house. Out of the windows, she saw the ghosts milling around nearby. All of them at least glanced her way. A few even gestured greetings towards her.

In the entrance to the den, a fading apparition of an elderly woman stood. Tara wasn't sure why this one had appeared until the woman smiled at her. That triggered a recognition. The smile had been on other members of her family. It was great-aunt Julie, visible to her senses at last.

Be happy, girlie.

The words of her deceased great-aunt echoed in the house even as the ghost faded in a silvery light. A light Tara knew meant her aunt had moved onto whatever came after death.

Tara smiled as she turned and watched Ross playing with the kittens.

Yeah. She could definitely be happy here.

"I think I might just do that," Tara finally replied.

end.

Love and Justice

By: William Joseph Roberts

I'd gotten a call two days ago from Travis Blankenship, an old military buddy of mine from back in the day. We'd served together overseas, did lots of stupid shit, and had one hell of a great time doing it.

When he called, I'd been working just south of Wheeling, West Virginia. He was a complete wreck, like rock bottom dumps, and had had so much to drink that I could barely understand any of his slurred, pig Latin.

I managed to understand enough of his drunken babble to put two and two together and figure out his wife Janice had left him.

I wasn't too surprised by that. She was one of those high-maintenance trailer park divas that needed nearly constant attention. And Travis, well… he liked to hunt, fish, and drink, none of which she thought a *proper* man should partake in. How in the hell she thought she could find someone in Southern West Virginia who didn't like any of those things was beyond me.

It didn't hurt my feelings whatsoever that I'd have to cruise through the twisty Appalachian roads to reach Travis's place. He'd set himself up a sweet little spot along the banks of the Guyandotte River in the unincorporated town of Justice. Where the fishing was choice and the scenery picturesque.

I made quick work of interviewing the locals and collecting evidence so I could close out the case. It turned out to be nothing more than another bogus run-of-the-mill Mothman sighting.

I figured that the *supposed* incident was most likely induced by the use of some sort of redneck chemical cocktail in an attempt to find that blissful nirvana where they could ignore the world and all of their problems one hit at a time. That sort of thing had become a serious problem in the area and wasn't within my jurisdiction or any of my damned business to start with. So I wrapped up the case, packed my gear on Jonie, my Harley-Davidson Road King, and headed south.

In my opinion, one of the best things in life is an easy, relaxing ride, and this ride ranked up there with some of the best I'd been on. The sun was out, and the temps were perfect, letting the wind wash away the cares and worries of the day as the engine pounded away. Not much else in this world even came close to matching the relaxation a little wind therapy provided.

The miles rolled along effortlessly as the sun slowly edged its way closer toward the ridgeline, casting long shadows in the valley by the time I pulled off of old State Route 52 and into the parking lot of the Justice Church of God.

The first time Travis had given me the directions, I must have made some sort of stupid noise, because he laughed into the phone and asked if he was wrong to have gotten some religion. He let me fumble with that for a few minutes before he told me the preacher was his fourth cousin twice removed on his mamma's side. Travis had won a houseboat in a poker game and talked his cousin, Brother John D. Browning, into letting him park the boat along the riverbank behind the church.

In exchange, Travis donated a hefty tithe to the church each paycheck and did a little work around the place. In order to put the boat into the river, he clear-cut the river bank and built a small launch ramp to the river that the church used to collect a little extra in charitable donations. With the influx of tourists and promotion for the Hatfield & McCoy riding trails, there were plenty of city folks coming into the area who wanted to kayak, paddleboard, or canoe down the now *"historic"* Guyandotte River.

I pulled in and parked next to Travis's old Ford Bronco. It was beautifully quiet. Nothing but the sound of the slow-flowing river down the hillside and songbirds filled the air.

"Can't say I blame him one bit for setting up shop back here," I mumbled to myself. "It's absolutely peaceful." I took my time along the steep path down the river bank to the water's edge. Travis had built a small dock of sorts and had several lines tied back to the larger trees along the riverbank to secure his houseboat.

On a covered upper deck of the dock that overhung a deeper section of the river, he'd built a smoker and a large grill from fifty-five-gallon drums and bricks. Several camping chairs surrounded an old wooden wire spool, a full sized fridge, and along the deck's railing were about a half dozen fishing rod holders made from PVC pipe and in the corner was a stack of rods.

"Almost heaven, West Virginia," I said, looking over Travis's setup. "Can't say I ain't a little bit jealous." I popped open the fridge and found it partially stocked with a mix of Miller Light, and Coors, the standard watered-down horse piss that passed for beer in these parts.

"Beggers can't be choosers." I shrugged and snagged a pair of beers from the fridge. Being the nosey sort I checked the drawers, and sure enough, found a small cup of nightcrawlers in the back of the cheese drawer. I baited a few lines and tossed them in before kicking back, lighting up a long overdue cigar, and making myself comfortable.

"Yup…" I said, popping the *p* extra sharp. "Travis has to be the richest man I know. This is nearly my perfect idea of heaven." I let out a sigh, took a long drink, kicked my feet up, and closed my eyes.

Of all the times I've tried to relax and visit folks, something always goes wrong. Maybe this will be the one time that the universe lets me take a break.

Taking my time I finished both the beer and the smoke, then lit several of the Tiki torches mounted around the deck before I grabbed an extra beer and headed down to the boat.

Stepping from the dock to the deck of the boat left my legs feeling a bit shaky, but it didn't take long to get used to the odd motion. Most of my childhood fishing was spent along river banks or wading along and fishing the hard-to-get-to pockets along small rivers and creeks of Northwest Georgia. It was a rare occasion that I'd fished from a boat.

I made my way to the rear and started to open the door into the cabin when Butch, Travis's bluetick hound let out one hell of a braying howl. I let the door clack closed and heard claws scratching at the inside of the aluminum door. With the way the sound carried down here, it wouldn't surprise me if half of the town of Justice heard Butch carrying on.

"Travis! Hey Travis! You in there buddy? Come on Trav, if you're in there say something. Butch won't let me in."

Something shifted inside the cabin. I could hear what sounded like empty cans being tossed about.

"Butch come," Travis said from inside.

"Well, at least you're on the right side of the green. I was starting to worry that you'd gotten drunk and fell over the side or something."

"Braxton?"

"Yeah, man."

"What the hell are you doing here?" I could hear him fumbling to stand, as he waded through what I expected to be a sea of empty beer cans. The door to the cabin opened and there stood Travis, eyes bloodshot, his features worn and ragged.

"You don't remember calling me, do you?"

He opened his mouth and started to say something, then just shook his head. "Nope, I don't. Come on in, man. Excuse the mess," he said, waving at the disaster surrounding him as he waded his way back through the flood of beer cans then flopped on the bed. He pressed the heels of his palms into his eyes and let out a slow groan. The small horse of a dog followed suit and flopped onto the rug next to the bed after kicking several cans out of his way.

Travis let out a long sigh, looking around at the mess surrounding the small bunk. "Ah, there you are," he said, grabbing a can from the shelf behind the bed. A small amount of liquid sloshed around the nearly empty can when he shook it. Travis shrugged and grimaced as he downed the remainder of what had to be lukewarm piss beer by this point.

"Hair of the dog," I asked, tossing him one of the beers as I stepped into the cabin.

"Mighty kind of you, Braxton. Free beer is good beer." He popped the pull tab and took a long drink from the fresh can before laying back on the bed.

"You wouldn't say that if you knew where I got the beer?"

He looked up at me with a confused curiosity, then shrugged and laid his head back. "At this point, I really don't care. Beer is beer."

I popped the top on my beer and cleared a space to sit at the small corner table to the right of the door. "So what's up, Trav? You sounded pretty torn up on the phone."

"Go home, Brax. It isn't your problem."

"It kinda is, man," I said, chuckling. "You called me, and I'm not the kinda guy that will ignore a brother when they need him the most."

Travis downed the rest of his beer, crumpled the can and tossed it against the far wall. "Well, maybe I need some time to think things over."

"You've had two days since you called me, Trav. You're alive, so I'll give you that much credit for not going skinny dipping with your toaster, but that don't make it any easier once you sober up."

Travis chuckled and held up his index finger, motioning me to wait. "Hold that thought." With great effort, he rolled over onto his side and reached for something amid the cans and other trash littering the cabin. He lifted a small hatch from the floor, then reached deep into the opening, retrieving a dripping can of beer.

"What's that?"

"Live well. It's great for keeping beer cold, too." He popped the top and downed the beer in a few gulps. "See," he started to say, then let out a rumbling burp. "Problem solved. I don't have to think about it if I'm not sober." Travis flashed a cheesy grin, then fished out another beer from the live well.

"That ain't exactly healthy either, Trav."

"Who cares." He shrugged.

"Do you really think that's a good idea? I mean, ain't you gotta go to work at some point?"

"Nope." The crack, pop, fizz of the beer can opening almost chimed within the confines of the small cabin. "Besides, like you said earlier. It's just a little hair of the dog to knock the cobwebs out of my head, is all."

"So what the hell is going on, Trav? You look like a complete trainwreck."

He let out a grunted laugh. "Life."

I stood, downed the beer, then crumpled and tossed the can at Travis. "Guess I wasted a trip all the way out here then." I turned and opened the door.

"Dammit, Brax…" An empty beer can hit me square in the back. "Sit your ass back down."

I turned and glared at him. "You sure? I have no problem jumping on the bike and scooting on down the road. I wanted to make a run over the twisty roads across Horsepen while I was up this way."

Travis stared back at me with baleful eyes. "Please, Brax."

I reached into the live well. The water was nice and cold. Probably something to do with natural springs in the area that fed into the river. Grabbing the last two beers from the makeshift cooler I tossed one to Travis, who fumbled the can several times before it landed on the bed.

I took up my previous seat and lit up the last cigar I had on me. "Alright, spill it."

"Hell, man. I'm not even sure where to start."

I shrugged, and leaned back, getting comfortable for story time. "Start at the beginning."

Travis sat quietly for a few moments, nursing the beer while he thought. "More than a few of the boys have seen Janice schmoozin' round town with that big banker from up north."

I shrugged. "Okay? Didn't you say she worked at the bank?"

"Yeah, she does. She's the head associate."

"Then maybe it's nothing, and you're worried for no reason. Did you confront her about it?"

"Nope," he said, then took another drink.

"Trav…"

"Don't," he said, cutting me off. "Janice pulled a fast one on me, Brax. She left a few days ago in a tizzy. She was going on about how I was worthless, lazy, and never going to amount to anything, not to mention how much of a mistake it was to have married me in the first place. She said that if she stuck around any longer, it would undoubtedly ruin the rest of her life. She's gone and gotten so spiteful about it all she even had that uppity Yankee banker repo my Peterbilt."

"What? You gotta be shitting me, man."

"Nope," Travis said, shaking his head slowly. He placed the cold beer can against his temple.

"Damn, man. That's a whole new level of petty." I let out a long hissing gasp then took a long draw from the cigar. "That just ain't right. You don't mess with a man's truck. She oughta know that."

"Hell, Brax, she even tried to take Butch."

I looked from him to Butch and back again. "I mean, he is a big loud stinky nuisance. But what in the ever-loving hell has gotten into her? She's always hated that dog. Is she trying to write the perfect country western song?"

"I don't know, Brax. But the funny thing was that Butch wouldn't budge an inch for her. I think he likes me more because I let him have a beer every now and then. Oh, and she filed for divorce and had me served. She couldn't bother to hand the papers to me herself." He chugged the rest of the beer, crushed the can, and tossed it over his shoulder.

"What the hell, man? You treated that woman like a queen." I grunted a laugh and slapped my knee. "If her daddy knew she was runnin' round with a yank, not to mention a banker, he'd roll over in his grave. A banker ain't much better than a lawyer or revenuer."

Travis let out a long sigh and let his shoulders slump. "Guess she just got tired of livin' on this old boat. I got the letter here someplace. The postman delivered it yesterday."

He craned his neck, glancing at the tiny kitchenette countertop, then shrugged. "Tell me this Brax, what does that banker fella have that I don't?" Tears glistened in his eyes. "It's incomprehensible how she could want to be with the likes of him. I'd be willing to bet he couldn't do a hard day's work to save his life."

"Want me to round up the boys and we'll teach him a thing or two about southern hospitality?"

"NO! I don't want you or any of the boys to do nothing." He started to stand, then unsteadily collapsed back onto the bed.

"We can't just sit by and watch you suffer, Trav. Not to mention, I only got a few days to kill before I need to head for the next gig."

"Your Mamma would shoot me if I let you get into trouble on account of me. Just go away and let me sleep it off."

"If that's what you really want I'll head out first thing in the morning. Otherwise, I'll go pick up some supper and another case of beer for tonight."

"That sounds like a plan." Travis laid back on his bunk and almost immediately began to snore, wrapped in the warm numbness of alcoholic slumber.

I stepped out of the small cabin and stopped at the end of the dock to relieve myself of a few of those beers before jumping back onto the bike. The darkness of night had fallen over the valley, letting the Milky Way shine bright overhead. It was amazing what the sky looked like without the light pollution of a big city nearby.

A low rumble grew in the distance, slowly vibrating the boards under my feet as I stood at the end of the dock. Downstream on the opposite side of the river, a bright white light came into view. The rumble grew more pronounced the closer the light got, approaching at a pretty good clip.

By the time I finished my business the head of the coal train had passed by, crossing the trestle bridge that crossed overhead of the river and road at the end of town. Quietly, I stood there for a few moments finishing my cigar as I watched the train chug on by and out of sight.

Taking one last puff, I tossed the cigar into the river and started to turn when I realized the low vibrating hum continued to drone on. I could have even sworn it was getting louder.

Strange lights appeared in the sky above the mountain range on the opposite side of the river to the south. It looked like something straight out of Star Trek. I couldn't say that I was a mega fan of any sort but I'd watched enough to know what was going on and recognize most characters and such.

The thing had to be the size of an aircraft carrier and looked wrong the way it just hung there motionless in the sky. The incessant hum perforated everything. What looked like search lights panned across the small mountain town and surrounding hillsides.

I rubbed my eyes to make sure I wasn't seeing things, but sure enough, it was still there when I looked back up.

"Hey, Travis," I shouted over my shoulder, not taking my eyes off the object. "Travis!"

He replied with a wincing shout. I could hear him grumbling under his breath, shuffling his feet among the beer cans littering the floor. Travis stepped out onto the dock and stopped. I could hear him behind me, struggling for the breath to make words. All he managed to get out was a strangled "Huh…" as he made his way down the dock to stand beside me.

"I'm guessing this isn't something normal around here, is it?"

"Nope." Reaching over the side of the dock Travis pulled on a rope, retrieving what looked like a minnow bucket from the water. After a moment of fighting with the top, he pulled a can of beer out and handed it to me, pocketed one, and took the last beer for himself. He dropped the bucket, popped the top of the beer in his hand, and finished it in a few gulps. Crushing the can, he tossed it overboard then retrieved a crumpled pack of smokes from his pocket. He looked down at Butch, who had followed him out of the cabin as he lit the smoke.

"Whatcha think, Butch?"

The dog let out one hell of a braying howl.

"Reckon we should head up the hill and see what that's about? Or should we stay here and throw an end-of-the-world party?"

Butch licked his nose, grumbled, then turned and hurried back onto the boat.

"Yeah, that's true. We are about out of beer." He took a long drag on the cheap generic cigarette. "I suppose I should toss on a clean shirt before we take off."

The unmistakable sound of a CB crackling to life broke through the eerie hum from above. "Breaker breaker one nine. This is Shag Nasty. Anyone out there got their ears on? Come on back. We be in a mess of hurt."

"Who the hell is that?"

"Shag." Travis rushed to the helm on the upper deck of the houseboat. I hurried behind, hanging back on the ladder. Travis picked up the mic and keyed it.

"Break one nine, this is T-dog, I gotcha loud and clear, Shag. What's up?"

"Did you not see the fucking mothership hanging up there in the sky?"

The voice on the radio sounded overly excited and flustered at the same time.

"It's exactly what I've warned everyone about all these years. It's finally happened! The aliens are here to invade! I've been making shielding for as many people as I can, but I'm out of foil. Can you bring some to me? I'm up on the hill at Mom and Dad's place."

Travis let out a long sigh. Rubbing at his temples, he slowly smacked the mic handset against the side of his head before he keyed it again. "You just sit tight, Shag. Is anyone else up there?"

"No, it's just me right now. Mom and Dad are in Charleston for a bowling tournament. Al is probably at the office still and there ain't no telling about Glen. He's probably back down there with Tammy all over again. I tell you what Travis, it wouldn't hurt my feelings none if them there aliens just up and took that woman. She ain't nothing but a no good cock teasing devil woman, I tell you what."

Travis looked at the radio and shook his head. "Will you shut up already you damned crazy ass." He retrieved the last beer from his pocket, popped the top, and stopped himself just as the edge of the can touched his lips.

Butch grumbled.

"Where are my manners? I'm sorry, buddy." Travis poured half of the can into the dog bowl sitting nearby then held the can up in salute.

"Cheers, bud."

He chugged the rest of the beer and tossed the crushed can over his shoulder. "Guess we should go save the world, hu?" He smiled back at me with that half-lit look of invincibility then headed below.

For the most part, I'd always been the law-abiding type, except in those moments where being law-abiding tended to be… inconvenient. After signing on with the KCG, Krypto, Cults, and Gangs, an offshoot department of the Federal Marshals, I had to make sure to follow the rules…more or less…because the bean counters really didn't like explaining to their superiors why one of their agents needed bail money.

But, hell, we're all guilty of bending the rules every now and then in some way. From speeding, to double parking, to selling a little moon shine on the side. It's just one of those things, ya know. So, I really didn't see where it would be much of an issue when Travis came back on deck toating an

M4 carbine with extended capacity magazines, targeting laser, and an underslung 40mm grenade launcher. Considering there were what looked to be honest-to-goodness aliens invading the backwoods of southern West Virginia, I took it as one of those times it was okay to bend the rules.

We hopped into Travis's old Ford Bronco and headed north along Route 52 toward Gilbert.

It seemed like a lot of other folks had seen the ship as well because the road was clogged with hastily loaded vehicles leaving the area as fast as they could.

The alien vessel hung in the air, twenty or thirty feet above the overgrown gravel field that took up a rare acre of flat land between the river and the only road leading out of Justice.

Travis pulled off the road, put it in park, and climbed halfway out the driver's window.

"Don't you deal with weird shit for the government," he asked, sliding back into his seat.

"Yup."

"So what do we do about this?"

I shrugged and shook my head then leaned out the window to take in the enormity of the craft. "I honestly don't have the faintest clue, Trav. This is way above my pay grade."

Travis shifted the old Bronco into gear and spun her around, kickup up a cloud of dust and gravel as he pulled back onto the highway.

"Where we going?"

"Let's go pay Shag a visit. Maybe his crazy ass will have some sort of bright idea."

I looked over to Travis and laughed. "What sort of crazy are we talking about exactly? Conspiracy theorist? Paranoid schizophrenic? Psychopathic megalomaniac?"

Travis's face twisted like he was thinking really hard about my question as we turned off the main road and continued up the hill onto Plum Street.

"I'd say he falls somewhere between conspiracy theorists and paranoid schizophrenic with prepper tendencies if that gives you any idea."

"Okay," I said, nodding. "Good to know he isn't the type that'll cut out my liver and wear my face."

"Naw, not even close. Shag is more or less harmless even if he is a little eccentric. But he knows lots of off-the-wall things that normal folks wouldn't even think about."

Travis gunned the engine and raced uphill like we had a load of homemade hooch in the back and a government man was hot on our ass.

We pulled off into the driveway of a three-story split level that looked like it had been built in the 80s. Travis slid out of the truck, slung his M4, and followed a sidewalk around the front side of the house that faced the hillside. A very large canvas yurt came into view just down the hillside on a weathered wooden deck as we rounded the corner of the house.

"What's the deal with that," I asked, motioning at the yurt.

"Shag never really left home, but did at the same time. He talked his folks into letting him build that down there after nobody cared about having a pool anymore.

"G…g…god, is p…p…punishing us!" came a stuttered shout from inside the yurt.

"Thought you said he wasn't the certifiable kinda crazy?"

Travis spun on his heel and poked a finger into my chest "I did not say that. I said he was mostly harmless, And besides, that ain't Shag, that's Red."

"Who the hell is Red?"

"He went to school with all of us and lives a few houses down the hill. He found Jesus a few years ago and turned into a bit of a bible thumper since."

Travis continued down the weathered wooden stairs toward the yurt.

"Hey Shag!"

"Travis? That you?" The canvas flap of the yurt flew open and there stood a ragged bum of a guy. Shaggy beard, long shaggy matted hair topped with a tin foil hat in the shape of a pirate's tricorn.

Travis fought to hold back a laugh but just couldn't help himself. "What the hell is up with that, Shag? Did you all of a sudden turn pirate on us?"

Another figure appeared in the doorway behind Shag. "His b…b…belief in false gods, will be his failing. The end is nigh brothers!"

"Dude!" Shag turned in the doorway and glared at Red. "Will you please, give your biblical doomsday bullshit a rest already. It ain't demons. It ain't Angels. It ain't even some kind of burning bush or some other fancy fantasy nonsense," he said counting off with his fingers. "It's an alien spaceship, plain and simple."

Shag turned his attention back to me and Travis. "And to answer your question, no I have not turned pirate. But there's nothing says you can't also be fashionable when protecting oneself from alien brain wave control." He flicked the brim of the tricorn and smiled wide.

"T..t..tin foil will not save you from God's wrath and fury."

Red stumbled forward with a little nudge from Shag assisting him out of the yurt's door. "Get out and don't come back unless you have a suggestion to save us from the alien invasion!" Red stormed past us, shouldering his way past me and up the hill.

I tapped Travis on the back of the shoulder and leaned forward to whisper to him. "Are you really sure about this, Trav? Tweedle Dee and Tweedle Dum don't exactly seem sane enough to be giving advice."

"Red, maybe not so much. But Shag…" Travis cocked his head and smiled. "Even if his hobbies are making tin foil hats and creative taxidermy on roadkill, he's the real freaking deal. If there's any truth to any of the conspiracy theories out there, I do not doubt that Shag will know something useful."

Shag snapped his fingers in our direction. "Hey, you two! Don't you know it's rude to be whispering around other folks?"

I nodded to Travis. "Alright, I trust ya, Trav. If you say he's a good source, I'll follow your lead."

"Good." Travis nodded then turned his attention back to Shag. "So what have you got? Bring us up to speed."

Shag let out an honest-to-goodness squee like some happy little feral gnome and then stepped aside, holding the flap open for us to enter. "Come on in and get comfy. It isn't often I get visitors down here, so look over the mess." The heavy flap slapped close behind him as he made his way to an old folding table with a stack of tin foil hats piled at least five deep. "Oh! Would either of you like a drink? I might have a few beers or cokes stashed away in the fridge."

"I'm good," I said, then noticed a low-toned beep that seemed to warble and fade in and out amid the sound of three dot matrix printers set up at the back of the yurt. "What is that?"

Shag flashed one of those excited lunatic smiles at me. "Caught your ear too, didn't it? I don't exactly know, but it started shortly before the mothership came over the ridgeline. It's on a repeating loop that lasts exactly four minutes, and twenty-two point two five five seconds with a point two two nine-second segment of silence before the next cycle begins."

I looked at Travis. "Automated message?"

Shag clapped and let out a triumphant shout. "That's exactly what I thought!"

Travis shrugged. "Possible. But the question is, what's the message."

"Ah," Shag proudly gushed. "I've already started translating it… Or, well…" he paused for a moment staring off into nothing as his eyes ticked back and forth. He licked his lips and turned back to us with a dead serious glare. "At least I'm pretty sure that's what I was doing before Red burst in preaching his hellfire and brimstone."

Shag picked up several large pieces of poster board with patterned grids of symbols placed on several folding tables in the middle of the room. "If I'm right, the key to the transmission is contained within the first three minutes of the signal, but it's hidden on a subsonic track buried within the message below the infrasonic frequency threshold. Similar to when the CIA slides subliminal messages into radio and television commercials. The main difference is whoever created this audio wanted it to be found."

"Why do you think they wanted it to be found?"

"Because the layering is as plain as day. They, whoever *they* are, wouldn't have made it so easy to find if they didn't want it found. It's also possible that there's some sort of data stream attached to that audio. The compression packets are tighter than anything I've ever seen before."

"Huh," I grunted, looking up at Travis. "You weren't shitting me, were you?"

Travis grinned. "Nope."

"Shitting him about what?" Shag looked up at us.

Travis waved off the question. "Nothing, Shag. Inside joke. Do we know anything else?"

"Not really…" Shag shuffled through several stacks of printouts that were still running on old dot matrix printers.

I stepped around Travis and scanned over the poster boards which were marked with different frequencies and instances showing the pattern. "Well, what do you think they want?"

"Oh, that's easy," Shag said matter of factly. "They're here for our women. They mean to breed us into submission and take over the planet for the resources and the breeding stock."

I chuckled. "There it is. That's exactly what I was expecting." I straightened and took a step back from the table.

"Well, maybe they're depraved explorers, and they see us as sheep on the galactic scale."

"Yeah, Trav. Galactic sheep," I prodded. "You know, all warm, soft, fuzzy, and if you catch one with its head stuck through the fence…"

Travis threw his hands up and rubbed his face in frustration. "Okay, I don't need that mental image."

Automatic gunfire erupted from somewhere in the distance.

Knowing how the people in this part of the country were, automatic gunfire at any hour of the day was not a surprise. But knowing that there was an alien ship hovering over the little mountain town, it could only mean two things. Either somebody snapped and they're killing everything in sight or some dumbass is shooting at the ship.

"That can't be good," I said to Travis.

"Nope."

A handheld radio on the end of the table with tinfoil hats suddenly came to life, crackling with static. "Break one nine. Shag, you got your ears on up there?"

The voice was almost as annoying as the sound of grinding brake pads on a second gen Chevy Silverado. It was nasally, high pitched, heavy with a backwoods West Virginia drawl, and I was pretty sure it was female.

"Dammit to hell, devil woman." Shag picked up the radio and keyed the mic. "The hell do you want now, Tammy?"

"Listen, Shag. Josh and his daddy are trying to start world war three or something."

Shag muttered something under his breath, then keyed the mic again. "Yeah. What you want me to do about it?"

"I want you to tell the damned green men to go away before Josh does something really stupid."

An explosion reverberated through the valley.

"Too late," Travis added as he hurried out of the yurt.

I turned and followed Travis. Sprinting up the steps two at a time we hurried across the driveway to the road just in time to see a rocket or RPG streak through the sky and impact on the nose of the alien vessel. Black smoke and flames roiled around the front of the ship, reaching high into the darkening sky.

What sounded like a crew-served heavy machine gun rattled away, flinging tracer rounds skyward from what I guessed was Josh's daddy's place. The rounds ricocheted in all directions off of the ship's hull.

Several rebel yells screeched above the noise of the machine guns then the night sky lit up from another rocket that raced skyward and exploded on the ship's lower hull.

"God dammit," Travis said through gritted teeth. "Those idiots are going to get us all killed."

I turned and laughed at him. "What are you gonna do? You gonna go down there and ask them to stop or something?"

Travis sighed. "Yeah, no. Josh and his daddy start something they see it through to the end."

A blinding flash of green light from the ship bathed the valley in an eerie glow. A green beam shot out from a point on the bottom of the spacecraft and passed over everything within sight of the ship.

"That can't be good," Shag said, puffing as he came up behind us.

"Nope, that can't be good at all," I replied.

Travis punched me in the arm. "You're the Star Trek nerd. What do you think that was?"

"Dude! What the fuck?"

"Well?"

I rubbed at the knot starting to form on my arm. "If I had to guess, I'd say they just scanned the area."

"Scanned for what?"

"How the hell should I know?"

"Aren't you the one that works for some semi-secret alphabet agency?"

"You do what?" Shag shuffled backwards. "You're a fucking spook?"

Travis turned and slapped Shag across the chest. "Hush. He's a good kinda spook," he said then turned back to me.

"Honestly I have no idea. I'm way over my head with this one. They could be doing some sort of terrain mapping… Maybe some sort of life form or weapons scan?"

There was a slight pause in the automatic gunfire. If I were a betting man, I'd say they'd run out of ammo and had to reload considering the rate they'd been flinging rounds at the alien vessel. In literal seconds the all too familiar rat-a-tat-tat began again.

Short-lived as it was…

Three points of green laser light flashed from the lower hull of the ship. Each beam tracked about separately for a moment before coming together, focusing on the source of the gunfire like the Death Star focusing its planet-killing death ray.

A pulsing ray of light discharged from the underside of the craft, bathing the valley in a blinding pinkish glow while the sudden discharge of energy sounded like a dragon's roar that reverberated off the mountainsides. The targeted area ignited, trees flashed to flickering flames, then the whole area burned white hot. Scorched earth and burnt ozone filled the air following the burning winds that rushed over the hillside to meet us.

I turned away, shielding my eyes from the blast. Silhouettes of trees, cars, and Travis who stood a few feet away shone through my closed eyelids. Even from this distance, the heat of the blast felt ten times hotter than an F-15 in full afterburner on a pad run. I could only imagine that the area was glassed as close to what a nuclear blast would cause without the radiation.

A sobbing murmur caught my ears as the howling wind died down. I blinked, trying to clear my vision. "Travis! Shag! Y'all still alive?"

"Here, I think," Travis responded.

Shag coughed, gasping for breath. His voice came out like a shaky hoarse wheeze. "Here, I think."

Shag's radio crackled then a faint voice came through amid the static.

"Shag! Where are you, you crazy sumbitch? You ain't gonna believe this shit." I recognized the voice. It was Tammy, the woman who'd called earlier. "You ain't gonna believe what Mama found when she was taking out the trash."

Travis laughed from somewhere beside me. "Did she find some sanity? Her mamma is as crazy as she is."

I blinked harder, still trying to get my eyes to clear. A white haze like a thick fog seemed to cover everything.

"Can anyone else see?"

"Just give it a sec, Brax," Travis replied. "Mine is getting there; it's just slow about it." I heard the beep as Shag keyed the mic.

"What the hell do you want, devil woman?"

"Trust me, Shag. You're gonna wanna see this," she said through the static. "I'm bringing it to you. Be there in a few minutes."

The mic keyed again. "Come up the back way. Pretty sure Pos's place and the whole west end are gone.

"Copy that. See you in a few."

My eyes were finally starting to clear, like the fog of war on a battlefield dissipating. The area downhill to the west of us was nothing but charred devastation. It looked like something out of a war movie. Nothing within a quarter mile of the strike point was left standing. Dozens of structures had been decimated to burning piles of slag as fires raced up the hillside in several places.

Motion caught my attention. A small craft separated from the larger craft and cruised up river, toward Towbar's gaming house and Ellis's Restaurant, the heart of Justice. Bracing myself against my knees I pushed myself upright and attempted to balance while my eyes finished adjusting. "That can't be good."

Shag tossed each of us a beer as he went over the translations again when Tammy stepped into the yurt, laughed, and let out a excited squeal. "Oh, damn, Travis. I didn't know you were up here. I heard tell that Janice ran off with that banker from up North. How you just going to let her go and do that?"

"Cause it's the least of my worries right now. Have you not noticed the alien ship floating over the Gravel Pit?"

Tammy shrugged. "Eh. I figured they wouldn't bother us too much if we didn't mess with them. And I figure if they were just here for a little light probing, that might not be so bad either."

All three of us turned and looked at her.

Travis chuckled. "You know, Tammy. Sometimes I wonder if you're crazier than Shag.

"We sort of have a situation here," I reminded them, taking control of the conversation. "What did you find?"

"I'll tell you what. It wasn't easy to get here. Those aliens look like something right out of one of those alien movies. Body armor, ray guns, the works. They're going door to door searching for something. We had to hide behind the log trucks parked over by Miranda's mommy's house.

They started with the hotel, gas station, Ellis's, and the Justonian diner. I don't think they've started going through trailers yet. We ducked out as soon as they weren't looking and cut up the little walking trail."

Shag let out a frustrated grunt and started toward Tammy. "So help me, woman…"

"So help you what, you crazy old coot?"

Travis stepped between the two of them, blocking Shag's advance. "Can we stop the bickering and get on with it already? What did you find, Tammy?"

She let out a cackling laugh, put her hands behind her back, and started rocking like an innocent schoolgirl. "I might know what they're after."

"Come on, now," I shouted. "If you're just going to keep leading us on, go on ahead and leave. We have things to figure out before anyone else gets hurt."

An angry glare twisted Tammy's face. She crossed her arms and tapped her foot for a moment before she turned her glare on Travis then looked back over her shoulder toward the entrance of the yurt. "Hey, Hairy. Come on in. It's safe."

The door flaps swung to the side and a massive mound of fur and flesh stepped through the opening. He was all of eight feet tall if not more, covered head to toe in thick brown fur, and easily recognized as what most would call a Sasquatch or Bigfoot, but dressed in some sort of high-tech jumpsuit.

Tammy crossed her arms and bowed up at us. "Mommy found him out back when she took the trash out. It didn't take me long to coax him inside. No man or beast can resist a good scratch and a stroke."

I shook my head, unsure of what I just heard her say. "Do what now?" I blurted out without thinking.

"Oh, don't go gettin' your hopes up, buddy." She flashed a wide, gap-toothed smile at me and waggled her eyebrows. I wiped my hand down my face in disbelief.

"We…are…friends," Shag began as he stepped closer to the hairy alien, sounding like an idiot talking to a native in an old-school western.

I slapped Shag across the back of the head. "Will you stop?"

"Hey! What was that for?"

"He's a space-faring alien, not an idiot. Where do you suppose he comes from? Nebraska?"

Travis shrugged, then leaned back on the table. "No telling. I've heard them egghead scientists have found hundreds of possible worlds out there that could sustain life."

"Well, all I know for sure is there ain't nothing *little* or green about this man," Tammy added as she snuggled up against the creature's side and ran her fingers across its chest.

Travis shook his head and laughed again before mumbling something and rubbing at his temples. "I'm sure that whatever you're talking about was inappropriate, even on a galactic scale. But don't you think molesting alien visitors would give them the wrong impression of us as a species?"

"Well, for your information Mister Wizard, he didn't complain one little bit while I…"

"Okay! Let's slow up a bit," I shouted, hoping that the visuals coming to mind were wrong, but I suspected every bit of rule 34 was in effect when it came to Tammy. "I think that's about enough for the moment. How about we get back to the problem at hand?"

"Oh, there's no problem at all from where I'm standing, Shug." She gazed up into the alien's eyes and squeezed him even harder. An odd, uncomfortable look suddenly washed over him, like the look of guilt and disgust a new troop shows the morning after spending a night in Bangkok, Thailand.

The creature peeled Tammy away from him then retrieved a small device about the size of a smartphone from a pocket and held it out. He pointed to his mouth and motioned like he wanted us to continue talking.

Tammy gasped at the creature's rejection. "Well, I never."

"Probably won't ever again according to the look on his face," Travis said, fighting back a laugh.

The creature motioned more excitedly. I stepped closer and looked at the object in the alien's massive palm. "What do you suppose that is?"

"Maybe it's one of those hidden camera prank things like you see on TV," Shag added. He flinched at the sideways glance I gave him. Travis took a step forward, joining me in examining the object. It was a small, black, and squarish with all edges rounded, almost giving it the look of a flattened egg. The creature touched the edge gently with a large bulbous fingertip and it emitted a cheerful beep. It opened its mouth and uttered a series of grunted growling barks.

"Hello," the device said in a robotic English that immediately brought Stephen Hawking to mind. *"My name is Larrs'Neytee. I am a Rohʙandī."* The last word rolled off the creature's tongue with a long sighing gasp.

Shag let out a shrill cry and collapsed to the floor, curling into the fetal position beneath the table.

"Freaking Nonner," Travis said over his shoulder then looked up at the large creature. "Sorry about that. Numbnuts down there has issues." Travis whistled and made the twirling motion of crazy along the side of his head.

"I, see."

I cleared my throat and broke into the conversation. "So… I'm no rocket scientist or anything, but I'm guessing those guys out there torching the place are hunting for you?"

The creature let out a cooing chortle and nodded. *"Indeed, they are,"* the device translated. *"They are known as the V'ril. They are ravenous and bloodthirsty. Their race is renowned throughout the galaxy for their vicious, indiscriminate methods, and as such are hired by most other races to fight their conflicts for them."*

"Nothing against you, man," Travis said, taking a step back. "But what kinda trouble have you brought down on us? I'm all about helping folks, but that generosity does have a limit."

"I am a political refugee," Larrs said. *"The Salorians and my people have been in conflict for several generations. Recently the V'ril were enlisted to overthrow my home world. Being one of the most outspoken dissidents to survive the invasion, they see my existence and message as a threat to their invasion. Upon entering this system, my ship was irreparably damaged. I landed in the valley just beyond the ridgeline to the southwest across the river."*

"Probably Lost Branch if I had to guess," Travis interjected to me as a side note.

"So, what's to keep us from turning you over to the… V'ril?"

Larrs flinched as the device translated my words back to him. He immediately took a step back in retreat. I put my hands up defensively, palms open. "I didn't say we *were* going to turn you over, I just asked what *keeps* us from turning you over?"

"Because now that they know that your people are here, and pose little threat, they will come back to enslave your race and conquer your planet for the available resources."

I turned to Travis. "Sounds like a pretty damn good reason to me. What do you think?"

"See, what did I tell you?" Shag shouted.

Travis mule kicked the table behind him. "Will you shut the hell up."

I turned back to the RohBandī. "So what happens if we help you?"

"If we succeed, freedom." He paused for a moment in thought. *"The V'ril have no way of alerting their people without connecting to the galactic network. We are light years beyond any consortium relay arrays. They would have to jump to a system with a relay in order to upload any data or messages."*

"And what happens if we fail," Travis asked.

"Pain…suffering, and death." Larrs drifted off in thought and shuddered. His eyes looked hollow and sad like a man who had seen too much suffering. *"So much death…"*

I turned and faced our alien visitor. "How many V'ril are aboard that ship?" The big guy waited patiently as the device translated for him and he began to speak back to it.

"Up to ten warriors at their maximum, with possibly three of them deployed to the ground with the drop shuttle."

I turned back to Travis. "What sort of armament do we have available?"

Travis shook his head. "I don't have anything but the M4 and a shotgun in the truck. If it hadn't all gotten blown up I'd say let's go down to Pos's and see what he's got, but that sorta got fragged quick. What all you got stashed away, Shag?"

Shag nervously tapped out of rhythm on the table. "Come on, Shag," Travis said. "Braxton is an old buddy of mine, and I trust him with my life. He's good people. I can vouch for him."

Shag hemmed and hawed for a moment before he looked back up at us. "If you say so Travis. I trust you, and I'll take your word on it."

"So what do we have?"

"A few boxes of flash bangs, several dozen home-brewed frag bombs, a few M4s, several shotguns, 9mm pistols, and plenty of ammo for each. Nothing really fancy but it'll get the job done in most cases."

"It'll be hours before we see the National Guard or any sort of reinforcements." I drew my .45 from its shoulder rig and pulled the magazine to double-check my rounds then slammed it back in the hole. "I guess that's settled then. We go on the attack and stop them here and now."

"Whoa," Travis said with a nervous laugh. "Hold your horses, Lone Ranger. What's this *we* shit? You got a mouse in your pocket or something?"

"You'd really let me take on an alien invasion by myself?"

"You got Shag, the big guy, and Tammy to work with."

I chuckled and wiped a hand down my face. "A crackhead, a crackpot, and Sasquatch walks into a bar…"

"Hey," Shag and Tammy both groused.

"See!" Travis punched me in the shoulder again. "It might not be the A-team, but it might be enough to get something done."

"Yeah… How about hell no, Trav. If we do this, I need you by my side."

"Then what's in it for me?"

I thought for a second, scratching at the scruff on my face. "Being the hero and saving the planet ain't enough?"

Travis tucked his hands in his pockets and shrugged. "Meh."

"Okay, then how about a chance to make a shitload of extra beer money?"

"Oh, hey. Now you're talking my language. But how you gonna guarantee that, mister fancy pants?"

I looked over at Shag. "You got a bible or anything like it in here?"

Shag drifted off in thought for a moment before his eyes lit up with excitement. "I might have the perfect thing." He scuttled away to a dark corner of the yurt and rummaged around in a pile of boxes, returning moments later with a small picture frame.

"How about this? Do you think it would work?" I was kind of surprised at the document he held out in front of me. It was a replica copy of the Constitution of the United States of America.

"All enemies foreign and domestic," Shag said with a wide, beaming smile.

"That'll do pretty well," I said, then took the document and turned back to Travis. "Hold up your right hand and place your left on the Constitution."

"What the hell you doing?"

"Swearing you in."

"How the hell you going to swear me in?"

"Remember that government agency I work for? Technically I'm a federal Marshal because we fall under their jurisdiction. Therefore I have the power to swear in deputies to aid me in my mission, which does come with pay and benefits."

Shag let out a worried squeal. Tammy turned on her heel, heading for the door. "Nope, ain't gonna have nothing to do with no government spooks," she said before disappearing out the door.

Travis tilted his head with a curious look. "Are you sure about this Braxton? It ain't like I really have anything left to live for. I could be that wild card that causes the mission to fail."

"Trust you with my life, brother. Then and now."

Travis placed his hand on the Constitution. "Alright, then. Let's do this. Come on, Shag. Get over here." Reluctantly the conspiracy theorist shuffled his way around the table and put a shaky hand on the Constitution.

"Alright, y'all. Repeat after me..."

Larrs might have looked like an eight-foot-tall hairy monster, but the more we chatted as we geared up, the more he sounded like my kinda people. Down to earth, level-headed, and enjoyed long rides on his people's equivalent to a motorcycle, even if it was a hoverbike. He'd just been caught up in some sketchy political shit of galactic proportions and ended up on the wrong people's shit list.

While we prepped for the op the small frigate, as Larrs had identified it, had moved upriver towards the dam. The drop shuttle on the other hand wasn't hard to find. It lit up the area around Towbars and the motel like a freaking Christmas tree with searchlights and drones running search patterns, scouring the area around it for our new fuzzy friend.

Larrs warned us that the search lasers coming from the drones were searching for his biological signs, which would be easy to pick out from all the human life signs in the area. The trick was that it was a line-of-sight system. As long as the beams couldn't touch him, they couldn't pick him up. Most metals blocked the scans, but then they relied on thermals to search within structures.

I didn't think that was such a bad plan. We could easily avoid those if we timed their movements. It wasn't any different than any good video game level, really.

The trick was going to be dealing with any of the V'ril warriors on the ground if we ran into them.

The way that Larrs described them, they sounded a lot like the Klingons from Star Trek, only they were ten times nastier. Raised from birth as warriors, they lived it every waking moment of their lives. He said the one thing that set them apart from the other warrior races in the galaxies, was that they thrived on keeping their prey alive. To let prey expire too swiftly was heretical. A talley was kept to record the duration a particular prey was kept in captivity and the number of procedures they'd managed to survive. The V'ril did this for two reasons. Experience of skill and technique, but mostly for the pure enjoyment of inflicting pain and suffering.

The V'ril were essentially evil incarnate on a galactic scale, and we had to stop them at all costs. We couldn't let the word of Earth and mankind reach the rest of their people.

Once we were ready, we cut down the back side of the hill and down the holler till it met with the old service road heading towards the dam before dropping down among the trailers behind Ellis's restaurant. Larrs ran point, even though he stuck out like a big hairy sore thumb.

From our position we could see several of the drones slowly hovering along Dolly Atkins Street just ahead of us, and along Old Route 52 on the other side of Ellis's Restaurant.

Larrs started forward then suddenly stopped, backpedaling into the shadows alongside the trailer. For a big dude, he moved super fast and slammed into me before I could come to a complete stop with Travis stumbling into me.

Larrs held up his hand, then turned and motioned for us to be quiet before pointing at something hiding in the shadows between Ellis's and The Justonian, the *other* diner in town.

It couldn't have been more than a few minutes that we remained motionless, but it felt like an eternity while I stared into the darkness, expecting to see some horrific xenomorph ready to pounce.

Larrs tapped at the device then quietly spoke into it. *"The warrior is moving away."*

"Moving away?" Travis stepped ahead, standing next to Larrs' elbow. "I didn't see anything at all besides shadows."

"That's because my people's eyes are better adapted to seeing in the dark."

Before I could ask him anything about the V'ril he sprinted ahead, quickly putting his back against the back of Ellis's restaurant.

"Let's go," I whispered over my shoulder before following Larrs across the street, Travis and Shag close on my heels. While Larrs made his way to the left side of the building, I hustled to the opposite corner and slowly peeked around the edge.

Further down the highway, I could see another drone scanning the area, heading our way from the west. I froze when I spotted the shuttle taking up several parking spots between other vehicles across the street at the motel. It was like something out of a movie. An eerie purple under light reflected off the pavement and the ship's dark, mirror-like surface.

"I'll be damned…"

A forceful release of breath and a sickly crack drew me out of my stupor. I turned to find Larrs restraining an individual by the neck, its head lolled limply to the side as it kicked and writhed.

The individual was short, even shorter than I was, but broad-shouldered and barrel-chested like one of the heaviest football linemen alive, and sported some of the most impressive-looking combat armor I'd ever seen.

That didn't necessarily mean it worked well, but it looked pretty badass. And being that it was made out of *space-age* material, there had to be other hidden benefits to it as well.

A popping hum of electrical discharge left the heavy stink of burning ozone in the air. Larrs let out a bestial roar. Dropping the alien soldier he stepped back from the corner of the building and cradled his right arm. Smoke rolled from a bloody and charred wound on the back of his right shoulder.

Another V'ril warrior sprinted around the corner and fired in our direction. A crackling ball of light sored by, striking the barrel of Travis's M4. The end of the carbine melted away like hot dripping wax.

Travis threw the ruined rifle at the alien then leveled the barrel of his daddy's old Remington slug gun at the creature's head and fired. The 12 gauge slug struck the creature's forehead with such force that its head snapped backward and slumped to the side in an oddly incorrect way. The alien dropped to its knees, collapsing sideways.

Shag slapped me across the chest and laughed. "Jesus Christ on a cracker, Travis. Ha ha! Did you see that, spook boy? That's how it's done!"

Larrs let out a moaning growl. *"Good riddance,"* the device translated. I knelt down next to the creature's body and rolled its head around where I could inspect the damage from the slug's impact. The body armor, including the helmet and face mask, looked like it was made with some sort of fancy carbon fiber material. The only difference was that there was barely a blemish on the facemask where the round struck. No cracks or dents whatsoever, only a broken neck from the impact of the round.

I looked up at Larrs. "Do these guys have notoriously weak necks or something?" He replied with several grunts.

"Yes, when not fully matured. It is the one flaw of their genetic design."

I shifted and turned the creature's head so Travis could see. Face shape was elongated similar to the snout of a bear or a dog, but with a large chin protrusion. "Headshots are the way to go."

Travis tipped his head side to side, examining the mask. "I'll be damned. And here we thought these guys would be a problem."

Larrs cooed and grunted. *"Do not let these young scouts put your fears at ease. The veteran warriors remaining on the ship will be much more skilled and difficult to dispatch."*

"Gotcha," Travis said. "The privates got stuck doing the shit work while the old guys waited to see what would happen."

"Sounds normal to me," I said. Letting the creature drop to the ground I turned back to Larrs. "Do you think there are any more of them left in the drop shuttle?"

This time his odd noises almost sounded melodic, like a song from some foreign opera. *"Most likely, yes, unless they are short manned. V'ril scouts normally operate in teams of three."*

Larrs reached down and fiddled with something on the back of the helmet that released it and the facemask. He pulled them away from the dead alien's face and tossed them to the side.

"Holy fucking shit, Batman. He looks like a Sleestak on crack."

The Vril's neck was made up of heavily corded muscles that continued into a broad jawline. The damn thing honestly looked like the bastard love child of a rhino and wild boar, with a rough horn on the end of its nose, and several tusk-like protrusions along its chin, all covered with a greenish sharklike skin that was damn near a perfect match to the green of one of those quiet river fishing holes. I looked back to Travis and smiled wide.

"What bat shit crazy idea is forming behind your ugly face, Brax?"

"Larrs, can you still fly that drop shuttle?"

He looked down at his arm, flexed it, rolled his shoulder then nodded, and growled.

"We're about to steal ourselves a spaceship."

"You want to fly in that thing?"

"Yeah, Shag," Travis answered for me. "He wants to fly in that thing."

"Does the shuttle have any external defenses we should know about?"

The hairy alien roared and grunted again. "No, unless it is a modified attack shuttle. That one does not appear to be so."

"Then let's go snag ourselves a new ride."

Larrs retrieved the weapon from the V'ril warrior and several of what I guessed were power packs before we continued around the building. We sprinted across the main road to the parking lot of the old motel and ducked behind several dump trucks parked in the parking lot. The big guy slowed as he approached the nose of the vessel, cautiously making his way to the open hatch on the side.

Before we could reach him, Larrs fired blindly into the opening and then sprinted inside the craft.

With my .45 drawn and aimed I crossed to the opposite side, keeping my sights steady in case Larrs wasn't as quick as he seemed.

I nearly pulled the trigger at the first sign of motion within the ship. Larrs had just gotten straight up stupid lucky. He dropped another of the V'ril soldiers onto the decking of the corridor and let out a barking growl as he stepped to the opening. *The ship is clear. Once we return to the frigate it will be all or nothing. There will be no return if we do not win. Move swiftly, strike true, and we may yet succeed.*

"May?" Shag said through panting breaths as he stumbled up alongside of us.

Larrs nodded. *"Yes."*

"I don't know about all that *may* return bullshit, y'all." Shag started backing away. "I think I'm just gonna leave the hero shit to you two. I'll go get on the horn and coordinate relief efforts with the National Guard." He hurried away back across the road and out of sight behind the restaurant.

"Fucking Nonner!" I shouted after Shag, holstered my sidearm, and smacked Travis across the chest. "You ready for this?"

"About as ready as I am to go get a vasectomy."

"That ready, huh?" I laughed and started to step into the ship. "Guess that's about as good as we're gonna get, big guy," I said, looking up at Larrs. "Let's get this show on the road before we change our minds."

Larrs let out a barking chortle. *"Agreed. The sooner this is over, the sooner I may return to my people."* The large alien turned and led us to the cockpit. It was just like something out of Star Wars. A vast array of controls, indicators, and displays covered every possible surface of the cockpit. Not really any different than the cockpit of the F-15 Strike Eagles I'd worked, only there were four independent stations spaced well enough apart to accommodate the wide-shouldered aliens.

Larrs slung the energy rifle across his shoulder and slid into the seat of the forward right station. I dropped into the seat to his left and buckled in, the harness wasn't much different than any of the five-point racing harnesses I'd ever seen in the past. Travis plopped into one of the rear stations and examined the console.

"Wow, that's a crazy layout."

Larrs turned in his seat to look at Travis and let out several barking trills. *"If you would, please do not touch any of the controls. Considering you are sitting at the engineering station, I wouldn't want you to accidentally destabilize the power matrix."*

"Yeah…," I said with a nervous laugh. "Let's not do what he said. Be a good little boy and look with your eyes, not your fingers. What do you say, Trav?"

"Sounds like a plan to me…" Travis settled in and secured his harness. Larrs cycled several controls and pushed what looked like throttles forward on the control console. The sound of the craft changed, from a low-frequency hum to a pulsating throb that resonated throughout the frame of the craft and we lifted off with a sickening lurch.

Larrs let out a chortled cooing. *"Once we are inside, if we are allowed to dock, our only chance is to catch them off guard. Strike fast and strike hard before they have an opportunity to respond."*

I looked back at Travis and he nodded in understanding. "That we can do, big guy," I responded to Larrs. "What can we expect once we're inside?"

The big guy shrugged one of those non-committal shrugs. *"The V'ril are minimalists in a sense. If it doesn't aid in their combat effectiveness, it is an excess. To the V'ril, anything in excess is sacrilegious to them and isn't to be tolerated. Expect dark corridors, a hot and humid atmosphere, and little space to move."*

"So, the worst-case scenario of alien flicks possible is what you're saying," Travis asked, interrupting.

Larrs turned, nodding to Travis before he continued. *"From the launch bay at the rear of the ship, two corridors will branch out and run the length of the vessel, meeting again in the forward section. There will be an upper deck with the command station, officer's quarters, and primary offensive systems. There is also a lower deck composed of cargo bays, holding cells, and rudimentary ship systems that will most likely be empty, but we will still need to clear the area to be sure."*

"Okay. Good to know," Travis said.

I leaned forward as best as I could in the harness and looked at Larrs. "What should we expect weapon-wise? Will they come at us with those ray guns or are we going old-school toe to toe back alley brawling?"

"Several of the officers may have sidearms, but otherwise expect close-quarters fighting with blades from any of the V'ril still aboard. They will fight with a ferocity you have never seen. Beyond any weapons, they still have claws and teeth that will tear flesh with a little effort."

The thought of going toe to toe with a crew of aliens wasn't what I had in mind when I was coming to help my buddy get over the fact that his wife left him for some uppity Yankee banker, but there's no guarantees what life is ever going to throw at any of us at any given time. All we can do is take the situation at hand, run with it, and do the best that we can with what the universe gives us.

It couldn't have been more than five minutes before we were approaching the rear of the V'ril vessel. A small hatch at the back of the ship opened as we approached, allowing us entry. Larrs tapped at the console controls, expertly maneuvering the small craft into the landing bay of the alien frigate alongside other drop shuttles in the bay.

"I'd rather this be a sawed-off," Travis said, gently patting his daddy's shotgun, "but I guess it is what it is."

"It might be better if me and Travis go one way to clear the corridors. We work well together and understand most of each other's hand signals."

Larrs let out a low growl and nodded. *"I am capable of holding my own in most cases. You have a sound strategy."*

"Game on," Travis said, loading fresh rounds into the shotgun.

We sat down in the bay with a light thud, and the engines of the drop shuttle powered down.

"Be on your guard. They will give no quarter. The V'ril have even been known to add unworthy prey to their larders."

"Fuck that noise," Travis blurted out.

"Agreed," I replied, reaching back for a fist bump from Trav.

Larrs stood and quickly looked about the bay through the windscreen, then hurried aft to the hatch. We slipped out of our harnesses and followed behind, weapons drawn.

The bay was as large as a truck garage with several other shuttles parked about. We followed Larrs to a blast door style hatch, sliding to the left side of the doorway while he accessed a control panel on the right. Getting our attention, he made sure to show us what button to hit on the panel before he depressed it. The hatch slid open with a mechanical whir of drive motors.

He turned and let out a low throat rumble. *"Remember, move swiftly, no quarter, and we may yet survive this night."*

The big guy moved as fast as a flash of lightning, sprinting out the door and down the right side of the corridor.

"Lock and load," Travis said, then slipped through the hatch to the left, his shotgun held at the ready.

I followed close behind with my .45 drawn, covering Travis as he advanced into the dark corridor.

It really was like something out of the Alien movies. Dark, barely backlit with a tropical fog that hung heavy in the air. I was already sweating like a stuck pig by the time we'd made it around the first corner. I couldn't imagine how miserable Larrs had to be with his heavy covering of fur.

Travis approached the first hatch on the left of the corridor. He swung wide, stepping to the right of the hatch while I positioned myself on the left, then he pressed the controls to open the doorway.

The door slid open, revealing a small equipment room that I didn't even want to try to understand. I continued down the corridor past Travis and adjusted my aim as I advanced to the next bulkhead hatch. Again we repeated the sequence, making our way through the belly of the ship.

We'd made it through several bulkheads heading forward before coming to a larger set of doors on either side of the corridor. The layout made me think of an equipment passage like I'd seen on a few older naval vessels that had been turned into floating museums.

I nudged Travis and chin nodded at the doors to the right. "Engineering space?"

"Could be the chow hall for all I know," he whispered. "The only thing I know for sure is I want off this boat as quick as we can get this over with. Between the heat and the stink of the place, it's all I can do to not barf."

He wasn't lying. It was worse than the stink of a rancid swamp in the middle of summer and twice as hot. Sweat poured from my pores, soaking through my clothes. It was easily worse than any Louisiana summer I'd endured.

I hurried to the control console and smacked the button. "Then let's get er' done." The door slid open with a grinding, labored moan. The three V'ril in the compartment looked up from their stations with surprise as we rushed in.

"Hey there sweet thang, pucker up for daddy," I shouted as I fired two rounds center mass on the first alien to my right.

"Say hello to my boomstick!" Travis fired several slugs into the V'ril to the left of the door as quickly as the action could cycle.

The third alien fumbled with something on its belt, drawing what looked like some sort of blaster pistol right out of Star Trek. The creature cleared the holster, aimed, and fired in our direction.

Travis let out a blood-curdling scream, dropped his gun, and collapsed to the deck. The heat generated by the beam was insane. It was as intense as any blast furnace I'd ever been around. Heat ripples like you'd see on a blacktop highway in the desert pulsated from the device. My sight blurred and stomach lurched as my knees buckled and I dropped to the floor. The stink of burning hair and scorched ozone invaded my nostrils.

"Travis!"

Three rapid-fire shots from a shotgun rang out in the small space.

"Dammit, Brax! Why couldn't we have just gone for beer and let well enough alone?"

My head throbbed and the world spun like I'd dunked my head in the punch bowl at a squadron party and gulped till it was empty.

"Because we're the good guys."

Travis laughed from somewhere to my left. "That's a big ballsack of bullshit, man. There ain't much good about either of us."

Even though my eyes were starting to clear, they burned something fierce. "Can you see?" Travis laughed. "I can't see shit. What the hell do you think he hit us with?"

I pressed my palms into my eyes and rubbed gently. Colorful swirls exploded in the darkness before my eyesight began to really clear. "If it was sonic, we'd both be deaf and bleeding from the ears. Probably some sort of radiation gun would be my guess."

"Great… So the lizard reject from the black lagoon tried to microwave us like chicken nuggets?"

Finally spotting Travis laying on the floor nearby I nodded in his direction and forced myself up onto one knee. "Yeah, I guess so."

"Let's not do that again."

"Agreed."

"You okay, Brax?"

I pushed myself upright and paused for a moment. "Besides slightly crispy, yeah, I think so. Nothing feels broken or missing. What about you, Travis?"

His chuckle quickly turned into a raspy wet cough. Cautiously I made my way over to his side, barely holding my balance.

"Travis?"

"Yeah, Brax?"

"That really doesn't sound good."

I could tell his shoulders moved up and down in a shrugging motion. "Meh, it's probably nothing. I still can't see a damn thing. I'm sure it ain't nothing a bottle of top shelf whiskey can't fix."

"Uh, hu…" Blinking, I wiped my eyes on my sleeves, trying to clear the haze that still clung there. It took several more moments, but they finally stopped watering enough that I was able to start making out details in the dark compartment. Travis's shirt and face looked like he'd single handedly took on a pissed off flamethrower. The upper half of his body was scorched. Crispy bits of flesh that had cracked and peeled itself back from the extreme exposure glistened from oozing open wounds.

"Well? What's the verdict, doc?"

"Um…"

"Come on, man. I already know it ain't good just by that response."

"Naw, man. It ain't nothing. You'll be up and running in no time. You've seen better days, but.."

"But nothing, Brax. Don't bullshit me. I can't feel anything in my upper body and I can't see a thing. Come on, man. How bad is it, really?"

That's when I noticed his eyes. Two dark voids stared back at me from his mangled visage.

I dryly swallowed, attempting to catch my breath. He didn't look real. More like some animatronic thing from a bad horror flick. I was surprised he could still form words as good as he could considering the amount of meat missing from his lips and cheeks. Blood stained teeth peeked through the holes in his face like some sort of undead thing from a zombie flick.

"I ain't no medic, man."

"For fuck's sake, Braxton. We've seen some shit in our time. Now grow some god damned balls and spit it out already."

"It don't look good, man. You're missing a whole lot of meat and…"

"And?"

"And your eyes are completely gone."

Travis shrugged once more and let out a long sigh. "Meh. Ain't nobody going to miss me anyhow."

He'd be lucky to survive the night, let alone land another hot psycho hose beast like Janice.

In the old self aid buddy care courses they taught us that attitude was everything. Keep their spirits up, keep that hope alive and even the most seriously fucked up grunt could pull through and live another day.

"Bullshit, Travis. I know for a fact you could score with that Kelly chick down in the bottom you talked about. She'd sleep with a dead man for a twinkie."

"No shit, Brax. I know I'm done. I can feel it. And aside from the alimony Janice might try to take me for, there ain't no one going to care one way or the other if I live or die."

"Hell, I'd miss your sorry hide, dumbass. You ever think about that? Doubly so now that you smell like crispy bacon."

That got a chuckle out of Travis.

"Come on man. We got to get you out of here." I knelt down and worked my hands under him to get a grip, then froze. What was left of the shirt was soaked completely through with blood. And greasy gore oozed through the ragged remains of his shirt.

"Braxton, dude. Stop already. I'm not going anywhere anytime soon. Did you forget that we're on an alien ship? Can you fly that shuttle we came here on?"

He was right. Without Larrs to fly the shuttle, there was no way I could get him back to the ground. The only chance Travis had was for us to finish this fight and take the ship.

"Mark it on the fucking calendar," I said sarcastically. "The dumb ass jarhead actually got something right for a change."

Travis let out a tired laugh. "Glad I got to be right at something for once."

I picked up his shotgun and quickly checked it for damage. Other than a little scorching on the wood it looked perfectly serviceable. I racked the action and checked the ammunition. Four rounds that still looked decent. I was glad the plastic shells hadn't melted in the tube or the gun would have been worthless.

"Where's the rest of your ammo, Trav?"

He wheezed then coughed out several bloody chunks that dribbled down his chin, onto his chest. "My right cargo pocket," he managed between straining breaths. "Should be a dozen or so rounds left."

I hurried, gathering the shells and tucking them into the breast pockets of my kutte after fully loading the shotgun.

I could hear commotion from somewhere else on the ship. The discharge of energy weapons and a bestial roar like nothing else I'd ever heard reverberated through the ship's bulkheads.

"Kick some alien ass for me, Brax." Weakly he slapped me across the arm.

"You're damn right I'm gonna. Stay put. I'll be back as soon as this is over and we'll get you off this ship."

Travis coughed through another raspy wet laugh. "Not like I've got a whole lot of choice, bud. Don't worry about me. Just finish the job so we can go get those beers."

Against the protest of my aching muscles, I pushed myself upright and rushed through the hatch we'd come through, activating the next hatch leading forward in the corridor.

Larrs had one of the V'ril Warriors pinned against the wall by the throat. His fingertips dug deep into the alien's flesh, threatening to puncture through the skin under the strain. Smoke roiled from what remained of Larrs's now patchy fur.

The massive walking carpet let out another bloodcurdling roar and ripped the alien's right arm clean from the socket. Tossing the V'ril against the opposite wall, Larrs lunged at the warrior and proceeded to beat it with its own dismembered appendage.

Another V'ril appeared from around the corner at the end of the corridor, aimed, and fired his ray gun at the Rohʙandī.

I stepped to the left side of the corridor out of his path of fire and brought the shotgun to my shoulder. "Not today, scale face!"

The blast from the shotgun resonated in the tight space, rattling my insides, but the .79 caliber slug slammed home, caving in the right side of the greenskin's face.

Larrs dropped to one knee and leaned against the side of the corridor. He let out several whimpering barks, then pulled himself together, forcing himself back to his feet. In two steps, he brought his size 20 boot down on the Vril's face, caving in what the slug hadn't.

"Remind me to never piss you off, big guy."

He mumbled something that was only echoed with static from the translation device he'd hung on his belt.

"That isn't good, but it isn't going to stop us from doing what we need to do." I nodded down the corridor and brought the shotgun back to ready hoping he understood the gesture. "You lead, I'll follow."

Larrs nodded, picked up the Vril's blaster pistol, and stalked forward toward the corner of the corridor.

The forward equipment compartment looked like it had already been cleared. Two bodies littered the floor, and sparks flew from several of the damaged consoles. Larrs was a one man wrecking crew. If the one V'ril warriors hadn't gotten a shot in when he did, I had no doubt Larrs would have already been on the upper deck wreaking havoc.

The Rohʙandī didn't waste any time. He leaped onto the hatchway steps leading to the next deck and took three at a time like it was nothing.

Reaching the next level, he disappeared from sight before I was even halfway up the ladder.

Something rock solid slammed into the side of my head as soon as I popped out of the hatchway, sending me sprawling forward across the deck.

The world spun as my head swam. For a split second I could have swore I saw Looney Toons stars circling my head like a Saturday morning cartoon. Whatever just hit me knocked the literal shit out of me, and felt worse than any bar fight I'd ever been in.

Something nearby let out a crocodile-like growl. Forcing myself back to my feet, I shook my head, clearing the cobwebs.

The V'ril was on me and toe to toe in a split second before I could bring the shotgun up. It swatted the barrel aside with its left and delivered another powerful punch to my chest.

I stumbled back, gasping.

The hit knocked the wind clean out of me. I gasped, struggling to get my breath back. If the hit hadn't cracked a few ribs, it was damn close. Cold pain radiated out from the impact point.

The V'ril let out something that sounded like a guttural barking laugh, then advanced again.

"I don't care if fifteen minutes can save me money. Fuck you and your insurance, buddy!"

It charged forward and I rotated the gun around, butt checking his ugly face square between the eyes. The V'ril took a step back, grasping its face in pain.

"Don't feel so good, does it, fuck face?"

The warrior crouched like a linebacker and flexed its massive muscles before letting out an ear-splitting shout. It rushed forward, nose down like the rhino-pig it looked like.

Sidestepping at the last minute I slammed the butt of the gun into the side of its head as it shoulder-checked me, sending me flying into the corridor wall.

The V'ril teetered, striking the opposite wall before it turned, shook its head, and galloped back toward me.

I raised the shotgun enough to fire it from the hip, pulling the trigger as fast as the action would cycle. Three slugs tore into the creature's torso. Black ichor and gore exploded from the creature's back.

Pain radiated across my shoulder and chest from the force of the shots. Maybe there were a few cracked ribs in there after all.

"Fuck, that hurt!"

I rolled my shoulders and pain shot through me. I staggered back and leaned against the corridor wall, still gasping for breath. "Check that. Pretty sure they're broken."

Larrs roared from somewhere deeper on this deck.

"Not sure if that was good or bad," I mumbled to myself as I dug fresh shells from my pocket. I forced a breath past the pain and stood upright, reloading the shotgun.

"This shit ain't gonna finish itself." I hurried in the direction of Larrs's roar, stepping over several more dead and dismembered V'ril.

"Mental note, never piss off a RohBandī." The sound of several energy blasts resounded from ahead. The guttural bellow of another V'ril overshadowed the roar from the RohBandī fugitive. It seriously sounded like Godzilla and King Kong were having one hell of a stand off ahead.

"That really doesn't sound good." Racing forward, I dodged broken equipment and several more bodies littering the corridor that lead to another large bulkhead hatch.

The RohBandī roared from the other side of the hatchway, but this time it sounded different. It wasn't a roar of anger. It sounded more like a wounded moose trying to escape the maw of a grizzly bear than anything else.

I tapped at the controls, and stepped through, shotgun at the ready before the door had fully opened to reveal what I guessed was the ship's bridge. Several stations surrounded what looked like Captain Kirk's chair in the center of the compartment.

Larrs lay back on the deck plating of the alien bridge, propped up on one elbow. A massive V'ril warrior loomed over him firing one of the alien energy pistols.

Smoke spewed forth from his jumpsuit as it smoldered and his flesh burned. Acrid smoke mingled with the stink of burnt ozone, filling the compartment with a bitter choking haze.

"Hey FUCK FACE!"

The V'ril quickly turned his attention to me and smiled. Rows of needle sharp teeth gleamed back at me from its massive maw. It was at least twice the size of any of the other V'ril warriors aboard. Large plates of a bronze like material covered its combat armor.

I had no doubts that this guy was the V'ril commander. None of the others wore anything similar. It snarled then lunged forward, bellowing out a saurian howl.

"Your mom screamed my name louder than that last night!"

Bracing myself, I hip fired the shotgun as fast as the action could cycle. The first three rounds struck the commander across the right side of his chest piece, denting the bronze-like plating.

Pain coursed across my chest and shoulder, drawing my aim to the right. The remaining rounds went wide, ricocheting off the walls of the compartment.

The commander lurched to the side and spun from the impact of the rounds.

Larrs rolled to his side and roared, forcing himself to his knees. He dove toward the V'ril, grappling it in what could only be described as a perfectly executed sleeper hold.

I pulled the shotgun close, stepping to my left and away from the commander as I reloaded another slug into the chamber, racked the action, and loaded the remaining slugs into the tube. Not a full load, but it would have to do.

Larrs roared and barked again. Leaning back, he placed his knee into the V'ril commander's lower back, lifting it off the ground.

The commander flailed helplessly in Larrs's grasp. It strained, massive muscles bulging against the RohBandī's hold.

Larrs barked something incomprehensible at me. I had no doubt what he wanted me to do and darted forward.

"Nighty night, pig boy!" I shoved the end of the shotgun into the Vril's mouth, crouched, and pulled the trigger.

The V'ril jerked violently. Black ichor exploded from the top of its scaly head. I pulled the trigger again, unloading the shotgun into the bastard's skull for good measure.

We as a race might be royally screwing ourselves over with wars and polluting the environment, but fuck anyone who might try to take over and enslave our planet.

The commander's limp body slipped from the RohBandī's grip and slumped to the floor with a hard thud. Larrs, exhausted, collapsed on top of the Vril's corpse.

Larrs was an absolute wreck after the fight. The exposed skin where the V'ril commander's ray gun had burned through was blistered and had begun to slough off in places. The guy must have had an insane level of pain tolerance. There was no way he wasn't in a massive amount of pain, but that didn't stop him from getting back to his feet and back to the job at hand.

The walking carpet had more balls and gumption than I did. After a beating like that, I'd have been curled up in a ball waiting for the reaper to come along and punch my ticket.

After a quick look over the ship's systems, he motioned for me to follow him. Both of us made our way to the next deck, limping, and bracing ourselves against the walls of the corridor.

We found Travis, cold and lifeless, even in the heat of the ship when we returned to the lower deck. It really didn't surprise me that he'd passed away after I left him. He'd taken a direct hit with the same kind of ray gun that had cooked Larrs so badly. At least now I didn't have to worry about him falling back into his depressive funk and drinking himself to death.

Larrs let out a series of soft chortles then lifted Travis over his shoulder with little effort before leading me to a small compartment on the lower deck that looked like something out of a psychopathic butcher's wet dream.

Dozens of bladed, spiked, and otherwise painful-looking tools hung all around the compartment. Dark stains covered the large metal worktable in the middle of the room and the floors surrounding it.

Gently, Larrs laid Travis's body on the table, then made his way to a cylindrical hatch at the back of the compartment. He motioned for me to approach then tapped at the controls for several minutes, cycling through numerous screens of information that looked like hieroglyphic gibberish to me.

The console beeped and the curved hatch slid away, revealing a small chamber. Larrs turned to me, muttering something in his language while pointing at a large green oval on the screen before he stepped into the chamber and nodded at me, motioning toward the control panel.

"You want me to hit the button," I asked, stepping toward the controls. Larrs nodded again and let out an approving growl.

The hatch instantly slid closed. A pale blue glow filled the viewport and the chamber filled with a thick viscous liquid. Pressurized air whistled from the edges of the door as it fully seated and sealed into the frame. Larrs closed his eyes and visibly relaxed, floating freely within the blue glowing fluid.

I watched in amazement through the viewport in the hatch as mechanical arms extended from the walls of the chamber and slowly scanned the RohBandī inch by inch.

Scorched, blistered skin visibly smoothed, then hair slowly sprouted and began to regrow before my eyes. The console beeped and I glanced over to see what looked like a visual readout of the damage Larrs had sustained.

"Well, I'll be damned…"

Several sections of the damage on the display flashed momentarily then highlighted. I stepped closer, leaning in to get a better look through the viewport. Tiny mechanical fingers worked the seriously damaged areas like they were weaving new flesh and bone into place.

A little over an hour passed before the console beeped again. The display now showing the damaged areas in green. Fluid within the chamber began draining, taking little time before the door seals hissed and the hatch slid to the side.

Other than the damage to his jumpsuit, Larrs looked as right as rain when he stepped out of the chamber.

"Damn, man. I hope you feel as good as you look." The large alien smiled and responded with another of his growling chortles. "Even though I can't understand a word you're saying, I'll take that as a yes."

He pointed at me, then stepped aside and pointed at the chamber.

"You want me to get into that thing?" I asked, pointing at the contraption. He nodded and let out a soothing cooing sound.

"I don't know about that man. I never was one for going to the doctor unless something was really busted. Hell, would it even know what to do with a human?"

Larrs poked me in the ribs I'd been cradling since the fight. Pain raced across my chest and shoulder.

"Dude, what the hell was that for?"

He motioned to the chamber once more and repeated the cooing sound.

"Yeah, you aren't wrong. I'm pretty sure I have at least a few cracked and broken ribs at best."

He urged me forward again.

"You sure it ain't going to give me a sex change or add a few extra arms or something weird like that?"

His urging was a little more insistent this time. Kinda like a grandmother at the end of her patience. If my ribs were cracked, it would be at least six weeks if I was lucky before they were healed. Not to mention I still had at least an eight-hour ride back to Georgia when all of this was over. Reluctantly I stepped into the chamber.

"Alright, alright. I get it. But I ain't doing it for you. I'm doing it 'cause I can't ride with busted ribs."

Larrs cooed another chortling phrase then tapped the control console. The hatch slid shut and the chamber filled with pale blue light.

I had no idea how long I'd been in the regeneration chamber, but I felt better than I had in years. Parts that had hurt since my time on the flightline, especially my knees, felt as good as when I was a teenager.

The massive RohΒandī smiled wide as I stepped out of the chamber and laughed, then said something in his language. *"Are you feeling better, little brother?"*

"You fixed the translator? How long was I out?"

"Long enough." He laughed again and slapped me on the back of the shoulder. "Help me with your friend."

"But he's dead."

He laughed again. *"Trust me. He's only mostly dead. You'd be surprised what this technology can do."*

After the results I'd seen, it sure as hell wouldn't hurt to try. Worst case, Travis was still dead. Mostly dead was better than all dead any day in my book. So we propped him into the chamber and Larrs activated it once more.

While the machine did its work, I helped Larrs collect the bodies and toss them into the ships' recycling system where the bodies would be broken down and used by various ship systems. He didn't go into the gory details of the process, but all I could think about was the bodies being used in some sort of protein resequencer or replicator-type contraption like you'd see on Star Trek.

Waste not, want not I guess?

By the time we'd finished with the clean up, the regenerator had finished. I expected my buddy to be just as dead as he was when we put him in there, but to my amazement, he yawned and stretched as if he'd just awakened from a long and refreshing nap.

"Travis?"

"Yeah, Brax. What's up?" He started to take a step out of the chamber and began to stumble.

I hurried forward and offered my hand. "How you feeling, man?"

Taking the offered hand he regained his balance and took a slow step out of the chamber. "Good," he said, thinking on the question for a moment as he studied the chamber and his surroundings. "Yeah, good, I think. A little dizzy, but otherwise nothing hurts. Hell, I honestly feel like I could pull off a ten-mile ruck in record time."

I laughed. "Okay, let's not get carried away now."

"What happened?"

"Um…," I started to say something but wasn't sure what to say. Hell, if it were me I'd want to know the truth, so I just rolled with it. "You kinda died, man. One of those scale heads hit you hard with one of their ray guns and cooked you like a microwaved potato."

"You're shitting me, Brax."

"Naw, man. You seriously think this is something I'd shit you about?"

Travis froze, absolute befuddlement showing across his face.

Larrs let our several smooth barks. *"Your friend is correct, Travis. You were not too far gone for the V'ril technology to work. The regeneration machine was able to repair your damaged systems and revive you."* He pointed at the screen readout that showed the damaged areas the unit had repaired and their current status.

"Looks like it even repaired all the damage we did to our livers over the years," I said jokingly, pointing at the bright green spot that indicated the over used organ.

A forlorn look washed over his face. "I guess that's at least something to celebrate."

"Dude, why the long face? You got a second chance at life after we kicked alien ass and saved the world."

Travis shrugged. "Yeah, but what good does that do me when I don't have anything to go back to? Or don't you remember that my wife left me for a no good Yankee banker?"

Larrs let out another series of cooing chortles. *I must leave soon before your government forces arrive. Several aircraft are enroute to our position. If you have no business to attend here, you are welcome to come along and see what the universe might hold for you out there.*

"Shit, Trav. You could be the next best thing to Captain James T. Kirk to the hot alien chicks out there."

Travis looked at me with confused surprise, then back to Larrs. "You serious?" The big guy nodded and let out another bark.

While Travis considered the offer, Larrs fired up the shuttle and took us back to the ground, landing in the church parking lot just behind my bike.

Hands tucked into his pockets, Travis slowly stepped off the shuttle. "Do you have any problems with pets?" He asked, turning back to the Rohʙandī.

Larrs cooed in reply. *"What do you mean by… pets?"*

"Like a small domesticated animal companion that you feed and take care of," I replied.

"Oh, yes," the large alien said then laughed. *"There are many creatures throughout the galaxy held in this esteem that you would consider a pet.."*

"Then hold that thought for a minute." Travis ran back toward the boat while we waited. He returned in a fresh change of clothes with a backpack strapped over his shoulders and Butch trailing behind him on a leash.

"Larrs, this is Butch. Butch, this is Larrs." The large hound let out a low growl and hunkered down behind Travis's leg.

"He's a good guy, Butch. Just wait and see."

The beating of helicopter blades in the distance cut our goodbyes short. I leaned back on Jonie's seat and watched the alien craft lift away into the beautiful mountain sunrise with my best friend for what I figured would be one hell of an adventure to tell over drinks the next time I saw him.

The Pie Piper

By: Brisco Woods

1
Mid 1980's
Mississippi Delta

The air was thick with humidity, but that was common for southern Mississippi in June. The ninety-five-degree temps were a little harsh, but not unheard of. It was evening and the normal crew was gathered around the porch of Dupree's General Store and Sundries off Yellow Jacket Rd.

Harold 'Harry' Howard laughed as he jumped his black checker over two red ones, landing in the coveted king's row. "King me, Freddy! Dumbass!"

"Shit!" Freddy Yoakum slammed his fist on the barrel, shaking the remaining disks around and causing several to clatter to the board floor.

"If you had your mind on the game instead of Tawny Kitain's ass in that stupid Indiana Jones knockoff." Stephan 'Sprig' Wilcamp chimed in.

Freddy flipped him a bird and scowled. "The Perils of Gwendoline In The Land Of The Yik Yak. It's not a knockoff, it's gonna be a classic, you just wait and see."

"Suuure it will. Just like Ghostchasers will."

Harry reseated himself after picking up the fallen checkers. "It's Ghostbusters, and you ain't even seen it yet, Sprig. Don't knock it 'til you tried it."

Sprig spat a stream of Redman in the sand. "Yeah, well, you like The Fall Guy too, or at least that Heather chick."

"Yes. Yes, I do." Harry said with a stupid grin.

A buzzing sound forced its way through the Live Oaks, Spanish moss, and thick evening air. Harry looked toward the woods and spat in the sand near his feet.

"It's about damned time. Where's that boy been?"

A three-wheeled minibike bounced through the trees. The lanky teen hunched over the handlebars, twisted the throttle and spun the three-wheeler in circles, kicking up sand and pinecones as he laughed hysterically.

The other three teens jumped off the wooden planked porch and ran for their own bikes, the checkerboard and game forgotten. A few quick minutes later a combined two hundred and seventy cc's of Honda two-cycle power buzzed off toward the swamp leaving a cloud of sand, sticks, and smoke in their wake.

Gazing out the open window over the bayou at the evening sky, she smiled. The moon would be full tonight and for the next few. There was some truth to the fear of the full moon, but it came from the fear itself more than any magic linked directly with the celestial orb. So many stories had been told connecting the full moon to evil things. The fear was nearly palatable. For one who practiced the arts as she did, anyway.

Her fingers were long and graceful as she deftly shaved small slices from the light wood. Changing tools, she began to carve the details. A small upright rectangle, placed exactly in the center with one of the shorter ends against the bottom. Midway between that rectangle and the outer edge, she carved a small square. Then duplicated it on the opposite side of the rectangle. She continued around the sides of the carving, placing a few different sized squares and then another rectangle on the opposite side of the cube.

Finally, a peaked top with lines horizontal to the bottom finished off the carving. She placed it carefully on the wooden topped table she used as a workstation and sat back on the dark green pickle bucket she'd acquired from the rear of a fast-food restaurant. It was nearly complete. Only the final steps to seal the talisman and incant the gift. Rachel Santee would be here within the hour with the last physical item required.

Her smile widened, stretching the dark skin of her face. She felt something coming, but she didn't know what, yet. Maybe it would show itself this cycle, maybe the next, but something wicked was most definitely on its way. The suspense was enticing all on its own and provided a satisfying high. But the 'something wicked' enticed her even more.

Soon, she thought to herself as she scratched behind the ear of a silver streaked black Maine Coon. The cat pressed its head into her hand, closing its yellow eyes, and purred quietly.

Four teenage boys sat around a small fire slowly turning hot dogs jabbed onto the ends of cypress twigs. Carl Dean hunched his shoulders up to try and appear larger than his hundred and thirty pounds. He pulled his head as low as could between them like he was imitating a turtle. Lowering his voice as much as he could manage, he tucked his chin into his chest and looked up through his eyebrows.

"You kids better not be out in the woods after dark. You know that's when the snakes and the gators eat."

He dropped his shoulders to their normally slouched position and sat back, laughing.

"Don't he know we've lived here our whole lives? I swear he's useless as tits on a boar hog," Sprig said as he spat a long stream of tobacco juice into the fire.

Not to be outdone, Harry spit his own stream of Levi Garrett into the flames and said, "useless as rabbit ears on a ham radio."

"Brakes on a shrimp boat." Freddy said with a similar hiss from the fire at his stream of Beech-Nut.

"Yup, a steering wheel on a coal train." Carl Dean agreed, checking the browning of his hot dog. "Hey, did y'all hear about that bass jig Billy Spencer had last year? They swore he caught a lunker ever' time he casted."

"No shit? Where'd he get that from?" Freddy asked, checking the black crust ringing his own hot dog.

Sprig spat again and kicked one of the rocks ringing the campfire. "Hell, he was lying. That shit-for-brains never caught a fish big enough to keep in his whole damned life."

Freddy gazed under thick eyebrows at his friend a moment before replying. "Oh, that's right. Y'all got that family feud going on. How long back's that go, Sprig? Your papaw's time, or before that?"

Sprig just grunted and stared into the fire.

"Yeah, that's right," Freddy said, refusing to let it go that easily. "The Wilcamps and the Spencers. Why they been quarreling since the war between the states. One of 'em kicked the other'n's dog or something."

Sprig flipped him off and kicked dirt at him, barely stifling his own laugh as the other two boys cackled. "No, it wasn't no dog. His great something granddaddy tried to run off with my great something granddaddy's girl when they was kids. That's what started it all and it just went downhill ever since."

"Hmph." Harry chimed in. "Figured it had to be a dog or a girl. They probably could've worked it out if it was a dog."

All four boys laughed as they stood to gather around the table. Someone had left an old card table on the little island long ago and two of the legs had rusted off. The two that worked held one side up while the other sat on an old cypress stump. It was never quite level, but it served their purposes.

Carl Dean was looking at the other three. "Seriously though, he said he had to quit fishing 'cause they started following his boat into the bank and flopping up out of the water. He finally burned that lure, but he won't even go fishing now."

Sprig wasn't buying it. He looked cross-eyed at Carl Dean. "Yeah, right. Like that really happened."

Carl Dean shook his head. "I heard him telling Smokey Calhoun about it. Billy said he'd paid that witch woman over in D'Iberville forty dollars for that plug. She guaranteed he'd catch a fish every cast, and damned if he didn't."

"Witch woman?" Freddy asked with a slight nervousness in his voice. He always was the first to get nervous when the ghost stories started.

"Yep, that Widow LePue. She lives out on the edge of the back bay."

Harry was nodding thoughtfully as he put the hot dog on a slice of light bread and added mustard from a bottle one of them had liberated from the Dairy Freeze.

"Yeah, now that you mention it, I heard that same story. 'Cept it was from Smiley Townes. He said that same thing about Billy not fishing no more, 'cept he said it was 'cause Billy had got bored with it. He said Billy'd used that lure to win all them tournaments, too. Every one he entered for three months straight."

Sprig still wasn't convinced. "I ain't never heard such a line of bullshit. That boy barely knows which side of the rod to cast. He probably had somebody stash them fish out in the bayou somewhere and just went and fetched 'em when he was supposed to be fishing."

Freddy ignored the other boy's tirade, focusing on the witch story. "All on account of one jig he got from the Widow LePue? She makes them little doodads and sells them at the flea market every weekend, right?"

Carl Dean's voice got a little lower as the darkness engulfed the swamp around the campfire. "She don't make 'em like this one though. It had a dark red ring around it. Like crimson colored, like blood. It probably *was* blood. Maybe from some animal, maybe from somewhere else."

Freddy stood up as he finished his hot dog. "Y'all are full of shit if you believe that bull. Ain't no magic lures helping no redneck like Billy Spencer catch no bass. You ain't believing this, are you, Harry?"

Harry had been quiet for most of the conversation, but he raised his head with a haunted look in his eyes. He looked at each of his friends before turning his face back down toward the fire for a minute before answering.

"It's true. I seen that plug he used in a couple of them tourneys. It was dark water-stained cypress with a red band around it 'bout a half inch wide. I also seen some other things that witch woman carved with that same red band around 'em."

Sprig was acting like he wasn't interested, but he and Carl Dean were leaning closer. Freddy just moved closer to the fire, then asked, "Where'd you see 'em? At the flea market?"

Harry spat into the fire, nodding at the satisfying hiss from the tobacco juice meeting the burning coals. He dug a nearly empty brown foil pouch from the pocket of his cutoff denim shorts. Pulling a small plug to freshen up the chew in his mouth, he tucked it in his cheek and faced his friends.

"She keeps 'em in that little shack out on the bayou next to her cabin. It's where she makes them little doodads you was talking about." He nodded at Freddy.

Freddy grunted and asked, "How would you know that?"

"My cousin Rooster and me, we went in there with her to get a little wooden jewelry box she'd made for Rooster's new stepdaddy. I reckon he was giving it to Rooster's ma for her birthday or something, but he sent Rooster over to pick it up and I tailed along. She had a bunch of stuff she'd made in there, but there was a couple of little carvings with that red band around 'em in a little box. I remember 'cause it was laying open on the table. Rooster pointed 'em out and asked what they was for. That Widow

LePue shut that lid up right quick and smiled at us with them black teeth and said 'never you mind Rooster Delaroe. Now you boys get.' Well, we got alright. I barely kept up to Rooster. I never seen him pedal so fast in my life."

Freddy was sweating, whether from sitting so close to the fire in the thick humid night air, or from the story the boys were telling, nobody commented.

"What happened after that?" He asked.

"Nothing. That was just before Rooster's new stepdaddy went to prison."

"What'd he go in for?" Carl Dean asked.

"Rooster said he was framed. Sherriff Calderwood claimed he'd killed some woman up in Jackson and stole her jewels. Hell, he was dumber than a box turtle. He probably couldn't find his way to Jackson. He had a bunch of jewelry he gave Rooster's ma though. At least 'til the Sheriff took it all."

Harry got real quiet for a couple of minutes before looking back up at the others.

"That jewelry box, though. It didn't have a red band around it. The whole belly of it was that color."

2

The boys had pulled over near the road just out of sight of the first mobile homes in Coastal Breeze Park to say their good-byes. The night had been a little weird for all of them, but especially Sprig. Freddy got scared first, but he was over it quicker than any of them too. Probably due to being scared so often by the other boys' stories.

Sprig, though. He had been a downer to the point Carl Dean and Harry had ribbed him about it. He took the ribbing and even gave back, but his attempts were half-hearted.

Freddy threw up his arm and smiled, white teeth flashing bright in the morning sunlight.

"See y'all this evening. Ma said I could do the whole weekend if y'all still wanna go down to Old Fort Bayou, Friday."

Carl Dean looked at Sprig, but the younger boy just shrugged. Harry pulled his last plug of Levi out of the aluminum foil bag and tucked it in his cheek.

"I'm in. I wanna snag some more of them alligator gar and they grow big in that bayou."

Carl Dean nodded enthusiastically. "I'll bring Mike's metal detector. We found them musket balls that one time. Maybe we'll find some pirate gold or something."

Sprig perked up a little at the mention of a metal detector. "I'm in, too. I'll snag ma's garden shovel. Hey, if we strike it rich, what'll you boys do with your share?"

Carl Dean was the first to speak up, as per usual. "I'd go to Vegas. I bet I could double it at them one-arm-bandits."

Freddy said, "I'd get a truck for Uncle Lewis, then spend the rest on a new trailer. I bet we could get that end lot in the park if we had a new trailer. The folks that run the Coastal Breeze would like to have a shiny new one out there to get attention."

The other boys all nodded and agreed enthusiastically.

Carl Dean said, "Jimmy's got that old swamp boat. It's still broke down, but I was thinking about working on that motor some this evening if y'all want to help. Maybe we can get it running. We could really have a blast in the swamp then!"

A huge smile spread across Harry's face and Sprig laughed. Pointing at the smiling boy, he said to Carl Dean, "Now look what you done. He's about to split his cheeks open with that grin."

All four laughed and kicked their bikes to life. Harry was still grinning as he said, "I'm in! We could ride that boat to Gulfport or even Pascagoula if we get that thing running."

Freddy gave two thumbs up as he laughed, and then buzzed off on his minibike toward the back of the mobile home park. His mom's place was the last one in line. She said it meant they had less grass to mow, but it was also the only one left when they moved in five years before.

Sprig waved and kicked the stand up on his Honda. "See y'all this evening. I'm gonna help old man Morris clean that ditch out today. I should have enough cash to get some Cokes and more hotdogs from Tommy over at the docks."

Carl Dean waved as the boy gunned the throttle and kicked up sand and gravel.

Harry looked at Carl Dean with a twisted little grin. "You wanna go see what that witch woman has hid away in her little shed? You reckon we might find something to spook Freddy with again?"

Carl Dean laughed and nodded. "Man, that'd be cool! I can't today though, I gotta help Momma get Granny to the doctor's office this afternoon. What about Friday?"

"Well, I do need to earn some money for gas, but we could meet back at Dupree's around one Friday, if you want. The widow'll be over at the interstate flea market all day, so we won't have to worry about her none."

"Sounds like a plan, Harry. And you know what Hannibal Smith always says, 'I love it when a plan comes together.' We'll do some A-Team shit this afternoon."

The shorter boy laughed and kicked his bike to life. "I should be able to help on that boat, too. See ya, Faceman."

Rachel Santee was tall for a woman at five feet and ten inches. She also referred to herself as big-boned. She didn't complain about the heat and humidity of the Mississippi gulf coast, but it was all she had ever known.

Her family had lived in Bay St. Louis all her life and her husband had moved her to Ocean Springs before their first child was borne. Some of her mom's family lived down in Baton Rouge though, and she remembered visiting them as a child. The gigantic old plantation style house with the tall ceilings and transoms over the doors for airflow. She had always loved the hurricane shutters and expansive wrap around porch.

She knew her family would never have such a home, but she was going to do whatever she had to, to get them an actual house of their own. Her husband was a hard worker and a good provider, but he would never earn the money needed to get them in their own house before their two kids were grown and moved out. Well, she hadn't told him yet, but three children in about six more months.

He would be overjoyed, but he'd also worry about the money. He was always torn between working as a plumber and being home nights, or driving a rig over-the-road and earning more money being gone a lot of the time. She preferred him home, but she did like more money. Well, maybe with a little help, she could have both. She didn't think it too much to ask. Other families had it.

Which was why she was here now, knocking on the door of this small cabin on the bayou. The Widow LePue had been a sympathetic ear when she had needed one several weeks back. She had also suggested she had an answer to Rachel's worries, and her dreams.

"Now Mrs. Santee, there's just no need for you and your," she gestured to the larger woman's stomach, "growing family to suffer. You all have worked for everything you have and it's high time you earned a break. And I know a way to help you."

The promise of help came exactly when needed most, having just found out she was pregnant again. It never occurred to her to wonder how the slim woman with the stained teeth had known of the baby. It also didn't occur to her to wonder if this woman could help her get a house for her family, why she lived in a rundown shack herself.

"What do you mean, Ms. LePue? How can I do anything to help? We can barely afford the rent on the place we live now, let alone a new house."

"Now, madam," The frail woman had said with a small smile and a knowing glint in her dark eyes. "This thing I'm speaking of, it can help you get what you desire most. It won't cost you anything you don't have plenty of to give, and you'll see results almost immediately. Within a few short days at the latest."

She remembered her excitement at the prospect of a new home for her family and the look on Lou's face when she told him. She felt the same excitement now as she knocked on the clap board door of the widow's cabin.

<u>3</u>

"Dammit!" Carl Dean exclaimed as his knuckles hit the metal crankcase of the air-cooled Volkswagen engine. "Why did he have to put all this metal around this dang motor?"

Freddy was sitting backwards inside the boat facing him across the small engine. "Pro'bly has to brace it so it don't shake all over the place." He offered helpfully.

"How would he know? I don't think this thing has ever run since he got it."

"Well, I don't guess we'll be going up to Pascagoula." Harry said over Carl Dean's shoulder, making the older boy jump and bump his head on a piece of the metal bracing he had just been complaining about.

"Don't sneak up on me like that, Dumbass!"

Harry laughed and gestured toward the boombox on the ground blasting Ozzy's Bark At The Moon. "If you didn't have that shit cranked so loud, you'd hear me coming up behind you." He shouted over the screeching guitar.

Carl Dean had just started his own shouted reply of, "That's Ozzy, not shit!" When Sprig pushed the volume control slide down to a more manageable level, resulting in the older boy finishing his statement in a shout much louder than was needed. All four boys laughed. Sprig looked at Carl Dean and raised an eyebrow.

"Well, does it look like something we can do?"

With his own eyebrows squinched together, Carl Dean shook his head.

"I do believe she's beyond our abilities to mend, my friends."

Freddy jumped down from the boat sitting on its homemade cement block maintenance stand. "What happened to 'we can rebuild him, we have the technologies.', from yesterday?"

"Well, you see, that was yesterday. We have discovered some new intel since then."

Sprig was caressing his new Redman pouch, mixing any of the chew that might have dried out around the edges in with the rest of the pack. Pulling it opened, he retrieved a pecan sized clump of the moist tobacco and stuffed it in his cheek.

"I reckon it's about time I headed home anyways. I'm helping dad this evening and tomorrow. We're mowing for Mr. Sandoval, the church, and cemetery. He said he'd pay me ten dollars if I helped him all day tomorrow. But I'll be done so we can go down to Old Fort Bayou for the weekend."

Freddy jumped into the air and slapped his leg with his open palm. "Cool! I got a feeling this time, boys. I think we'll find some of that pirate gold."

Sprig and Harry looked at each other and laughed. Harry said

"You always have a feeling. And we ain't never found any yet."

Freddy's dark face shined with sweat as he smiled, ignoring the jab.

"This time's different. I got a real strong feeling this time."

Harry slapped him on the back.

"We'll see. It sure would be nice to get into a string of good luck for once."

Carl Dean broke into a poor rendition of, "If it weren't for bad luck, I wouldn't have no luck at all." And all the boys laughed as they headed away from the airboat and toward their parked minibikes.

As the other two buzzed off toward their own destinations, Harry paused long enough to say to Carl Dean,

"Don't forget about Friday."

The older boy nodded and smiled.

"Oh, I ain't forgetting that. Surely that witch woman's got something in there we can scare Freddy with."

Harry laughed and twisted his throttle, spitting sand and dirt toward the busted airboat.

Thursday morning brought the drawing and notification she had been waiting for. The local mayor, along with a nonprofit organization out of Texas, had partnered with local contractors to build a home to be given to a needy family via a raffle drawing.

Rachel had heard something about it on the evening news, but like all such things, she hadn't given it much thought. That was until her visit with the Widow LePue earlier in the week.

The frail looking woman drew a slim blade from her workbench and motioned for Rachel to place her hand on the smooth work surface. She had hesitated, naturally, but the small woman insisted.

"Now Mrs. Santee, this only requires a couple of drops in this cup of stain here. It'll just be a slight sting. Nothing like the pain you tolerated when you birthed those two beautiful young'uns."

Rachel nodded, remembering the hours of labor with Carolyn and the near breach with Charlie. She never told her husband she named the boy after the actor Charles Bronson, who she'd had a crush on since high school. That was okay, she had a great uncle named Charles too. It was a convenient enough story to get his agreement.

As the carving blade pricked her finger, she yelped. Then watched in amazement as the woman squeezed the tip of the digit just enough for three crimson drops to fall into the dark stain in the old wooden cup. After the third drop settled into the stain, the Widow LePue placed a clean white cotton ball onto the small hole in her skin and smiled.

"Now, I have some work to do, so you take this and head on home. Of course, this is our secret now. Don't go telling the ladies down at the PTA."

The same smile was there on her taut skin, but her eyes were different somehow. Rachel shivered as she took the small ticket the woman handed her and closed her fist over the cotton ball. "Of course not. But when will I know anything?"

The eyes turned harder and the frail woman gestured to the door. "You'll know when you know. Don't go frettin' none. Now go on and get. I got to make this quick, and the sooner I get my part done, the sooner you'll get your reward."

Rachel headed back to Ocean Springs. Later that evening, she had looked closer at what LePue had given her. It was a raffle ticket for the house she had heard about on the news. A newly built three bedroom with central heat and air, just a mile or so from the trailer-house they currently rented from Lou's cousin.

She felt a chill along her spine as she studied the raffle ticket now and listened to the mayor talk about all the volunteers who had come forth to make this happen. They had given three hundred raffle tickets to folks nominated by the townspeople and they were drawing for immediate occupancy and full ownership of the home

She held her breath and read the numbers on her ticket as he said them aloud. Down to the last number they were all matching, but when he read the last as a five, her heart sank, and she felt all the excitement and hope drain from her like someone had pulled the plug from a bathtub.

She stood for a few minutes as everyone applauded and congratulated the winner. She felt lower and lower, listening to all the hubbub. As she turned to leave, she saw the Widow LePue standing in the back of the crowd watching her.

As their eyes met, she felt an anger like she had rarely felt before. The slim woman met her eyes and shook her head once, then gestured with her chin to the stage where some sort of ruckus was going on. The mayor, in his blue and white seersucker suit, having retrieved his megaphone, he was hurrying back to the center of the platform. Rachel thought she may as well celebrate with the other folks. It wasn't like it had cost her much except the rollercoaster of emotions.

Raising it to his face, he called out, "Ladies and gentlemen, ladies and gentlemen. Please let me have your attention. Please listen up, now."

As the celebratory noise quickly died away, he continued, "I have some terrible news that's just been delivered to me. Mr. Jessie Bartley and his young bride, who were the holders of this winning ticket, were both tragically killed this very morning in a car accident down in Biloxi."

He paused as disbelief and sadness spilled from the gathered crowd. When the noise grew manageable for his megaphone, he continued. "Now the tickets have all been dumped in the trash already, so what we're going to do is take the next highest ticket. The ticket with the next number. All the same digits except the last one, which is a six. Does someone here hold that ticket?"

She felt her arm raise hesitantly as goosebumps covered her body. She suddenly felt chilled as she glanced back to see no one where the Widow LePue had just stood. Within a few seconds she found herself in shock as she was led on stage and her ticket verified. The mayor again stood with the megaphone to his mouth.

"Ladies and Gentlemen, we have the lucky winner right here. Mrs. Rachel Santee, congratulations! You and your family now own a new house!"

4

It was a quarter after one on Friday when Harry rode up on his Honda. The two boys waved at the store's owner, old Dupree, and took the backwoods trails toward D'Iberville and Saint Martin Bayou. Their teen laughs rang among the Cypress trees as they splashed through puddles from a midday shower and spun the fat minibike tires, throwing rooster tails of wet sand in the air. The trip took twice as long as it should have, but they had fun. And, for teenage boys, that is one of the most important things in life.

Luck was with them as they found a couple of palmetto bushes to leave their bikes hidden behind, just a quarter mile up the dirt road from the Widow LePue's place. She lived in a little three-room cabin on stilts, right on the banks of the water. Out back of the cabin was the smaller one room shack that Harry mentioned the night before. The door had a padlock on it, but the windows didn't have any glass, just heavy curtains keeping the less invasive bugs out. The two boys snuck in easily.

Carl Dean snickered as he stood up from crawling through one of the windows. "I guess that lock keeps the honest folk out."

Harry laughed as they checked the place out. The small shack was less than ten feet on a side and held only a bucket for a stool, a workbench against one wall, and a shelf. A plastic window fan hung from a string near the window facing the water. The workbench displayed a half dozen projects started but unfinished and several scraps of wood that the Widow LePue probably planned to carve into some doodad or other.

"Duuuude." Carl Dean said, squatting to pull something from under the table.

He plopped the small chest on the workbench with a big Cheshire cat's grin. Harry stepped up to examine the chest and grunted.

"I bet that's where she keeps the good stuff. Problem is, it's locked. We could bust it open, I reckon, but do you want to leave obvious evidence like that?"

Carl Dean's smile just got bigger as he pulled a couple of paper clips from his pocket.

"You remember my brother, Leroy?"

"Yeah, I seen him around a few times before he went off to the army."

"It's the Marines, and he had to go because he got caught stealing some stuff over in Gulfport. Anyways, before he left, he taught me how to pick a little lock like this one, and like momma has on the bathroom door."

"Why would he teach you how to do that?"

"Well, we started on this one and moved up to that one." He was busy studying the small lock on the chest and spoke distractedly, "Momma passes out in the bathroom sometimes, and I gotta get her to the couch."

Harry nodded gravely and looked back at the little chest, not really knowing what to say. He'd heard folks talk about Carl Dean's momma in ways folks shouldn't talk about a boy's momma, but he had kept his mouth shut because he didn't want Carl Dean to know.

They sat in awkward silence, broken only by a dog barking up the bayou. Carl Dean unfolded the two paper clips and poked them in the hole of the chest latch, wiggling them around. After a couple of minutes, Harry was about to say something when he heard a slight click from the latch and the lid popped open.

"Ha!" Carl Dean leaned back, teeth showing again.

Harry stepped up and peered into the small chest. There were four carvings lying on a green felt cloth glued to the bottom of the chest. One was a tiny car, about the size of one of the matchbox cars he'd seen other kids at school playing with. The next was a carving of a pony, mane and tail and all. The third one was a building. It wasn't a trailer like he and his friends lived in, it was an honest to goodness, stick built house. He could distinguish the changes in the siding on the walls. Something about it was familiar, but his attention was pulled from it by the last wooden carving in the box.

The largest of the four by far, was a dark wooden flute. He knew it was a flute because that's what Carolyn Santee played in the high school band. Carl Dean was studying the pony statue in amazement while Harry picked up the flute, noticing the crimson rings around the body between each finger hole. Placing it to his mouth like he'd seen Carolyn do many times, he gently blew into the slit on the side of the instrument.

The music generated by the instrument was low and beautiful and filled the small shack. He had never heard anything sound as wonderful as the notes coming from that small piece of carved wood. He gently breathed into the tiny slot on one end and moved his fingers randomly across several of the holes down the trunk of the instrument, like he had seen Carolyn do. Heavenly sound drifted through the small shack and out the windows.

After what seemed like forever, Carl Dean placed his hand over the instrument and pressed down to move it away from his friend's mouth.

Immediately, the music stopped and there was a flash of lightning and a clap of thunder over the water, just outside of the shack. Both boys jumped and ran to the window, looking out over the water. Several ripples of disturbed water splashed around the bayou, but only a few puffy white clouds floated in the otherwise blue sky several miles to the south over the gulf. Harry looked at Carl Dean with his eyebrows scrunched up in a frown.

"Didn't that sound like it was right outside?"

"Sure as shit!" He looked around the shack nervously, with his eyes stopping on the small house the widow lived in. "Let's get outta here Harry. I feel like something really bad's about to happen."

"Yeah. Let's get!"

Carl Dean shut the lid on the little chest and shoved it back under the workbench as Harry climbed out the window on the opposite side from the bay. Both boys ducked low and ran through the trees and palmetto bushes back to their bikes. Carl Dean jumped on his three-wheeler from the rear as Harry kicked the stand up on his minibike.

"Harry, I'm gonna check on momma, but I'll meet y'all this evening at Dupree's."

Harry jerked his chin up, nodding at his friend.

"See ya there, dude"

As the two motorbikes sped east, Harry was extremely conscious of the dark wooden flute with small red lines around it, tucked under his shirt in the back pocket of his shorts.

Back at the shack, the two-cycle Honda's buzzing dissipated in the distance as several huge swamp rats scurried from the water of the bayou to the cool darkness under the cabin. Thirteen pairs of glowing red eyes stared out from the black crawlspace.

The flea market's sounds and aromas filled the city block. Some were beginning to try and rebrand the get-together of local craftsmen and hobby farmers as a farmer's market, but most folks around D'Iberville still called it a flea market.

Folding tables filled to near collapsing with melons, tomatoes, cucumbers, okra. All manner of peppers, from sweet to slap-your-granny hot, lined both sides of the block. Other tables, stacked high with wooden birdhouses roofed in old license plates from Mississippi, Alabama, and Louisiana, sat among real and plastic flower arrangements. Locals peddled stacks of candles and soaps of various fragrances.

A fat man in a grease-stained t-shirt that had probably once been white, stood over and stirred a huge pot of gumbo, spiced with the occasional drop of sweat from his forehead. Laid out on the table next to him were loaves of French bread, pans of cornbread, and cardboard bowls and plastic spoons.

All the way at the end, several empty spots conspicuously separating it from its nearest neighbor, stood a rackety card table with a couple dozen carved statues and replicas spaced neatly across a bright white tablecloth.

Behind the table, a tarp spread across a two-by-four frame about the height of a short man. The canvas of the tarp was dark and cast a deep shadow over the woman sitting beneath it. Her thin frame hunched forward on an old five-gallon pickle bucket, seemingly haphazardly carving a small figurine from a piece of ancient water-logged cypress. Her wide mouth split into a smile across stained, black teeth.

Suddenly, the deft movement of the narrow fingers stopped. She sat for a moment as still as one of the statues on the small table in front of her. In the distance a crack of thunder shattered the silence of the steamy afternoon, causing several heads to lean back and peer toward the mostly blue sky. She looked toward the sound, and the smile grew a little wider. An astute person might have noticed the faint hint of a red glow from behind the tinted spectacles.

Just north and east of New Orleans, directly across Lake Pontchartrain, highway one ninety crossed the Lake Pontchartrain Causeway. The road made a bee-line through Mandeville to Lacombe and then slanted over to Slidell. Just off the highway and on the edge of the Fontainebleau State Park, was a small subdivision of about forty or fifty small houses. The homes in the subdivision had been there for well over thirty years. They were all similar in size and in layout, with elevated floors on small lots.

Somewhere in the middle of one of the nearly identical rows, a small white house sat. It was much like any of the other small white houses in the neighborhood, sprinkled among the yellow, teal, and maroon. In fact, it was much like all the houses of different colors, too. The only real noticeable difference was the extensive herb garden in the tiny backyard.

A tall, slim woman with dark skin in a flower print dress and a motherly look about her smiled as she worked the garden as she did every day, caring for the herbs and flowers. Suddenly, her long fingers stopped moving, and she looked east and slightly north. The crack of thunder near D'Iberville,

Mississippi wasn't audible sixty miles away, but she seemed to be aware of it, nonetheless.

Her face settled into a slight frown as she stood from the gardening stool, wiping her hands on the apron.

"Child, what have you done?" She asked the thick Louisiana afternoon air.

Harry and Carl Dean made it back to the Dupree's in record time. They stopped off the road and to the side of the old general store just long enough to say their so-longs and make plans for the night in the bayou. Then gunning their minibikes, they sped off toward the Coastal Breeze.

Harry pulled into the shade of the ancient live oak tree that stood behind his family's home. It was one of only two double wide trailers in Coastal Breeze Mobile Home Park, courtesy of his Uncle Petey's job at the post office. Uncle Petey lived with him and his parents and as far as he knew, was the only reason they had a home at all.

Lankin, his dad, and Petey's older brother, had been in a motorcycle accident when Harry was nine and had lost all use of his legs. It hadn't kept him from doing what he could to support his family, but there just wasn't much call for a man who couldn't walk. He made enough commission selling cars to feed them, barely. And with Harry's mom's money from the beauty salon, they survived.

Petey was in the living room when Harry slammed the door and kicked off his shoes in the mud room/laundry room. He looked up long enough for his nephew's face to register, then focused back on the football game. He yelled over his shoulder as the game continued on the nineteen-inch Zenith TV, six feet in front of him, "Gail, the boy's home!"

Harry sighed heavily as he changed direction from the hallway leading to his room, and toward the kitchen where he knew his momma would be this time of day. Making sure the flute was tucked inconspicuously under his shirt, he wondered why he was in trouble now.

Curly blonde hair preceded his mom out of the kitchen, bouncing as it circled her round face and upturned nose. She was part Choctaw Indian she had once claimed, but she kept her hair a bright blonde with the help of chemicals and her fellow hairdressers. The curls ran in the family, or at least to him, as his jet-black hair ran in long curls down to his shoulders in the back. She insisted he keep it cut short on the sides, but curls would show up in the front if it got a little long.

The frown he expected was replaced by a wide smile as his mom embraced him in a huge mom hug, "Did you hear the news? Rachel and Lou Santee won a new house! They won that raffle yesterday morning that's been all over the six o'clock news. That new house up on Restlin Drive, it's theirs now. What do you think about that?"

Harry thought of the flute in his back pocket and turned a little red. He had never mentioned his crush on Carolyn to his mom, but it was like she knew. He never was able to keep anything secret from her. Luckily, she made it easy on him, usually.

"Well, I guess that's lucky for them." He stammered as she smiled at him like she knew every thought going through his teenage head.

"That's just right up the road, sweety. Maybe you can offer to help them move this weekend."

He turned redder still as she turned back into the kitchen. That would be a way to get in with Carolyn's folks, but he told the boys he would spend the weekend in the bayou, and he wasn't about to let them down.

"I made plans with the guys, mom, remember? We're camping."

"Oh yeah, I did forget about that. Oh well. I think they get the help of a moving company anyway, so that'll be fine. You can go by next week and see if you can help Carolyn and her parents with any settling in. I'm sure they'll appreciate that, now, won't they?"

He nodded and hurried back to his room to hide the flute under his mattress. He didn't know if they would, but he would surely be able to spend a little time with Carolyn, and maybe even play her some music on the flute. She would be impressed by that, he was certain.

5

Heat and humidity were keeping folks inside Friday afternoon, in the air conditioning if they had it and in front of a window fan if they didn't. Most folks, anyway. Four teenage boys on their minibikes sped down familiar trails leading from civilization to someplace not so civilized. The inland swamps around Old Fort Bayou had limited hard ground, and it seemed, to these four teenage boys at least, unlimited swamp and marsh.

The boys knew right where they were going, however. A little dry spot they called Dewey's Island was out in the marsh just about as far as you could ride on a bike. It was no more than a quarter acre of dry ground, but it was high enough out of the swamp that it stayed mostly that way. A small, natural causeway connected it to the dryer land where the boys parked their Hondas.

They started digging in for the weekend. Sprig seemed to have recovered from his mood of the day before and was giving Freddy his usual hard time.

"Why do you want to bring a feather pillow out in the swamp? It'll be ruined after one night out here. Hell, maybe even before then, with all this moisture in the air. Feels like we're walking around under that swamp water all the time."

"Well, least there's a breeze from the gulf. It ain't cool, but it feels good still."

"You ain't lying, Freddy. Let's get that metal detector and see what we can find before it gets dark. Let's detect around that log over there where we ain't been yet."

Carl Dean was snapping some twigs for a fire, but pointed to his bag.

"It's in there."

Harry, gathering some semi dry sticks from the edges of the woods, said, "Y'all find some of them Spanish coins or something. We'll all go up to Mobile and get one of them Smokey and The Bandit cars."

Carl Dean snorted. "Ain't nobody wants a Pontiac. We need to get one of them sixty-nine Challengers like the Duke boys got."

Sprig laughed. "It's a Charger, dumbass. Not a Challenger, a Charger."

Freddy trotted over to the log after securing his pillow in a rolled-up blanket and retrieving the metal detector from Carl Dean's pack. "We could get one of them A-Team vans. That's what I'd do."

Sprig was kicking dirt around looking for any stray Spanish silver that might be laying on top of the ground. "Do y'all remember that big Torino, on Starsky and Hutch? That thing kicked ass."

They kept going back and forth for a few minutes while Freddy got the detector ready to go and Harry used an old Bic lighter to start the campfire.

Freddy and Sprig started waving the detector over the sand as they walked around the log, Freddy going on about the advantages of an El Camino, car in the front and truck in the back.

Harry pulled the flute out of his pocket and started studying it. He knew he couldn't have been responsible for the music that had come out of the thing when he played it, but the fact that he had held it and blew into it made him feel just a little more confident. He had never known much about music, and less about anything like what'd come out of a flute. Now if it started playing Marshall Tucker or Lynyrd Skynyrd, he might sing along, but nothing like what the ancient wooden instrument had produced earlier.

"You kept it, huh?"

Carl Dean had come back with some bigger firewood and glanced from the flute to Harry.

"Did you hear that earlier? It was real, right? I didn't imagine it, right?"

"I don't know, Harry. I heard music like I ain't never heard before and you was the one with that flute up to your face. But yeah, I heard it." He dropped his armful of sticks and looked sideways at his friend. "I heard that thunder too."

"Yeah, I wonder what was up with that."

"I don't know, dude. But that witch probably had some kind of alarm on her shack or something. That was magic lightning I bet."

Sprig shouted from near the water. "Woo-hoo! Lookie here boys, we got us a coin!"

Freddy peered at the metal disk in Sprig's hand as he splashed murky swamp water on it to rub through the dirt and grime.

"Aw shit, Sprig. That's just an old washer."

Harry and Carl Dean had come running at Sprig's excitement, but the boys all started kicking dirt at him and laughing.

Carl Dean said, "shit, we're rich now."

Sprig spat tobacco juice in the water and laughed. "Hey Carl Dean, didn't your momma want a new washer?"

The bigger boy flipped Sprig the bird. "Suck it, Sprig. Find us some real riches."

Harry and Carl Dean dug out the hotdogs they had brought and began sharpening the ends of some cypress twigs with Carl Dean's pocketknife.

"We got some dawgs, boys!" Carl Dean yelled as he poked the fire with a larger stick to get coals spread out for some good hot dog cooking.

The good-natured ribbing continued among the friends as they each took a stick and held hot dogs over the hot coals.

"Did y'all see The Fall Guy last week? You think there's any of them orangutans out in the swamp?" Freddy asked as he looked around nervously between bites of Oscar Meyer's best.

Sprig jabbed Carl Dean in the ribs gently with an elbow before saying, "I think I heard something about some of them in the swamp down by Bellefontaine. There was a circus train wrecked down there years ago. I think it was old Dupree that said they had been killing people's dogs down there."

Carl Dean nodded gravely. "Yeah, I heard that too. And you know they won't stop with family pets. It's only a matter of time 'til they get braver."

"Or meaner." Sprig said, chomping on a hot dog. "But, you know, they'll hit places with lots of dogs first, I'm sure."

Freddy looked around the swamp, peering into the dusk at the growing shadows. "Daaamn. Ma's only got four. That should be alright though, right?"

When nobody answered, he looked back at his friends, who were barely covering their laughter.

"Shit! Y'all suck." He said as he took the last bite of his hot dog, realizing the other two had been teasing him. He joined as the other boys burst out in laughter.

Unnoticed by the other three, Harry retreated to the fire ring and pulled the flute from his pocket again. Placing it against his lips, he blew gently.

A sweet ringing melody filled the air and all noise from swamp critters slowly ceased as they became as entranced as the teenagers. The music was soft and floated through the trees like a dragonfly along the reeds. All three of the other boys stood mesmerized as Harry played the red-banded flute like someone from the New Orleans Symphony.

As for Harry, he was just as fascinated at the music, maybe more so that he was the one playing it. His fingers danced and his breath never faltered. It seemed like it would go on forever, and he was certain he could keep playing that long.

The small shack on the water was dark except for one dim and yellowed bulb over what might have been considered a small dining table. Herbs dried in glass dishes and hung about the small kitchen by fishing line. In the distance, a dog screamed from some awful pain until the howling quieted to whimpers, and then those disappeared.

The rail thin scarecrow of a woman listened to the dog's whines and smiled sadly. Then suddenly, her head turned to the east and cocked to one side. She listened intently for a few moments as her smile broadened. Turning her focus back to the carving she was working on in the near darkness, she waited patiently, her sharp blade poised to shave another delicate flake of cypress from the stained stub. Then, hearing the clap of thunder, her blade continued the deft swipes along the near petrified wood. The anticipation was even more malleable in the air than the evening humidity.

A bus wasn't the quickest way to move from place to place, but she had no driver's license or identification, so it was the most dependable. The back row was her choice, but it was also next to the lavatory, which carried distinct disadvantages. The seat was straight backed and not very comfortable, but it allowed her to watch all that happened up front. And there were very few who wanted to sit in the most uncomfortable seats on the bus.

As the big vehicle lumbered up onto highway one ninety in Lacombe and pointed the painted grey dog on the side toward Bay St Louis and Gulfport, she knew she would reach her destination within a few hours. There were ways she could have traveled there more quickly, but they were vastly more expensive. And not necessarily in the monetary sense.

She had felt the second clap of thunder not long before. That 'thunder' she knew, and when it sounded, there was a cost. She would get there when she got there. Over her years of life, she had learned patience, and the cost would be paid, regardless. It was up to her to make sure that the cost was paid by the appropriate individual.

"What the hell! It ain't spose' to storm tonight." Freddy was looking at the sky, a puzzled look on his dark face.

Carl Dean was eye-locked with Harry, both boys beginning to sweat a little bit more than the humid night air demanded. Harry's hands were shaking as he placed the flute back in his pocket and the night sounds of the swamp slowly returned to the normal chorus. A gator bellowed out on the bayou. Lightning bugs started flashing in the woods.

Suddenly, another bellow sounded within yards of where the boys stood, and they all backed toward Harry's fire and the opposite side of the island from the deep roar. Four sets of young and sharp eyes, accustomed to the sights of the swamp, scanned the water at the island's edge for the source of the sound.

"What in the hell?" Sprig was pointing out over the swamp water past where the gator should have been. Bouncing through the swamp, coming quickly in their direction, were several pairs of glowing red orbs. The boys all froze as thirteen pairs of eyes moved toward them, bobbing up and down and dodging around reeds and logs.

Again, a deep bellow sounded from between the red glowing eyes and the frightened teenagers. As the eyes converged on the sound, a huge splash disturbed the calm water about twenty feet out from their fire ring of safety. All four teens stood staring with mouths open as a gator at least sixteen feet long caught several swamp rats with glowing eyes in its mighty jaws.

While the gator caught several, the rest of the rodents spread out too far for it to get them all. The glowing-eyed rats seemed to falter in their mission for a moment as several of their comrades perished in the gator's maw. Turning back toward the attacker, they screeched unholy screams and swarmed the much larger beast from multiple directions.

A swamp rat could get to be as big as a small dog, but these weren't normal swamp rats. Whatever evil magic gave them glowing red eyes also made them as big as coons and provided unnatural strength. Even so, the combined weight of the remaining rats was less than a tenth that of the huge gator. Their size, however, was augmented by sheer ferocity.

Nine small mouths full of magically enhanced, razor-sharp teeth bit through the tough hide of the monster gator. It shrieked like the devil himself had reached up from hell to clamp eternally damned claws through its skin. Thrashing around in the water, the gator flung rat after rat into the swamp. Occasionally it would clamp powerful jaws onto one of the red-eyed brethren, but they were too fast.

Carl Dean was the first to break his frozen stance and yelled at his friends. "Let's get the hell outta here!"

Nobody argued and all four teens ran for their motor bikes, campfire and treasure forgotten. Carl Dean's three-wheeler was the only one with a headlight, and it was just dark enough to make a mad scramble through the swamp trails dangerous even to the boys who knew it well. He led the group, with the three minibikes too close on his tail for comfort, yet none of them were making any moves to open up that distance.

The mad whirlwind of a trail race through the swamp seemed to take hours. All four bikes pulled up at Dupree's and cut their engines. Nobody said anything as the four boys watched the way they had come. After a few minutes, Harry let out a sigh and pulled the flute out from his pocket. Staring at it, he shook his head.

"Carl Dean, you reckon that thunder called them ghost swamp rats? That witch woman has surely put a spell on this flute."

Freddy was looking at the flute wide eyed, sweat standing out in beads against his dark skin.

"Harry, that there's one of them flutes like in the fairy tale. That Pie Piper feller."

"What are you gabbing about, Freddy? What's a pie pipe?"

"That fairy tale. That guy that played his flute and led all them rats outta town." He gestured back toward the swamp they had just vacated. "That was all them rats!"

Sprig stared at the instrument, nodding. "Yeah, the Pied Piper. And when the town wouldn't pay him like they said they would, he came back and played his flute to lead all the young'uns out of town. They was never, any of 'em, seen again."

Harry was still staring at the flute.

"Look," Carl Dean said to the group. "Let's all go over to my place and crash for the night. My mommas out on Uncle Turtles boat fishing all weekend. We'll figure out what to do tomorrow. When it's daylight, we can think more clear."

"Yeah, let's go find some cokes and build a fire in your backyard. That'll be almost like camping." Freddy swung a leg over his bike as he was talking.

The other boys mounted up and started their bikes. Sprig held his hand up to get their attention.

"I'm gonna go get us those cokes. I'll see y'all there in a hour or so."

"Hell, yeah!" Freddy exclaimed. "I need a coke after that."

Harry looked at Sprig for a minute, then nodded. "I'm gonna make a stop at the house and grab some snacks, I didn't get to eat my hot dog."

The other three laughed at Harry's sad tone.

He thought about the flute in his pocket and Carolyn Santee. Angling his bike north and west, he decided to swing by the new house on Restlin Drive and see if they had gotten moved in yet. He wouldn't stop, but he could buzz by just to check.

<u>6</u>

Saturday afternoon, the boys had all gone their separate ways for the weekend work. Teenage boys had chores and they had to complete in order to get to spend nights camping in the swamp. Or at a friend's house, like last night had played out. Harry finished helping his mom with household chores and moving some trash to the road for his uncle. His dad was in a mood, as he tended to be after a day off, so Harry went for a ride on his bike.

Just past the outskirts of the trailer park, he headed toward a row of small, two-story houses near the edge of the swamp. The rock and sand road contained enough ground up shale to keep most of the dust down. He idled along until he got out past the last house, then pulled off the road next to an old wood-sided shed and pushed his minibike around behind it.

Leaning the Honda against the board plank wall, he took a couple of deep breaths and pulled the flute from his back pocket. He wanted Carolyn to hear the music it played. He knew she would appreciate it, and well, he needed her to hear it before he took it back to the widow LePues place and put it back in that box.

Running his fingers over the surface of the dark wood, he marveled again at the smoothness. Harry didn't know a lot about woodworking or carving, but he was certain this was old from the look of the wood. The finger holes were worn, and the fluted end of the instrument showed small dents and dings from rough handling through the years.

It differed from the other carvings in the widow's shed. They had all seemed fresh, newly carved. This one was much older. As beautiful as it was, it was obviously well used.

He ran his hands across the flute and felt a shiver of anticipation as he looked at the small two-story house at the end of the row. He'd snuck in one night with the other boys a couple weeks earlier after the contractors had all gone home for the evening, so he had a good idea of the layout. Harry remembered the bedrooms were all upstairs, with the smaller ones in the back. That left a fifty-fifty chance at which one was Carolyn's, and which was her little brothers.

Palmetto bushes broke the small clearing up behind the house, before it gave way to the pines and cypresses of a small wash that led out to one of the tributary creeks dumping into the swamp. Harry walked quietly in the sandy, orange dirt between palmettos, nearly turning back to the hidden minibike several times. Eventually, he worked his courage up, moving until he made it to a spot directly behind the Santee home. The bush he stood near was in the middle of the windows, more or less, so he picked a spot off to the side an arm's length or so, with enough room to duck behind quickly if necessary.

The dark wooden flute seemed to find its own way up to Harry's lips, and as he breathed out the low melody began. He nearly stopped at the clear beauty of the music, but his eyes locked on the upstairs windows, and he kept on. His fingers moved deftly along the woodwind instrument as if he were a master and had played for decades. The notes sang clear, low, and sophisticated in a way he didn't even understand.

Movement from the left window caught his eye and he almost froze when he saw Carolyn push the curtains aside and lean her elbows on the open windowsill. Now he was committed, so he added purposeful breath to his efforts. The music changed slightly, quickening the tempo. Harry found his heel tapping to the tune and a feeling of lightness and joy spread throughout his body as a sense of urgency tightened his chest. Pushing through, he breathed deeply again and continued to play.

Carolyn kneeled with her eyes closed and elbows on the windowsill, soaking in the melody, so familiar yet totally strange to her. Her head swayed from side to side, taking her shoulders along for the gentle ride. This was something she had longed for, a tune she had dreamed of, forgetting the cadence the moment she awoke. She could hardly believe what she was hearing, what she was feeling.

Harry continued to play until he heard the slamming of the screen door at the front of the Santee's house. That sudden smack of wood on wood, propelled by a stout steel spring, pulled him out of the flute's trance. Jerking with the realization that the Santee's were about to catch him behind their house, Harry ducked behind the palmetto and pulled the flute to his chest.

As his butt hit the sand, a loud clap of thunder and the electrical smack of lightning striking a live oak out in the woods startled him to the point his flight reflex kicked in and he temporarily forgot about Carolyn Santee and her parents. Luckily, the thunder and lightning drew their attention from the backyard, and as they paused in their trek down the right side of the house, he sprinted through the palmettos across the left.

Carolyn had been staring out toward the lightning strike when movement caught her attention. The boy was too far away by then and ducking around the palmettos, but she swore the curly black hair looked like that Howard boy from school. The one that always hung around his friends, chewing tobacco and telling stories about the swamps and motorcycles. She smiled, thinking about that curly black hair, tan face, and upturned nose.

Harry chanced a quick glance toward the house as he ducked behind the abandoned shed. Not seeing anyone following him, he trotted as he pushed his minibike down the road and into the trees before starting it up and heading toward home. He felt the flute's weight in his pocket and grunted. He could have sworn he had dropped it when he took off running.

Unseen by anyone, thirteen large swamp rats with glowing red eyes splashed into the creek behind Carolyn Santee's house and skittered downstream toward the marshier areas of the swamp.

The flea market was winding down for the evening. As frail looking as she was, the widow LePue moved with a graceful ease. She wrapped each carving in its own soft rag and placed them in the small storage locker that came with her table rent. Sunday was usually the slower of the three weekend days selling her trinkets, but she used the time to catch up on the local gossip from the other townspeople, so she was looking forward to it.

They didn't talk to her directly, of course, but she listened in on the conversations and kept mental notes. She smiled as she thought of all of the useful information she had picked up on past weekends doing just that. Her real business, the work that brought her the most money and the most satisfaction, was from the individuals she approached after hearing one of the locals talk of some trouble someone was having. Needing a new job, wanting a new significant other, issues with a current boss or current significant other.

The clap of thunder was barely audible this far away, but there was no mistaking the source. She smiled again as she locked the storage locker and hung the key to the padlock around her thin neck. It was a child then, a teenager probably. They didn't learn as quickly from their mistakes as most adults did. Shuffling to the worn Volkswagen Thing that got her from place to place, she cranked the motor over and on the second attempt just under sixteen hundred cc's of German engineered technology sputtered to life.

7

"I know this flute is cursed, Carl Dean, I just know it. And now I've done gone and cursed Carolyn's family with it, too."

The two boys were already at work on the airboat again, expecting Freddy and Sprig to ride up any minute.

Harry kept twisting at the ratchet, loosening one of the metal supports holding the engine in place. "I just heard her brother took sick a couple days ago and they can't figure out what's ailing him. And her daddy got laid off from his work. I know it's all 'cause I played this flute out behind her place to show it off to her. I know it is."

Carl Dean sat backwards in the boat, holding the wrench tight against the support.

"I don't know Harry. That stuff happens, you know. My cousin got laid off a couple of weeks ago too, and he lives up in Pascagoula. I don't think it's because of you and that flute. 'Sides, that was all Friday, and you just played out there today."

Harry grunted as he continued to twist the rachet back and forth.

The other boy continued, "Now them rats. I do think they came from that flute. That thunderclap just when you quit playing, and them appearing in the swamp at that minute. Yeah, they came from it."

Harry stopped turning as the nut came off in the socket. "So, do you think they came from that thunder all three times? I mean, the thunder happened all three times."

Sprig spoke over his shoulder, "I bet they did."

Harry jumped, bumping his head on the same metal brace Carl Dean had lost scalp skin to.

"Dammit, Sprig. You'll give a guy a heart attack sneaking up like that." He said as he rubbed his head.

The other two boys laughed as David Lee Roth screamed about having a crush on his teacher. Harry slid the volume down and kept rubbing the knot forming on top of his head.

"Look boys, I screwed up when I took that flute and I gotta put it back. I'm sneaking back in there and putting it right back in that little box I took it from."

Carl Dean hopped down from the airboat and slapped him on the shoulder. "You'll need me to go with you and pick that lock again."

Head hanging, Harry nodded. "Thanks. I do need that, I'll never learn how to pick a lock, I just ain't got it in me."

Freddy stomped in as the boys each pulled Dr. Peppers from an old cooler Carl Dean's brother had left in his tool shed.

"What lock are we picking?"

Sprig gestured toward Harry with his Dr. Pepper can. "Harry's gonna sneak back in the widow LePue's place and put that flute back. He said it ain't been nothing but bad mojo since he 'borrowed' it last week."

"I'm in." he said as he popped the top on his own cold drink. "Y'all don't think we'll see no more of them rats, do you? They were some serious creatures attacking ole' Wally Gator like they done."

Sprig sipped from the cold brown can and said, "Something's been killing dogs around the swamp last couple of nights. I bet it was them rats. How many do y'all think are left after that gator ate his fill?"

Carl Dean rubbed his chin and looked toward the tree line. "Well, that's the thing. Harry played that flute three times and got three cracks of thunder. We was wondering if there weren't more of them than just from the time in the swamp."

Harry was nodding, a sad look on his round face. "I reckon there was a dozen out there in the swamp, so if they come from the thunder, there's got to be three times that now. What's that, Freddy? Thirty something?"

"Thirty-six if it's a dozen each time. Minus whatever Wally ate. That's a lot of damn demon rats, boys."

Harry threw his empty can on the ground as he stood up. "I've got to do something to get rid of them, I just don't know what. Do y'all reckon they'll go away once I put that flute back?"

Four pairs of teenage eyes traded looks with each other, all carrying worried expressions. Worried for their friend and worried for their neighbors. None of the four had an answer, but one of the boys left a little earlier than normal that evening, claiming to have to run a chore for his momma.

The other three figured Sprig was going to get her some beer, like was often the case. But he had another destination in mind as he buzzed off on the dusty minibike.

A small house with wood lap siding hanging loose in several places sat just far enough from downtown to be considered the wrong side of the tracks. Even though the nearest railroad was a half-mile closer to the gulf. Sprig killed the motor on his Honda and dropped the kickstand.

As he walked up the steps of the porch to the screen door, a thick dark-haired boy about his own age stood looking back through the screen at him.

"Sup, Sprig? What brings you over to town?"

"Hey, Billy. You got a minute? I could use your help."

Billy scrunched his eyebrows up and shrugged. "Sure. If you're asking a Spencer for help, it must be a powerful problem."

It was Sprig's turn to shrug. Billy pushed through the screen door, letting it slam shut behind him, and sat in the rocker next to the front porch window. Sprig sat on the swing and looked out into the growing darkness.

After a minute, he returned his gaze to Billy. "I don't know what all's true, but I heard about a fishing lure you mighta got off the Widow LePue."

Billy stopped rocking and leaned forward. "Look Sprig, that was over a year ago and I don't really know what to tell you. I really don't want to talk about it."

Sprig held up his hand shaking his head. "I don't care about the lure. I just want to know how you made it stop when you were done using it."

Billy looked at him for a long minute before he said anything. "You got into something bad, ain't you? Did you get one of them from her, too?"

"No. But a friend of mine may have got into something and I need to know how to help get him out of it."

"A friend, huh?"

"Yes, Billy. I'm trying to help a friend out." Sprig insisted, frustrated. "I need to know how you got rid of it."

Billy Spencer looked at Sprig Wilcamp and grunted.

Sprig said "Look, Billy. That whole feud was our grandaddy's fight. I ain't got nothing against you and your family, and I really need to know what to do. I heard you burned it, is that right?"

Billy nodded. "Yeah, that was their fight. I don't even know what it was all about."

A small smile crossed Sprig's face. "Probably some girl."

"Ha!" Billy laughed. "Probably right."

After a long pause, he continued. "Look, some woman showed up when I was out walking one night and told me I had to crush it and then burn it. I don't know who she was, but she wasn't the LePue woman. She seemed kinda nice in a scary sorta way. But that's what I did. I smashed it with daddy's big hammer then burned it in a campfire. And that was it. I ain't been fishing since."

Sprig felt a shiver up his spine as the other boy slumped back in the rocker.

"Thanks, Billy. I really appreciate it." He got up to leave and turned back as he stepped down off the porch. "We're getting together at Dupree's tomorrow evening if you want to come along. You still got your minibike?"

Sitting up straighter in the rocker, Billy smiled. "Seriously? The Out-to-Lunch Bunch?"

"Who?"

"Well," he laughed as he stood from the chair. "That's what Ms. Lewis calls y'all."

"Huh. We might start using that."

Sprig swung his leg over the Honda as he tried to tie the six-pack of RC Cola across the tank in front of him.

"I have a strap here if it would help you."

"Shit!" He looked around to see a tall dark-skinned woman in a colorful dress holding out the mentioned strap. "Uh, sorry about the language, ma'am. I didn't hear you come up."

"That's alright, child. I tend to surprise folks from time to time." She smiled as she held out the strap. He looked from it to the paper bag haphazardly tied to his gas tank with a piece of string.

"Ma'am, I don't know how I'd get it back to you."

"Don't you worry about that either, child. You have a task in front of you that will pay for this strap many times over, once you complete it."

Sprig accepted the strap with a nod of thanks and was just finishing securing the package when what she said registered.

"Um, what task do you mean, ma'am?"

"Destroying that evil little instrument your friend has in his possession, of course. But it needs to be done correctly, Stephan, in order to repair the damage that it has already caused." She paused and looked into his eyes. "I'm not sure how to ask this next question. Emotions are so strong in young men of your age. Is he seeing anyone? Does he have a girlfriend?"

He shrugged as he tugged on the strap to make sure it would hold. "He does like a girl at school, but she ain't ever paid him no mind."

She nodded thoughtfully. "How many times have you heard the flute play?"

"Just the once. Carl Dean and him talked about him playing it when they broke into…" Sprig stopped suddenly, worried he had said too much.

She smiled warmly at him. "Don't worry about how he came into possession of the flute, Stephen. It didn't belong to the one who had it, either."

Sprig liked this woman. She had a comforting way about her.

"Well, when they got it, Harry played it. Carl Dean said there was some magic thunder. Then when he played it in the swamp, we all heard it. Then he said he played it for that Santee girl, outside her house the other night. Far as I know, it was just them three times."

Sprig looked at the woman closer in the dim light of the marina's lamp post. She was taller than most women, but fit. Her face was round and her smile motherly, to the point of making him trust her almost automatically.

"Other than the thunder, have you seen anything else strange?"

"Are you talking about them rats, ma'am?"

She smiled sadly and moved a step closer. "In part. You won't understand, but that instrument, in different guises, has been around for a very long time. It has caused much heartbreak and much damage. People who knew of it, thought it lost to time. Then it turned up in your friend's hands and he has no idea what he's in possession of. It's past time it was permanently retired."

He looked into her warm brown eyes and nodded. "I think he has an idea. And, I was just discussing with a friend of mine how to destroy it. He advised that we smash it, then burn it to ash. I was going to meet with my friends this evening and do what he suggested."

The strange woman stepped closer, placing a long slender hand on the handlebar of his bike. "There is something very important you and your friends must do before you damage the flute. It is the same in many ways as William's fishing lure, but it is much. much older and more dangerous. It must be handled carefully when it's destroyed. And the creatures it called here must be destroyed before the flute is."

Sprig was paying sharp attention to this woman he had never met, as if she spoke the gospel right from the book. "Who are you, ma'am? And how do you know all of this?"

"You may call me Marie, child. And it is my business to know."

"Marie? Like that New Orleans witch back in the eighteen hundreds?"

"Well, 'witch' is such an unfriendly term. Although she has been called many things, during her time and since. Many of them... unfriendly. But yes, just like her. Now, you must follow these directions exactly, child. Can you do that?"

Sprig nodded without hesitation as she carefully detailed the directions for him.

<u>8</u>

Rachel Santee cradled her son in her arms and tried to comfort him from the coughs.

"Mrs. Santee?"

She looked up at her name and smiled tiredly at the nurse.

"Yes?" She asked hopefully.

"I'm sorry, but we don't have any new news as of yet. The tests are ordered, and we should have results in a couple of days. We had to send off to Pensacola for them. We just don't have the labs they do, but they'll let us know as soon as they have results."

Rachel had hoped for answers, but she had expected this. Dr. Ryan had said as much when he checked Charlie earlier, but she had been hopeful.

"Thank you. You have our phone number? The new one?" The new house wasn't even settled into yet, with boxes from the moving company piled up in every room. But they had a phone the first day they were there. That was how Lou had gotten his call.

"Yes, ma'am. You get this little fella home and keep him comfortable. We'll call as soon as we hear anything, I promise."

Rachel stood with a helping hand from the nurse, and lifted Charlie to her shoulder. She stiffened her back as she accepted her bag and Charlie's blanket with a nod and a sad smile of gratitude.

As she stood from settling Charlie into the back seat of the station wagon, she turned to find a woman she didn't know standing near the front of her car. The fog from the lack of sleep lifted slightly from the adrenaline as she closed the rear door and faced the stranger.

She was tall, a couple inches taller even than Rachel, but where Rachel was a little thick, by her own admission, this woman was slender. The flower print dress was several years out of date but made well and was still available if a woman knew where to look. She wore it well, Rachel had to admit. The motherly smile and kind eyes made one feel right at home in this woman's presence.

"Ms. Santee, can you spare me a few moments of your time? I promise to keep it short, but it is important that we speak."

Rachel was about to decline, telling this stranger she had to take care of her sick son, but something about the motherly woman in the flower print dress made her pause. Glancing at her son, she saw he had settled in across the back seat with the blanket pulled up over his shoulders.

"What can I help you with, ma'am?" Rachel asked as she stepped forward and leaned against the hood of the station wagon.

"It's more about what I can help you with, really. I fear you've fallen into a situation that requires a little work on both of our parts to rectify. I know your son is ailing, and I also believe I can help with what is ailing him. But I need your help as well."

Straightening from the hood, she looked into the dark eyes with hope creeping into her heart. Then the Widow LePue's narrow face and black toothed smile crept into her mind, giving her second thoughts.

"What kind of help are you talking about, ma'am? I've had a mess of trouble since the last time I accepted someone's help."

"I see." Compassion shown in the tall woman's face. "Would you care to tell me about it?"

As Rachel hopped up onto the hood and dangled her legs from the side, she glanced over her shoulder at Charlie, sleeping in the back seat. She felt a comfort from this woman she hadn't felt from LePue.

She admitted that she had wanted what the widow offered so much that she had probably overlooked any red flags that may have been waving in her face. This woman emitted a different feeling altogether, however. Rachel looked into friendly, dark eyes and told her story.

"So that's all we gotta do, fellers. And once we do that, we come back here, smash that flute and burn it to ash."

The three other boys were nodding slowly and looking around at each other. Freddy stood up and spat a stream of Beech-Nut into the fire.

"Only problem I see is where we gonna get a boat? I mean, pops got a john boat, but we need something that'll float us all four in the gulf. That john boat ain't it, and that airboat ain't going nowhere soon."

"Yeah, ain't none of us got any kind of boat that big."

Sprig was grinning as he heard the buzzing off down the main trailer park road. "Here comes your answer right now."

He pulled two fingers of Levi Garrett out of the brown aluminum foil bag and stuffed it in his cheek. He had just worked up enough spit to make a stream when Billy Spencer buzzed around the front of the trailer on his Honda.

Carl Dean was smiling, Freddy and Harry stared with their mouths open.

"Well, I guess that feuds over." Harry said with a smile, looking at Sprig.

Sprig shrugged. "I figured we needed somebody that had some experience with this sort a thing. Y'all know the story. So, I went to the only one I knew of."

Freddy nodded at Billy. "Good to see you again, Billy. Did you give him all them directions on what to do?"

Billy looked at Sprig and shrugged. Sprig said, "It was a woman at the marina. She sure knew about it and how to get rid of it."

"From the way he described her, she was the same woman who told me what to do with that fishing lure. Tall woman with a kind way about her. Even wearing a bright colored dress like the one who spoke to me." Billy looked around the group and shrugged again.

"So, Billy can get his old man's boat keys. We can use that to get out in the bay far enough."

"That'll be up to y'all." Billy spoke again. "I don't go out there no more, but I can ride around the shore and make sure we get all them red-eye's out there."

Freddy spat in the fire and listened to the sizzle for a moment. "I reckon I'm in."

Harry stepped up next to him. "Since I took it and played it in the first place, I gotta be in. I should have left that damned thing in the damned box."

Carl Dean slapped his friend on the shoulder. "You was just thinking about impressing that girl."

All five boys laughed as Sprig stepped up to the fire. "All right! Let's hear it for the Out-To-Lunch Bunch!"

"So, here we are. My boy's sick with something no one can figure out. My husband lost his job. And that young couple lost their lives. But. I got a new house." The frustration was clear in her voice, buried among the dread, guilt, and fear.

She found she had closed her eyes and had a hard time opening them, knowing the tall, motherly woman would be staring at her with judgement in her own eyes. Or worse, pity.

But as she parted her lids and the midday sun shone in, she saw something she hadn't expected. Deep brown eyes, like milk chocolate, investigating her own. Eyes filled with compassion and empathy.

"This isn't your doing, child. You had the desire for improving your family's lives, but others took advantage of that desire and took advantage of your lack of knowledge. Took advantage of your situation. Took advantage of you. Yours are not the first dreams to be exploited for another's evil aspirations."

The tall woman stepped around to the passenger side of Rachel's station wagon and glanced through the open window at the boy asleep in the back seat. Bowing her head slightly, she began to hum and extended an arm, palm open and fingers wide.

Rachel slid from the hood and watched warily through the driver's window, but the stranger remained totally outside of the Datsun. Charlie's face, pinched in pain and discomfort, eased. Lying on his side in a near fetal position, she could see his entire body relax. After a couple of minutes, the tenseness between her own shoulder blades seemed to slacken as well,.

She noticed the woman's humming had stopped and looked up to see her back on the sidewalk in front of the Datsun.

"What did you do with the gris gris, child?"

Rachel's confused frown caused the other woman to smile gently.

"The talisman, the carving."

"Oh, the little house. It's on the mantle above our fireplace. Right where the widow told me to place it." She wondered how this woman had known of the carving, but the lady continued before Rachel could ask.

"The widow, you say? Mrs. LePue, then." It was a statement as plain as saying the day was hot. The tall woman paused for a few minutes in thought. Rachel, waiting, became restless and checked on Charlie again. She swore his temperature was down from just a few minutes earlier, even in the midday heat.

As she gently closed the back door, the stranger stepped from the sidewalk and gently grasped Rachel's arm with a surprising strength.

"I can help you and yours, but you must be willing, child." Her eyes were clear and bright as she peered into Rachels. "If you want my help, I'll need a gift. It needn't be anything of any worth. Actually, that little carving of your new home will work just fine."

Rachel shuddered as she stared back into the motherly gaze. She felt as if this woman could see into her soul, but she also felt a trust in her, an honesty that she had never felt in the presence of the widow LePue.

"If you can help my son, we will survive the rest. I need him to be better or nothing I've done would ever be worth the cost."

The long fingers squeezed her arm gently, reassuringly. "You have a good heart, Rachel Catherine de Fontaine-Santee. Yours is a strong yet loving spirit. The very kind vodou was intended to help."

The tall woman stepped back, releasing Rachel's arm. "Now, get your son home and put him in a tepid bath. There are some flowers growing near the edge of the wood line behind your home. They are baby blue and pale yellow. I want you to pluck seven of the largest leaves, one from seven different plants. It may take some searching, but they must be different plants. Bake them in your oven for about a half hour on low heat. The edges will just begin to crisp. Then grind them with a half teaspoon of white distilled vinegar until they form a paste. Are you with me?"

"Yes, ma'am." Rachel said quickly, remembering admiring the flowers this woman spoke of.

"Good. Now let the paste sit for a time and come to room temperature. Don't fret, it will work it's best after it sautés a bit." That smile. "After a bit, just rub a small amount on the soles of Charles' feet, then replace his socks. Let him sleep for as long as he will. Your bedroom may have a smell of vinegar for the night, but you should start to see improvement by the morning."

Rachel nodded, eyes never straying from the woman's gaze.

"Now go, child. I have some work of my own to manage and a few more visits. It's very important that we get all of this taken care of before the weekend's over."

"What should I do with the carving? Do you need me to bring it to you somewhere?"

"You can just leave it outside your back door when you collect those leaves. There's no need for me to alarm any of your family and you'll want to be by the little one's side."

Charlie coughed as if on cue and Rachel said as she turned her head to check on him. "Of course. I don't know how to thank you…"

She trailed off as she looked back to the strange motherly woman, only to find that she disappeared, almost as if she was never there. Rachel walked all the way around the small station wagon, mouth open, eyes wide.

As she shook her head and settled into the well-worn vinyl of the driver's seat, she breathed in a hint of jasmine in the air, mixed with cloves and vanilla.

2

Four boys left the marina in a fifteen-year-old center-console Sea Craft as the sun sank in the west. Billy waved from the dock and ran off toward the parking lot where he'd left his minibike. He knew he needed to be out at Fort Point by the time they started their music. Slinging his grandfather's heavy Navy binoculars across his back on the thick leather strap, he gunned the Honda, getting all he could out of the seventy cc's available to him.

Harry watched the minibike headlight bounce along Harbor Road and crossed his fingers. They didn't know how many rats were out there, but the best guess was about thirty. Freddy figured they had seen between ten and fifteen in the swamp, but that monster gator had eaten at least five. If they were released from wherever they came from when the flute played, or stopped playing if that strange lady was right, there would be several more from earlier at the widow's shack and out behind Carolyn's. He hadn't played it but those three times, so they hoped that was all.

"Alright guys, we got this. Y'all got your weapons?"

Carl Dean held up a long-handled shovel, Freddy raised a baseball bat and smiled wide. Sprig had a tater fork from his momma's garden, missing one spine.

Harry held his own shovel in one hand, and the flute in the other. He pointed the flute toward the bridge where highway ninety crossed the Biloxi Bay inlet. "I think we can get in that open water between Fort Point and Big Island. Rats can't swim far, so that'll be the best place, I reckon."

"Let's do this!" Freddy yelled and gunned the outboard, dropping everyone back in their seats.

Monday evening had fallen calmly on Restlin Drive but Rachel Santee was restless. The little carving that looked like her new house had disappeared seemingly between breaths, earlier in the day. A small note lay in its place, held down by a small, beautifully tooled leather bag on a thick piece of string. The note, written in flourishing script, read:

Thank you for your trust, child.
Place this charm about your neck and tuck it beneath your shirt, against your skin. It will bring you comfort and clarity when most needed and offer some protection.
Find a reason to leave your house this evening and spend the night elsewhere. Your home should be fine, it is but a measure of safety.
By tomorrow, all should be well, and your life will improve soon.
Marie

Rachel hugged Charlie close as she placed him in the backseat of the Datsun station wagon. He'd improved immensely over the last twelve hours, but still had a mild fever and was weaker than normal. He'd shown some interest in the cartoons on the television this afternoon, but fell asleep on the sofa before the half-hour show was over.

"Where are we going, momma?" Carolyn asked as she settled into the passenger seat.

"We're going down to Granny Fontaine's." She had dropped the 'de' years before she was married, but remembered the motherly woman using it when addressing her earlier. She had used Rachel's middle name as well, now that she thought about it. Remembering the conversation clearly, she thought she should have been nervous or wary, at least, but the other woman's demeanor had put her totally at ease.

"On a Monday night? Well, I guess it is summer, but I wanted to spend the night in the new house again. Don't you like the way it smells? New house smell everywhere."

Rachel smiled at her daughter. "You can tell her and Pap all about the new house, Sweety. I'm sure they'd love to hear about it."

Her mom sounded concerned when she mentioned an overnight stay. She hadn't told anyone but Lou that she planned to stay for a couple of nights at least. Her schedule was clear until Thursday evening at the salon, thanks to Shelly Howard taking her clients for Tuesday. So she told him she wanted to visit her folks, and didn't like the idea of staying in the new house all alone with the kids. And with Charlie sick, well, she could use the help.

Lou had gone up to Hattiesburg the night before to interview with the union. That call had come on Sunday afternoon, and he hadn't even thought to ask how they had his new number. She suspected she knew.

As Carolyne plopped into the passenger seat, Rachel mashed the clutch pedal to the floor and pumped the gas as she turned the key. The little engine growled to life, and she accelerated up Restlin Drive into the setting sun toward highway ninety and Bay St Louis.

The little car sputtered and coughed a small cloud of white smoke as it moved west down the road. Marie watched with a small smile, clutching a leather bag with some tools of the trade. She felt her own gris gris against her skin beneath the flower print dress and closed her eyes for a moment.

One of her daughter's daughters had married into the de Fontaine family a few generations earlier. Rachel, and her own daughter Carolyn, were offspring from that union. She would have aided them whether Rachel had agreed to help her do so or not, but this made it, at least somewhat, easier.

Walking carefully around the home, she began to hum. It was just a building, a construct, not alive. Yet it carried a wicked energy she knew would cause more and more grief if left unattended to. That wouldn't do at all. Not for family.

She smiled again as she felt the wickedness begin to fade. She channeled it into a small compartment in her soul and prayed for help from the saint who many would be celebrating this very evening, asking him to aid her though his relationship with the virgin borned.

She would have a use for the energy soon, she suspected.

Fifteen minutes after leaving Billy on the dock, the boys were drifting with the current straight out in the bay from Saint Martin Bayou. Harry looked at the still faces of his friends and lifted the flute to his mouth.

"Hold up, Harry. You reckon Billy's got over there yet?"

Four sets of eyes turned to the point of land reaching out into the bay from Ocean Springs. All four chuckled as the minibike light bounced along the rough terrain of the point to stop at the edge of the water and flash three times.

"There he is. I knew he'd make it!" Sprig claimed.

Carl Dean and Freddy looked at each other and rolled their eyes.

Harry looked around at the crew again and nodded. "Ready, boys?"

Three heads nodded, and Harry placed the flute against his mouth and blew gently.

Mellow notes floated out across the water, almost visible in the moon lit darkness. That single wooden flute sounded like a symphony or maybe an angel's harp. Echoes played off the water of the bay sounding like an orchestra house.

Harry continued to blow softly into the flute as his friends kept a watch out across the water toward D'Iberville. After a couple of long minutes, they saw Billy's flashlight blinking quickly.

Then Carl Dean called out, "Here they come!"

All three boys moved to the side of the boat and readied their makeshift weapons as Harry kept playing. Within moments, they saw pairs of red eyes bobbing in the water, getting ever closer to the boat.

Harry continued to play, looking occasionally for a sign from Billy out on the point. Shortly, the sign came, but it wasn't the one he had hoped for. Stomping on the deck of the boat, he got Sprig's attention and gestured toward the point with his chin.

"Shit! Here come the ones from the swamp, too."

The other two boys looked where he was pointing his shovel. Shifting focus from one set of red eyes bobbing in the water, to the other, they paced, rocking the boat.

The eyes had just left the shore when Freddy called out and pointed toward a spot in the middle of the two groups of rats. Scurrying down the bank were several pairs of red eyes. "And here are the ones from Carolyn's house!"

The rats were drawn to the instrument that spawned them, just as it had been created to do a very long time before. Unfortunately for them, even with the strength and size they had been granted supernaturally, the length of time they could exist in water was still limited. Pair by pair, glowing red eyes disappeared beneath the smooth dark water of Biloxi Bay.

After several long moments, Billy's light flashed the all-clear signal and Harry stopped playing. Laying the flute down on the captain's seat, he retrieved the shovel he had brought along for this step of the plan.

"Alright fellers, this is the part where we earn our money."

Lightning flashed and thunder cracked over the water less than fifty feet from the boat, temporarily blinding the boys and sending stray electricity sizzling through their clothes and hair. As their sight quickly returned, thirteen pairs of red eyes bobbed in the water moving rapidly toward the boat.

Harry jumped into the pilot's seat and turned the key. The motor spun and spun, but didn't catch, and the smell of gasoline and oil wafted up from the outboard.

"Dammit! It's flooded!

"Choke it!" Sprig yelled from the front of the boat.

"I tried that, it ain't working!"

Freddy yelled out, "Here they come, boys!"

As the rats moved closer to the boat, Carl Dean and Harry struck first with their long shovels, knocking the first few on the head as hard as they could swing without falling in the water. As hard and as fast as they swung the shovels, it wasn't enough for the otherworldly creatures. By that time, the rats were getting desperate, and the boat was their only hope, so they were upping their efforts.

Anything that reached into the water near a rat became the possible salvation and immediate target of long, sharp claws. They grasped at fork prongs and shovel heads, three of them simultaneously grabbing Harry's shovel and ripping it from his hands. Carl Dean stepped up and knocked two of them away as Freddy smashed the third against the hull of the boat with his Louisville Slugger. Sprig's tater fork stabbed into another that squealed an unholy scream as it was ripped off the fork and into the water with the help of Carl Dean's momma's shovel.

As suddenly as the rats had attacked, they were gone. The boys spent several minutes searching around the sides of the boat to make sure there were no hangers-on. Once they were convinced all the rats had sunk into the bay, Harry hit the start button again and the outboard purred to life like the day it was uncrated from the factory. He grunted and flashed the navigation lights on and off three times and waited for Billy's reply. Once he saw the flashlight on the point, he sank down into the floor by the captain's seat and leaned his head back.

Freddy, Sprig, and Carl Dean joined him on the floor of the boat, somber to the last teen. They sat for at least five minutes, not looking at each other or saying a word.

Finally, Sprig spoke up. "I hate to say it, but we ain't done yet, dudes. We got us a flute to smash and burn."

Carl Dean looked up and nodded with determination. "Let's do it boys. Billy's gonna meet us back at Dewey's Island as soon as we can get there."

Harry stood and looked around the boat before gazing out into the dark water. "I think I lost momma's shovel."

The others all laughed and patted him on the back as they scrambled past him to take their seats. If the laughter was slightly hysterical, no one noticed, or at least, no one said anything.

Sprig checked the nav lights and gunned the outboard as he pointed the boat back toward Harbor Road.

Five teenage boys stood around a small but roaring fire on a tiny island in the southern Mississippi swamp outside of Ocean Springs. Harry placed the flute on a flat stone they had borrowed from the ring of rocks around the fire. Hefting a larger rock to measure the weight, he looked around the circle of friends. Each one nodded as their eyes met.

He nodded himself, and lifted the stone over his head.

"Well, here goes nothing, fellers."

Thrusting down with all his strength, he let go just before the rock landed. The wood of the flute was old and strong, but it was no match for two stones meeting at such a speed and with such force. The wood splintered and split into several smaller pieces, scattering about the flat stone in the sand.

Five pairs of eyes looked expectantly at the pieces for several moments.

"Well." Freddy drawled

"Yeah, I kinda expected more." Carl Dean said, looking around at the others.

Billy shrugged and knelt to start gathering pieces.

"Let's get all of these in the fire and go have some Mountain Dew."

As all four of the others jumped to help, Sprig said, "Now that sounds like a plan."

To which Harry replied, "I love it when a plan comes together."

The sparks and coals of the campfire were nearly gone. The boys had been for some time. The night was nearing the time it turned into morning when the slight, scarecrow of a woman silently stepped from the trees. She walked slowly up to the fading coals, looking closely around where the flat stone lay apart from the rest of the fire ring. A tight smile stretched across blackened teeth and her thin face as she knelt to retrieve a small splinter of ancient wood.

From behind her, near a thicker portion of swamp vegetation, a soft voice spoke. "You've been busy, Child."

The frail Widow LePue straightened quickly to her feet. "Who…Marie?"

The pleasant smile was noticeably colder as she gazed down at the thin woman.

"Indeed." Her mentor replied. "Did you not expect to be held accountable for your doings? You know voodoo was never meant to do harm, and yet you have done so much."

Desperation was thick in the smaller woman's voice. "I…I can atone, madam. I will if you but give me the chance."

"You've had countless chances, child. You could've stopped any of it, at any time, had you but chosen to. Your opportunities for atonement were many, yet you ignored them. Ignored them and continued to cause others pain, and even death. Yet, now, you ask for another? On this night? The Eve of Saint John? You have misbehaved, child."

As the words ended, the motherly woman in the flower print dress began to hum. As she hummed, she moved her hands in a quick and seemingly random pattern. Random yet precise motion, planned and learned through many, many decades of use.

Marissa LePue gasped an intake of breath as a sharp clap of thunder sounded in the nearby darkness of the swamp. The lightning flash was blinding, but darkness quickly regained its grip of the night.

Marie smiled sadly as the thin sliver of ancient wood floated gracefully to the ground, landing on the dimming coals. A slight breeze brightened the coals just enough to start the flame and allow nature's destroyer and cleanser to do what fire does. The motherly woman in the flower print dress silently turned from the now empty clearing and walked into the swamp as if she were part of it.

"No, child. You have been given your chances. Now, just as all who strive to gain personally from the gift they were given to help others, you must pay the piper."

Space Chicken BBQ

By: Sarah Arnette

<u>1</u>

Teresa was on her butt, looking up at the big chestnut mare who had dumped her, once again. Her horse, Runner, liked to dump people and then stare down at them like they were the idiot who decided to jump in the mud rather than the human she just tossed down there. She was fully capable of keeping a rider on her back when she felt like it and was especially good at keeping children up there, but put an experienced rider on her, and it was game over. Someone was going for a tumble, and it wasn't her.

That didn't stop Runner from being Teresa's favorite. When she felt like being a good horse, her canter was smooth as glass. If she thought there was a potential for danger, she would do anything to keep her rider safe. She was a great mamma to her babies and an experienced training horse for newbie riders. She was also great at knocking down egos if she thought her rider was too uppity.

Teresa picked herself out of the mud with a groan. She wasn't hurt, but that was beside the point. She just got tossed off the big mare for the third time this morning. Teresa had no idea what she was doing wrong to irritate the mare, but she was certain it was something. Dusting her hands off, she reached over to the horse to grab the reins and get back up onto Runner's back when a flash of light in the sky caught her attention.

"What in tarnation is that?" Teresa asked Runner, as if the horse could possibly answer her. In answer, Runner shook her mane, catching Teresa square in the face. She swore the horse was laughing at her. "Just for that, we're going to go check that out," Teresa grumbled. Straightening her John Deere hat, she danced on one leg before she was able to catch the stirrup and after a couple of warm-up bounces, she managed to hoist herself into the saddle.

She turned the horse around so that they were in the direction of whatever that flash of light was. Teresa took a good look around her, pressing her heels to Runner's side They began heading towards what could possibly be an adventure.

"Depending on what that was and where it went, it looked like it was heading towards the McDonald farm," Teresa told Runner. She was really just talking to keep herself calm, but everyone who ever rode Runner knew that talking to her was a good idea. It helped to keep them on her back and not eating dirt.

"Maybe it was some sort of weather balloon. I heard that there is a hefty reward if you find one of them things. That reward could come in handy in getting you some grain and alfalfa. It might even be enough to get you some new tack or a new pair of cowboy boots for me." Teresa kept going on in that frame as they rode along the trail heading towards the McDonald farm. It wasn't a difficult trail, although it hadn't been used as much now that the McDonald boy, Tyler, and the Dickson girl, Rosey, got married and moved away, leaving old Ethal and Benny to tend that old trailer of theirs. They used to use this trail all the time for their secret rendezvous before it became official that they were together.

The weird thing that Teresa saw was not in the McDonald field, but rather one field over, the commercial cow farm. There was a lot of open land in that field, with nothing but corn stalks for almost as far as she could see. She knew there were cows there, too, but they were in the barn all the time. It didn't seem normal to keep cows in the barn all the time, but she's been to the farm. If the cows wanted out, they could get out. Instead, the only thing outside of the barn was corn, normally.

Now, there was a real, live flying saucer sitting in the middle of the field. "Holy Crap, Runner, we're going to see aliens make real live crop circles!" Teresa always thought that the idea of little green men from Mars making crop circles was a load of bullpucky. She's seen her brother make crop circles in harvested fields with nothing more than a couple of boards and ropes.

She smiled, remembering the way that the old folks in the trailer park were convinced that the circles were some type of communication from aliens, showing the best place to land their UFOs and kidnap people for anal probing. Old Crazy Silas walked around with a butt plug for weeks, saying that no alien was going to be probing him, he was protecting himself.

She pulled out her cell phone to take a video of what she was seeing. There was no way that anyone was going to believe her, that she saw real live aliens making crop circles. Her Nokia flip phone had horrible graphics, but it was hard not to recognize the pie-tin shape of an alien craft, no matter how horrible the graphics.

Just as she was considering getting closer, a panel in the ship opened. A ramp slid down, looking like nothing more than a bad CGI animation. In a cloud of steamy air, the very first alien stepped onto the ramp. Once the air was clear, she was able to see him in all of his feathered glory.

"Holy Clucking, he's a chicken!" Teresa was in shock. Of all the things she expected to see, a giant white chicken dressed in a silver space suit was not one of them. He didn't have a helmet on, making his comb and wattles extremely visible, even from across the field. He stood exceptionally tall, taller than a man. His yellow-scaled legs were bare, showing off large fighting spurs tipped in some type of chrome-like material. His eyes, besides his sheer size, were what set him apart from a regular chicken. Chickens have small, beady eyes. This alien had huge, round, and protruding eyes.

When he crowed upon touching Earth's soil, she knew they were all in trouble.

Runner was not named for her ability to race or gallop for long periods. She was named because if her rider wasn't careful and there was something more interesting to do, she'd dump them and run off to have fun or get something to eat. She knew where her barn was, and knew where safety could be had. She knew that a giant-sized chicken would be nothing but trouble and there was no stopping her on her way home.

Runner was lathered, and both of them were panting by the time they made it back to the Pleasant Mountains Trailer Park. The whole thing was a big circle with trailers on the outside of the big road that circled the inside of the park. Each of the trailers had a large yard and most of them had a garage sitting just behind the trailer. The inside of the road was a field where the kids would play and the adults would drink together. It was one big, happy, redneck community. There was not a mountain in sight.

Runner didn't stop when they got to the trailer park. Instead, she ran, without any guidance from Teresa, right to her barn. It was a garage, but her Papi made it into a barn for her when all she said was that she wanted a horse every time she was asked about birthdays, Christmas, or any other type of presents. It was an expensive present, but Ronnie, also known as Papi by just about everyone, could deny his princess nothing.

When Runner finally skidded to a stop, Teresa did something she never considered before. She abandoned her horse, still tacked and sweating, to run to her Papi. Clutching her Nokia as tight as she could, she ran to the trailer, hoping he didn't pick today to go to the store. No one would believe her like her Papi would, even though she had video evidence of giant alien chickens.

Teresa bound up the old wooden steps leading to the trailer. She never used the bottom step if she could help it. It was just a little jinky, wobbling at the most opportune times. The last thing she wanted to do was to trip on the stairs and get hurt. She needed to talk to her dad and then see to Runner. Papi would know what to do about the giant chickens.

The front door of the trailer was wide open, leaving nothing but the screen door between the occupants and the biting flies of the outside. Waving them away quickly, she opened the door as little as possible and then slipped inside the darkened interior. "Papi! Come quick, something bad's happening at the cow farm!" she called out before allowing her eyes to adjust to the sudden darkness. She didn't know her Papi was sitting right next to the door, cleaning his rifles for the upcoming hunting season. She practically screamed in his ear.

Papi is a big man. He was a Marine back in his younger days. That's when he met Teresa's mom, God rest her soul. His hair might have fled with time and his ponch might have grown a bit, but he was still as solid as they came. He was a hard worker, and that made him a hard man for everyone but Teresa.

Every time he saw his daughter, he was struck again by how perfect and beautiful she was. She looked just like his Ellie did all those years ago, back before the cancer ate away at her. It darkens his heart that Teresa never really got to know her mama. He was certain that they'd have gotten along like peas in a pod. Either that or hair would be flying daily. Moments like this when she was standing in the light, her red hair shining, it almost brought tears to his eyes.

"What you be hollering about?" Just because his heart was bursting with love for her didn't mean he was thrilled to have her screaming in his ears.

He was hoping that he had left that time behind him, along with the diapers. He really should have known better.

"Giant alien chickens landed a spaceship at the cow farm. They don't look friendly," Teresa turned and looked down at her dad. He was the best dad a girl like her could have ever hoped for. He would believe her. Even with that, though, "I have proof." Teresa thrust her hand out, showing him her phone.

Papi took a good look at his daughter. If she were any other kid, he'd worry about what drugs she managed to get into. His little Teresa didn't mess with that stuff. She didn't even like it when he drank in the circle with his buddies, although she never came out and said it. Keeping eye contact with her, he reached up and took the offered phone. "Alien chickens, you say."

Papi liked to pretend that he was technologically illiterate with Teresa. He'd often pretend he didn't know how to turn on a cellphone or open a file on his computer. She'd make a big show of helping him and explaining how it worked. She always forgot that he was the one who showed her how to do it all those years ago. This time, he just opened the latest video and played it without her help. She sounded serious, and it was his duty to take those concerns seriously, no matter how weird they sounded.

Papi started out leaning back against the couch when he first hit play. He was fully expecting to see some props for some type of game the boys were playing on the commercial farmers. The local boys don't like them as a rule, even though they're not competition for what their parents do and the farm often employs people from the park in the fall to help with harvest. As he watched the video he started to pay more attention. By the time he played it for a third time straight, he was leaning forward, elbows on his knees, and a deadly serious expression on his face.

"You take care of Runner. You don't want her catching a cold." Papi stood up from the couch, pocketing Teresa's phone as he went. "I'll go grab Billy and we'll take a truck out that way. It certainly looks like we have an alien invasion, but for all we know, they might be just lost travelers or actors in some Hollywood movie." He didn't wait for her to acknowledge what he said before he picked up the rifle he had been working on, assembled it, and strode out the door. She was hot on his heels, racing off to the barn. A cold for her mare would be a serious headache for her. The last time Runner was sick, she was a very demanding patient.

2

Billy was Papi's old Marine buddy. Billy moved out to Pleasant Mountains shortly after Papi and Ellie did, and just in time for Teresa to be born. He was instrumental in keeping Papi sane and helping out with the baby while Ellie underwent her cancer treatments. For that, Billy treated Teresa like the niece he never would have, being an only child and single to boot.

"Are you sure that Teresa saw an alien ship? I mean, I shouldn't be surprised there are aliens, but why land in the middle of nowhere instead of, you know, the capital? Or New York, LA, somewhere with people." Billy had watched the video, but he was more skeptical than Papi.

"Your guess is as good as mine. It leads me to think that they're up to no good and don't want to be noticed. If they were on the up and up, they'd land where the population leaders are. If they're smart enough to cross space, then they have to be smart enough to figure out that cows aren't going to be the governing body on Earth." Papi had been wrestling with the same question. Landing in a cornfield, in an area where the largest city is two hours away and could barely be considered a city, doesn't sound like a bright move. It screamed deception.

Billy drove his truck down the only asphalt road towards the cow farm. "If there are aliens, I don't think approaching the farm straight on is the best route," he said as they were getting closer to the farm. The route Teresa took with Runner was as the crow flew and was considerably shorter than the roundabout route that the truck was forced to take.

"There is a road that runs parallel to the farm's property line over by the McDonald trailer. Teresa said it was in the field and we can get a good look at the field from that road," Papi suggested. He was pretty sure that Billy knew about that road, but if not, he thought it was a better idea than riding straight up onto the farm, too. Besides not having to deal with the people at the farm, it also had the advantage of some cover in case there really were aliens. Some trees, set up to be a wind block a few years back, lined the road on that side.

Billy nodded his agreement about the boarding road being a better idea. He knew about the road and he was in the process of turning onto it even before Papi pointed it out. It was a stony dirt road, so he had to slow his speed considerably once he was off the asphalt. Not only was the road too slick due to the loose dirt to drive quickly on, but if he went too fast, the dust trail would be far more obvious than it was when he was going slowly. They waved as they passed the McDonald trailer with Benny and Ethal sitting on rocking chairs out front. If nothing was going on at the farm, maybe they'd stop by for some of their famous hard cider.

They saw the alien ship well before they reached the back fields. It was much bigger than it looked in the video that Teresa had taken. It was at least the size of the barn, if not bigger. It was certainly taller than the barn. The ship looked like nothing so much as two aluminum pie pans stacked opening to opening. The only thing it was missing from the traditional alien ship were two antennas standing off the top of it. Instead, the top of the ship was more of a domed shape in contrast to the very flat bottom of the ship.

Billy gave a low whistle as the two men sat in the cab of the truck. "Well, that's an alien ship if I've ever seen one."

"Have you ever seen an alien ship before?" Papi asked.

"Not that I can say, but seriously, if this isn't an alien ship, then I'll eat my hat."

Papi refrained from mentioning that Billy wasn't wearing a hat.

They sat there for a while before they finally saw their first alien. Just as Teresa said, it was a giant chicken. If the alien chicken was anything like the Earth ones, this was a male. He had a large comb over his beak and large waddles hanging from his face. He bobbed his head back and forth as he walked. His large feet were unshod and even from a considerable distance, the men could see talons on the ends of his feet. His spurs, large back spikes that protruded from his leg, facing backward, were tipped in what appeared to be chrome, although for all they knew it could be silver or some unknown alloy that is only found in space. His beak was slightly hooked and the bright yellow contrasted sharply with the blood red of the comb and waddles.

The strangest thing was that the chicken wore clothes much like a human astronaut might. His space suit was silver, although it had openings for his wings rather than sleeves. It covered him from neck to knees, except for his butt. It had an opening to allow him to show off his tail feathers. The men didn't see any identifying markers on the bird, but even if they did, they were pretty sure they'd not have been able to identify them.

Shortly after the first Chicken appeared from the barn, three more followed him. In front of these Chickens were the workers who ensured the safety and welfare of the cattle living on the farm. They were each bound hand-to-hand, creating a chain of fifteen unhappy men and one miserable woman. They appeared to be in good condition, despite having been captured and tied together. They were quickly guided to the spaceship and shoved inside.

"Well, shit. It looks like we have casualties," Billy remarked to Papi as they watched helplessly. Papi simply nodded as he pulled out the cell phone he borrowed from his daughter. He'd better call the authorities on this one, they were going to need help if they were going to rescue those people that were just put on the alien ship.

"911, what's your emergency?" came the voice over the cellphone. It was a woman on the other end of the conversation and she sounded tired and just a little tinny over the phone.

"There are giant alien chickens taking people prisoner over at the Daisy Free farm. Their spaceship is currently parked in the backfield. There are four chickens that I've seen so far and they have sixteen hostages." As Papi spoke, he realized how insane he sounded. There was no way that this woman was going to send help unless it was to haul him in for an emergency mental evaluation.

"You are telling me that there are giant chickens taking people hostage over at the cow farm?" The woman sounded incredulous and rather offended. "Okay. What's your name and where are you?"

"I'm out by the field, far enough way that I'm hoping the chickens don't see me, but where I can see the ship. Are you going to send help?" Papi was hoping that the woman did not notice that he didn't give his name or a solid description of his location.

"I'm going to send you some help. I just need to know where you are and what your name is." Crap, she did notice.

Papi knew when he lost, and he certainly was not going to be winning that woman over. He should have realized there was no way that she was going to believe him that there were alien chickens, the size of men, running around. Heck, Teresa brought him video proof, and he had not wanted to believe it. There was no way a woman who most likely heard every far-fetched idea ever thought of was going to believe him.

"I think we're on our own." Papi turned to Billy, unsure as to what to do next. Billy, however, looked like he might be thinking of some type of a plan.

"We're going to have to protect our own first, and then we can see about getting those people out. There's no sense in getting them out just for all of us to be captured immediately afterward because we don't have a safe spot to hole up in for a bit." Billy spoke without taking his eyes off the ship.

"That's what I'm thinking, too. We need to head home and get things secured. Secure the whole park with a wall and man it. I'm sure there are some people with guns down at Pleasant Mountains. It'll just be a matter of convincing them that the threat is real."

"That shouldn't be too hard. Remember Silas? He already firmly believes. Plus, we have video proof and our word. If anyone doubts, I guess they can call the farm. Most of them already have the number. When no one answers there, they'll believe us." Billy put the truck in reverse and carefully navigated a proper K-turn so they could head back the way they came. When the cell phone rang from the 911 operator calling back, neither man answered.

It was only when they were nearing the McDonald trailer that they realized they were going to need to stop by, even if it wasn't to enjoy some cider. They had to convince the old couple to leave with them.

<u>3</u>

"Nope. Not gonna happen. Ethal and I have lived in this here trailer all our married lives. We've raised six children, ten dogs, eight cats, and more hamsters and guinea pigs than I can count. If those giant chickens are going to come to try to pry us out of our home, we'll go down shooting." Benny was crotchety and cranky when it came to the idea of change, even temporary change.

"Look, it's just for a little while. Just to be safe," Papi pleaded with the old man. "Think of Ethal. You wouldn't want anything to happen to her, would ya?" Papi knew that the old man loved his wife, so while it may be playing dirty, he was willing to do anything to make sure the two made it to the relative safety of the trailer park.

"It won't matter what I say. Ethal ain't gonna leave her trailer. Even if you could convince her that it'd be life or death, she ain't gonna leave. Heck, her favorite cat just had kittens a week past and she won't leave them and mama cat ain't gonna let you move them. Not to mention the horses." Papi thought he saw some progress being made when Benny started talking, but the big black man shot that down with every excuse in the book as to why his wife wouldn't leave.

Papi looked over to Ethal and knew it was going to be a lost cause trying to get her out of the house. She might look like a doddering old woman, but she, a tiny white woman, married a black man, in the South, against her parents' wishes. They raised their kids on their own without any help from their respective families. She had it rough for most of her life and it made her stubborn. He'd heard that she was able to out stubborn a mule, and he didn't doubt it.

Realizing that Ethal was the deciding factor in getting the couple out, Papi tried to convince her instead. While he worked on trying to get the people to leave their home, Billy began to think outside of the box. Making a point not to attract attention, he stepped outside.

The McDonald's had a small farm, of a sort. There was half an acre of corn growing off to one side of the trailer. There was a small vegetable patch alongside the trailer. The pole barn had a small paddock next to it, with four draft horses. In the barn was a large cart with a removable pole set up for the four horses. A plan was beginning to form in his mind.

Heading over to the front of the mobile home, he checked the spot where the hitch was supposed to have been. It was still a solid area with no rust. Pushing aside some of the skirting, he slipped under the trailer. The tongue was still intact. The axils were still present and appeared to be in good condition. The utility connections looked easy enough to detach.

Crawling out from under the trailer, he dusted himself off and plucked a few random cobwebs from his hair before going down the side of the trailer. The tires had been cleverly hidden behind flower boxes, but to his surprise, they were all well-inflated and cared for. He figured that Benny was checking on them as something to do now that he was retired, a lot like the half acre of corn and the fancy cart pulled by too many horses.

Billy would have gone over to the paddock and checked the horses for soundness, but while he might know how to move a trailer, he had no idea about horses. Unless they were limping or dead, he wouldn't be able to tell if they were in good condition or not. He simply wasn't a horseman. He wasn't even sure that Papi would be able to tell since the only horse he had ever dealt with was Runner. He figures that the four horses could move the trailer, although he might be wrong. If so, maybe a tractor could be found.

Billy walked into the trailer and found Papi, Benny, and Ethal all leaning against the kitchen counters, looking frustrated. "I take it that no one is willing to leave the trailer?" Billy asked into the silence. It was obvious that Papi hadn't won his argument. If he had, he'd have been busily bustling the old couple out the door and to safety. It was equally clear that he didn't think that Benny and Ethal won since he had not left the kitchen. No one answered Billy.

"I think I have a solution," Billy hazarded. Sometimes people don't want answers when they're angry, they just want to be angry and he was hoping this wasn't one of those times. "I think we should take the trailer with us. Those horses look like they can haul the trailer and the trailer itself looks in good enough condition to make the trip."

"There isn't a hitch on the trailer, Billy, remember?" Papi reminded him. He had begun to rub his forehead in anticipation of the headache he felt coming on.

"No, the hitch is gone." Billy sounded hesitant to make his suggestions, but nothing ventured, nothing gained. "But the tongue is still in place. The carriage out in the pole barn has a tongue we can weld onto the trailer tongue. Those horses look like they can pull the trailer relatively easily. If not, maybe there is a tractor we can borrow or steal. I'm sure the cow farm has one."

"You want to hitch four horses to the trailer and drive it to Pleasant Mountains? Do you even know how to drive a team of horses?" Papi sounded incredulous. Images of the disaster this could be were racing through his mind. He could all too easily picture all four of them dead with four draft horses wandering around, eating grass around them. He wasn't sure what kind of disaster would result with the horses being fine, but that didn't stop the image.

"I know only so much as what end of the horse bites and which end poops. But, I am betting that Benny here could drive that team without any problem." Billy never even considered the possibility that he'd be the one driving the team. He figured Papi and he would be providing some sort of security for the move, ensuring that no giant alien chickens attacked them while they were trying to get to safety.

He was certain that the dust trail that they'd be kicking up would be enough to attract their attention unless they were only going for the people at the farm, although that sounded like a waste. Why fly a huge spaceship all the way to Earth for sixteen people and some cows? More than likely, they'd grab as many people and cows as they could fit in the ship, comfortably or not. Heck, there might even be a mothership out there leading to multiple runs.

The kitchen had been silent while he was thinking about the spaceship and the giant alien chickens stealing people and cows. It was not the brooding kind of silence that he had walked into, but rather the thoughtful silence of people thinking of a way to make sure the plan worked. "Those horses will have no problem moving the trailer. Each one of them could move the trailer on their own if they had to. Between the four of them, it would barely be considered exercise. If you can get the hitch onto the trailer, I think this plan just might work," Benny finally concluded. Ethal humped at them, but she didn't voice an objection.

Getting the tongue off the cart wasn't difficult. It was designed to be able to be switched out as necessary. Attaching it to the trailer was another matter completely. "When you said you were going to weld it onto the trailer, I kind of thought you had welding equipment with you," Papi grumped as they dug through the barn. Benny swore there was some welding equipment in there, somewhere. He just used it last year to fix something. They were hoping he was right.

"Well, I thought I did. I must have taken it out when I went hunting," Billy snapped back. He was a welder by trade, and although he didn't take his work equipment home with him, he generally kept welding supplies in his truck. He never knew when a project might pop into his head and he would find himself needing to build something random. His whole property was littered with smallish sculptures that he'd made over the years.

Papi snorted in frustration, but never stopped looking through the mounds of stuff that Benny and Ethal had collected over the years. The side of the barn that kept the horses and cart was pristine. Nothing was out of place there. The side that they used as storage was another matter completely. It had become a catch-all for any and everything that might at some point become of use.

After what seemed like forever,, they were able to find the welder, electrodes, a grinder, and even the helmet and gloves. It wasn't the nicest kit in the world, but it would be effective for what they needed to do. Without a filler material, Billy was going to have to use a fusion welding process, but he was confident in the success of the project.

Keeping the tongue steady was the next difficult part, but once they were able to stabilize the metals in place, Billy was able to start his work. While he worked, Papi went with Benny to prepare the horses. Ethal began gathering up the things she couldn't leave, including her new mama cat and kittens.

"These are beautiful animals," Papi said, admiring the four draft horses standing unbothered by the noise and fuss going on at the trailer. They looked like they didn't have a care in the world. They were Belgium draft horses and they looked near enough alike that Papi wasn't sure he would be able to tell them apart if pressed. Benny named them off easily enough, but neither the names nor which horse they went with stuck to Papi.

"They're stubborn and they eat too much," Papi groused as he grabbed what appeared to Papi to be miles of leather. "The cart could be driven by one horse, without him even breaking a sweat. But no, Ethal said we couldn't buy just one horse. He'd be lonely. So we bought two. But, that left two horses in the pen, calling out to the ones we bought. Guess what happened after that?"

"Ethal made you buy those two?" Papi guessed.

"Nope. Someone else bought them. He was some farmer who was going to use them to haul trees out of the woods. I had to buy them from him at twice the price." Benny sounded irritated about the whole thing, but Papi could tell that he didn't mind buying four horses for his wife. He's the type of man who'd move a mountain for her.

"Do you know what it means to have four horses?" Benny continued.

"Four times the amount of poop?" Runner pooped a lot. It was enough to keep Teresa busy cleaning the horse's stall every morning. Runner was half the size of these monster horses. He couldn't imagine how much they popped.

"Four times the poop. Four times the vet bills. Four times the food bills. Four times the tack." Benny chuckled. "That little lady best be glad I love her." Benny laid each of the harnesses out in a specific pattern, but Papi couldn't make heads nor tails of it. Then he grabbed four collars out of the barn. Walking into the paddock, he slipped a collar and a halter on each horse, tying them to the wooden fence surrounding their paddock.

Papi admittedly tried to help Benny harness the horses. After the third time of getting in the old man's way, he stepped aside and just watched the man work. He kept a running commentary as he worked, explaining the entire process, but Papi wasn't sure if he was talking to him or to the horses. If he had any confusion whether the horses minded being harnessed or not, it was laid to rest as they picked up their feet for him and moved to make the process easier Once the horses were ready, Benny led them over to the trailer, leaving Papi to grab their spreader bars and other equipment that was needed to guide the team.

4

Hitching the horses was another task that Papi couldn't help with. The best he could do was stand there with Billy and hold the horses while Benny put them all in their places and attached them to the pole that now jutted out from the trailer.

"Are you sure that it's gonna hold?" Papi asked, looking at the contraption. He could just picture the horses taking off and the trailer staying in place.

"You *doubting* my welding skills?" Billy emphasized the word 'doubting' as though it were a true insult rather than a good question. "I will have you know that my welds don't fail," he continued arrogantly. Then, in a more normal voice, he amended his statement. "I also bolted the pole to the tongue and used some cable ties to keep everything tight. There isn't a lot of time for letting the weld settle and cool properly. I didn't want to risk it, so I did my best to keep everything in place so that the trailer moves safely."

"I'm sure it will work." Papi looked over at Billy, who was staring at the pole with concern. There was a lot that could go wrong, and if it did, they'd have lost a lot of time that they could have used to secure their homes. If the chickens arrived while they were messing around here... well, that's a thought that wasn't worth bearing.

It didn't take long to hitch the horses up to the trailer. Benny handed the reins over to his wife, who was standing inside the trailer, leaning out of an open window, waiting for them. He was going to steer the team from there, standing in the spare bedroom, leaning out the front window of the little trailer. It wasn't the safest way to drive a team of horses, but it was the only feasible way to drive this team and this trailer. With any luck, they wouldn't have to go fast, so Benny should be able to keep his footing.

"Utilities disconnected?" Papi asked Billy while they walked to Billy's truck. They were going to provide security for the trailer. It wouldn't be maneuverable, so if the giant alien chickens arrived, they were going to get between them and the trailer, protecting them the best they could.

"Yep, I did that before I crawled out from under the trailer after bolting everything in place. You wanna drive or you wanna be the shooter?" They were Papi's guns and Billy's truck, but they both knew that Billy was the better shot. Some people don't like others using their guns, though.

"I'll drive. You can hit a fly's wings off on a windy day from the back of a boat." Papi was exaggerating, but not by much. With a slap to Billy's shoulder, he turned and got in the truck. Billy didn't even consider getting in the cab of the truck. Instead, he went right to the bed. He would have more maneuverability back there and a better line of sight. Papi handed him the rifle through the cab's rear window, and they were ready to go.

It didn't take long for Benny to get the horses going. They knew how to pull the cart, so the trailer wasn't that much of a change for them. With a short clicking noise and a commanding, "Forward," Benny got them going. Even with the tires being full and everything in good condition, it took a moment to get the house moving. The house had sunk into the field just a bit, meaning the horses were going to have to pull the house up a bit as well as forward.

Four thousand pounds worth of horse leaning against eight thousand pounds worth of home should have been a one-sided outcome, and it was, just not in the way that most people would expect. With barely a grunt from the horses, the house lifted out of its divots and began to roll forward through the field. Benny deftly steered the house towards the driveway, giving the horses an easier route and himself a smoother ride. Papi and Billy followed just behind them in the truck.

The dirt kicked up by four horses, a mobile home, and a truck on the dirt driveway was substantial. If the giant alien chickens didn't already know where they were, they could easily hazard a guess based on the dust cloud. It made Papi and Billy nervous, but there was nothing to do about it. Even if they had stuck to the field, which would have taken longer, they would have eventually needed to drive on the road, and dust would still be present. Papi focused on driving, but Billy kept a wary eye out towards the cow farm. If the alien chickens were to attack, they'd most likely attack from that direction.

They were a mile from the trailer park when they spotted the chickens. They burst from the trees almost right behind Papi and his truck, startling both of the men who had been watching for them. Papi nearly swerved off the road in his surprise, but quickly got control of himself and the truck. He hoped that Billy was okay in the truck bed behind him.

Billy, after being tossed around like a ball with Papi's sudden jerk of the wheel, was quick to take a kneeling position and level the rifle at the oncoming alien. It was fast. This chicken looked like it might be female, being slightly smaller and more darkly colored than the previous chicken he saw. She also had a much smaller comb and wattle. She was moving far too fast for him to tell if she had spurs or not. Instead, he started shooting.

The first chicken he shot went down quickly with a shot right to her head, as she passed him, aiming for the mobile home in front of them. Once she went down though, the threats were reassessed almost as though by telepathy and they were all going after the truck. Once he was fairly sure he had everyone's attention, Papi took them off the road and away from the trailer.

Chickens are fast. They are much faster than people are, in most cases, Usain Bolt aside. The giant alien chickens are no exception. They were fast. Papi did his best to keep in front of them as he drove them off the road and onto the field. With Billy in the bed of the truck, he didn't want to push past forty miles an hour, and they were in a field. Catching a hole and ripping an axle out was a very real concern for the truck. Ruining the truck would be bad, but not as bad as letting the aliens catch them because he broke the truck.

Billy had a full magazine, minus the round he already shot. It was a big magazine, far bigger than what was initially available with the gun. This might have been overkill while hunting, but while fighting off half a dozen chickens, he wasn't sure it was going to be enough. There were five left, but they moved fast, never running in a straight line. The rough terrain that the truck was going over didn't help. Every time he thought he had a shot ready to go, they'd hit a bump, and he'd go flying.

It was beginning to look dire for Billy and Papi as they raced across the field, leading the chickens away from the mobile home. That was until they heard a shotgun firing and the lead chicken burst into a cloud of feathers. That gave Billy just enough room to line up his shot and blast the one right behind.

Without any warning, Papi adjusted his angle, bringing them almost parallel to the road. He had to know who was shooting the chickens besides Billy. What he saw burned into his brain for the rest of his life. There, in the afternoon light, he saw all four horses cantering with practiced precision. Behind them, leaning out the front window of the mobile home, was Benny, driving for all he was worth. The most surprising thing though, was seeing Ethal standing on the top of the trailer, feet spread wide, rocking with the motion under her, shotgun on her shoulder, laughing like a fool.

"God damn it, woman," Papi screamed out the window of Billy's truck. "Get off that trailer before you fall and break a hip!" He was pretty sure she couldn't hear him over the racket going on around them. Not that she would have heard him if it had been silent out, her being hard of hearing and all. That didn't stop him from hearing her, though.

"Take that, you varmints!" Ethal screamed at the top of her lungs before firing the shotgun again, resulting in another cloud of feathers. "I've been plucking your kind all my life, you don't scare me!" Papi had to hand it to her. She didn't look scared. He was certainly scared enough for both of them.

The last two of the giant alien chickens knew they had lost a battle. With a few flaps of their wings, they took off back the way they came. They were quickly out of reasonable firing range, but that didn't mean they slowed down. Instead, they used a flapping-run, and raced all the way back to the cow farm, from what it looked like.

Once the running battle quit, Papi pulled the truck in behind the mobile home. They were almost back to Pleasant Mountains. The horses weren't slowing down, though. When it was apparent that the chickens were not going to attack again, Ethal decided to go back into the trailer. Slipping the gun's shoulder strap diagonally behind her, she began climbing down the side of the trailer.

Papi nearly threw Billy out of the truck as he hit the brakes, trying to give them enough room to stop in case Ethal slipped as she climbed down the side of the moving mobile home. It looked for a second like she was going to slip just as she made it to the open window that she must have climbed out to get to the roof. There was another breathless moment for Papi as she got the shotgun stuck in the window frame. He could just imagine her accidentally discharging the shotgun and either getting herself shot or being hurt by the recoil. Hell, with his luck, she'd shoot her own husband, leaving them with a set of charging horses and no way to control them. He didn't dare to breathe until she waved at him from inside the trailer before closing the window.

"That's one tough broad," he whispered to himself as he passed the sign for home.

<u>5</u>

Benny finally slowed his team of horses when they made the turn onto the driveway for the trailer park. The road was plenty big enough, but he needed time to see where he was going to park the mobile home. He hoped he was not going to have to move it again once he got it stopped. One good look around the park showed him that there was only one spot where he could park it, and that was in the center circle.

People rushed out of their homes, some in bathrobes, some in white tank tops and boxers, and some few in jeans and tee shirts. They were called by the sounds of the horses' harnesses jingling like Christmas bells. He had forgotten how cheery that sound could be to those who don't hear it in their sleep like he did. He and Ethal didn't know most of the people in the park, just Papi and his daughter, Billy, and Uncle Jasper, even if they were pretty sure that wasn't his real name. He looked around expectantly for those he knew and was not disappointed to see Teresa running up to him, ready to help with the horses.

"What are you guys doing here?" Teresa asked as she caught the first horse in line. She gave him an affectionate scratch while holding him still. "Papi and Billy find you guys? Did you see the giant alien chickens? Is that why you're here? You drove the whole trailer here?" Teresa never gave Benny a chance to answer any of the questions before asking more questions. "Where is Papi and Billy?"

Just as she asked that last question, Papi pulled Billy's truck into his parking spot, saving Benny the trouble of explaining what happened to Teresa. It would be her Papi's responsibility to tell her as much or as little as she was to know about the whole thing.

As soon as Papi put Billy's truck in park, Teresa opened the door and hugged him. She was evidently worried that he might come into some harm against the aliens. There was no way that he was going to tell her how close of a call he and Billy had actually had. Once she had squeezed the stuffings out of her Papi, she let him go and helped Billy out of the bed of the truck, not that he needed her help.

"Well, that was scary," Billy said without thinking. The glare that Papi shot him would have killed a lesser man. "I don't miss riding in the bed of a truck," Billy amended. Apparently, he was not supposed to talk about the giant alien chickens chasing them down the road. It was a shame, too, because that had the makings of a good story, he thought.

"Yeah, Papi says that I'm not allowed to ride in the bed of the truck because I could get hurt," Teresa agreed with him. She had done it a few times with her friend's older brother, but she didn't like to disobey her Papi, so she didn't do it often. Besides, it was scary. Even when they went slow, it felt like they were flying and that every bump was going to toss her out of the truck.

"Did you see Ethal?" Billy asked Papi as they walked towards the mobile home.

"Yeah. I saw her. Of all of the foolish things to do, climbing on the roof of a moving trailer. All I could think was that she's gonna slip and break a hip or fall off of the trailer and I'd hit her." Papi rubbed his forehead, hoping to calm what felt like a killer headache coming on. He could feel his heart rate pick up at just the thought of Ethal climbing off the roof. That would be visiting his nightmares, he was sure of it. "That being said, it did look awfully cool."

"Ethal climbed the mobile home while Benny drove it down the road?" Teresa sounded in awe of the woman. Ethal had always impressed her before, but now she might hit hero-worship status. Then came the obvious question, "Why did she do that?"

"Well, ah…" Billy floundered. He couldn't come up with a good reason for her to do that without mentioning the alien chickens and their narrow escape.

"Well…" Papi weighed his options. Lie and not scare Teresa, or tell the truth and potentially scare her. She did already see the chickens. She was the one who discovered them. Without her, the McDonalds would have most likely already been taken and the trailer park would not even know that the chickens were on their way. Not unless it hit the news, but even then, who would believe that.

"Well, we ran into some chickens. Ethal decided that the roof of the mobile home gave her the right angles to hit the chickens without becoming a target. She was right. She was able to hit the chickens without the chickens turning and attacking her. She may have saved our butts. That being said, it was a very dangerous thing for her to do." Papi decided to go with the truth. She would be better off prepared.

"ETHAL SHOT THE CHICKENS FROM THE ROOF OF THE TRAILER…WHILE IT WAS MOVING!" Teresa practically screamed in excitement. Yep, the woman had reached the hero worship status.

"You did what now?" Benny demanded of his wife. She was supposed to be safely in the trailer while he did the dangerous part of driving the horses while standing half out a window.

"You never mind that. I did what was necessary," Ethal downplayed her role to her husband. "I assure you, I was perfectly safe."

"So you weren't on the roof of the trailer? Papi and Billy are mistaken?" Benny grumbled to her.

"I was perfectly safe," was all that Ethal was willing to say on the matter. There was no way that either Billy or Papi were going to gainsay her. Anyone who could consider climbing any moving vehicle "safe" was not someone they were willing to tangle with. Besides, they were pretty sure that Benny knew the truth. He had to have heard the shotgun and the rifle and known that they were not the same gun. They were coming from two different locations. He wasn't stupid.

"Let's get these horses taken care of. This is a good place to park, right?" Ethal moved away from that discussion with all of the grace of a bull in a china shop, abruptly and rather jarringly.

"Well, the circle doesn't have any hookups, but it will work for the moment, I guess. We'll have to move one of the empty trailers out of the way later and let you guys have that spot if you are gonna be staying here." Papi answered, thinking aloud.

"We'll take the horses over to Papi's barn. They can bunk with Runner for a bit," Billy suggested. He wasn't sure where else they could put the horses unless they just stood in the field. Would they even just stay put if they were in a field? He remembered something about hobbling a horse, but he wasn't sure what that all entailed.

"Runner would love to have the company," Teresa agreed, bouncing up and down with her excitement. She loved the big draft horses almost as much as she loved Runner. It would be like a sleepover with all of her best friends if her best friends were all horses.

Benny had to show Billy how to take all of the tack off the horses, leaving the bridles on until the horses led to the barn where Runner had previously ruled alone. To say that she was unimpressed by the sheer size of the horses in comparison to herself would be an understatement. Runner could not have cared if each of the horses were twice her size or not. This was her barn, and she was in charge. She stood in the middle of the paddock while all four of the drafts crowded themselves into a single corner.

"Friendly, isn't she?" Benny remarked as he watched the mare bare her teeth at one of the drafts who dared to consider eating some grass.

"Not especially," Papi had to agree. It was a good thought to have all of the horses living together. The reality did not look promising, though. He'd have to talk to some of his neighbors and see who would be able to watch over some horses for the night until they were able to figure out what to do with them.

"Leave them there. My boys are nice. They'll wear her down. Either that or they'll finally have enough of her behavior and remind her that they're bigger than she is." Benny huffed out a small laugh as he watched the horses. It always amazed him how much trouble a single chestnut mare could cause.

"Well, now that the horses are taken care of, we need to get a park meeting going. We gotta prepare for the chickens." Papi slapped the wooden fence surrounding the paddock as he spoke, spooking the horses a bit, but emphasizing what he said. This was going to be a hard sell, convincing people that there were giant chickens and they needed to outfit the park against them. Everyone thought there might be aliens out there, but even then, giant alien chickens were a heck of a stretch even for the most conspiracist of their group.

Papi left it to Billy to gather the residents of Pleasant Mountain while he hunted down a soap box to preach from. He figured that a milkcrate was close enough for his purpose and walked over to where Billy had everyone gathered. It was up to him to convince them of the impossible, or if not the impossible, the highly improvable, giant alien chickens.

<u>6</u>

"...so now you know what we know. There are giant, man-sized chickens from outer space who are here to steal people. We don't know what they're doing with those people, but I rather doubt it is something healthy for them. It is up to us to protect ourselves." Papi had spent the past ten minutes explaining everything that had occurred so far. No one wandered away, and no one was handing him tin-foil. So he figured that people were getting the picture. It helped that neither he nor Billy were known to fly off the handle at just any old conspiracy.

"So what's the plan?" someone asked once Papi finished talking. He wasn't sure who it was that asked, but it was a good question. Too bad he didn't have a good answer.

"I think our first step should be to fortify the park. If we build a wall connecting all of the trailers together, we can mitigate the chances of them getting into the park and abducting someone. Then we need to think about firepower. We know they can be killed and protecting our own is vitally important. Only once we're safe can we even consider a rescue mission for those who have been taken." Not having a plan ready to go before he started talking, Papi was able to think up an outline of a plan fairly quickly. It helped that he had thought about how to defend the park before.

"Billy, you're in charge of gathering people and building the barricades. I'm sure someone here has some spare steel lying around, although anything will work. We just need to prevent them from running in, forcing them to go up and over the barricade. Trailer height would be preferred. The higher, the better." Papi was on a roll now. He had a plan, of a sort, and he was going to make it work.

"I've got me some extra steel you guys can use. I was going to use it to build a few things, but this sounds more important," Silas offered. A few others spoke up, offering what they had. Several more offered up their building skills to help get the barricade constructed. As Billy followed Silas to his scrap pile, they all followed Billy, giving their opinions as to how it should be built. Papi watched them go, amazed by how easy it had been to convince them of the plan.

As Papi watched Silas and Billy lead a crowd of people away from their impromptu meeting spot, another man walked up to him. It was the man everyone called Uncle Jasper, much like everyone called him Papi, even though he was only one person's Papi.

"What can I do for you, Jasper?" There was no way Papi was going to call the man uncle.

Uncle Jasper smiled at Papi, although it was impossible to tell if the smile touched his eyes or not. Jasper was never without his sunglasses on. He looked friendly enough, even with the golden front teeth, lost and replaced from some fight back in his younger days. The only thing Papi knew for sure about Jasper was that, like himself, Jasper was a Marine.

"We're gonna need some guns," Jasper said as he smiled. Papi smiled right back at him. They were going to need some guns. He was hoping that Jasper had an idea about where to get some. Jasper looked like someone who might know where to get some guns.

Jasper led Papi back towards his garage. It looked just like every other garage in the trailer park. The main difference was the boat that was stuck up in the rafters. It wasn't a big boat, just a simple row boat, stuck right-side up, wedged between the joists and the roof of the garage.

"How in the hell did that get up there?" Papi asked in astonishment. He'd seen a lot of things, but for the life of him, he could not imagine how the boat got up there. It didn't look like there was enough room between the joists for the boat to slide in. Even if there was, there wasn't enough room between the joists and the roof for it to have tipped in without damaging anything.

"It was a boating accident," Jasper answered with a smile. He looked rather proud of his little accident.

"That's a special kind of stupid boating accident," Papi muttered. He didn't think that Jasper heard him. He was wrong.

"The type of stupid that wraps all the way back around to brilliant." Jasper's smile got even brighter as he grabbed the ladder that was leaning against the back wall of the garage.

"What do you mean?" Papi was confused. He's never heard of stupidity being anything close to brilliant.

"Why don't you take a look up in that there boat." Jasper settled the ladder near the stern of the boat, looking up to make sure it was aligned and close enough to the boat for Papi to look in, even to grab whatever he might see of interest up there.

With a frown, Papi climbed the ladder. He was picturing all of the things that could possibly be in a right-side-up boat. Something like that would make a great home for all sorts of critters, and while he had nothing against raccoons when they were out in the field, he didn't particularly want to run into one while he was balanced on a ladder. Not to mention the possibility of spiders. Heck, after dealing with alien chickens, he was all crittered out for the day.

Papi's concern didn't lessen when he reached the top of the ladder and found a blue tarp lying over something in the boat. The tarp looked dusty, but clean. There was no sign of any animals making the boat its home, but he knew that it could be deceptive. How many times has he been certain that nothing was outside, only to practically walk into a deer or a cow?

Cautiously, Papi lifted the tarp, keeping one hand on the boat just in case something jumped out at him and he lost his balance. If he slipped, he wanted some chance to catch himself before falling off the ladder. Jasper looked strong, but even if he caught Papi, they'd both get hurt. The first peek under the tarp made Papi smile. That smile grew as he pulled the tarp completely away from the prize that it covered. There, in pristine cases, were enough guns and ammunition to supply most of the park.

"You lost your guns in a boating accident?" Papi called down to Jasper as he reached for the first box of ammunition.

"Yep, and the ammunition." Jasper was smiling as he took the first case from Papi. It'd been a trick getting the boat up there. It started when he slammed on the brakes to avoid hitting his dog, who had run in front of the truck. That shifted the boat that was in the back of his truck, not really tied down. It didn't quite hit the rafters, but it was a close thing and it gave him the idea. The fact that the boat had a leak sealed its fate.

It'd been exhausting moving most of his guns up there. Guns aren't heavy, but they can be awkward on a ladder. The rounds were heavy. Getting the guns and bullets for target practice every week was almost enough to make him rethink storing them up there, but it did make him smile every time he thought of the joke. Having someone else help him get everything down was a lot easier than getting them down himself.

Once everything was unloaded, Papi was able to get a good look at what was currently available for them to defend the park with. Jasper, believing that anything worth doing was worth overdoing, had ten M-4s and three AR-15s, as well as their respective ammunition. There was a lot of ammo for the guns. If Papi hadn't been the one to pull them out of the boat, he wasn't sure that he'd have believed that anyone could fit that much in a simple row boat.

"You must be a master packer to have gotten everything in there." Papi was looking at the various guns and boxes that he had handed down to Jasper. The garage floor was practically covered with the boat's contents. "I'd have never expected to find all this in a boat."

"That's the point, isn't it?" Jasper laughed. It's been a while since he's seen everything pulled out at once. Most of the time, he just took what he was using that day and put it all back after it'd been used and then cleaned. No point in having guns that aren't usable because they've not been serviced and cleaned.

As they walked out of the garage, leaving everything on the floor, Billy jogged up to them.

"I have people building the fence, but Silas says he has something he has to show you. I think you're going to want to see it." As they walked over to Silas's trailer, the three men talked about how best to defend the trailer park.

"You know, having a fence is good, but we need a way to see over that fence and see far enough to be able to stop the chickens before they ever get to the park," Papi reasoned aloud.

"Deer stands," Jasper answered without elaborating.

"Deer stands? You mean tree stands?" Billy asked. He'd never heard of a deer stand before, but he knew about tree stands.

"Do you use them for anything but hunting deer?" Jasper asked. He didn't look at Billy, but he did smile.

"I can't say that I do. I guess that makes them deer stands," Papi answered with a sigh. He knew when people were just messing with each other. "What does that have to do with the situation at hand?"

"We should put deer stands up in the trees that surround the park. They're not very noticeable, but they are very secure. They make great shooting spots and they can be positioned so we can see the chickens well before they see us. They're effective against deer, and they'll be effective against some aliens unless they come with things like heat-sensitive eyesight," Jasper explained. "I'm pretty sure that there are some hunters here with spare stands."

"That's a pretty good idea. If not, we could always stand on the trailers, although that's just inviting someone to trip and fall off one of them. The stands come with a belt to prevent you from falling," Billy elaborated, picturing the situation. He'd rather be in a tree stand than on a trailer. He might have more maneuverability on the trailer, but the chances of falling off are higher.

"I like it. After we talk to Silas, we'll ask around and try to find deer stands," Papi agreed, deliberately using Jasper's word for the device.

7

The trailer park wasn't big. It didn't take long for them to reach Silas's trailer, even when taking their time to get there. They found the toothless man standing there, looking for all the world like a cat who had gotten a canary. He was fair vibrating with excitement.

"I got something to show yous," he started waving the men towards the back, turning to lead them at the same time. He was oldandspry, but old. His back was bent from years of working construction. His legs bowed, and he walked with a bit of a limp. None of that seemed to bother him as he led them to his backyard. His apparently empty backyard.

"What ya think?" Silas did not point to anything in particular once they all reached the backyard. Instead, he seemed to simply smile brighter and expect them to know what he was talking about. They, unfortunately, had no idea what he was talking about.

Jasper looked long and hard at the man, not that Silas could tell. Jasper never took off his sunglasses. Papi didn't look at Jasper at all. instead, he kept looking at the yard like it might open up and point to what Silas was talking about. Billy simply scuffed the ground, embarrassed for the old man. At least he was until he noticed that there was a line in the dirt. "What's this?" Billy asked as he bent down to feel along the line.

It wasn't a hook-up for the trailer. It wasn't a lost paving stone. This was a large metal door, hidden in the dirt and grass in the backyard. "That's my underground bunker for when the zombies come a calling. I figure giant alien chickens are close enough to zombies to break this baby out." With a magnetic key, Silas managed to unlock and open the hatch, revealing a marvel that was only outmatched by the volume of Jasper's stash.

"Silas, what were you going to do with a rocket launcher? How in the hell did you even acquire one?" Papi asked cautiously. There, on a metal table in the middle of the room was a rocket launcher, although he couldn't immediately identify the make or model. Along the walls were guns hung up, ready to use from the looks of them. There was even a mini fridge tucked in the corner. If they all survived this invasion, maybe he'd be moving him and Teresa out of the park. Guns in boating accidents were one thing, but rocket launchers owned by the most insane person he'd ever met was a bit too much for the father part of him.

"Just you not worry about where I got it. As for what I was planning on using it against, well, the zombies, of course. I told ya, they're on their way. They're gonna fall on us like locusts and eat our brains! Better to have a rocket launcher and not need it than need it and not have it." Silas smiled his toothless grin. Papi wasn't so sure about that, but then again, he was pretty sure that aliens were not supposed to be man-sized chickens, but he was wrong about that so he could be wrong about zombies.

"How in the hell did you keep all this dry and safe?" Jasper asked, looking into the pit. It was a cold white pit with four solidly constructed walls. For being a hole in the ground, the whole thing had that professional look. It was well-lit, deep enough to stand comfortably in, and there was no indication of dampness, at all.

"I'm a contractor. I know how to build things," Silas looked at Papi indignantly while Papi stared at the man's trailer in absolute confusion.

"So, let me get this straight. You built a leak-proof, well-lit, comfortable bunker for your guns, and rocket launcher because we can't forget that thing, but you live in a trailer that is falling apart." It sounded even worse than it appeared when Papi said it aloud. He looked over at the trailer as he was talking. The trailer was slightly canted to one side, looking more like a parallelogram than the more standard rectangle shape. He was pretty sure that a stiff wind would bring the whole thing toppling down.

"I'm comfortable enough in that there trailer. There's nothing wrong with it. The gov'ment ain't coming to take me away. But they might my guns," Silas lost all use of his grammar as he spoke, slipping further and further into the Hillbilly speak that he grew up with in the middle of the mountains. That was usually a bad sign for the man. It meant he was gearing up to do something spectacularly unexpected. However, the last time he did it, he predicted aliens, and by golly, he was correct.

"Well, the gov'ment isn't here to take your guns right now. Instead, they might thank us for being so well supplied, if they ever learn about the alien invasion. Have you ever fired the rocket launcher?" For some reason, Papi was very interested in the rocket launcher. He hadn't seen one since his Marine Corps days, and even then he had not gotten the opportunity to fire one. He could see his chance today, depending on how the day played out.

"Did anyone check the radios to see if anyone else is reporting a giant chicken invasion?" Jasper asked, looking back and forth between the men. He had fired a rocket launcher and thoroughly enjoyed it.

"Ah, I can't say that I have. I didn't even think about the radio. The dispatcher didn't sound like she believed me when I called it in a few hours ago," Papi admitted. Who knows, maybe they were not going to have to fight the aliens alone. Maybe the gov'ment, as Silas put it, was already making plans to rescue the captives and the whole world was being informed about the alien invasion. "Let's go to my trailer, I have cable and we can check FOX News. If anyone is going to report on the aliens, it will be them."

When Silas, Billy, Jasper, and Papi got to Papi's trailer, they found Teresa and the youngest of the kids huddled around the television watching cartoons. "What's going on here?" Papi asked, surprised to find his home taken over by rugrats.

"Oh, I volunteered to watch everyone's kids while they worked to build the fence. A lot of the moms sent over snacks." Teresa raised her hand that was holding a Capri Sun that he hadn't bought. None of the other kids even acknowledged that the men came into the trailer. They were so intent on watching the cartoons and eating from the small bags of chips that they all held.

"That was very good of you. Nice, helpful, and mature of you to think of this." Papi was fairly glowing with paternal pride. His daughter, stepping up to a challenge that he hadn't even thought of yet. Not that he'd had much time to think of all of the challenges that the invasion presented.

"We still need to see what's going on outside of here," Jasper reminded him quietly. That many children in one area fairly terrified him. He'd seen what a bunch of kids can do when they decide to set their mind to it. Hell, he had been one of those kids.

"I have a small television in my bedroom," Papi indicated the room towards the back of the trailer. It was the smaller of the two rooms, but without his wife, he didn't need a lot of room. Meanwhile, Teresa seemed to need the whole trailer to hold everything she had.

Watching FOX News was anticlimactic. It took them less than half an hour to realize that the rest of the world didn't know a thing about the invading chickens. They must have snuck down onto Earth and gone after locations of low habitation.

"They might be avoiding a fight," Billy suggested after watching a news anchor talk about the English Royal family for the second time in thirty minutes. Who was marrying who an ocean away was of no interest to him.

"That might indicate that they don't have a lot of firepower, they have limited personnel, or that their ships are more fragile than they look," Papi agreed.

"Let's hope for all three, but prepare for none," Jasper added to the discussion. He was the more pragmatic of the group. Hope for the best, but prepare for the worst.

"Right you are," Billy agreed. "What's next, boss?" he asked Papi.

"Jasper had the right about the deer stands. Let's get them up some trees and post some crack shots on them. The further from home we can engage the enemy, the better. We have too many vulnerable people here to risk them getting into the park." Papi led them out of his bedroom and past the most vulnerable of the community, the children, and out the door. The world would burn before he would let some chicken get his daughter.

In all, they were able to find eight deer stands. Getting them up and into the trees was a bit of a challenge. There were not too many large trees inside the perimeter that were going up between the trailers. Jasper found himself sitting in a deer stand just outside of the perimeter, rifle in hand and a case of Bang energy drinks dangling from a cord. Shades on, he watched the woods with the same singular intensity that kept him alive during all three of his deployments into hostile territory. No chicken was going to get past him.

<u>8</u>

It was loud in the trailer park most of the day, with people building walls and others consolidating resources to make sure everyone got fed in the community. By the time night fell, the community was ready for war. They had worked out rotation schedules for the guards and set up spotlights to make sure that no chickens approached unseen. They might not have built a true fortress, but it would not be an easy victory for the birds if the chickens came calling. If there was one thing to be said about a bunch of hillbillies living in a trailer park, it was that they knew how to work together when they had to.

Papi spent a restless night in his living room, trying to catnap. He'd have slept in his bed, but it was down a narrow hall and he didn't want to navigate that in the dark if there was an attack. He had sent Teresa to her bed, along with three of her girlfriends, who had decided to sleep there while their parents helped patrol the area. No one wanted to be alone when there was a real possibility of being abducted by aliens.

Every time he would fall asleep, he thought he heard a noise. A scratching outside of the fence, a clucking bird, or the creak of the trailer as it moved ever so slightly on its foundation. The only comfort was that none of the dogs in the park, and there were a fair number of them, made a peep. He might question his senses, but he's never questioned a dog's ability to spot danger.

Papi stopped trying to sleep when the sun began to brighten the skies. Teresa was a deep sleeper, so he was not particularly worried about being quiet as he brewed a pot of coffee and stepped out of the trailer. This was always his favorite part of the day, the golden hour when everything was still dewy and the fog was still clinging to the trees. Sometimes he'd even see deer in the field behind his trailer. But not today. Today everything was still, almost as though it was anticipating the possibility of battle.

Looking around the park, he could see other people were up and moving. Most of them had probably been up all night, keeping watch over their loved ones. He hoped that there were enough functionally awake people to keep everyone safe for the day. Papi figured that even if they had been up all night, they'd be alert enough if they had to kill some chickens. Not much will wake you up like seeing the enemy will.

It wasn't long before the smell of someone making an egg bake wafted through the park. It was enough to make him hungry. He turned and went back into his home, set on making some pancakes for the girls. Being a father didn't stop just because there were some invading giant chickens just a couple of lots away. Besides, Teresa wasn't safe to be around if she didn't have her coffee and some food in her. Just like her mama in that way.

As he was flipping the last of the pancakes, Billy walked in, kicking dirt off his boots at the door. Papi flinched as he did so, knowing that Teresa would be awake now, and the pot of coffee wasn't done brewing.

"Talk fast, that little woman will be waking up soon and the coffee isn't done yet," he warned.

Billy cast a terrified look over at the pot that was just under half full. He helped raise that little girl and he was terrified of her sometimes. The coffee addiction wasn't his fault. It was a tradition in Teresa's Mom's family to give kids as young as two a little bit of coffee with their milk. That didn't mean that he did anything to curb the kid's cravings. Heck, he went out and bought her luxury coffees whenever he went into town. He helped create the monster that would be coming from her room soon.

"Cheater cup," he said suddenly, thinking of a way to avoid her ire. With a quick step over to where Papi stored the mugs, he grabbed the first mug he found and replaced the pot with it. It was a cute mug, most certainly one of Teresa's, with horses of unlikely colors dancing across it. He vaguely remembered a cartoon that she liked that had those same characters on it.

"What's a cheater cup?" Papi asked, as he eyed Billy suspiciously. He was hoping that the hotplate on the coffee maker wasn't too much for that cup. Finding another one of those would be difficult, although with Amazon, not impossible. Who knew that there were so many adults who were addicted to a cartoon about ponies?

"It's when you take one of the first cups from the pot before the grounds have lost their potency. It's cheating the pot out of that first cup," Billy replaced the cup with the pot once the mug was mostly full, leaving just enough room for some creamer. If Billy wasn't practically family, Papi might have been a bit worried that the man knew his daughter's coffee order so well. As it was, he was pretty sure that knowing Teresa's coffee was a survival skill more than anything else.

"I've never heard of it before," Papi answered, just as his daughter, in all of her good morning glory walked into the kitchen. Her hair was mussed and she had a crease mark on her cheek where she must have slept on a wrinkle in her pillowcase. She moved like the walking dead with one of his old tee-shirts and a pair of sleep shorts on. She looked adorable and terrifying at the same time.

"I got your coffee," Billy said, presenting her with the cup even before she asked. Her friends must've still been sleeping since they did not come out with her.

"Thanks, Uncle Billy," Teresa muttered as she took the cup and pulled over a stool to sit at the counter, awaiting the pancakes her dad was making. Looking at her sitting there, waiting for food and drinking coffee, Papi could hardly believe that his little princess was now a thirteen-year-old young lady. He still saw the little three-year-old who would climb up on the stool to "help" him make pancakes when her Mama was so sick she could barely get out of bed.

"Papi, if you don't pay attention to those pancakes, they're going to burn. Do you need me to finish them for you?" Teresa grumped.

This morning appeared to be full of horrors.

"Nope, I got them," Papi said, turning his attention to the pan in front of him. She was right, the pancakes were nearly done. That didn't mean that the idea of her behind a stove terrified him any less.

The last time she'd thought to help make something, she nearly set the whole trailer on fire. Luckily, he was there when the pan caught on fire and she didn't panic. Instead, he calmly took the pan outside and doused it with water, putting out the fire. His heart might have been going a mile a minute, but he made sure to look calm since his panic would only panic her and make her feel bad and she already had felt bad about catching the French toast on fire.

No sooner did Papi shovel his last bite of food into his mouth than he heard it. It sounded like it was pretty far away, but that didn't stop the hairs on the back of his neck from rising. It was the loudest, deepest rooster crow he'd ever heard. He was used to the mind-numbing scream of the roosters around there screaming when they woke up. It was loud, annoyingly so, but not terrifying. The sound that he heard that morning was more like what he would expect a dinosaur to sound like.

"That's the big chicken I saw yesterday," Teresa said in a quiet, scared voice. She sounded as though she expected him to be able to hear her and find her.

"Well, that'd be a big chicken. Good thing we're prepared for him." Papi didn't lower his voice. He knew that the rooster was pretty far away. If he were closer, he'd hear people shooting at the bird. He was not going to act afraid of that thing in front of his daughter and scare her even more.

"We'd better make sure everyone is ready. That sounded like he was getting ready to declare war." Billy took his cue from Papi, finishing his food and talking normally. Truth be told, he was just a bit scared, though. He had gotten a good look at those beaks when they were chasing the truck. There might not have been teeth in those mouths, but they still looked like they could do some serious damage.

"We'll make more coffee and find you later with your thermos. Go take care of business, Papi." Teresa took her confidence from her Papi and adopted Uncle. They weren't afraid, neither would she be.

<u>9</u>

Jasper didn't sleep well, even on the best of days. Yesterday was far from the best of days. He had hoped that he left the people who wanted to kill him behind in the desert, but while they're not the same people, they were certainly his enemy. He went over his plans again and again, making sure that he knew what he was supposed to do and had every contingency planned out. Granted, no plan ever survived contact with the enemy, but it helped to calm him down enough to get some sleep.

Well before he was supposed to be on watch, he wandered out of his trailer and surveyed the park. Everything was quiet. Papi was up, but that old man always woke early. Someone else was up and cooking, but that wasn't all that surprising either. He doubted that there were too many people who got a full night's rest that night.

Since he was up, he figured he might as well start his watch a little bit early. A half an hour is not long most of the time, but it can feel like half a lifetime when trying to stay alert, alone, and in the dark. The sun had just risen when he heard it. It was the crow of what had to be the biggest rooster ever. It echoed through the fields, letting everything around it know that he was awake on the hunt. Jasper smiled.

Waiting is the hardest part of every war, Jasper thought as he watched the field for any trace of movement. He had heard the other guards switch places, shuffling around to get comfortable. He didn't look around. Instead, he stayed focused. He had a feeling that the attack wouldn't be long off. He was not to be disappointed.

They came in a square formation with the huge rooster in front. They looked for all the world like chickens dressed as astronauts from a distance. It was only as they got closer that their size became apparent. Papi had said that the chickens were at least man-sized. Jasper figured that he meant in height because the body sizes of those monsters were far more than any single person he had ever seen. They were huge. Their feathers made them look even bigger.

While the M-4 that he was holding was accurate up to 800 meters, that still meant that the operator had to be able to hit a target at that distance. He didn't want to give away his position to the chickens by attempting to shoot the head rooster, as tempting as it was. The damned thing was making itself a target, parading out in front of the rest of them. He might hit the target, and hopefully kill it, but there was too high of a chance that the others would follow his example and start shooting. They were less likely to be successful. While he had not heard that the chickens had weapons, he had to assume that they weren't stupid enough to attack the park unarmed.

There was something he could do, though. He radioed Papi and the rest of the guards on an open channel. "Chickens ahead, about half a mile out."

"Got it. Hold steady. No sense in wasting bullets if you don't have a clear shot." Papi knew that Jasper knew this, but he figured that since they were on an open channel, he'd remind the others in the tree stands.

What Jasper was not anticipating was Silas climbing up his tree a few minutes later. "Boss man says you might like something to keep you company," the old man grunted as he tried unsuccessfully to lug a huge canvas tote up with him.

"Something? Not someone, right?" Jasper asked. He would not like to try to share the tree stand with someone else. There was not a lot of room up there, and only one strap.

"Nope, he specifically said 'something' and told me to go fetch it." This was followed by even more grunting and shifting around, making the tree sway dangerously.

"Hold still. If they don't know we're up here, they will by the time you settle down. You're rocking the tree." Jasper reached down to seize the strap of the canvas, surprised by the weight of the thing. It was close to thirty pounds, and while that isn't much to carry, it is a lot to climb with, especially if that person happened to be an old man.

"What you got here?" Jasper asked. He thought Silas would continue his way up the tree now that he wasn't hampered by the bag, but instead, the man started working his way down the tree.

"Something to keep you company!" With that, the man was gone.

Glancing up at the oncoming chickens, Jasper figured that he had a few more minutes before he would be engaging them. He had just enough time to check to see what was in the tote. It brought a smile to his face. It was certainly something to keep him company and disrupt the chickens from their attack. It was the rocket launcher.

There are a lot of rocket launchers out there. Some of them are better than others, but Jasper had shot them all. He had his favorites, and the RPG-7 happened to be right up there. It was lighter and better constructed than some others on the market. He never thought he would get to shoot one as a civilian, and he didn't even begin to question how Silas got one, but he was glad he did.

Silas had not set up the rocket launcher for use. He had just brought all of the necessary components, leaving Jasper to assemble it, sitting twenty feet in the air. It had been a few years since Jasper had used one of these things, but just like riding a bike, his hands knew what they were doing before his brain even began to process everything. Within seconds he had the device armed and ready to go. With a smile, he lifted it to his shoulder and looked down the scope. He was going to shred some chickens today.

The shot was deafening. Despite being prepared for it, Jasper was still surprised by how loud it was in the relative silence of the morning. The recoil was even more concerning if that was even possible. The air around him felt as though it was his own private hurricane-force winds. His hair was short, but even then it lifted in the currents. His glasses were knocked askew, and he was thankful for the belt that kept him tethered to the tree stand. That was until he heard a sharp crack.

Issac Newton said that the force of an object is equal to the mass times its acceleration. The RPG-7 Warhead was not a small object. It also had a very fast acceleration. The force of that object was significant, to say the least. The last time Jasper did the math he came out with something like 384 feet per second and while there is a socket to reduce the recoil, no one expected it to be shot from a tree. The initial movement in the tree was minor, but as Jasper corrected himself for it, it intensified resulting in a snap similar to the sound of a bone breaking and he found himself falling backward.

This is not how I thought I'd die, Jasper thought as he went from swaying in the tree to falling. The sudden change in inertia tore a gasp from him and it was only through training and luck that he didn't drop everything he was holding, potentially hurting himself further. His gun was loaded, dropping it could cause an accidental misfire, and that bullet wasn't going to stop unless something made it stop.

Jasper braced for the impact that he knew had to be coming. Twenty feet didn't seem like a lot until he was falling with half a tree coming down with him. Just as he thought he'd hit the ground, he felt the tree snag, dragging his tree stand to a not ungentle stop just before the ground. The surrounding trees caught him, snagging their branches in the half trunk that snapped from the tree he was in. Unfortunately, it left him practically dangling out of the tree stand, facing the ground that was now less than five feet away from his face. Looking up, he could see where the top of his tree caught in the "Y" of another tree. It had been a close thing, but he'd survive.

<u>10</u>

Papi watched as the rocket that he had sent Silas out with left the trees. He couldn't see Jasper, but he figured out where he was by following the trail the warhead had left behind it. He hoped that Jasper had enough time to move before the Chickens figured out where he was and launched a counterattack.

Watching the warhead streak toward the chicken was the longest seconds of his life. If Jasper missed… Well, Papi just had to hope that Jasper didn't miss. He didn't have long to wait to find out though. The warhead landed in the middle of the square of Chickens, just slightly more toward the head chicken in the lead. Blood vaporized in a sudden mist. Feathers, meat, and bone flew everywhere, spraying the area surrounding them with chicken parts. It was a devastating attack.

It, unfortunately, didn't take out the head chicken. Instead of dying, he puffed up his chest and crowed. The sound of it echoed through the field in the eeriest manner, striking terror in small game. What this chicken didn't think of was that the people living in Pleasant Mountains Trailer Park were used to roosters and had a love of defiance. True to their form, at least half of the people in the park raised their own voices, calling back to the rooster in several animal noises. He heard wolf howls, chicken crows, and even a few cow moos.

When he came rushing to the trailer park with his few remaining chickens, Papi thought it would all be over quickly. He was surprised when he heard gunshots coming from the other side of the park. It looked like the chickens decided to use a two-pronged attack. Not being able to be at two places at once, Papi chose to race to where the head chicken was and hoped to put a stop to his attack. Maybe if they cut off the head of the chicken, it'd actually die.

Billy heard the gunshots over to the east and the north. It wasn't his job to set up guards, his had been to get the fence set up. Without anything specific to do at that moment, he turned to where he thought he'd find Papi, looking for instructions as to where to reinforce the men. Instead, he found the man racing towards the north, where the rooster was. It didn't take long for Billy to decide to head east and help those guys out.

Billy grabbed his gun and took off towards the newly built wall and the more inexperienced guards to help prevent a breach. The devastation that those chickens could cause if they got into the park didn't bear thinking about. He would just have to prevent it at all costs.

Billy climbed one of the mobile homes so that he could look over the fence and have the high ground shooting the chickens. With their wings, they could jump the fence and even change direction once in the air, but he had gone hunting before. He was pretty confident that he could hit a giant chicken from a stable base. He had managed it from the bed of a moving truck, after all.

Just as he had his first chicken lined up, he heard the rumbling roar of a zero-turn John Deere riding lawn mower gone wrong. It had gone so wrong that it belched black smoke and sounded more like a monster truck than a mower. The average zero-turn mower clocks in at a whopping eight miles an hour at full speed. This monstrosity was clocking nearly forty, and the cackling man on top did not look like he was planning on slowing down.

"Who the hell is that?" Billy asked nobody in particular. He was not expecting an answer.

"Oh, that's Nathan Rogowski. He just moved here last month. He's a retired Army Ranger. He mowed the field behind his trailer once before declaring that there had to be a better way. Apparently, that's what he came up with," Silas answered. Where the old man had come from, Billy didn't know, but he was glad to have another witness to the chaos going on below.

Nathan had tied the controls together, much like the reins of a horse, and was using his knees to steer the mower. All the while, he was shooting at the chickens with his rifle. He was actively chasing the chickens with the full intention of running them over with the mower.

"He doesn't think that will work, does he?" Billy asked Silas as they watched. He had managed to shoot two of them, but he hadn't run any over yet.

"It looks like it's an effective way to counter their speed," Silas pointed out. "I'm not so sure that running them over will work, though."

It took a few more minutes of dumbfounded staring before they had their answer. Nathan had lined his mower up to a chicken. It was too close for the bird to get away. It fell when he shot it, but he was too close to avoid running it over. The spray of feathers, fabric, and blood exploded from under the mower in an impressive burst. Everyone flinched, everyone except for the man who was simply having the time of his life riding on the mower, chasing giant alien chickens.

"At least he's having fun," Billy commented as he turned to check on the rest of the perimeter.

"WATCH OUT!" someone shouted over the noise that the mower was making. Nathan didn't have a chance to hear them, though. The engine was simply too loud, plus the ear protection he was wearing. He didn't see the last chicken coming up behind him, but Billy did. Without thinking about it, he raised his rifle and fired. The chicken's head burst like a melon, sending the beak flying and hitting Nathan in the back of the head, but not hurting him. With a startled jump, he looked around and found the dead chicken behind him. With a smile and a thumbs up, he conveyed his thanks as he continued to ride around his portion of the perimeter.

Billy stood there for a few more minutes, making sure that the chickens were not planning another attack. As he stood there, he noticed that the sounds of gunfire from the North were increasing. He had thought that the attack would have been quick-lived like this one was. Instead, the head rooster was giving them some trouble.

Billy thought about jumping from trailer to trailer. It'd have looked cool as heck, but one look at the distance between the trailers, and the roofing conditions of some of them, and he realized that he'd never make it.

Instead, he climbed down the trailer and ran towards where Papi was standing on a trailer.

As he was running over, he saw Papi point his gun almost straight down. The chickens were almost to the fence line. Before he could shoot the gun, the giant rooster jumped straight up. If it had been an anime, it could not have looked any cooler or any more terrifying. The bird was huge. His feathers were red where he was bleeding through his space uniform. His tail feathers were a wild mess behind him, some broken and others sticky with his command's gore. From the view Billy had as he watched the chicken rear over Papi, he had to be twice the size of the average man. "PAPI!" he screamed, knowing he was about to watch the death of his best friend.

Papi didn't panic when the rooster jumped in front of him. Panicking is how people end up dead. He took a step back, keeping the bird in front of him. The rooster looked so much bigger as he landed on the trailer, standing several feet taller than Papi. He was thick and there was a lot of blood leaking from him, but it didn't seem to slow him down at all.

Papi thrust his gun up and towards the chicken's head. He shoved it forward and up as if it had a bayonet, but it was just the open end of the barrel. With the stroke of his finger, the trigger depressed, and a burst of flame leaped forth. The rooster, whose body had soaked up the damage done by the same bullets, didn't survive the blast. With a thud like thunder, the rooster toppled.

11

The silence was deafening. No one moved for several minutes after the rooster died. Even Nathan on his souped-up mower sat silent. Everyone was expecting another attack, that there would be more chickens. The battle was not long, but it was long enough and terrifying. Everything seemed to have happened all at once, and now there was nothing left to do.

"Is that it?" Billy asked as he climbed the trailer that Papi was on so he could get a good look at the rooster. He was a mess. His head was gone and there was blood everywhere. He had one good tail feather left out of what was once an impressive display.

"I'm thinking that was it," Papi answered after a few more minutes. If there was going to be another attack, they'd have done it by now. Granted, if he was attacking, he'd have made sure to have backup ready to strike when the enemy got complacent, most likely in the evening. That's when he'd strike. He also could not imagine that the ship had that many chickens on board.

"We should check out that ship and see if we can rescue the people from the farm." It was barely eight in the morning, and he was already exhausted. Today was going to be a very long day.

"I reckon we'd have better luck finding survivors if we go sooner rather than later," Billy agreed.

"We'd better find Jasper," Papi though aloud. If they wanted the mission to be successful, they needed help. Two people against a spaceship was just asking for trouble. Plus, if anyone needed medical attention, it was better to have more people who could administer first aid than not enough. Granted, three might not be enough, but it was better than two. Papi rubbed his face with his hands. He'd kill for another cup of coffee and an hour's nap.

"We should find Jasper first, then we'll get that new guy, Nathan," Billy added.

"New guy? Oh, that's right, he moved into Rosie's trailer. I don't know anything about him yet. Seems to keep to himself."

"Silas knew him. Apparently, he was an Army Ranger. He rigged his mower to drive almost as fast as those chickens could run. He managed to run one of them over. It was concerning, terrifying, and gratifying all at the same time. If he can come up with that, and he initially did it just so he didn't have to spend an hour cutting his grass, then I'm sure he'll come in handy trying to rescue people from the ship."

"I'm pretty sure being an Army Ranger isn't something you recover from. I understand it's something like being a Marine, a terminal condition." Both men laughed at that. Marines until the end, in or out of uniform.

They found Jasper still hanging by the strap on the tree stand. Even though he was able to hang onto the rocket launcher, he had managed to drop his knife. He could not cut himself down and there was too much pressure on the latch for him to unclip it. He couldn't shimmy out of it either, the strap being too tight for that, and him not having anything to grab hold of to work against the strap with. He was well and truly stuck. Billy climbed the nearest tree and started to cut the strap securing Jasper in the seat.

"Wait, wait, wait. I don't want to land face first!" Jasper called as he felt the first pieces of the strap give up the ghost. Just as he reached behind him to grab hold of something, the rest of the strap broke.

One moment Billy had been watching Jasper squirm in the seat, trying to find some way to control his approaching fall, and the next, the man was just gone and there was the sound of crashing below him. Jasper had fallen, practically face first, in front of Papi. Papi had tried to catch the man, but since no one was expecting him to fall right then, no one was prepared. Jasper was just lucky he was able to get his hands in front of him and break the fall a bit.

"We should have gone back and gotten a mattress or something before attempting to cut him out of the deer stand." Papi reflected with his 20/20 hindsight.

"Did I miss everything?" Jasper asked once he was done spitting out dirt and brushing off leaves and twigs.

"Well, kind of. We're about to go wandering out to the cow farm to see if we can rescue the people in the ship," Billy answered for Papi.

"You think they're still alive?" Jasper asked. He had a good point. They might not be alive. If they were caught to be food, keeping them alive would require a lot more work than just processing them immediately. If they were going to be used as labor on the chickens' home planet, that'd be a different matter. Either way, there was only one way to know for sure if they were alive or dead.

"We have to check." Billy led the way back through the trailer park.

"I'm Billy, this is Papi and Jasper." Billy introduced himself and his friends to the stranger who stood in front of him. The man wasn't particularly tall, but he had the type of fighting building that spoke of years in the military. There was only as much fat as was necessary to be healthy. The rest of him was bone and muscle. His piercing blue eyes took in the group with an appraising glance, and then his whole face burst into a smile.

"I'm Nate. What can I do for you guys?" His smile changed his whole persona. He went from looking like someone who'd pick a fight just to pick a fight, to someone who would go out of his way to help people.

"I saw you on the mower. Silas also says that you are an Army Ranger. We're Marines, but we figure that just this once, a mud dog could work with some crayon eaters. We might have some people to go save."

Nate grew serious. Billy wasn't sure if it was because he called him a mud dog, or if it was that there were more people in need of help. The longer the man took to answer, the higher the tension rose between the men. Just when Billy was going to call the whole thing off, Nate answered.

"I say we're going to have to work together. I don't know where the people are and if I leave it to you guys, you might get distracted by a coloring book. Nope, we're going to have to work together." Nate spoke with a dead serious voice, but there was a twinkle in his eyes to let them know he was joking. "Lead on."

Getting Billy's truck out of the trailer park proved to be a bit of a challenge. For the security of the park, they had not added gates. Gates are a point of weakness in a wall and since they were unsure of the strength of the chickens, there was no way they were going to make the wall intentionally weaker than it had to be. That left them with no way to get the truck out and get themselves to the cow farm. With none of them being the best of riders, and with only one horse having a saddle, cowboying it up wasn't going to be an option either. They had to cut the fence.

"Make sure you close it up tight, but don't weld it shut after us. We might have casualties riding with us, and we don't want to be stuck outside the fence. The same goes for if we're being followed by chickens." Billy guided several people through the process of cutting open the fence and how to secure it after them. While he worked on that, Nate and Jasper decided that two trucks were better than one.

"If we take two, we can guard each other and provide support when necessary. Besides, we might need the extra room," Nate reasoned. "I have a club cab truck. It'd be ideal if we need to move a lot of people. You can ride with me."

It was almost noon before the two trucks were able to leave the park. They didn't hurry; they didn't rush. Doing something stupid like racing across the fields as opposed to doing things right by taking the road was just asking for them to break an axle and get stuck in the worst possible moment. Instead, Papi led the tiny caravan while Nate drove the truck behind him. Billy and Jasper rode in the truck beds, one each, keeping an eye out on the surrounding terrain for any stray chickens.

It did not take long to get to the farm. They used the same road alongside the McDonald farm where they had previously seen the spaceship. Billy and Papi found it hard to believe that it had only been one day since they first heard about the spaceship. It was easily the longest day ever, and it wasn't even over yet. At least they were able to get some sleep, and they now had coffee, so it was not a total wash.

From the trucks, they stared at the spaceship for a while. They noted the flashing lights on the ship, as well as what appeared to be an antenna coming from the top of the disc-shaped craft. The ramp was still down.

"I swear, if I had asked a bunch of preschoolers to draw a UFO for me, this is exactly what they'd have drawn," Jasper observed.

"Yeah, makes me wonder if there isn't some type of genetic memory of them coming down to Earth before," Nate continued that thought.

"Like what? they came down to steal humans and maybe leave chickens as their spies?" Billy wanted to laugh at the idea, but even he had to admit that it made a certain type of sense.

"I thought we had evidence that chickens came from dinosaurs," Papi interjected. He was all for the idea that maybe there had been alien abductions by these creatures before, but the idea that he might have been eating alien meat his entire life was a bit too much for him at the moment.

"It'd make a type of sense if they originated from Earth first. I mean, we lost a lot of history. Maybe there were smart chickens who developed space travel and just left the dumb chickens here." Billy felt he might be stretching things a bit much, but who knows, maybe he's on the right track. Papi just grunted, not wanting to continue the pointless discussion.

"Anyone see anything yet?" Nate asked. He had been listening to their discussion, but without anything solid to contribute, he remained silent. No sense in speculating, especially since it had no bearing on saving the people trapped inside.

"Nope, not a thing. There doesn't appear to be anyone home." Jasper jumped out of the bed of Nate's truck. He was going to get closer.

"Where are you going?" Billy whisper yelled to him.

"I'm going to find out if anyone's home. We're not doing any good from here." Jasper had a point, but it was a dangerous thing to do. Just because the chickens that attacked the trailer park didn't have weapons didn't mean that the ship or whoever was on the ship didn't.

"I'm coming with you." Nate quietly climbed out of his truck and silently closed the door behind him.

"We'll all go," Billy reluctantly said as he climbed out of his truck bed. He waited a moment for Papi to join him, and then they followed the two men in front of them towards the spaceship.

Walking at a crouch was hard for Papi. It'd been a long time since he had done it consistently as part of his strength training. By the time they made it to the ship, his legs were on fire, and he wasn't positive he was going to be able to stand without his knees cracking. The fact that everyone else looked like they were comfortable just rankled him even further. The fact that nothing had happened between the trucks and the ship was the only highlight of the entire trek.

"I don't see a door," Papi informed the group when he leaned over the ramp and peered into the ship. He didn't see much, just that there did not appear to be a door baring their way into the ship.

"Rather cocky to leave your ship wide open," Nate noted.

"Cocky…" Jasper laughed. Everyone else smiled and laughed at the terrible pun.

Once the men were settled back down, they decided it was time to ascend the ramp and see what they could find inside the ship. If they were lucky, the captives would be right up front, but no one actually thought they were going to get out of there without a fight.

The men knew that they were going to have to be fast. The ramp offered considerable risk to their safety. Once they were on the ramp, the only place they could go was up and into the ship, or off the ramp. There would be no cover and if anyone cast even a causal glance their way, they'd be spotted. Without cover, it'd be like shooting fish in a barrel, just easier. A couple deep breaths each, and they stormed the ship.

Jasper and Nate were the first up the ramp. Papi and Billy were right on their heels and almost ran into the men when they stopped suddenly. The ship was dark and going from the bright day into the dark ship was jarring. The men couldn't see much of anything, not that there was much to see. There was nothing in the center of the ship except for sixteen humans sitting in what appeared to be hay.

"Thank God, someone came to rescue us," one of the humans said.

"How come there are only four of you guys?" another person asked.

"Tell me you aren't the rednecks from Pleasant Mountain," the only girl in the group groaned.

"Uh, yeah. We're here to rescue you. Why didn't you just leave the ship? The door is open," Papi decided to ignore the last statement.

"Because of the force field, obviously," the girl stated as though it were obvious. Papi could not see a force field. All he saw were walls covered in buttons with a few chairs in front of them, and openings that most likely lead to the crew quarters and mess. Most of the ship seemed to be designed for the transport of livestock.

"Step forward a bit," the girl said with a smile.

Papi knew whatever was going to happen was going to be less than pleasant. He was braced for what would likely be an electric shock. He kept an eye out, figuring that maybe there would be some warning as to when he'd run into the barrier, but he didn't see anything. Just as he figured that maybe he was wrong, and that there was nothing but a psychological block stopping the people from moving, he ran into it. He expected electricity, but what he got was a solid wall of something. He crashed into it full bodily.

"See?" the woman asked.

"Actually, I don't see it, but I certainly felt it." Even though Papi knew where the wall was, he couldn't see it, or even hear it, when he knocked on it.

"Exactly, which is why we aren't moving. We're not sure where the wall is, and it is flexible enough that the aliens sometimes move them just to mess with us. At least that's what we think they're doing. Moving the wall from the inside is impossible."

"Well, we'll just have to work on getting you guys out. Are there any chickens in the ship?" Papi should have asked that question right away, but the invisible wall had distracted him. Once he thought of the question, he realized how vulnerable he had left his team. Just because he didn't see the aliens, didn't mean they didn't see him.

"Just the one. We've named him Bobby. He's been taking care of us. He seems nicer than the others. He also seems to be the one being picked on the most. I think he's afraid of the other chickens."

"So, there is only one chicken left? We killed the others when they attacked the trailer park," Jasper explained.

"Bobby should be back shortly. Maybe we can convince him to let us go," the girl suggested. She had grown to like Bobby and didn't want these men to hurt him.

"Maybe," Billy partially agreed. He would love nothing more than a peaceful solution, but he wasn't counting on it.

Bobby arrived a few moments later. He was a balding rooster with small cuts and bruises from where the other chickens had been plucking at his feathers. He was skinnier than the other chickens had been and looked thoroughly miserable. He brought oats with him in hopes of finding something that the humans in his care could eat. He saw the cows eat it, so he thought it might be a promising option.

"Bobby!" the girl called over to him. He looked up sharply at the name that she had given him and looked as joyful as a creature who didn't have facial expressions could look. Then he noticed the four new humans.

12

Bobby threw himself between the humans in his care and the new humans. As he launched himself between them, oats scattered everywhere, marking the boundary of the force field. He began to cluck and scratch at the ground wildly, almost as though he was trying to intimidate the men standing in front of him. It almost made Papi laugh. It reminded him of the kids in the park and their posturing.

"Calm down, Bobby. We're not here to hurt anyone. We're just here to get these people home." Papi knew that Bobby was unlikely to understand them, but he felt the need to explain, anyway. It was clear as day to him that Bobby would not be a threat.

"Bobby! They're friends," the woman explained, using hand gestures to get her point across. She even hugged one of her co-workers to express affection and friendship. Papi wasn't sure that any of this made any sense to the alien, their culture being potentially so far removed from their own, but the captives had a full day's more experience with the aliens than he did. They'd know better.

It took quite a bit of gesturing, but finally, the woman, who Papi learned was named Crystal, managed to convince the alien that his co-workers were not coming back and that he should let them all go. The minutes that it took Bobby to figure out how to open the force field were stressful for the would-be rescuers. They knew all too well how some people viewed failure, and they worried that Bobby might just kill the captives out of spite. Luckily for everyone, Bobby was far more compassionate. He let everyone go without any fuss or bother.

As the sixteen people who had been held captive left the ship, Bobby drooped lower and lower. When Crystal was about to leave, his head was practically on the floor and his wings were spread on either side of him. If he were any more despondent, she'd worry that he had just given up on life and died. It broke her heart.

"You guys should take him back to your place, and let him live in your community," she told Jasper, not taking her eyes off the giant chicken. Somehow even his cream-colored feathers had appeared to dull before her eyes.

"He likes you. You like him. You should keep him," Jasper countered. He'd just got done fighting a bunch of these birds. He didn't want to take one home as a pet.

"I can't. I live in an apartment. I'm not allowed to have pets." Crystal's argument wasn't completely sound. Bobby wouldn't be a pet. He'd be an alien invader whom she decided to let live with her.

"I live in a trailer, not a chicken coop." Jasper's answer was just as valid.

"What are we going to do with the spaceship?" Billy asked, cutting into the conversation.

"Blow it up?" Jasper answered, but he answered it as a question. He had not thought about what to do with the spaceship. Papi wandered over to join the conversation when he heard Billy's question. It was a good question, and Papi figured that the government would be mighty eager to get their hands on some alien technology, but since they refused to help, maybe he'd refuse to give it to them.

"We could turn it into a roadside attraction," Papi answered, thinking about the spaceship he saw at Roswald.

"Charge people to see it?" Billy liked that idea.

"We could have Bobby here show people around. He'd hide himself in plain sight!" Crystal was getting excited about the idea.

"Well now, wait. We didn't agree to take Bobby home with us," Jasper reminded her.

"It would be an easy solution. I don't think I could bring myself to kill the bird. He is harmless, and he did try to protect everyone when he thought we were a threat," Papi reasoned. Jasper knew he had lost that battle. He'd just have to get used to having a chicken as a neighbor.

"Come on, Bobby, we'll show you where you're going to be living from now on," Jasper called over to the bird, invitingly waving his arm. Almost as though he understood what the man said, Bobby perked up and came half leaping, half flying over to the group. Jasper had to admit, he did look rather pathetic and nothing like a threat.

When everyone got back to the trailer park, they were greeted with the best smell on Earth, barbeque.

"Someone's cooking an awful lot of food," Billy commented as they began smelling the food quite a ways away from the park. Billy was driving his truck with Papi in the passenger seat. Bobby couldn't fit in the truck, so he was riding in the bed of the truck, trailing feathers as they went.

"Must be a potluck or something. Everyone is likely hungry after this morning's battle." Papi was a little surprised though, even if everyone pitched in together, getting enough meat ready to cook at the same time was surprising.

"Smells like chicken," Billy mumbled as they got closer to the park.

"They wouldn't have." Papi began to rub his forehead. He was too tired to deal with the headache he knew was coming.

"Are you kidding? There is nothing that Silas wouldn't eat," Billy disagreed.

Just as they were about to get within sight of the park, Billy hit the brakes. "We've got a problem."

"What problem?" Papi asked. He really didn't want to deal with any more problems, yet, they kept coming.

"We have a live chicken in the back of my truck. What's to stop anyone from just shooting him?" If any of them had anywhere near enough sleep, they'd have seen the problem it was well before they got so close to the trailer park.

"Shit. One of us will have to go in and explain it first. Rock, Paper, Scissors?"

Sitting in Nate's truck, Nate and Jasper just stared at the two men in front of them. "They've lost their minds," Nate casually noted, watching the two men start round three of a best of three. When Papi won again, Billy started for a fourth time, hoping to get four out of seven.

"They might be entitled to that. They did fight some giant chickens today," Jasper agreed.

"Yeah," Nate laughed. They fought giant alien chickens. Who would have guessed that his retirement would be so adventurous?

"Like I said, Bobby is a chicken, but he's our friend, not our enemy. He helped the people who were kidnapped, and he seems to be a gentle soul. No picking on Bobby. No shooting Bobby. Everyone will be nice to Bobby." Billy intentionally used the name that Crystal had given the bird when he spoke. He wanted everyone to think of the chicken they were bringing in as an individual, not as one of the beings that tried to invade their home. Judging from the blank looks, he wasn't sure that his message was getting through. No time like the present to see if they got the message or not.

Papi drove carefully through the gate when Billy signaled to him to come forward. He was prepared to put the truck in reverse and retreat if it looked like people were going to go after Bobby. He just hoped that Billy had made it clear that Bobby wasn't to be hurt, that he was one of the good guys. He also hoped that he could do this quickly. Whatever was cooking was beginning to smell almost too good to his starved body.

Papi put the truck in park once he got clear of the gate. He held still, not wanting to trigger anyone into any rash actions. No one moved in the entire park. Glancing up into his rearview mirror he saw something rather disarming. Bobby was in a submissive crouch. His legs were bent, and his body was pressed against the bed of the truck, wings spread out on either side of him. It looked both ridiculous and impressive at the same time. Papi smiled to himself and began to laugh.

"Well, Bobby, welcome to your new home. We'll move your spaceship here and make it a tourist attraction that you can live in," Papi said as he got out of the truck, breaking the spell of immobility that seemed to have settled on everyone. As a sign of his trust in the chicken, he reached up into the bed of the truck, ruffling the few feathers that Bobby had on the top of his head. They were surprisingly soft.

Just like that, everyone else accepted the bird.

"Dinner's ready!" screamed one of the children who lived in the park. It was obvious that his mom told him to pass the message along that the food was ready, but he decided that shouting it was the most effective way to get the message to everyone.

"What's been cooking?" Papi asked Silas as they walked towards the series of tables that had been set up in front of the McDonald trailer. They'd have to move that back out to the McDonald farm in the next couple of days. The trailer didn't have any hookups in the middle of the park, making it impossible to even go to the bathroom there. Instead, Ethal and Benny had to go to someone else's home for the slightest thing.

"Well, we decided that the chickens would be good eating," Silas answered as he took his place in line, in front of Papi.

"Say what?" Papi was hungry, but he wasn't sure he was hungry enough to eat alien chickens.

"Well, the dogs had been out in the field making good work on the chickens that Jasper blew up, and we all got a thinking. If the dogs are willing to eat the birds, and they didn't get sick, maybe we could eat them. It sure beat burying the things and we had to do something with him. Waste not, want not, and all of that," Silas explained.

"You deemed the chickens safe to eat...based on the fact that the dogs ate them and didn't get sick?" Papi repeated, looking for clarification.

"Yepper. That'd be the gist of it. When the lady folks began cleaning the birds, they found that they were exactly like normal chickens, just bigger. It should be fine. No way that Emma was going to use her famous bar-be-que sauce on some meat she didn't think would be good." Silas pronounced barbeque with three distinct syllables.

With panic-filled eyes, he turned to see how Bobby was dealing with his former shipmates now being dinner. He was startled when he found the bird pecking at the ground, softly clucking to himself. He apparently didn't care that there was a pile of feathers off to one end of the park and the heads of several birds were sitting by that pile. Throwing caution to the wind, Papi decided to just go along with it and enjoy his meal.

It was the best barbeque he ever had.

254 | Page

Hydra King:

Darkleaf Exotic Animal Rescue

By Jesse James Fain

For my Pop and the Fain brothers, wild at heart and wild in action

"Dolly, baby, for the love of the Gods, put a jacket on. We've got a hydra to deal with, and that's not half as bad as a crowd of riled up Marines." Buckthorn Robindriel Darkleaf argued with his daughter, pausing to light a new cigarette as he guided the big truck and trailer down the gravel road. In the passenger seat, Dollanduriel Elouise Darkleaf ran a frustrated hand through her tall red mohawk. She gestured to the shredded *Unleash the Archers* shirt and scandalously small jean shorts.

"Daddy, you haven't told me how to dress since I was twenty. This is my style, and I'm not changing for a bunch of crazy young men. Besides, you ain't never had a bad thing to say about the Marines. Rough men like that, I might actually find a date." Bucky fought off the urge to massage the growing ache behind his eyes and took the previously instructed right turn to one of the Camp Lejeune firing ranges.

"I love the Marines, Hun. Best damn men I ever fought beside, but them boys are going to have to grow up into mustangs or experienced men before I want them around my daughter." He blew a puff of smoke. "Just listen to your Daddy one time. I'm already exhausted."

"Fine, but I'm telling Mamma you stopped for burritos and didn't get her one."

Bucky took his turn, sliding a hand through his mass of blonde braids, causing bones and feathers to shimmer and clack together, but kept his silence and took another drag instead. Dolly gave her father a mischievous smile before stealing one of his cigarettes and lighting it with a zippo from her boot. "Ain't you and mamma about to go on vacation?"

"Yep, got us a fancy stateroom for a Caribbean cruise. Nothing but sunshine, fruity drinks, and bikinis."

"If we don't get eaten?"

"If we don't get eaten."

Bucky didn't get much of a chance to speak past that, slamming on his brakes as another big truck with a trailer spiraled out into the road. He cursed as he struggled to bring the vehicle to a stop, and his anger boiled over even more when he saw the writing on the side of the offending vehicle. *Berkin's Bestiary* flashed sunlight back at Bucky's angry glare. The other truck wobbled slightly as it ran off the road to make the turn, then stopped, and the tinted driver window lowered to reveal a beady eyed man wearing a bright yellow sun visor and ratty polo. The man gazed at Bucky with all but murderous intent. Bucky dropped his own window and growled at the man.

"Damn it, Carl! You nearly wrecked us both. If you can't drive a truck, use some of that trust fund money to hire someone who can. Besides, what the hell are you doing here?"

"I was here to make sure the job actually got taken care of, Bucko! To let them know when you inevitably screw the pooch, they can call me instead of you and your inbred clan of hicks." Carl spat back in a thick New York accent.

"Carl, I've never seen you do anything but fornicate, Fido. Now get your ugly ass out of the way. The longer you stand in my way, the more likely good men will get slaughtered. Not that you ever bothered to care about that!"

"I swear to Christ, Bucko, I'll drive you and your clan of rednecks out of this business. Just you wait."

While the men were arguing, Dolly calmly fished into the glove box, gently withdrawing a heavy caliber revolver. Bucky caught the gleam of the blued steel in the corner of his eye and gestured for her to put it away with a shake of his hand.

"Fuck off, Carl, I have people to watch out for." The big man stated, choking down on an old, deep-seated rage that bordered on demonic. Bucky rolled the window up.

Carl took his sweet time getting the truck out of the way, doing his level best to murder every Darkleaf in history with the daggers in his gaze. Bucky held up a single finger salute throughout the process. Dolly spat out her own window as their rival's truck bounced down the road.

"That **bastard**. Should've just let me shoot him Daddy, I got an ole .38 in my boot. I could've planted it on him, no prints. He cut us off and pulled it. I had to act."

"You're too pretty for jail, Baby, and he'll screw another job up eventually and get eaten, just like all those poor people from the last three times." Bucky put the truck in gear and a few minutes later, they reached the job site.

The big *Darkleaf Exotic Animal Rescue* truck rolled to a stop, pulling up and around a crowd of Humvees and newer JLTV transports. The big trucks transported the Marines of the 1st Battalion, 8th Marine Regiment out for machine gun practice. Range day turned rapidly into another kind of special event, which led to Bucky and his daughter traveling up from Georgia with a plexiglass lined trailer.

The duo climbed out of their transport and scanned around, both had sharp noses and the same curve to their lips. They made an odd pair even with the family resemblance. Bucky stood near seven feet. Tall enough to worry about cracking his noggin on a door frame if it was out of spec. Covered in scrolling knotwork tattoos, Bucky's shoulders were broad under his black *Strigil Simpson* T-shirt. He stuffed his cigarettes into his jeans and looked over at his daughter to make sure she was following his request.

Dolly listened to her pa, tossing on a denim battle jacket covered in heavy metal band patches. Dolly's mohawk was tall enough to cover her father's nose, placing the lithe woman over six feet. Where her father decorated himself with knotwork, metal adorned the conservationist's eldest daughter. Piercings spangled across her ears and dark skulls and gravestones covered her skin.

"Well, I'll be damned," slipped gently from Dolly as she strode up next to her father.

Out on the target range, the United States Marine Corps engaged in a tug-of-war. On one side of the long rope, a dozen grunts hauled for all they were worth, young men of all shapes and backgrounds with combat boots dug into the wet grass, undershirts laden with sweat. On the other side of the rope, a massive double headed reptilian beast bit onto a makeshift grip, tossed together with exercise mats and duct tape.

Near the size of a truck already, the young swamp monster was the dark green of bog water with brown freckles adorning its matte scales. A single shirtless Marine with a great bristling mustache rode atop the base of the beast's neck, shouting encouragement.

Two great rivers of corrosive saliva ate into the grass under the creature's twin maws. Long spines ran down the tapered necks that led to a squat, powerful body supported by six thick legs and lethally clawed feet. Each neck sported a camouflage shirt, and each noggin wore a human sized battle helmet secured with more hundred-mile-an-hour tape.

Bucky scratched the back of his neck and shrugged at his daughter's exclamation. "I expected them all to be holed up in the trucks or scattered by now."

A pair of warriors walked up to the new arrivals, covered in sweat and grime from the day's exercise. The bigger of the two stepped forward and extended a hand to Bucky, then Dolly.

"Thanks for coming out, Mr. Darkleaf. You got here damn fast. I'm Staff Sergeant Ramirez, and this is Corporal Kilpatrick. The Major I talked to on the phone about getting someone out here seemed really freaked out, but so far, Corporal Doubledome hasn't been much of a problem. Though that Carl guy almost pissed him off."

"That *bastard* has a tendency to get people mauled to death… Just Bucky is fine, Staff Sergeant, and this here is Dolly," Dolly nodded and interjected before her father could continue.

"He ain't tried to eat y'all yet?"

Both Marines laughed and cast a guilty glance. Kilpatrick explained, rubbing his forearm as a nervous tick. "You ever had an MRE?"

"Can't say I've had the pleasure."

"Well, some of them are just plain Fu-" The Corporal caught himself. "Just nasty, so we do everything we can out here to avoid them. We had this one crate full of the worst flavors, and we set it off on the edge of the field. That's what Corporal Doubledome got into. Slipped out of the bushes and ate the whole crate. Handles and all. Trust me, nothing he could do would frighten the men worse than getting stuck with *Veggie Omelet*." Kilpatrick shivered, his eyes going to a faraway place, before he remembered to continue. "Well, Lance Corporal Keeper, over there." A hand guided them to look at the man on the hydra's back. "He deals with dangerous animals all the time back home. He took a few more decent flavors over to the big guy, fed both heads, and then asked us for a toy. Said that alligators and some other big reptiles were fine to hang around if they had a full belly and had something to do. So, we started working on a toy."

"Y'all made the giant, two headed, venomous, acid spitting lizard a Corporal?" Bucky asked in confusion.

"Wanted to make him a Second Lieutenant, but they don't let us give commissions," Ramirez snarked. Dolly changed the subject back to the matter at hand. "That's about right for a lot of critters, but hydras are territorial and predatory to a fault. How'd y'all get the rope to stop burning away from the venom? Hydra spit will melt rock."

Ramirez spoke up for that one. "CLP. Gun lube makes the spit slick right off."

Dolly pulled out her phone and took notes. She'd need that one for later. Her father jumped in.

"Sad as it is, Staff Sergeant, we need to get the good Corporal out of here before his appetite comes back or he gets bored."

Both Marines' shoulders sank as they saddened visibly.

"Could we build him a habitat or something, have the brass call it an experimental testing zone and rope the place off?" Kilpatrick offered. Bucky slipped to the side and patted the man on the shoulders. He knew the look and the love Kilpatrick suffered right now. Magical creatures like this terrified people. The sheer power and lethality of them shook a person to the core. There were a chosen few, like the Marines here, who saw that power and marveled instead of fleeing. They'd talk about the range day with Corporal Doubledome until the day they died.

"Much as I'd love to see it, Marine, he'd eat someone, eventually. Dolly's trained her whole life to handle them, and I worry about her every day. Class One critters need specially built facilities or lots of terrain away from people, but if y'all are ever down in Georgia, you can come see him and even feed him."

Both Marines nodded then, and Dolly broke off to the back of the trailer. The heavy metal monster tamer opened up the back of the long transport and dropped a massive ramp down from a hidden roll out. She walked out a moment later roughly carrying a half side of beef. Her father and the two NCOs walked ahead of her.

Back at the tug-of-war, Corporal Doubledome overwhelmed the men. The colossal beast dragged them through the wet grass, either digging boot sized divots or sliding them on their asses. Lance Corporal Keeper gave a great rebel yell from the monster's back as they claimed victory and his new friend remained undefeated. He hopped down and patted the hydra as it panted, scratching one head and then the other under its great chin. The Staff Sergeant piped up to give new orders.

"Alright, Devils! Fun's over for today. We have to get back to training and Corporal Doubledome is getting set up with a new barracks. Clean it up!"

The bitching started immediately, as was every warrior's sacred right. Ramirez waved the complaints away.

Keeper took the news the worst, some deep instinct bonding him to the giant predator, and he lingered for another moment, scratching and patting the monster. Shockingly, the two-headed creature appeared to enjoy the attention, and leaned into the mighty mustached Lance Corporal. The Marine laid his forehead to the creature for a few breaths, gently took off the helmets, gathered the rope carefully from each mouth, and walked away. Confusion and irritation seemed to strike the giant monster, but Dolly soon captured its attention. She and her father both tapped a talisman at their necks, a smooth stone carved with an ornate leaf, and then she let out a series of clicks and whistles.

Corporal Doubledome returned the clicks, both heads turning to the denim clad woman, and she awkwardly waved the great mass of beef enticingly.

"Come on, big fella. Let's get you into the trailer and on the way home." Dolly added softly. "He sure is pretty, Daddy. I ain't seen a two header that big since training in Greece. He's gonna make Odie look small in another twenty years."

"Let's hope he's got more brains than Odie. For having five heads, that critters only got two brain cells, and they can't even rub together."

"Don't you talk about my Odie that way."

"Focus, please!"

Slowly Dolly and Bucky walked back to the trailer. With another whistle and click she tossed the beef slab right into the back where a pile of treats awaited the good Corporal. The hydra seemed happy enough as he followed the tossed treat into the massive trailer, and the wrangling duo shut the ramp and doors peacefully. Bucky pulled a piece of Damascus steel from his pocket then, the pattern waving and weaving with beautiful craftsmanship and polish. He signed the steel over the door from corner to corner and around the edges, speaking in a rolling and flowing foreign language. The approaching Staff Sergeant thought it might be Gaelic or Welsh.

"Do you two need anything else from us?"

Dolly produced a clipboard from the cab of the big truck.

"Sign right here, and we are all set." The Staff Sergeant signed and gave the paperwork back with a nod. "Just a reminder I'm sure Major Faraday gave y'all; the big guy is classified, hydras don't exist, and we just needed to move a lost alligator."

"We're all sworn to it." Ramierez said and started to walk away, but he paused for just a moment as the two animal handlers were climbing into the big truck.

"You take care of them or relocate them, right? He's not going to end up as a fancy pair of boots?"

Dolly shut the door but rolled the window of the cab down and lit a cigarette.

"Haven't put one down in years, Staff Sergeant." She blew out a cloud of smoke between sentences. "That one was blood drunk on half a tour party Carl kindly led into its den. Killed my sister." Dolly's eyes misted for a moment. "Ole Dubby is gonna be just fine. Y'all holler if anything else shows up."

The window rolled up, and they rolled away. The two sat in companionable silence for a while, hearing the clicks and calls of the hydra occasionally as it ate or played with the toys inside the trailer. Dolly heard it make a companion call, and bang around some, it sounded irritated or lonely. She whistled through her teeth, telling the great beast she wasn't far.

"You want me to start the teleport spell, Daddy?"

"Hell, naw." Bucky replied with playful irritation.

"Any reason why not?"

"Gotta stop and get your mother a damn burrito."

Dolly chuckled before turning on the radio, and soon she and her father were both singing along. From the trailer, two heads and a tail bobbed and banged along with the beat.

"Major Faraday, our contract states plainly that we charge an extra recovery fee for Class One critters." Pamtriel Jolene Darkleaf did her best to keep a neutral tone. The Major enjoyed being a pain in the ass on the best of days, but today's attempt to wheedle her down from the government paying its due bordered on egregious.

"You can't possibly plan to charge us the same amount for this incident as you would for a wyvern breakout, Mrs. Darkleaf. Not a single person was injured in the incident. By all accounts, the men had *fun*." The Major cleared his throat. "I've got it on good authority that the contract between your company and The Department of the Navy is about to be renewed. Surely you would want to retain a good working relationship and not leave an opening for the competition."

"What competition?" The woman laughed at the audacity of it, the question coming out as a cruel bark as she lit another cigarette and tossed back her giant mass of blonde curls.

"Mr. Carl Berkins has already sent an interesting proposal to my office. Your family is not the only game in town."

"We're the only professionals, Major. There isn't anyone else that cares for the animals or provides safe and professional containment like us, like we have for the past two hundred and fifty years. No one, especially not *THAT BASTARD*, Carl Berkins, can claim that. Hence why his past three wives ended up eaten!"

The outburst scared the hell out of the six-legged wampus kitten that lounged lazily on the closest corner of her desk. The kitten jumped up hissing and spinning, trying to find the threat, but saw only the tall, hourglass shaped woman in her spandex shorts and leopard print blouse grumbling angrily with a Marlboro red hanging out of her mouth.

"Before you go and do something stupid, Major Faraday, let me tell you a story about Carl Berkins."

Jenna Mariethriel Darkleaf had been taking over the wildlife tours to take some of the weight off her parents. She and several of the staff swore they could handle anything out in the swampy south Georgia game ranch. They'd done a great job for months.

The tour group had left that morning like any other, every one of the guides packed with weapons and medical supplies, and the side-by-sides loaded with well-sealed food and water. Part of the tour would need a fan boat, also safely stocked for the two families and one newlywed couple setting out for a day of wonder at hydras, kelpies, and skunk apes.

Jenna Marie led the way through the wetland paths, Eric and Connor following at the rear of the heavy booted group of authorized tourists. Her black hair and gray eyes made her a stark contrast to both her parents, latent gifts from her great grandmother. Tall and regal, she seemed to float despite the combat boots, generic guide khakis, and a long shotgun.

"Alright y'all, gather up." She gestured, pulling everyone close as the other guides kept watchful eyes on the surrounding wilderness. "We are getting close to where we see a lot of the Altamaha-ha river creatures, giant catfish, and even some hydra activity. Please check your cameras and phones to make sure your flash is off, keep to a whisper, and listen to your guides at all times. We don't want to startle or disturb the wildlife. Remember, the safe path is marked with the white home logos, and the arrow will show the direction back to the vehicles. Please keep to the path and stay together."

"What the fuck evah, lady, this place sucks, and so far we haven't seen anything. Now you wanna tell us we can't even take decent photos if we see something. What am I paying for?" The beady eyes and ball cap would become all too familiar accessories on the man who spoke up, purposely too loud. He nudged the much younger woman next to him. "Take pictures however you want sweetheart, we paid a fortune to be here."

Jenna Marie scowled at the jackass, wondering what possessed some people to act like idiots around wildlife.

"I can promise you, Mr. Berkins, we will do all we can to make the tour as memorable and exciting as possible, but all the rules we have are for your safety. Camera flash can get your liver torn out in this swamp, so please follow the path and keep noise to a minimum."

Carl Berkins rolled his eyes, but Jenna Marie left no room for rebuttals as she turned with a nod, weapon in hand, and led them into the proverbial lion's den. It wasn't long until they came to a small grass covered rise that quickly dipped into a large swath of green and black water, lily pads and reeds dotting the brackish drink. The group hovered at Jenna's hand signals, and she whispered to the group.

"This is a great spot to see the catfish. They often surface in this pool while hunting. If we are lucky, the skunk apes and some of the local predators come here to fish as well. Let's sit for a while."

The group waited, quietly murmuring between bird calls and the occasional cheep or chirp. They did not have to wait long before a small flight of cranes came by, and they snapped photos of the beautiful birds as they fished and stalked. A group of ducks landed a few moments later, and that was when the real show began. The ducks rested on the pool, paddling and dipping as the waterfowl fed. One of the ducks wandered slightly, floating gracefully through the pads by itself, and the already dark green waters below it turned to a deep, almost black as something shifted below the surface. The water beneath the duck seemed to almost part as the massive fish emerged with a thwap of its great mouth, bulbous eyes, and meter long whiskers. The duck was there one moment, and then it was gone, replaced by the monstrous bottom feeder.

"Did you see that?" One of the children gasped at her father. "It's bigger than me!"

"There it is y'all, the Georgia Giant Catfish. Attacks on humans are rare, but even the bobcats aren't safe," Jenna Marie said in her best tour guide whisper, her sharp eyes zeroing in on one of the small islands of vegetation. "It looks like we are going to get a display of another hunter's prowess as well. Watch just behind the fish," she quietly told her group.

Silent as butterfly wings, a massive feline shape hurtled from the small island of mud and flora. The tawny cat spread its six paws wide, hurtling hundreds of pounds of muscle down onto the fish with a combination of crunch and splash. Dark blood pooled in the water as the giant wampus cat, and its prey battled beneath the brackish ripples and frothing churn. A few moments later, the mystical cat surfaced with fish in tow, all six of its legs paddling to haul the great prize back to some semblance of shore.

The excitement was infectious beyond just the children in the tour group. Everyone, even the guides, were abuzz at the rare sight. Jenna Marie let them all chatter excitedly for a moment before quietly continuing the tour.

"We call that one Wally. He's one of the oldest wampus cats on the preserve. Records and estimates have him at least sixty-five years old. I've been blessed to get close to Wally a few times, and he has several successful children all around the swamp and preserve. His mate, Brunhilda, will be somewhere nearby.

"Remember folks, if you encounter a Wampus cat, be respectful, bow gently, and slowly make your way onward. Wampus cats are intelligent and commonly understand intent. If you are passing through, they almost never attack. We will have smaller Wampys back at the Zoo you can even pet. Alright y'all, stay together and let's get moving. We have lots more to see." Jenna Marie checked with her fellow guides, a quick nod to make sure nothing was amiss, and the group continued down the trail.

An hour of exploration, critters, and a light lunch later, the guides lost some of their casual swagger and kept their eyes roaming. The part of the preserve they were heading into was the most dangerous. Connor scanned the trees, and Eric changed the shells out in his long-barreled shotgun, loading specially built armor piercing slugs. Jenna took a knee in the trail, twirling a talisman absently in her hand, a shining pendant of gold and silver with an ornate obsidian leaf.

"Alright everyone. This is the most dangerous part of the woods, and where most of the big predators have found their dens. We are going to try and find our biggest hydra. We call her Hexen. She's old, powerful, and wise. She will know we are here, but she knows all of us that work here, and if we respect her, she will leave us alone. Remember to keep to a whisper, and no flash photography."

The group nodded in silence, though Carl rolled his eyes with skepticism despite the earlier encounters.

They traveled down the trail in relative silence, besides the occasional cough or swatting of a mosquito. Jenna Marie had long perfected the magic to drive off the small bloodsuckers. She needed all her focus on much bigger monsters. She eventually brought the group to a halt on another small ridge. They stared down the dirt slope over an open clearing, observing the moss and vine strung trees that shaded long grasses. While still damp, the ground was drier here, able to hold the weight of both man and beast more easily. Jenna pointed for the group, quietly announcing they had found their apex predator with reverence.

"There's our girl," the guide said simply, taking a knee and keeping her weapon in an easy low ready. Still, she offered all the tour participants a big smile. "Hexen gets more beautiful every time I see her."

Hexen was a massive specimen, coming in at the same weight class as an eighteen wheeler with six serpentine heads. The brown and green beast occupied itself by gnawing on the rapidly melting bones of some creature as it sat outside its lair, a tree shadowed borough. The group snapped pictures quietly, all the guides still scanning to make sure no other predator decided to introduce itself while they observed the preserve's biggest monster. Everyone was almost silent, besides Carl Berkins, who struggled and fussed at a low whisper with the settings on his phone camera.

One by one, the great heads took notice of the group, zeroing in on the tour with predatory eyes, but distance and quiet were enough that the beast carried on about its meal. That boded well enough with the guides, and after a few minutes the great creature had polished off its snack, and with another scan, turned and slipped into its shadowy den.

"Beautiful, she's probably going to nap and shelter for a while after her snack, everyone. Let's head back, and we can tour the facility. We have tons of magical beasts left to see, including more hydras. Those are the ones we can't yet release, and the exhibit will offer a much closer look. Everyone, please follow the guides and stick together."

The closest of the group turned, but Carl Berkins' feet stayed in place. His wife looked at him with minor concern.

"I didn't get a single damn photo. What a rip off. I'm not giving up that easy," Carl said, and with a quick scan of the ground, took a step off the marked path and down the short slope towards the now occupied monster den.

"Carl, what are you doing?" his wife blurted.

"Going to get my picture. You coming?"

The confused woman, torn between the moving group and her husband, sighed and moved to follow her beloved. Jenna Marie had started to move as well but quickly caught that the two had separated from the group.

"Mr. and Mrs. Berkins!" She hissed out, trying to drive urgency without yelling. "You have to come back, and return with us, it's not safe out here, and it's sure as shit not safe that way!" Jenna Marie's professionalism slipped slightly at the stupidity.

"I'm going to get my picture! She already saw us. She just ate. We're fine. We'll get a closer look and catch up." The man waved an arrogant hand at her as the couple walked off into the muddy clearing.

Jenna Marie was torn, she had other charges to keep, and the two grown adults had been informed. If they wanted to get killed, it was on them. She started to turn away, until the children heard "closer look," and members of each family were excitedly darting and sliding down the small embankment.

As the children followed the Berkins, the guide's control of the situation fell like a string of dominos. Confused calls turned to yelling. Leisurely strolling turned to panicked steps, and suddenly all the tour was heading towards the burrow. Ignoring all the calls and the excited little ones at his heels, Carl handed his wife a flashlight.

"It's darker than a whore's heart," Carl exclaimed as he got close to the hole, and nodded to his wife. "Shine some light in there, Margie, so I can snap a photo."

It took Margie only a moment to flash the light into the den, a light that shone on six teeth and venom filled mouths, rearing back to strike. That moment of light was the beginning of Margie's last. A head lashed out to sink its fangs through her arm, the limb both tearing and burning away in an eruption of fright and blood. Another head tore through her torso as Carl fell back and screamed. His phone snapped a panicked burst of photos, capturing the gruesome scene from several odd angles.

The hydra stormed out, enraged at the intrusion into its territory and even deeper intrusion into its own resting place. With six jaws and its massive claws, the tourist fell like a raccoon before an F-150. A massive foot punted Carl away. Parents and children fell in a venomous rage. Jenna Marie was the first guide there, dashing in with inhuman speed. Her shotgun roared, slamming a heavy slug into one of the heads as it ripped apart what had once been a young man. The young woman charged, fired and screamed to gain the attention of the beast. Pain and thunder captured all of Hexen's focus, and for just a moment the two faced off, woman and wondrous creature; Death and Defender.

Eric and Connor spread out to each side, fear and hesitation on their faces and features. Then a fang filled maw lunged, and the shooting began.

"My Jenna Marie was fast, Major. Hexen only touched her once before the specialty slugs put her down. Grazed her side with those hellish teeth. She died an hour later from the venom, ate up from the inside out. So, you tell me, do you think you can hire ***that bastard?***' Pam Jo let the silence hang for a moment, then continued. "I'm sending the invoice for the proper service rendered to your branch. Not a dime more, or less, than was in the contract stipulations. If you can find someone to respond to a hydra encounter in less than an hour, anywhere in the world, you are welcome to sign them up. The fact nobody got eaten is a testament to the men, and our services, not an excuse for you to fleece our pockets."

"Very well Mrs. Darkleaf, I… I'm sorry for your loss, and I'm sure we'll be in touch." Pam Jo all but slammed the phone down, barely stopping herself from breaking the expensive device.

"Forty-eight hours, two damn sleeps, and I'm off to Nassau," she growled and wiped away the budding tears from her eyes. After a few steady breaths, she sat to pet the riled up cat. "I'm so sorry, Blender, mama didn't mean to scare you. Those stupid old Pencil Pushers just really stress her out." She petted the purple-eyed swamp kitten with her left hand and flipped through invoices with her right.

She needed to hunt down how much they had billed the Marines for the last hydra's removal. They sat like that for a while, Pam Jo scratching Blender behind the ears and doing paperwork. Occasionally, another six legged cat would wander out from the office furniture, or shelving of the double-wide trailer Pamtriel ran the business from. After half an hour of quiet, her cell phone rang. AC/DC's *Thunderstruck* blared from its twin speakers.

"Darkleaf Exotic Animal Rescue and Rehabilitation, this is Pam Jo speakin'. How can we help yah darlin?" She said as she pressed the phone to her ear.

"Good afternoon…Pam Jo," the man said, as if the name confused him. "I'm Reginald Simpson Beauregard III from the Greenville Arcane Academy. I've heard you have a wide selection of cryptids and exotic creatures for students and events?"

"Yes, sir, we have chupacabras, carbuncles, and mimics available for offsite educational classes, and offer onsite field trips including 'Night at the Zoo' opportunities. We need proof of the school's 52543-41 forms and licensing. We also have an extensive selection of wampus cats." She scritched the black and purple kitten.

"That's splendid, Mrs. Darkleaf, but my students are young men more than children. I was hoping for something more formidable. Something with teeth or claw. Something to inspire them with its power. A prodigious school such as ours has a reputation to uphold, after all."

Pam Jo bit her tongue for a moment, *prodigious enough to get them all killed.* "We have a few more exciting creatures, and we can provide handlers for shows and arenas as well. We have a griffin, though they need a lot of space for a proper showing and we advise against children under twelve.

You will also want to clear any pets or livestock. Griffins like cows and horses enough to ignore what anybody, including the handler, says."

Blender stretched and slinked into the woman's lap as she spoke. When the man on the other end of the line prattled some more, Pam Jo's eyes rolled.

"That is certainly better, though I shall have to weigh my options. I've seen on your advertisements that you have Hydra's, Van Meter creatures, and Honey Island Maulers. Are none of them available?"

"Class One Creatures have to be viewed on site, Mr. Beauregard, there are no exceptions. That's federal law. Honey Island Maulers and Van Meters are not safely transportable for things like that. We take a risk every time we pick one up from an incident, much less driving a few thousand pounds of killing machine around for kicks and giggles."

"Please, Pam Jo, call me Reginald. Mr. Beauregard is my father." The man's attempt at a charming chuckle almost had her puke.

"Are there really no provisions for special events? My own little Reggie is dying to have a manticore at his birthday party, and your organization just famously recovered one from DeSoto Caverns not too long ago. I assure you we will spare no expense."

"Not something we can do, Reginald, but I'm sure a man of your station will think of something. You think on that griffin and let us know."

She hung up the phone more gently this time, though her exasperation was just as prevalent.

"Can you believe the nerve of that idiot wanting to have a manticore for a birthday party?" she said to the monster cat, who blinked at her slowly with his purple eyes. "Happy birthday Reggie, ready to watch all your friends get impaled and devoured?!"

She was just finishing her tirade to the creature when the trailer door swung open and her husband walked in, nearly having to duck to get through the door to avoid bumping his head. Bucky made a beeline for his wife, dropping a foil wrapped burrito on the desk. He leaned over to kiss her, letting his work and war calloused hands roam mischievously before getting swatted by her long nails.

"Bucky Bob Darkleaf, you cut that out in front of the children!" She gestured to Blender and the other bizarre cats that lounged or wandered about the large office trailer.

"Pam, wampus cats don't care about PDA. And the damn things multiply like mice anyway… speaking of… who is *THAT*?" Bucky pointed a long finger at the black-haired kitten that was sniffing and blinking at him from his wife's lap.

Pam's eyes widened for just a moment, looking like she was doing her best to swallow a softball before she caught herself, and covered the surprise panic with fake indignation.

"You don't recognize my sweet Blender? You don't know your own babies? Next, you will be asking me the names of our biological children!"

"Pam Jo, I have never seen that Wampy before in my God bless-ed life. We talked about this! You've got to stop taking in every stray creature smaller than a damn Rock Drake. We make good money, but it's getting to where you can't spit without hitting a critter around here." Bucky flopped his arms in frustration. "I'm never going to financially recover from this."

Pam deflated at her husband's admonition.

"I know, *I KNOW*, but I couldn't just leave him there on the highway, and if he came out to me like he did, you know that means his parents are gone. I promise this will be the last one."

Bucky nodded and dropped into his chair, propping his boots up on his own desk. He stopped short to toss a large orange and white wampus cat out of his chair as it gave an indignant rowl.

"Damn it, Horus, git!" Bucky said with casual annoyance in his voice. The feline glared at him, Bucky glared back, and then it prowled off with a steam kettle hiss. Bucky loved animals. You couldn't do what he did every day and not care for critters, but every man just didn't get along with somebody. Horus, the wampus cat, was that somebody.

"Shithead cat," Bucky grumbled. "Me and the kids shovel enough unicorn shit around here, Pam. We need a break, not more work."

"That's what this cruise is for Robindriel, and don't you lecture me about it. I run this office, so you don't have to."

"And I punch swamp monsters in the face, so you don't have to. I ain't downplaying your work, baby, but I'm getting too old for this."

"My handsome man, you don't even look a day over three hundred."

A black ball of purring fur thumped onto Bucky's chest, interrupting their laughter. Blender circled several times on the man as his four front paws clawed about, adjusting the small wrinkles in Bucky's T-shirt. The motion, despite the sharp prickles, reminded Bucky of his grandmother mixing up biscuit dough. Blender settled down soon after, staring and blinking lazily at Bucky with low lidded eyes.

Bucky eyed the kitten for a moment, watching the sleepy expression on its midnight face, and then slowly started to scratch behind the tiny monster's ears. For a few blissful minutes, they all sat there in companionable silence. Bucky himself was dangerously close to dreamland when Pam Jo picked up the ringing phone again. As Pam Jo got the details on another job, he let out an exhausted growl.

Bucky stomped out of the trailer, cursing under his breath. He cursed the entire way down the steps. The Darkleaf's zoo and rehabilitation facility was tucked away deep in south Georgia, down among the pecan groves and swampland, a paradise of dirt roads, double wide trailers, and massive animal exhibits and enclosures. The bugs were big enough to carry off small children, and the gnats could get so thick you killed them when you blinked, but it provided all the space and secrecy the Darkleaf family needed. Its Owner/Operator cursed the entire way down past the griffin paddock. He cursed past the unicorn corral and the serpent pit. He cursed as he passed the hydra enclosure, where he stopped. That woke a cradled and carried Blender, so Bucky sat the six-legged cat down and told him to go back to Pam Jo. Bucky scanned the enclosure, tapping his feet to the thundering heavy metal that blasted through the enclosure.

The Hydra enclosure was a mix of dark swamp and dry mountain rock, to accommodate both the Lowland Hydras like Corporal Doubledome, and the Highland Striped Hydra, like Odie. The former hydra was playing with his rope, a gift from his fellow marines, and bouncing and strutting to the music. Hydras, some breeds of hellhound, and a few other critters loved music. The genre and style didn't matter much. If it had a rhythm, they calmed noticeably. Dolly stood on a rock in the middle of the enclosure, facing the cave that their five-headed Highland Hydra liked to call home. The young woman wore a belt of tools around her waist over her jean shorts and had a large bucket set aside. She let out a shrill pattern of whistles.

"Odie, come on, dude! It's practice time!"

From the depths of the cave, a chorus of clicks and whistles replied and out came the Darkleaf family's prized hydra. While the good corporal was the size of a truck, Odie rivaled a bus. Five massive, toothed heads of charcoal grey and obsidian black bobbed and pulsed around one another as their shared body strutted and joggled to the thundering double pedal and wailing electric guitar.

The creature bounced up to his trainer, who in turn bobbed and swayed. She raised her hands high into the sky and whistled. All five heads rose to their limit, and Dolly began to give commands.

"Spear!" she called, and the hungry faces adjusted, forming a spear shaped flying V. "Good," the woman called before tossing each maw a decent sized fish from the bucket. "Now Cigarette!" The heads adjusted, lining up one atop the other in a straight line. Again, she fed the critter. The cycle continued through multiple other commands. "Beer Can… Triforce… Fishhook… Symphony of Destruction!"

Each time, Odie's heads shifted and swayed to be rewarded with a treat. The far left noggin, however, eventually lost interest in waiting, and started to slowly creep towards the bucket of tasty fish. Dolly chirped and whistled, not fooled by the ruse, but the muzzle still came on. She pulled a long steel rod from her belt and whacked the offending head across the dome. The head recoiled, annoyed, and while all the others continued to move in proper pattern, the offended head lunged.

"Damn it Odie, get your shit together!" Dolly cursed as she leapt into the air. She vaulted over the strike of the washing machine sized cranium and smacked it again with the iron rod. The other heads stopped at that point, waiting patiently, as Dolly and the left head dueled over fish driven hunger and fury. Finally, a particularly meaty thwack of the rod saw the unruly maw give up. Dolly fed the other four one handed, sternly watching the last before finally giving it a fish, too.

"Alright, Odie, go have fun!" Dolly scratched each muzzle under the jaw before clicking on a remote. The remote triggered three massive rubber balls to release from the mountain side, and soon the hydra was bouncing and oscillating as it played with its toys.

Lesson done, Bucky called out to his daughter.

"Hey Hun, got another call. You want to hit the road again?"

"I can't Daddy, I gotta give Dubby his first lesson, and get an order in for his enrichment toys. We ain't had a Lowlands in a long time, so a lot needs updating or replacement. Take Hoss. He's over in the Onikuma enclosure. Oh, can you get me a shit ton of CLP while you are out?"

"Yeah baby, I'll get it. Be safe! Love you!"

"Love you too, Daddy!"

Bucky decided to get the van from the shop first. The big open air workspace held multiple vehicles, and almost every tool known to man: welders, fabricators, and 3-D printers; cauldrons and chemical beakers. Still a little surly, the monster wrangler grumbled as he fired up the old van, and tossed a one eyed, tabby wampus cat out of the passenger window. The A/C running, he hopped out once again.

The grumbling finally stopped when he got the back doors open to check his supplies. A small arsenal of weapons, silver, gems, minerals, feathers, and potions. Restraints and traps for everything from your normal raccoon to fifteen-foot-tall sasquatches. Satisfied with the bags of tools, he tossed out one last calico colored monster cat and hit the road. Bucky didn't mind Roscoe, but the cat hated water, and they were going to a naval base.

Bucky stopped by another habitat on his way down the long dirt row of enclosures. He hopped out and gave a sharp whistle. Over the sounds of a nearby brook, a gigantic roar followed the whistle. Another booming baritone voice called behind it.

"Wait one, Pa!"

Bucky scanned the enclosure from a high vantage point, looking down into a dense Japanese forest. Moss covered the imported maple trees and ginkgos with wide leafed laurels. They worked tirelessly to do this for all the animals, but despite coming from a forest thousands of miles away, the Onikuma's enclosure felt the most like home to Bucky, who still missed his native Highlands.

A great thundering crash echoed, and two figures burst through the trees in a tumble of limbs and fur. A mountain of a man, taller even than Bucky and half again as wide, barrel chested and bearded, twisted and turned with a massive bear. Black midnight fur covered the magnificent beast, decorated with red and purple swirls and tendrils of dark energy. Its jaws were full of dagger-like fangs and paws tipped in scything claws. The bear easily reached fifteen feet as it stood on its hind legs from the grapple, dwarfing the gigantic man as he arose to face the beast. They squared off with each other in unwavering focus, locked in a world that only included the two combatants.

Bucky leaned on the railing of the enclosure, enraptured by the clash.

"Get em, Hoss!"

Hoss lunged, grabbing the massive bear, wrapping his arms around the monster, and heaved. With a fierce bellow, the beast moved. It lashed back, slinging the man around. They wrestled, tumbled, and thrashed, rolled, and crashed, finally coming to an exhausted halt. Dirt stained and sweat drenched, Hoss lay on the bear's back as it turned to look at him, panting jovially.

"Good, Daisuke," Hoss said, patting the bear's back. "Go eat." He slid down from the animal's back, and the beast stood, nuzzled its keeper affectionately, and headed back into the forest. The giant stripped off his shirt, revealing long scars and thick muscle. He turned up to Bucky after a few deep breaths.

"Yes, Pa?"

"Got a call, Kings Bay. Want to ride with your old man?"

"Mhmm," Hoss said. He held up his shirt. "Be right back."

Bucky's eldest son walked off to change his wardrobe. Ten minutes later, the gigantic man sat next to his smaller father, a cigarette on his lip as they rode off to another call. Bucky honked his horn to scatter the pack of chupacabras in the road, and they were off to King's Bay Naval Base.

Hey all you hotshot hydras and hellhounds, it's your favorite crypto-conservationist, Carl Berkins. From Maine to Miami, if you need help with a paranormal creature, Berkins has your back.

Bucky stared at the radio in disgust, struggling to even focus on the road. T-103-Wk The Warlock was his favorite radio station for the magic community. Accessible only with an enchanted radio. "They let him have a commercial on the damn radio. What is wrong with people!"

Other conservationist services may try to tell you they have more experience, those competitors may act like they are autumn leaves, but they are really just dull compost. When you need help, Call Berkins Bestiary for fast, fun, and HUMAN service.

Bucky's eyes rolled so hard Hoss could hear the bowling pins scattering. "*THAT-**BASTARD,***" both Bucky and Hoss supplied the last word at the same time. The fatigue that rolled over Bucky in that moment was soul deep. The weight of a thousand years of oaths, wars, and worries wore heavy on him lately. "Forty-eight hours, two damn sleeps, and I'm off to

Nassau." Bucky muttered to himself as he parked. His massive son gave him a sideways glance.

"What's wrong, Pa?"

"I'm worn out Hoss, I just need some time to myself, some time with your ma."

"Been a Guardian for a long time. Want to retire?"

It was a powerful question. Bucky had the right to retire. Pass things on to Dolly or Hoss and move back to just the occasional spell. He could sit it out from now on. Let his children take the mantle. Was he ready to return to the trunk and let his new leaves handle the winds alone?

"Not yet Hoss, your grandfather would spin in his grave if I retired this early."

Hoss gave a simple grunt and hugged his father over the shoulder.

"I know, Hoss. You've always carried more than your weight. I'm just tired, son." The two just leaned into one another for a moment with only the quiet tick of the settling engine.

"Love you. Beer after." Hoss broke the silence and tossed on his sunglasses while he climbed out.

"Love you too, buddy," Bucky said, took a deep breath, and left the cab for the back of the van. Hoss and Bucky both fished out a bag of tools before turning to the concrete pier leading down to the brackish waters of King's Bay Naval base. Charging up the pier was a powerful young woman with dark hair, a frazzled attitude, and a sailor's uniform.

"Thank God you're here. I'm Petty Officer First Class Sarah King. My team and the creatures are this way. Please follow me," she spoke rapidly, and barely waited for the two men to acknowledge her words before turning about face and ripping back down the gangway.

Despite being staggeringly taller, Buckthorn's pace distinctly failed to match Sarah's urgency. Both the men were graceful as hunting cats, but Bucky's face was mostly annoyed under his long blonde braided mullet and *Lost Dog Street Band* trucker cap. Beads, feathers, and bone clanked in the twisted strands as he *moseyed*. He was clearly feeling as lazy as a Maine coon with a full belly. By his reckoning, he was hellaciously overdue for the coming vacation, and with the heat being worse than two rabbits fucking in a wool sock, he wasn't going anywhere fast. He knew he should have talked Pam Jo into living in Texas. At least it would have been a dry heat on the other side of Fort Worth.

Hoss kept pace with his father, taking in the sights and examining everything around him, but saying little. The big bag of tools and talismans seemed to weigh nothing to him. After a minute of what Hoss's old unit would have called *dragging ass,* there was a subtle annoyance in the slight cock of his brow. He gave his father a hard look.

"Pa?" Hoss said, his empty hand making a gesture that spoke volumes. *Can we hurry the hell up?*

"What?" Bucky asked, defensive at his son for calling him out. Sarah spoke as Hoss just shook his head.

"Mr. Darkleaf, please, we really need to hurry. Those things have got my entire crew mesmerized and I'm sure they are why Seaman Smith went missing last week."

"Call me Bucky, or Bucky Bob, Petty Officer, and this here is Hoss." Hoss gave a nod and a "Hooyah," before his father continued. "You said he'd been spending a lot of time out staring at the water?"

Sarah nodded, nervously tucking a stray strand of her brunette hair under her brown and tan patterned cap. Bucky couldn't remember the name of the pattern, but it crossed him as about as useless as tits on a bull for sailors to be camouflaged. At least it wasn't that ocean pattern anymore. 'Cause if anyone fell in or needed to be fished out, they sure as shit would want to *BLEND IN* to the water from a distance. Shaking the sarcastic thought off, he felt a pang of sympathy for the fear and pain in her blue eyes. Sarah was scared. Not for herself, but for the men she spent years of her life working and fighting beside. He knew that fear all too well, and it perked up his pace a little bit.

Sarah was a powerful woman, broad in shoulders and hips, managing to make even the goofy ass navy uniform look filled out. She clearly spent time in the gym. She was strong in both arm and conviction from the look of it. Concern like that didn't sit well on her, and to a man with sensibilities as old as Bucky's; it lit a fire under his ass a lot faster than his son's complaint.

"I hate to tell you, Petty Officer King, but Smith is probably already off to fair winds and following seas. If it's what I think they are, they only take men for two reasons, and both of them end up at the bottom of the water never to come back up."

"Mhmm." Hoss added. "Bones in the ocean."

"Sarah is fine, Bucky, and I appreciate your honesty. Can we please hurry? I don't want the others joining Smith."

Bucky's stride lengthened and suddenly he was moving almost too fast for Sarah to keep up. Hoss matched the stride gladly, his big mechanic's bag of tools jingling and clanging as he took off.

"We'll get everyone else sorted, though. Sure as shit," Bucky assured Sarah.

Kings Naval Base was a big place, thousands of acres of protected wetlands and the flowing waters that hosted a nice chunk of the American submarine fleet and other small boats that could fit into the dark coastal river waters. The Petty Officer and her civilian companions strolled right into the giant dock building at the end of one of those massive piers and walked into something from an ancient Greek fever dream.

A small platoon of sailors all set at the water's edge, most of them in various stages of undress, their tools discarded, workstations and diagnostics abandoned. They all lounged around the dock as a beautiful and haunting melody arose from the midnight waters. In the water, and among them, other *things* moved. Long hair flowing past sharp and aquiline features, a dozen deep purple scaled creatures moved languidly through the water, singing to the heavens a lament filled aria.

The words meant nothing to mortal ears, a language never meant to be understood by anything that roamed on land. The solos intertwined, soaring around and above each other. Purple tails, thick and powerful like a dolphin's, powered them both on land and through the dark pools. Those creatures not singing had emerged onto the dock and were cuddled in among the sailors. Wide, black eyes and mouths full of sharp teeth curled into smiles and giggles at the sweet nothings passed between man and monstrosity. Slowly, the enrapturement complete, gleeful black eyes sparkled with delight as the monsters sank their needled teeth into a few of the sailors, drinking blood to satisfy their dark hunger

"What the hell are they, Bucky?" Sarah's voice roiled with fear and disgust. Her Boston accent came out with the emotion. "How do we get them off of my crew?"

"Those are Sirens, Ms. Sarah." Bucky sighed as Hoss dropped his tool bag and smoothed his beard. "Iberian Sirens to be specific, haven't seen them in the states for a long time. Family must have migrated with a breeder at some point. They feed on human men. Lure them to the water for feeding or fu…fornication… for the purpose of reproduction. That song they sing gets men all twitterpated. Makes them look like whatever a man's taste is. Poor Seaman over there thinks he's got Marilyn Monroe on his lap and not Elvira's sharp toothed aquatic cousin."

Bucky himself turned and dug through the bag for a moment, then sat up with a snap and a triumphant cry. "Haha! Found 'em!" He proffered a two-foot cylinder to the Petty Officer. Sarah took the offered object and studied it. The object was a small bat, painted in a dark blue and emblazoned with a cursive "A" crossed with a tomahawk. Dark metal studs had been added to the bat about every inch, leaving only the logo untouched.

"Why am I holding an *Atlanta Braves* catfish bat?" Sarah's Misson Hill accent once again crept out with incredulity.

Bucky shrugged. "Well, I didn't know you were a Red Sox fan when we left the house."

"What? No, what do I do with the bat?"

"Holler a lot and go start bappin' Betty and her ballad barking bitch brigade on the noggin till they leave."

"Mhmm. Bonk'em." Hoss added, drawing a much larger version of the bat, studded with spikes instead of simple balls.

"You're both men, won't the song get you, too?"

"I'm a man, but I ain't a hu-man, and I know I don't look old enough, but Hoss is my eldest son." Bucky smiled his silver tooth studded grin, then brushed back his wild mass of beads, feathers and braids. The shift in his hair revealed the long-pointed ears that so notably distinguished his race.

"You're in the service, so you already got oaths. Your command is going to ask you for another one. People ain't supposed to know about us anymore. Or them sirens, or anything else that ain't normal, but we'll be fine, Ms. Sarah, sure as shit. True as toasted toads. I've been doing this longer than your branch existed. Now let's get to bonkin'."

Bucky gave a cry then, loud and long. A roar that would have given justice to Hercules as he slayed the Nemean Lion or Leonidas and the Three Hundred as they leveled the next wave of Persians. He roared to his ancestors so many thousands of years distant from his long life, and for the days when he was so much more than the man you called when the thing you were looking at wasn't a normal creature. Ancient magic, blood and bone deep, radiated from the elf as he roared. Around his neck, the leaf pendant flashed.

"YEEEEEEEEEE HAAAAAAAAAAAAAAAWWWWW, GO ON NOW, GIT!"

He charged the siren that was already snacking. The bat smacked right across her wet hair covered crown with a wooden thunk. The siren recoiled immediately at the impact and touch of the cold iron. Hoss followed as a silent force on his father's heels, smacking a creature with calculated strength.

"Skit!" he barked, giving the shocked siren another wack, and prodding it in the tail with the big club.

Sirens were slow eaters, and their bites didn't often cause normal infection, but of the victims he could reach first, the bitten were in the most danger. The real threat would be if one of the sirens didn't get spooked enough, and tried to take a sailor souvenir before the rescuers could get to her.

Sarah watched the "Exotic Animal Experts," momentarily stunned at the bizarre scene as the tall country elves proceeded to bash, thrash, and cuss the sea creatures that were feasting on or copulating with her crew. She shook her head sharply, looked at the bat in her hands once, and then gave a mental shrug. *Screw it.*

"HOOYAH!" Sarah added the Navy's war cry to the mix, then rushed the nearest of the water witches. Together the three of them drove the predatory creatures back, Sarah brutally cudgeling any of them she could reach, Bucky dancing between them with his powerful height and inhuman precision. Hoss simply tossed them by the tail most of the time, or thunked them with his version of restraint. Bucky fell into a rhythm, something in his past taking hold of his movements. He flowed and slipped where his son worked on raw aggression.

"HA NOW, GIT! SAIL ON YA BLOOD SUCKING SEA SLUTS! GIT, GIT, GIT!" The cry was almost jubilant, this moment of skill and savagery letting the tired elf exercise some frustration.

The sirens shrieked then, a terrible wailing sound somehow intermixed with its own melody. Agony and anger laced with some nightmarish seduction. From the swirling waters, one massive hand emerged, then another and with a splash, a gigantic siren emerged from the waters, at least as heavy as a bear and impossibly tall on her massive tail. Several more of the creatures followed her, hissing while bearing long fangs and short taloned hands. Bucky planted a boot approximately where a fleeing siren's ass should have been, eliciting a yelp from the creature, and turned to face the giant. He started to step forward, but Hoss cut in front of him.

The bearded giant's glamor fell, exposing his long, pointed, rune tattooed ears. He casually removed his sunglasses and glared at the massive siren with emerald green eyes.

"Chan abair mi seo ach aon turas. Fàg, no brisidh mi thu. Chan eil na seòladairean seo dhutsa!" Hoss rumbled. The massive siren gave a haughty laugh and jabbed an accusing claw in Hoss's direction.

"Cò thusa a dh'iarras dad air **Banrigh***, elf?"* The sea creature demanded.

"Uh, Bucky, what the hell are they talking about?" Sarah whispered, watching the exchange with a mix of anger, awe, and fear.

"Hoss told her she had one chance to sod off, and she asked him who he thought he was to tell a Siren Queen what to do." Bucky walked over and lit a fresh cigarette, offering one to Sarah, who accepted. "Hoss don't talk much, but he gets really touchy about boundaries. Sirens are sentient, they are part of our accords. Hoss is *real* particular about them, and real particular about watchin' out for the troops."

Hoss held his massive club to the sky as he replied to the Siren Queen.

"Is mise **Hoss***, de dhuilleag* **Chlann Duilleachdorcha***, Mac* **Robindriel** *is* **Pamriel***. Mharbh mi dràgonan, agus chuir mi às deamhain. Ghlèidh mi na tìrean seo airson dà cheud bliadhna. Gleidhidh mi mile eile iad. Cha bhi thu 'n am measg."* He rumbled, lowering the club to smack it ominously over and over again into his palm.

"He introduced himself in a boast." Bucky supplied to Sarah. "In the same way you do when you're about to duel someone if they don't scram."

"I got that part, Bucky, but thank you."

"Bheir thu biadh dha mo nigheanan." The queen hissed with clear violent intent

"Yeah, that's what I figured… back to work." Bucky said and lunged with the still lit cigarette on his lip, cracking another siren over the head and dragging a sailor back to safety.

"Get'em out of the way, Ms. Sarah, so we can let Hoss work. He's got his mama's temper. Takes seventy-five years to piss him off and then it's genocide."

The Siren Queen lunged on her tail, surging forward with nightmarish power and slamming into Hoss with the force of a train wreck. The gigantic elf met her with the end of the spike studded club, and twisted his powerful hips. They both went hurtling and crashing, but the big man was on his feet in an instant. He swung fast as lightning and crashed like thunder, and the Siren Queen screamed as her ribs cracked. She returned a scything blow with her claws, a blast of dark green light flaring as some magic protected Hoss. Again, the force sent him rolling, but he came to his feet with little more than a bloody nose instead of shredded flesh. He lunged back into the fight, his weapon slamming into the giant creature again and again.

One by one, Sarah and Bucky carried her fellow sailors away, still in a mesmerized stupor from the magic song that carried up from the waters. Bucky gently settled a sailor as best he could and then rummaged through the bag. A sea of tools and equipment passed his hands; blades, books, and bobbles. He even pulled out a multicolored beanie.

"Shit!" He spat and shrugged his shoulders. "Guess I left 'em in the van."

"What?" Sarah asked as she lowered a comrade down to the deck.

"Sure would be nice if we had some grenades."

*"You have **grenades**?"* Sarah asked in shock.

"Yeah, hard to deal with some kinds of vampires without 'em. It's possible, but thermite makes it a damn sight easier."

Sarah only shook her head and went back for another man.

The siren queen whipped her tail and slashed with her claws as Hoss slipped and struck. Magic swirled and bones cracked. For another few deadly seconds, they struggled until the Queen's strike missed its mark, and Hoss slammed his club across her wet temple, like Dale Sr. into the wall. *God rest #3's soul.*

She wobbled, dazed and enraged, and Hoss hammered her skull again, laying the queen low. The massive elf gently set his weapon aside, magic swirling as he uttered an incantation in elvish, and grabbed the queen's massive tail in both hands. He drug her without ceremony back toward the edge, and with a pivot and a mighty roar, hurled her into the waters like a Highlander with a hammer. **The sirens keened in despair at the defeat of their queen.**

Cussing, smacking and dodging, Sarah and Bucky drove the sirens back until none remained on the shore, and most had fled into the murky depths of the river and the sea beyond. Sarah smacked one particularly stubborn siren across the back of the head as she finally fled.

With the song absent, the men came to their senses and got to their feet. Some startled, while others simply blinked for a few moments and then looked around, confused. The shock of what happened wore off quickly enough. Everyone started getting dressed and grumbling.

Bucky walked over to the crew's Lieutenant as he hastily fixed his pants and patted the man lightly on the shoulder. He was the man in charge when all this had gone wrong, and now that he was back to his senses, they had a lot to talk about. Still keeping one eye on the waters, Bucky stuck out a hand.

"We need to have a talk here, LT. First, about your new siren protocol, and no, I don't mean the electronic ones. Then, about how Petty Officer King deserves a promotion. Also, you need to tell your liaison to expect an invoice for a real expensive Red Sox catfish bat."

The officer flushed, embarrassed on multiple fronts, but simply nodded and shook the elf's hand. Bucky gave the man credit for that. Lesser men would not handle embarrassment well and might have snubbed the gesture.

"We can talk in one of the side offices. I take it you are the contractor for supernatural creatures?"

"That's me, call me Bucky."

There was a gentle ripple of water and Bucky whipped around, launching his bat in an overhand throw that smacked right into the temple of a slinking siren with a high-pitched squeak of "EOW!"

"I SAID FUCK OFF, BITCH!" the elf roared, before turning back to the LT. "Make that two catfish bats. I ain't going swimming for that one."

No other creatures or jobs presented themselves. The following days passed in the relative peace of normal rescue duties: feeding, watering, and caring for the various critters. Bucky Bob and Pam Jo left for the cruise at 6:00 am sharp, saying goodbye to the land of swamps and gnats to leave for sunny Florida. They climbed into Pam Jo's bright pink Ram 1500, and after tossing two chupacabras out of the truck bed they hit the road. Dolly was up by the serpent pit and waved her parents goodbye.

The teleportation spell made the trip drastically shorter, and Bucky smiled as they hit the Tampa line. Finally, the break he needed was happening.

"What do you think Baby," Bucky asked his wife casually. "You think the food will be better or the scenery?"

"Honey, I'm just looking forward to not taking a phone call for five days."

"Thank you for runnin' the office, Pam Jo. I know it ain't nothing like the war front, but I know it ain't easy, most days. It's boring." Bucky placed a loving hand on her thigh as she weaved through the harbor traffic. "I've been bitchin a lot lately, but you've been workin' just as hard."

"Buckthorn Robindriel Darkleaf, we've been married four hundred and twenty-three years. You've fought, bled, and damn near died next to me every step of the way. You may get pissy at times, but you ain't failed me yet."

"Ain't gunna," Bucky chirped pridefully, and squeezed her leg. Pam Jo parked the car and kissed her husband.

"Come on, Honey. Let's get settled in and hit the buffet before all the old farts steal the banana puddin'."

"Pam Jo, we are the old farts."

"Speak for your damn self. I still got another 300 years of modeling in me," she said and ran both hands up through her blonde locks, flashing her husband a ruby smile and a wink. "Grab the bags, Baby, and let's go!"

The two elves bailed from the truck, and Bucky fished the bags out, loading up both his shoulders and hands with heavy luggage. He learned several hundred years ago not to highlight his wife's undying habit of over packing. It just pissed her off and made it worse. It wasn't long till they checked in with a smartly dressed young lady in a sailor's uniform, and a crew of burly, sun tanned men took the bags away.

A few passport checks and a final confirmation later and they were heading down a massive dock and walking alongside the *Siren's Call.* Bucky couldn't help but find the name ironic, considering his last job. It was a beautiful marvel of a ship. Doubly so to an elf that lived through the golden age of sail. Cargo cranes and salty crew were still loading on the final supplies as the early bird passengers made their way to the ship. In Bucky's mind, the ropes and shipping containers rang with the echoes of long forgotten songs.

"veyra veyra veyra veyra
gentil gallandis gentil gallandis
veynde i see hym veynd i see hym
pourbossa pourbossa

hail al ande ane hail al and ane"

Pam laughed as her husband sang lightly and leaned on him as they walked, a comfortable swagger taking both of them. The sleek steel giant washed Bucky and Pam both in memory. Some were lovely, and some were full of blood and flame, but they smiled all the same. At least until a gruff New Yorker called out.

"What the hell are you doing here, Bucko?"

Both elves tracked the radio-famous voice to the middle-aged man with dark beady eyes and a hairline that stayed behind in his home state. Pam Jo let just a bit of wide-eyed shock hit her face, while Bucky Bob simply stopped to calmly stare at the drastically smaller man who glared up at him with thinly veiled malice. He scanned his arch nemesis, the two decades younger woman attached to his side, the ramp up to the ship, and all the prying eyes around him. For just a moment, a cold and familiar call to rend and destroy washed through Bucky, showing only in the depths of his eyes. Then he closed his green orbs off to the world, took a breath, and spoke.

*"Too many **witnesses**,"* he hissed out with a steadying breath, quiet enough only his wife heard it. Instead of strangling the Yankee, he opened his eyes and plastered on a grin that carried little friendly or happy intent.

"I asked you a question, Darkleaf." The man placed both hands on his hips, shrugging off the brunette woman he was with.

"Well, Carl, until the interrogation started, I was heading for a vacation." Bucky swept a free hand down the edge of his body in presentation, emphasizing his cargo shorts and *Gone Fishin* t-shirt. "I ain't exactly in a three piece or my work clothes."

"I wouldn't put it past you to work in your pajamas."

"Funny thing about it, dumbass, I'd still get more done faster than you."

"You dirty needle eared-" Berkins was cut off before he could finish his name calling. Pam Jo slid halfway between the two men and greeted the woman Carl had shouldered with a bright smile and thick southern charm.

"Why Melanie, it's so good to see you. I love what you did with your hair! It looks better than the red did on you. Who styled it?" She asked with all the concern of an old friend. The young woman looked between all of them with obvious confusion, and replied in a soft voice.

"I'm sorry, but I don't think we have met, I'm Hanna."

"Oh, goodness, Heather, I am so sorry. Carl Berkins here goes through wives so fast I have a hard time keeping up. I guess Melanie was the last one to get eaten. Or was it Margie, no Margie was the one that got eaten when Carl got my daughter killed."

Hanna sputtered with horror, looking back and forth between the blonde elf beauty and Carl, who was turning red enough to wave in a Chinese parade. Pam Jo calmly slid back to take her husband's arm. "Well Carl, I'm sure you two are busy as can be on your adventure, just like we are. Was nice catching up with you."

She steered Bucky onward, leaving the rival animal wrangler behind. The man sputtered for another moment before turning to yell at the retreating couple.

"You just stay out of my way, Bucko! This is my expedition, my job, and I'll be damned if I let you ruin it! You watch yourself or-" Pam Jo was smiling in Carl's face in an instant, towering over the average sized man as the sunlight glinted off her golden earrings and pearlescent teeth.

"Let me make something clear, you moronic **bastard.** My husband and I are on vacation. We are here to relax and have a wonderful time." Her voice was a low smooth whisper as her focus all but bore a hole through his near black gaze. "Speak to him like that again, and I'll feed your kidneys to the sharks while you watch and bleed. I swear on all the Gods and my ancestors. You breathe by my grace alone."

Carl became conspicuously quiet and simply nodded to the woman. She returned to Bucky, and they began the ascent up the massive ramps to the *Siren's Call.*

Bucky Bob sprawled out on a beach chair, an umbrella securely in place to shield him from the oppressive sun and allow him to sip his mojito in peace. The crash of the waves soothed the elf deeply. Even the chatter of all the tourists and the incessant thwack of a bartender smashing coconuts with a machete couldn't disturb his calm. He cosplayed his favorite wizard, wearing palm tree patterned yellow shorts, and blood red converses. The fake beard had been too hot, but he'd already gotten more than one smile from parents and children alike when they saw him dressed as a cartoon character.

His rainbow pattern beach shirt hung behind his head as his sunglasses covered green eyes watched his wife frolic in the surf. He lit a Marlboro red while watching her in the ocean. The camouflage bikini left little to the imagination as the tall elf woman splashed around in the surf, looking for shells.

Pam Jo was noticeably shorter than her husband, but still taller than ninety-nine percent of women. Gleaming in the Caribbean sun, she towered well over six feet. Her blond curls lifted into a bun that hung down just enough to cover her pointed ears. She could have modeled for any agency in the world. Her gold cat eye shades turned his way, and she blew him a kiss. It was going to be a good day, watching her and a few of the other ladies' frolic while he drank until the sunset and the fireworks show started.

Bucky adjusted his red *Raise Hell and Praise Dale* cap after returning the flirtation, looking to take a nap as his wife soaked up some sun, but just as he settled in his keen ears picked up a small squeak of delight from the woman, and the sound of her approaching footsteps in the packed sand.

"Bucky, would you look at this? I ain't seen one of them in person before, and it's as sweet as it can be!"

Already expecting tomfoolery, Bucky opened his eyes to see his wife cradling what looked like a cross between an otter and a raccoon. About the size of a large rabbit, the water slicked creature waved a long tail about, a tail that happened to have an extra hand on the end of it.

"What the hell is an ahuizotl doing out here? Little guy belongs in a Mexican river," Bucky said in a low hushed tone to his wife, moving to shield the creature from view of all the normal cruisers and vacationers.

"I don't know, but the poor thing is scared to death and way too far from home." Pam wasn't wrong. The little creature was shaking, eyes darting nervously as it glared at the water from over the elf's shoulder. She let her long blonde curls down from the updo, and lifted the water dog. All three raccoon hands and both feet scrambled as the little creature hid under her flowing, sunlight colored hair.

"Pam, I know you care about anything small and cute, but we are on a *CRUISE*. You can't take that thing back on the boat, we don't have a carrier for it, and if I was going to go through all the trouble of working a glamor on the critter for the next four days, I'd have brought Blender!"

"And you didn't want another Wampy!" Pam said conspiratorially.

"He's the only one I like, and that's beside the point!" Bucky pointed out to the water. "It's probably some shark that's got him spooked, we can give it an hour for Jaws to screw off and then…" The roar of a speed boat caught the couple's sensitive ears and they ceased the debate, looking out to see Carl, Hanna, and two other men pull up to the beach and climb out.

"Bucko, you get your ass over here!" Carl roared, causing exactly the kind of scene Bucky didn't want.

*"This **bastard.**"* Pam and Bucky both muttered before Bucky raised his voice and his temper.

"What in all twelve hells do you want, Carl? I'm trying to drink and enjoy the sun here."

"Where is it?"

"Got a mojito right there." Bucky gestured with an angry finger. "And the sun is the bright ball in the sky. You need a drink that bad you can take mine. I'll order another."

"Not the alcohol, you inbred hick, where's the creature?" Carl said, stepping up to try and intimidate his rival.

"Considering all the people around Carl, I was smart enough to leave all mine at home, because I'm off work…ON *Vacation,"* Bucky hissed. His temper rapidly made him wish he'd better studied self-defense laws in the Caribbean.

"Don't play dumb with me, Bucko! You and that whore wife of yours need to cough it up beferrrk-" A rage filled hook rattled Carl's head like a dashboard hula girl, dropping him on his ass as Bucky's left hand slammed across his jaw. The dam that held back the grief filled rage finally shattered, and it was only by chance that the blow wasn't enough to snap Carl's neck. The tall man let his weight carry, firing off with a right footed front kick that hammered the man next to Carl and sent him rolling and gasping as his diaphragm suddenly refused to function. Surprised at the sudden speed of the violence, the last of the men in Carl's band of fools crumpled when Bucky's right cross blended his thoughts like a milkshake.

Bucky checked both of Carl's escorts before returning to the man and hauled him up by his neck. Hanna gazed on in horror and shock. Pam Jo circled around slowly and touched her on the shoulder gently.

"Let's give the boys some space, Honey," she said as Bucky manhandled Carl. He pulled the concussed conservationist onto his beach chair, sitting him up and slapping him for attention. Bucky snapped his fingers in Carl's face a few times before pointing to himself. "Bucky Bob," he moved the pointing finger to his wife. "Pam Jo. I'll even cut you some slack with Bucky and Pam. If I hear any other name, slur, or derogatory remark used in place of our names, I'll end your entire bloodline. I spared you after your idiocy killed Jenna Marie, I spared you when you tried to take me to court for it, and I spared you when you insulted me to my face. Next time, I will cave your skull in. So, say it with me, you stupid *bastard*."

"**bUcKy bOb…PaM jO,**" Carl slurred along with Bucky, his blurred eyes and face awash with pain, fear, and embarrassment.

"Good. Now what the hell is going on with this critter?" Bucky shoved the dazed man down to lie back in the chair, and placed the cold mojito glass against the man's jaw. He lit a cigarette, figuring it would be a few minutes till the cops came. Carl took the drink, but it was Hanna who spoke up.

"Poachers hired Carl to help hunt down a monster. The cruise was just a cover for getting down here. They took a submarine and were gone for a while. They had all kinds of critters, but when they came back up, something attacked the camp."

"They don't need to know all that, Hanna!" Carl yelled, trying to rise on concussion addled legs and getting roughly planted back into his seat by Bucky's massive hand. Bucky stuck a finger in his face to tell him to shut up.

"Continue darlin'. What happened next?"

"Well, we saw this little raccoon looking thing as we were jumping in the boat to get away, but it dove under the water really fast, and we only caught glimpses of it till we got here."

Carl glared daggers at the woman, but found the stare interrupted by a big, violent elf.

"What did y'all run into Carl?"

"I don't know."

"The hell do you mean you don't know?"

"There was a lot of them, and at least one big one! I don't know what they were."

"Well give me-"

A chorus of shrieks from the water drowned Bucky out and he snapped his gaze around to find the sea frothing with multiple swirling red clouds spreading out from the ever-growing number of tourists disappearing under the waves. Men, women, and children scrambled to the shore while fighting to run in the soft toss of the waters, only to scream as something pulled their legs from beneath them.

Carl tried to bolt again, and Bucky slapped him down with casual contempt.

"What was it Carl?" The elf barked at his nemesis.

"Just a shark!" Carl said in a daze.

"That's no damn shark, Bucky!" Pam Jo hollered and launched herself forward, making a mad rush for a group of children still gawking with their toes in the very tip of the wave wash. Bucky cursed, and scanned the water, searching desperately for something, anything, that would tell him what he was dealing with in those crimson waves. Lacking all tools and preparations, there were some things even an elf with hundreds of years of experience couldn't fight. If it was something like a dragon turtle, luska, or one of the monsters of The Deep, he didn't have the tools on hand to save anyone.

The hesitation cost lives, but he had no choice. He had to know what was eating people to stop it. Finally, one muscular man made it to the shore and emerged with the creatures devouring him. Dinner platter sized crustaceans ripped chunks from the man with nightmarish mandibles and razor-sharp claws, swarming over the slowest of the beach goers with crablike legs.

"Pamtriel! Get that beautiful ass back here. We can't fight that many by the water!"

Carl tried to stagger to his feet but was still wobbling from the repeated blows. He looked at his wife and held up a hand.

"Help me, Hanna baby, we gotta go!" but Hanna only gave the man a look of disgust.

"Help yourself, Carl Berkins, you told me your wife died of cancer. Not getting eaten just like those people. Consider this our divorce." She slapped him across the face and ran for the ship.

Bucky scrambled, charging back to the bar about fifty yards away, weaving with inhuman grace between the panicking travelers and waitstaff. He snatched up the coconut machete and a pair of kitchen knives, still covered in lime juice. It was way better than nothing, and nowhere near enough. He needed something that would drive them off or take a group of them out at once. It was then he saw the bar rags and his own reflection in the liquor shelf mirrors. The lightbulb clicked on in his mind, and he snatched up an arm full of ouzo, scotch, and one hundred proof whiskey.

He began lining out anything one hundred proof or over in a glass bottle, and all the dry rags or napkins he could find. Pam Jo arrived seconds later as he was gathering supplies, setting three children down along with one terrified ahuizotl. Bucky slid the machete towards her.

"Git the hell out of here, run to the ship!" Pam Jo screamed to the children, before standing with her husband, and taking up the blade. Bucky Bob was already stuffing rags and napkins into the top of the liquor bottles. He only paused long enough to kiss his wife deeply, and press his forehead to hers. He pressed their leaf pendants together, both of them flashing with protective magic.

"If one of these firebombs fucks up, or it ain't enough, you run, you hear me? I've fought in five wars, won thirty-two duels, killed hundreds of men and beasts. I've sailed all seven seas, and stared living nightmares in the eyes, but I have only ever loved one woman, and that's you. I'll go to my grave and my ancestors with a smile before I lose you. You take care of our kids, and the critters. It goes sideways, you run like a scalded dog. Promise me."

"Bucky, it won't come to that, we've fought together a thous-"

"Promise me!"

"I promise." She whispered, and then they were running back to the snapping jaws of death together.

The issue with pure alcohol Molotovs was that liquor bottle glass was often a pain in the ass to break, and the rags often struggled to ignite well and hold the flames. You could make it work, and even work well when you needed something lit on fire, but it was a constant hazard from the time you struck the lighter. Bucky had done this a lot, for fun, profit, or otherwise, and that experience scared him more than anything. Burning to death probably wasn't any more fun than getting eaten alive by giant sand fleas.

So, Buc-cee's Bic lighter in hand, they charged out to meet the skittering horde, and started tossing flaming liquor bottles. Thankfully, the shells of the ugly bastards were hard enough and with a crackle and hiss, the fires began. The feasting sea beasts screamed in blood curdling high-pitched shrieks, the smell of roasting crab filling the air. Flaming creatures scattered in all directions, lighting up the cabanas and beach side furniture.

A particularly stubborn set of screams caught the couple's attention, drawing it back to the lounge chair where they had left a dazed and confused Carl. Carl battled with one of the giant crustaceans. Blood ran from the man's arms as he rolled with the monster.

"Shit! I forgot about *that **bastard**!*"

"Well, looks like Hanna did, too," Pam Jo snarked.

"Come on then, let's go save him."

Bucky and Pam rushed through tossed over furniture, flaming creatures and the dead looking to rescue the moronic monster keeper, but the remains of the swarm were relentless and even larger monsters, up to the size of large dogs, came from the ocean still. The swarm washed over Carl and his cries for help turned to panicked keens of pain and fear.

Bucky dove in with blade and foot, kicking and stabbing. He ripped and hammered, but the blood frenzied creatures would not relent. Claws raked at Bucky's skin, but his protective magics held the snapping pincers at bay. Pam Jo finally kicked one of the beasts for a field goal and pulled her husband back.

"Bucky." She called, but he dove back in, stabbing and bashing as blood flew in weak splashes. "Bucky!" She tried again, killing a monster as it tried to take her husband's back.

"Buckthorn!" She finally bellowed, and he stepped back and whipped around to look at her.

*"**What?**"*

Pam Jo shook her head and held up a liquor bottle.

"He's doomed. Send him out."

Bucky kicked one final guard dog sized crab for a field goal, shook the blood from his hands, and took the bottle from Pam Jo. They stepped back and Bucky spoke with a weary breath as he lit the improvised weapon.

"I always knew the stupid bastard would get eaten. Never thought I'd be there to see it. He smashed the bottle into the writhing pile of man and monster. The chorus of screams noticeably lacked a human voice. Bucky and Pam heard another cry, and rushed further down the beach.

Three rescued vacationers later, Bucky scanned the beach and still saw too many critters.

"You know I can't figure out if it would be cannibalism or justice if we ate them back." Pam Jo remarked while she hurled one of the last flaming liquor bottles to shatter in the midst of the creatures and readied her blade.

"Probably haven't digested the people yet, but we ain't human anyway, so technically it's justice. Probably be pretty good if there is any lemon juice left after the fires." Bucky slid to her left side with the instinct of long practice, a knife in each hand. "You remember how to do this?"

"Do you? We ain't fought together with blades in fifty years."

"Well, they made me leave the twelve gauge at home, Pamtriel Jolene! Despite my complaints! That's exactly why we moved to the U.S.A. in the first place!"

"It wasn't even a colony then!"

"Still didn't have any idiots getting nervous about a man being armed, did it?"

Most of the crawling horrors were burning or fleeing back to the ocean, but the stubborn and brave came on, seeking the flesh of the few people still in sight, and the two elves who had spent so long in the swamps of South Georgia. The pair readied themselves, Bucky guarding Pam's left from old habit.

"I love you," were the last words they said to each other as they dove into the fight.

Bucky met the leap of the first jackal sized crustacean, impaling its soft underbelly and slinging it aside as Pam Jo slashed down on another flaming creature that charged her from the right. Gore splattered as the fire wreathed monstrosity's shell crushed in with a gout of blood. She twisted the machete to slash another. Together they stepped and dodged, slashed and stabbed as the creatures poured forth. Bucky's right-hand knife snapped off in another crab, then the tip of Pam's machete shattered on another carapace, and still one or two at a time, the creatures came on.

"Might be time to cut and run baby, anyone still out here is dead." Pam faked a slash at one crab, then carved half the legs off another.

"I can't let em' get to the ship. Who knows how many of them are out there in the water waiting to see if the others come back full?" Bucky stabbed another.

"Well then, we are going to have to do somethin' real stupid." They both looked to the restaurant sized propane tank out back behind the bar.

"I'll run the rabbit; you rig it." Bucky punted the closest creature into the flames. He slipped the lighter into his wife's hand and dashed out to the beach.

"YEEEEEE HAAAAWWWWWW SUEEEEEEEEEEEEEEE HERE CRAB CRAB CRAB CRAB" The elf cried as he dashed between the flames, waving his hands like a moron.

"GET OVER HERE YOU BOTTOM FEEDING FECES MUNCHERS!"

He leapt clear over a pair of crabs, then skirted a fire to dodge another three, scorching the side of his leg.

Pam worked frantically, tossing the bar over worse than if she was robbing the place. Still manning the bar, the ahuizotl also dug through cabinets and drawers, though Pam Jo had no idea if the little critter understood. She was overturning and upending anything that might contain some material to help. The water dog slipped out the back entrance, but she had little time to pay attention. Blowing up a propane tank was an easy Tuesday night. Blowing it up after they could get away was going to take some trailer park ingenuity. Rags would burn too fast or lose the flame; paper wouldn't be any better.

A few agonized moments later, she was looking at a tablecloth wondering if she could set it up some kind of way. Her plotting stopped when a furry blur darted on top of the bar and a little tail hand dumped a box of sparklers onto the beer soaked wood.

"You brilliant little beast!" Pam cried and placed the water dog back on her shoulder. "Are there more?" With a chirp, her new furry friend pointed the way.

Bucky was running out of space and gas. Wheezing like a stuck hog, he'd had way too many years of beer and Marlboros between him and the last time he was in true fighting shape. Pam was going to have to come up with something quick. Magic talisman overloaded, forearms already bleeding, his inhuman physiology could only make up for so much.

"Swear on the Mother Tree, if I make it out of here, I'm picking the sword up again. This is what I get for leaving the kids at home. Shoulda brought the twins." He huffed from the top of the lifeguard shack and kicked another Assault Crab from climbing up. It waved and snapped comically as it fell back into the small sea of its peers.

"Pam Jo, baby, if you are going to do something, it needs to damn well be soon. How long does it take to rig a propane tank? Uncle Joey used to blow up two a week. Then again, he never kept his eyebrows either."

For just one moment, as the creatures swarmed, Bucky thought he was going to die, and then he saw his beautiful wife waving and nearly bouncing out of her camo swimwear. Any other time, he would have enjoyed the show, but getting torn to pieces by Doberman Crabs just put a damper on the display.

"Sumbitch, maybe I am getting old," he said, and with a running step, he leapt from the top of the shack and rolled onto the sands. The hungry horde followed right behind him; the alcohol fires were mostly spent unless they spread to some other material. He hurtled a severed leg, and stepped past a set of still feeding crabs, stabbing his now half broken knife into one as he ran by. The other crabs squealed and gave chase, following the small drops of blood trailing down his pumping arms onto the sand. He watched Pam Jo disappear behind the bar towards the tank and heard the telltale hiss of a partially cut line.

"Keep running, Baby!" she yelled as he turned the corner to see a massive pile of fireworks next to the hissing coffin sized tank. She stopped long enough to light a shit ton of sparklers and dart in behind him. They stopped some distance away, praying the crab's appearance would line up right with the sparklers igniting the gas. The first of them showed, then another and another. They swarmed for Bucky's blood, but still nothing happened.

"Piss!" Pam Jo yelled. "I put them too far away from the cut! It's right by where the line meets the tank."

The couple lamented then, there was nothing left to do but flee or die. Bucky held his hand out.

"Give it here Pam, tell the boys I love them," he said, but instead of a fire source, an all too familiar cylinder filled his hands from a little furred helper underneath her hair. A bundle of five long, bright colored packages screamed *Roman Candle* to his eyes, and his wife smugly held out a lighter.

"He's coming home," she snarked.

"Both of you get behind something." Bucky bristled his mustache and lit the whole bundle, pretending he was trying to shoot his cousin Bernthal in the ass just like any other Fourth of July. "Snip this," he cracked as the red, white, and blue fireballs began to fly. The whole world shook.

A week later, rested and returned to his home, Bucky sat snoring in his workshop, Blender perched on his chest as he reclined with his feet up on an old workbench covered in Pabst Blue Ribbon cans and one single, beautiful saber.

"Buckthorn Robinriel Darkleaf!" His wife hollered from the office trailer door, and he leapt up with a start, catching the panicking wampus cat and enduring all six pairs of claws until the black and purple feline was stable on his shoulder and head.

"What is it Pam Jo! I'm training over here!" he called as he wiped the drool from his face. In his defense, he had gone through forms for an hour.

"I got a Staff Sergeant Jackson calling from over at Fort Stewart. Sounds like a Jabberwock is interrupting 1st Battalion's artillery practice!"

"Sumbitch," the wildlife wrangler muttered. "Tell him me and Blender will be there in two hours! Have everybody leave it the hell alone. Shooting it is just gonna piss it off." Bucky headed to his work van.

"Ok, love you!"

"Love you too." He said as he opened up the driver door to the work van, tossed out the one eyed tabby wampus cat, and climbed up with Blender into the van. The swamp kitten sat patiently in the passenger seat as they pulled off into the afternoon sun.

We hope that you enjoyed this title and look forward to many more to come. Please, leave us a review! Reviews matter to all of our authors.

And don't forget to check out the latest edition of *Car Wars*

http://www.sjgames.com/car-wars/

Or the other amazing titles from
Steve Jackson Games

http://www.sjgames.com

…or the latest in the Car Warriors: Autoduel Chronicle fiction series.
https://threeravenspublishing.com/car-warriors-autoduel-chronicles/

Take a look at some of our other award-winning series at
https://threeravenspublishing.com/series-universes/

Visit us at https://www.threeravenspublishing.com and sign up for our
newsletter for the latest and greatest news on upcoming titles and events.

Other series and titles you might enjoy.

DECLAN FINN
DECLAN FINN
DECLAN FINN
DECLAN FINN
HONOR AT STAKE
LOVE AT FIRST BITE ONE
The Dragon Award Nominated Series
FREE on Kindle Unlimited!

AVAILABLE ON AMAZON
JOINT TASK FORCE
13
HOLDING THE LINE
BETWEEN HEAVEN AND HELL
13

MYSTERY,
MAGIC &
MAYHEM
WITH A TWIST
OF ROMANCE
J.F. POSTHUMUS
ON AMAZON
FIND ME
B.E.N.T.
BIOLOGIC   ENHANCED   NASCENT   TALENT

THE RAVEN
AND
THE CROW
MICHAEL K. FALCIANI
FIND ME
ON AMAZON

STARFLIGHT
IT CAME FROM THE
TRAILER PARK

3R
Three Ravens Publishing
Are you looking for fun, new fiction?
L.N. Hunter
The FEATHER and the LAMP
JONATHAN MABERRY
A GAME FROM THE TRAILER PARK
LEGENDS
A JOINT TASK FORCE 13 ANTHOLOGY
Edited by:
William Joseph Roberts
Philip K. Booker
CROSSWAYS
THE WAYMAN CHRONICLES
MICHAEL J ALLEN
USA TODAY BESTSELLING AUTHOR
THE RAVEN AND THE CROW
DARK STORM RISING
J.F. POSTHUMUS
STAFF OF CHAOS
The Written Word Will Never Be The Same…
https://www.threeravenspublishing.com
Veteran Owned and Operated

You can also keep up to date with our latest release announcements on Scifi.radio and get some of the best fandom programing on the planet.

Scifi for your Wifi

And don't forget to check out our other Sponsors and Affiliates

A southern Appalachian jewel for craft beer lovers, Buck Bald Brewing offers something for everyone. With delicious, locally brewed beverages from across the spectrum, Buck Bald Brewing offers craft brews that are consistently amazing.

From the dark and smooth Shesquatch Scottish ale, to the intense hops of Hippibilly IPA, to the puckering sour of the blackberry and cinnamon in Berry My Heart at the Trailer Park, and more than 60+ rotating brews, you'll find what you're looking for and more.

With smiling faces behind the bar ready to help you find your next favorite brew, a constantly rotating selection of delicious craft beverages, toe-tapping tunes always playing, and the biggest games on TV, you can kick your feet up in either Copperhill, Tennessee or Murphy, North Carolina and immerse yourself in the Buck Bald Brewing experience. So, come out, fill a pint, fill a growler, and fill your mind at your new favorite family-owned craft brewery.

To discover more visit us at buckbaldbrewing.com or follow us on Facebook @buckbaldbrewing and @buckbaldbrewingmurphy.

Vesper Wren's
TRAILER PARK
PIXIE
PUNCH
· A PEACH STRAWBERRY SELTZER ·
BUCK BALD BREWING

BRAXTON
HICKS
MIDNIGHT MOCHA MILK
STOUT
BUCK BALD BREWING

Peanut Butter Paws
Peanut Butter
CHOCOLATE
STOUT
BUCK BALD BREWING
BUCK BALD BREWING